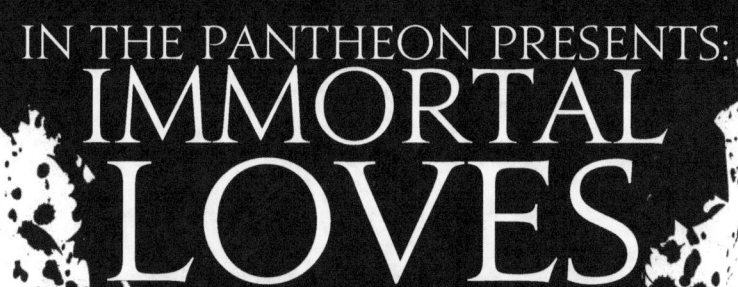

IN THE PANTHEON PRESENTS:
IMMORTAL
LOVES

First paperback edition February 2021

ISBN (paperback) 978-1-953256-05-8

ISBN (eBook) 978-1-953256-03-4

www.inthepantheon.com

ЯR

REWRITTEN REALMS

EROS

ROMANTIC

LOVE

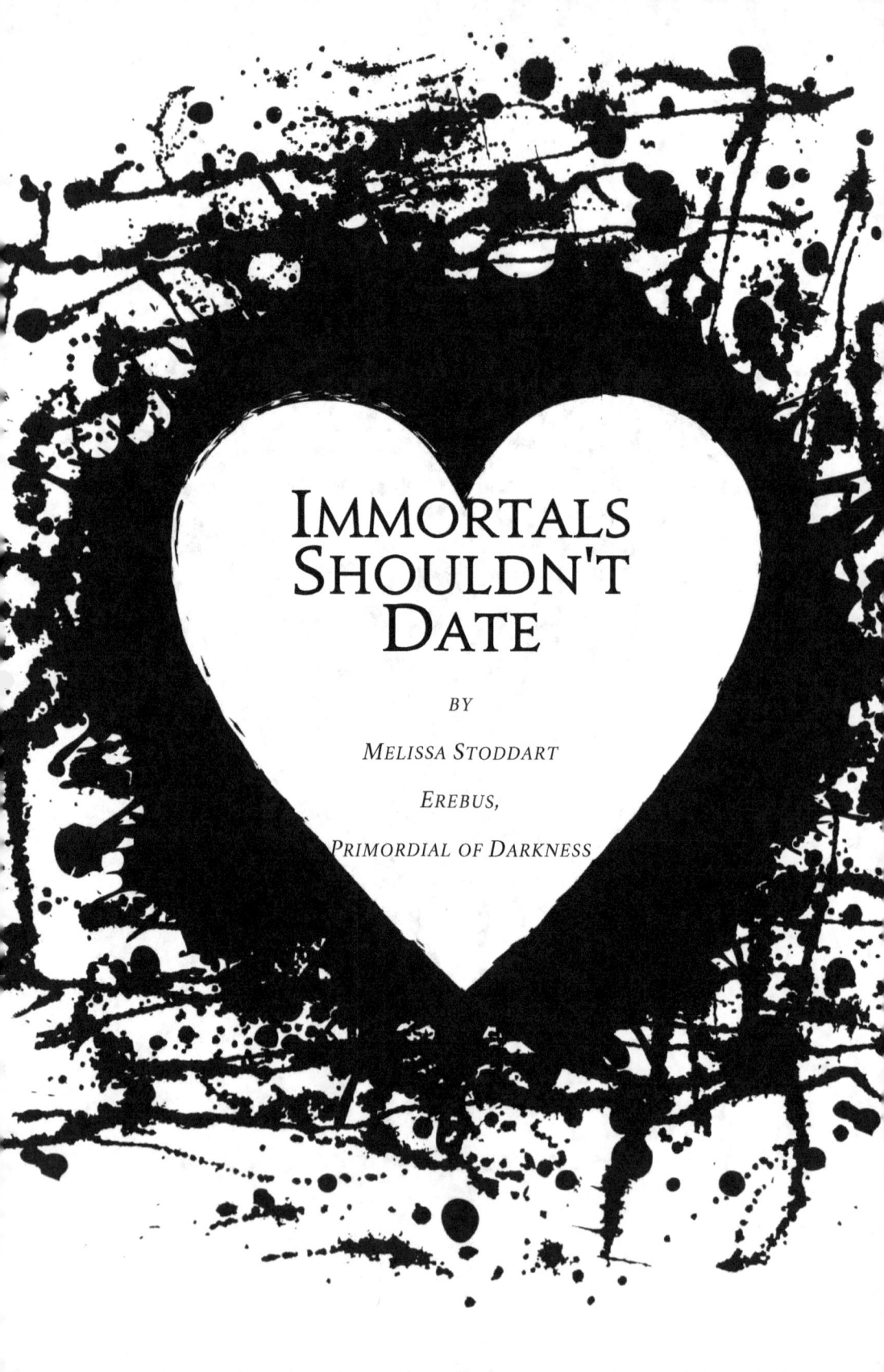

IMMORTALS SHOULDN'T DATE

BY

MELISSA STODDART

EREBUS,

PRIMORDIAL OF DARKNESS

I tore apart my drawers, trying to find something to wear, my frustration reaching new levels. This was such a ridiculous idea. Whoever heard of hot tantric yoga on a first date? I shook my head. I'm never listening to Eros again. This was the last time I would take his advice. I just hoped everything would go well.

It had taken so long for Atë and me to get to this point, and I didn't want to mess things up. After months of living together, in a completely platonic manner... Oh, who was I kidding? We still fought like cats and dogs, but in the last month, things had finally started to turn around. She had finally gotten control of her anger and didn't want to kill me, so that was a bonus. It felt less and less like she had been *court ordered* to live with me and more like she actually didn't mind having a roommate. I thought getting a place that didn't have meaning or ownership to either one of us would help her feel more at home, but I had never really understood until living with her that she'd never had a home. After being booted from Olympus, it was one city after the next for her. Sure, things weren't always rosy between us, but I'd like to think it was the small things I did around the house that warmed her up.

There was no refuting our connection. Even when we bickered, the heat and tension between us was undeniable, at least for me. Atë had spent the last several months with her head stuck up her ass. I don't even know why she agreed to go on this date with me.

I stood up straight. *Maybe she doesn't know it's a date?*

I thought I had made myself pretty clear. My brow furrowed, and thoughts raced through my mind. *Gods don't date.* That was my immediate response to Eros when he suggested I take Atë out. Dates were for mortals to get to know each other and pretend they weren't trying to get into each other's pants. *I'm a fool.* Frustration settled in. I went back to rifling through my drawers, looking for a particular pair of shorts. Clothes started flying left and right over my shoulders. I could hear Ebhot screeching at Atë down the hall.

For fuck's sake! I chucked a shoe across the room, hitting the lamp on my bedside table. It crashed to the floor, shattering into pieces. I let out a mad groan. Maybe I should just call this off. *Yoga is a dumb idea.* Of course, as I thought that, I finally found what I was looking for. I slipped into them and realized that they probably went out of style in the nineties. I never wore shorts, not unless I was going to the beach. *Could I wear swim shorts to yoga?* Slipping a black t-shirt over my head, I stood back to look at myself in the mirror and grumbled loudly. A screech sounded from behind my door, followed by a small knock.

"Everything okay in there?"

I could hear the sass in her voice. Giving myself a last once over, I exhaled and stalked towards the bedroom door, pulling it open. "Yeah," I mumbled, "just knocked something over accidentally." I nodded at my broken lamp. "It didn't survive."

Atë stuck out her bottom lip in a fake pout, Ebhot circling her leg and snickering. I gave him a sinister look before shrugging it off. "It's okay. I hated it anyway."

"Okay, well, I'll be downstairs...when you are done, ya know, knocking stuff over."

Her comment took a second to register as I took in every inch of her. She was in a light grey sports bra and matching leggings. I gulped as my eyes reached her bare midriff.

She swayed from side to side, one hand resting on her hip. "Or are you ready now? You did say yoga, right?" She tugged self-consciously at the waistband of her leggings. "Is this alright then?" she said as her lips moved into a Cheshire grin. She wasn't fooling me. She knew damn well she looked fine as hell.

I gave her a smirk and answered, "Yes, yes, of course. What you have on is fine." Idiot. *Tell her she looks better than fine.* "I mean, you look great."

"Thanks. You're not so bad yourself." She playfully slapped my arm before looking down at Ebhot, who was now doing circles at our feet like a tiny horned kitten. "Ebhot wants to go too, but I told him no."

I looked down at our tiny imp, shaking my head at him. "Not this time, little buddy."

"So, are you ready?" she asked, pointing with a thumb over her shoulder towards the downstairs.

It's now or never. I smile, placing my hand on the small of her back. "Yes, let's go."

We headed down the hall and to the stairs. Our oceanside house was bigger than any home I've had. When I picked it out, I wanted something reclusive, hidden away from the rest of the world. The structure itself was half-buried into the side of a cliff, two stories with a walkout basement that led straight to the beach. There would be no more dark caves for me. If I wanted to hide, this was better than any stupid suite in the God Complex. Plus, we didn't have to run into any other big egos out here. Between the two of us, we had all that we could manage.

I rubbed the palm of my free hand subtly on the back of my shorts, my nerves starting to show. If not for the ridiculous reality dating show I had been on at the end of summer, I wouldn't have the slightest clue what to do. Not that I had gained much knowledge there. Everything had been set up for me by the producer Chuck, and I hadn't planned a single date. Most of the girls were so chatty I barely spoke a word. Mortal girls were easy to please, I just had to shine my pearly whites at them, and they swooned.

This was different, though. Atë wasn't like mortal girls, or for that matter, most goddesses in Olympus. Being with Atë would be an adventure. Before she and I became roommates, we were on the verge of solidifying our friendship. Then, she went and let out a few dozen Titans and blew up Olympus. She did manage to lock me up for a few months in the dream realm, to keep me out of the way. She was a clever minx. I had to give her that. Dating her would be a challenge that I welcomed wholeheartedly.

"So, why yoga?"

"I took some advice from the God of Love," I said, rolling my eyes.

Atë let out a snort. "Again? Have you learned nothing?!"

"My friend pool is on the low side."

We stepped outside into the brisk air, something I welcomed. Atë quickly jumped into the passenger seat of my black escalade and put on her sunglasses. I flipped through the radio, trying to find something to fill the silence. The polite thing would be to let her choose, so I relaxed and sat back in the big leather seat.

"I don't even know what kind of music you like."

Atë looked over at me, sliding her sunglasses down the bridge of her nose, holding my stare. "A little bit of everything. It depends on my mood. Being alive as long as we have music changes like everything…" she let her voice trail off.

Looking out the windshield, I nervously tapped the steering wheel. "Yeah, I suppose you're right." *Could I be any more lame?*

Atë shifted in her seat so that she was somewhat facing me. "What about you? What do you like?"

I cleared my throat before glancing at her. "I like the classics."

"Classics like rock-and-roll classics or classics like ballroom jazz classics?"

"Ella, Miles, Duke." And before I could stop it from happening, I heard myself say, "You know I used to run with that crowd." The words slipped from my mouth, and I bit back a groan. Am I really

11

fucking name dropping a bunch of dead mortals she could probably care less about? *Kill me now.*

"Pffftt, no way!" she said in a tone that was hard to decipher. Was she mocking me? Likely.

I slid the car into reverse and backed out of the garage. We drove for about a mile in awkward silence before Atë looked at me again and asked, "How long have you been deejaying?"

"Oh, not that long." Every question she asked, I turned to see if she was serious or if she was secretly judging me. After I determined she wasn't, I averted my eyes back to the road. "It was cool in the beginning. I loved the rush. I mean, what god doesn't like to be worshipped, am I right?" I couldn't help but let my eyes wander back to her. She was so beautiful.

She smiled softly, giving me a once over before she turned her attention back to the road ahead.

"I wouldn't know," she said with some bite. "I've never been worshipped. Can't really do that with no statues, or memories, you know."

I knew exactly what she meant. I could barely hide the contempt in my voice, "Mortals don't remember me, not a single one. They don't understand what it means to be the God of Darkness and Shadows. Even Zeus's immortals, you think they quake when they hear my name?" I couldn't help but snort. "Mortals are only familiar with what the textbooks tell them of the Olympian Gods. And for everyone on

12

Olympus now...well, let's just say there's no love lost for those who think they are better and stronger than an Original."

Atë rested her arm on the window, placing a hand behind her head as she turned to watch me rant. "You don't want it."

"Don't want it?" I was confused.

"That power you seek...to have everyone fear you. I mean, sure, you get a certain level of respect, so to say, but no one ever sees you for who you really are anymore. You are just something they fear."

I realized we were no longer talking about me. Atë was reflecting on herself and what it had been like since she tried to kill half of her family. She was processing who she was becoming since being released from Tartarus.

"Even if they deny it, they all act differently around you. Like you're a ticking time bomb just waiting to go off." She turned and looked sadly out the window.

I wanted to reach over to her and squeeze her hand. I wanted to let her know that I didn't fear her the way others did. She certainly wasn't alone anymore. I think I had proven that to her month after month, comforting her when no one else could. She had to know I cared and didn't think poorly of her.

"I-I..." *Fuck, you nit-wit, stammer much?* I was an idiot, I knew this had been a sore spot for her, and here the very thing I craved was something she wanted to be rid of. "I'm sorry, Atë."

We pulled into the empty parking lot of the yoga studio.

13

"I hope you don't mind, but on the advice of one love god, I booked the entire studio just for us."

Atë looked at the studio before turning and smirking wickedly at me. "The entire studio?" She gave a fake gasp. "Erebus, are you trying to seduce me?" she said in her best southern-belle accent.

"Are you flirting with me?" I chuckled, but before she could answer, I continued talking nervously. "Well, our instructor will be here, but other than that, yes, it will just be us."

She looked back out the window at the studio, then back at me. "Just us, huh? Hmm, so you either are trying to seduce me or are afraid to have that many people around me."

I gave her a terse look, which she quickly dismissed. "So, which is it?"

"You've proven you can handle yourself. I think you did that in Paris." A few months back, Atë disappeared for a few days with her best friend on an impromptu trip. It caused a serious fight between us. After I retrieved her from good ol' Pari, I knew she was ready and wouldn't knock down any more buildings with her anger. Not to mention, kill anyone.

I stepped out, jogging around the car to open Atë's door. Showing her that chivalry wasn't dead, I held my hand out for her. She seemed a bit surprised, perhaps even confused. Or maybe she was secretly judging me, laughing at me on the inside, and being polite on the outside. Either way, I didn't let go of her hand as we walked toward the studio with my heart pounding. It was another new development in the Atë/Erebus saga.

"This is nice." Atë smiled.

I wasn't sure if she was referring to the studio or holding my hand.

"Chaos knows I could use some relaxation time. Who better to share it with? And tantric...well enough said." Could I be any cheesier? Atë would be running for the hills in no time if I kept this up. I opened the studio door, feeling a little more comfortable, trying to get in a groove.

As if she were aware of my insecurity, she answered, "You know, I think this is the longest we have gone where I haven't tried to stab you or throw something at you."

A beautiful, full-figured blonde welcomed us as we walked in. She was wearing what I could only assume was an outfit to allow for absolute flexibility. It looked as though it had been painted onto her skin. A low-lying zipper revealed a bounty of cleavage where most mortal men would love to bury their faces. I squeezed Atë's hand, hoping she would behave.

I smiled at our instructor. "Hello?"

"I changed my mind. I'm going to kill you," Atë said in a low enough whisper that only I could hear.

I glanced at Atë. "Relax. This is probably one of Eros's jokes."

15

Atë stepped forward to shake the overly perky instructor's hand. However, the blonde didn't meet her gaze. She was fixated on me. *I'm a dead man.*

"I'm sorry, I didn't catch your name. Also, do you have any next of kin?" Atë said through gritted teeth.

I chuckled and stuck out my hand to introduce myself. "I'm Erebus, and this one is Atë. Don't mind her. She's a bit territorial."

The instructor laughed hesitantly. "Eros said you two could be a handful. I'm Kiki."

"I bet he did." I laughed, keeping a close eye on Atë.

I could feel Atë's eyes narrow on me before turning back to the instructor. "So, what are we learning today? Some Pilates? Downward dog? Kama Sutra?"

The instructor silently led us to the middle of the room, where some mats lay flat on the floor. "As you can tell, this is hot yoga with a bit of a twist. You two are overdressed. In our yoga classes, things can get pretty hot. You may want to strip down." Kiki looked me up and down, the corners of her mouth twitching. And with that, I could feel just how hot the studio was.

"Strip down? To what?" I laughed nervously.

"Well, other couples that have taken this class usually just wear their underwear," she said matter-of-factly.

"Oh wait, we were supposed to wear underwear?" Atë was sizing up Kiki.

Kiki looked like she disapproved of Atë's choice to go footloose and fancy-free and gave her a disgusted look. Clearly, she didn't know who she was messing with. "Yes, well...we do have bicycle shorts available in our store you can purchase."

Atë folded her arms, narrowing her gaze at the soon to be ill-fated yoga instructor. "I survived hell, sweetheart. I think I can handle a little heat. "But," she turned, smirking at me, "if Erebus would like to take his shirt off, I'm sure no one would mind."

I gulped, looking back and forth between the two women. The tension between them was almost palpable. "Yes, well. If you want to get the full effect, the more bare skin touching, the better." Kiki smiled at me, completely ignoring the death stares Atë was throwing her way. "We are looking for the ultimate intimate experience."

Atë let out a snort, and I figured it was best just to get on with the instruction. I was having flashbacks to the reality show and being forced into ridiculous dating situations. If it weren't for fear of disappointing Atë, I would have called this off right then and there. Instead, I decided to be a team player. I looked at Atë and smiled, giving her a shrug. "I wouldn't mind getting the full effect." I slipped my shirt off and removed my shorts, standing in the studio in just my boxer briefs.

Atë smiled, something hidden behind her eyes. Maybe a memory from our past? Her eyes went back and forth between Kiki and me. I silently hoped she wasn't angry.

"Fine."

I held my breath as Atë walked past the instructor. I hoped she would keep her claws in. When she turned around, my shadows were ready. But to my surprise, I didn't need them.

Atë leaned over and spoke directly to Kiki. "He tastes even better than he looks." Then she disappeared into the back.

My heart hammered in my chest at the memory of the last time we were together in an intimate setting. At least now I knew she had fond memories of it, too. I stretched out on my mat, waiting for Atë to return. Kiki went off to grab some essential oils for the session to *set the mood*.

When Atë returned, she was wearing new attire. She had taken a pair of bicycle shorts but made a few adjustments, cutting them super short, so half her ass cheeks stuck out. She stopped in front of me, spinning for dramatic effect.

"All better?"

I had to pick my jaw up from the floor and remember we weren't alone.

A satisfied smirk spread across her face as she sat on the mat beside me. She glared at Kiki as she adjusted the bun on the top of her head.

Kiki had set up candles around the studio, slipping into a more professional mode. She asked us to lay down on the mats side by side. She continued with her instructions, encouraging us to mimic her as she thrust her pelvis and hips into the air, making some grunting noises. I could think of nothing more awkward than this. I looked at

18

Atë to see if I could guess what she was thinking. Kiki was completely immersed in it, and her grunting noises grew louder.

"Hey, hey, hey. You need to feel the release from deep within. Hey, hey, hey."

Atë and I watched Kiki thrust her hips. I was trying my best to stifle a laugh. Kiki continued with her ridiculous instructions.

"Then, I want you to release it all, like you're having a tantrum." Kiki let loose on the floor, flailing her body, kicking and screaming.

This had to be a joke. Eros really thought this was the perfect first date? Kiki looked over to us after her release. "It's kind of like an angergasm."

Atë lifted herself onto her elbows, raising an eyebrow. "A what?"

I leaned close to Atë and whispered with a laugh, "I think she said an angergasm."

Kiki turned to us. "Okay, your turn."

Confused, Atë looked at me and then back at KiKi. "Wait...seriously?"

Kiki smiled smugly at Atë. "Yes, seriously." Then she looked at me expectantly. Reluctantly, I lay back and started thrusting my hips into the air, making the ridiculous grunting noises. There is nothing sexy about this, and I'm going to kill Eros. It's shit like this that makes the other immortals not fear me.

Atë lay back down, her arms behind her head as she watched me thrust my hips in the air like a fool. "No, no, please keep going. I'm actually enjoying myself now."

I looked at her, rolling my eyes. "Just do it."

"Say please." She smiled.

I stopped for a second, sitting up in a half crunch. "Pleeaaaasssse."

She winked before copying my movements. But of course, in true Atë style. She was adding a little oomph to it, giving an extra loud and obnoxious yelp, and I wanted to laugh. It looked like we were having an exorcism, not an angergasm. If anyone saw me, I'd hibernate for the next millennia.

After the nonsense was over, a man walked into the room and introduced himself as Marco. Kiki explained he would be assisting in showing us how to do couples yoga poses.

"Ooo, hot." Atë licked her lips. "Now this will be fun."

I turned to Atë and smirked, thankful that she was open to this even though it's extremely awkward.

Atë sat up, adjusting the bun on top of her head. She leaned over to whisper, "Fifty drachma Marco has boned Kiki in this very studio."

"Sshhhhh," I said on a low chuckle as Marco and Kiki got into the position of downward dog, one moving back on top of the other.

She pointed her finger, waving it back and forth. "Hey, doesn't that kind of look like that one time—"

"A-ah, ah," I scolded Atë but then snickered as I looked at Marco and Kiki.

Atë readied herself, brushing her hands off before getting into position and mimicking the instructors. "Alright, let's do this, hottie."

I bent down into downward dog while Atë stood in front of me, bending over. Her ass looked like a juicy peach. I needed to focus. I looked down as Marco helped place Atë's feet onto my shoulders. Holding the position for us was less than challenging. I looked up to see the underside of Atë. Her tight abs flexed, tightening her core. Sweat began to roll off me. "Looking good."

"I can honestly say this is new," Atë called over to Kiki, being a little cheeky. "So, what does this do, instructor?" She hung her head back down and muttered, "Help relieve stress or form a mild concussion if dropped?"

Kiki gave Atë a curt smile. "Is it too challenging for you?"

Atë looked up, glaring at Kiki, her comeback quick. "No, no, I've been upside down for hours before. I think I'm good," she said with a smirk.

Marco cleared his throat. "Okay, we're going to demonstrate something called Yab Yum. This," Marco looked at me, "is where you leave your ego at the door."

I growled at Marco, not liking his alpha attitude.

Marco continued, "We will demonstrate first." Marco sat on the floor, and Kiki lowered onto his lap, facing him. Straddling his hips, she wrapped her arms around him, so they were no more than a few centimeters apart. Kiki looked over, waiting for us to mirror them. "This is the intimate part we discussed. Your hearts will be in alignment, as will your third eye. This is about deep intimacy. Hold your breath at the top."

21

Atë slipped onto my lap, her scent surrounding me as my hands cupped her hips. Kiki's voice washed away as I focused on Atë, our faces mere inches apart. My heart thundered again in my chest. Even though Atë and I had been together on more than one occasion, this felt different. I suddenly became preoccupied with the sweat dripping down my forehead and back. *Do I smell?*

Atë settled herself by scooching deeper into my lap. Looking more at ease, I could feel her body go heavy as she got more comfortable. She wrapped her arms around the back of my neck, her chest pushing against my own. I could feel her heart hammer away, like a caged animal trying to break free. Her brow furrowed as she looked into my eyes. What I wouldn't give to know what she was thinking. *A penny for your thoughts?* The last time we had been this close, we had been fighting...and the time before that, the same. This was entirely a new experience. We weren't yelling at each other. She smiled at me briefly before looking back at the instructors, and my mind raced with paranoia. I could feel every inch of Atë's legs wrapped around my waist.

Kiki looked at us. "You'll, of course, want to train your eyes on Erebus, Atë. Really feel the spirit of the exercise. Use your third eye."

Atë turned her head back to me, but her eyes remained averted, trying to hide the nervousness vibrating through her. I sucked in a deep breath, willing her to bring her gaze up to meet mine. I needed to reassure her with no words, just my touch and my *third eye,* whatever the hell that was. I needed her to know I wasn't going anywhere. I leaned in, pressing my forehead to hers, the tips of our noses brushing.

Atë's breathing slowed. Either she was really getting into the exercise, or she was overthinking. I had come to gauge her range of emotions since living with her. Sarah, Atë's shrink, had nothing on me. I was better for Atë than any therapy session, and we knew it. She had come so far these last several months. But this seemed too much for her to handle. Intimacy was not something we had dealt with properly.

Atë shot up, almost toppling me over. She looked at me as if she was a caged beast. The building began to shake as she struggled to rein in her powers. Her emotions were showing, but she wouldn't lose control. I had faith in her. The scared look on our instructors' faces said they had their doubts.

"Nope. I can't do this." She shook her head. "This is too much."

My shadows were prepared, spreading out, keeping the walls from crumbling and the roof from caving in. But I did not hold her back from running. I had become all too familiar with Atë's anxiety. I'd pushed too hard, and it was too much, too fast. I looked over to the scared instructors and raised my hand. "It's okay. I got this."

"Atë…" I called after her. I followed her out the doors of the studio and into the crisp air of the afternoon day. "Atë! Would you stop?"

She stopped, bending over to place her hands on her knees to catch her breath. The lights and sounds of cars seemed to break through her panic. She continued to take deep breaths, one after another, just

23

like we practiced. Closing her eyes tight, she stood straight and placed her hands on her hips, turning to face me. Atë shook her head. "I can't...I can't do this, Erebus. Dates? We go on dates now? That wasn't a date."

I stood in front of her, taking her hands from her hips. "You're right, that wasn't a date," I said, rolling my eyes and all the while swearing Eros's name under my breath. "But I did think it started to go well…"

Atë nodded slowly before closing her eyes briefly. "It just reminded me of…" her voice trailed off. "Never mind, it doesn't matter."

Squeezing her hands in mine, I tried grounding her. "Yes, it does matter. Tell me what's going on? Did I push too hard? It was a bit much, wasn't it?"

Pulling her hands from mine, she stepped back. "What is this supposed to be? We're supposed to bond over yoga now? Open our fucking third eye? What does that even mean?"

A breeze picked up, reminding me we were standing in the middle of the street half-naked. Normally I would have shoved my hands in my pockets, but I had none. All I could do was shrug. "I don't know."

"What are we even doing? I've tried to kill you repeatedly. I've locked you away, and now we're bonding over music in your car? Going on yoga dates? Like we're normal?"

"Atë, you're panicking. I thought we had passed all this? We've been living together for six months. I know we aren't normal, but I thought some normalcy in our lives would be good for us. It's not healthy to scream at each other or throw the other across a city and into buildings."

"Exactly, Erebus. Exactly, and that's what I do. What we've done since the beginning." Her eyes glazed over, tears threatening to spill. "You want normal. I can feel it, and I don't think I can give you that."

I shifted back and forth on my feet. "Don't you think it's time for a change?"

"What does that even mean?" Her voice sounded as if she had lost all hope.

"I mean you and me. We have to move forward. If we keep living in the past and reliving our mistakes, we can never build a foundation. No, we don't date. But why can't we? I spent millennia with Nyx. Everything went so stale, and it's because we both stopped trying." I was rambling. "But you and I are different," I said, grabbing her hands again. "I know this. The feeling in my gut, the passion we felt months ago when we were together, the reasons why you push me away like you do. All of it, it's because you and I are more right for each other than anyone I know. I know you feel it, too. We are connected."

Atë leaned forward, and before I realized what she was doing, her lips pressed against mine. "I don't know how you do that. You always know exactly what I am worried about without me ever having to say it out loud." She took a step back. "Okay, but no more group dates or

25

whatever the fuck this is." She made a gesture towards the studio. "If we do this, I want you to myself."

I was about to correct her but thought better of it. "Deal." I smiled and leaned toward her for another kiss.

She let an uncharacteristic giggle escape against my lips and then playfully pushed me away. "Alright, don't get greedy. Also, I need my actual clothes. Those pants were like, a hundred drachmas." She looked at the street behind us and smiled. "Also, I'm pretty sure you've stopped traffic like, five times." She pointed to the cars and random mortals staring behind us.

I turned to see the crowd that had gathered, my face turning warm. "Well, you're the one with half her ass cheeks out for the entire world to see." I spun to face the crowd, angrily addressing them and shooing them away with my hands. "Move along. There's nothing to see here!" I let out an exasperated sigh. "Now, let's try this again," I said, turning back to Atë. "But first, let me go tell Marco and Kiki we won't be needing their services anymore."

We entered the studio, and Atë calmly walked back to the changing rooms while I told Kiki and Marco we would be leaving. They seemed relieved. I hurriedly pulled my shirt and pants back on, hoping to salvage the rest of our date.

Atë emerged fully clothed, a smile on her face as she approached. "This was so enlightening, Kiwi." Atë's voice dripped with sarcasm as she purposely addressed our instructor incorrectly. "Remind me never to do this again."

AN INCONVENIENT ATTACHMENT

BY

AMBER ALBRIGHT

ATË,

GODDESS OF MISCHIEF &

RUIN

I stare out the kitchen window, my bowl of cereal sitting forgotten before me. I am still a bit in shock at being here with Erebus. Yes, we live together. Has it been all sunshine and kittens? No, absolutely not.

When I was freed from Tartarus, I had to choose, either be sent back to my Hell prison or go to therapy. I chose the latter. Well, actually, after a brief discussion of my feelings, loss of control of my powers, and close examination of what had gone on in my life since my release, my therapist decided for me. Her solution was, *Hey, why not shove you in the same house with the man you can't stop thinking about? You know, for fun.* But it wasn't fun. I had escaped Tartarus and went to find the one person who, at the time, I thought cared for me. I found Erebus on a dating show. I slaughtered most of the contestants and staff, then ended up sleeping with him. Yes, I know, I have issues.

The moral of the story is that Erebus and I have not gotten along well. I still have a lot of feelings and emotions that I've not discussed, and why would I? I am the Goddess of Ruin and Mischief, not kind and fluffy feelings. Besides, it doesn't really matter. I know I am not good for him. I am bad news with flashing neon signs. But still, even with that knowledge, I can't leave because I know the truth even if he doesn't. This is the closest thing I've ever had to a home.

I stir the same bowl of cereal I made twenty minutes ago, the metal spoon scraping against the glass. I am not even hungry. I am sitting at the kitchen table in my oversized pajamas and lopsided bun, my head resting on one hand as I continue to think about everything and nothing in particular. Erebus isn't home and hasn't been for a day or so. He often has business elsewhere that I don't ask about. Sure, I am curious, but it would just result in another fight and me admitting more of those damned feelings I currently want to take to my grave.

The doorbell rings, drawing me out of my haze. Who rings a doorbell? I narrow my eyes before shrugging and turning back to my cereal. It is more like soggy soup now. A short burst of repetitive knocks has me sighing. I roll my eyes as I push off the counter, my bare feet slapping against the floor. Two of my nightgoyles stand at the front door, growling and alert. I speak a command in Latin, and they settle. They are unruly beasts, that's for sure, resembling gargoyles from mortal legends. I open the door, and a brown-haired man about 5'7" hurries past me. Chuck. He is one of the producers from that lovely dating show I mentioned earlier. Well, after I killed almost everyone, he had no job and nowhere to go. So out of the kindness of my cold, dead heart, I gave him a job. He is like an assistant to Erebus and me. Plus, he is loyal, and that always receives high points in my book. I hold my hand out, sarcastically ushering him into the room before closing the door and turning.

"Well, come right in."

"Sorry." He stops, looking around the room before turning back to me. "Have you heard from Erebus? I have called like fifteen times, and I didn't see his car out front."

I shrug, heading back into the kitchen and grabbing my cereal bowl. "No, I haven't, but he often disappears for work stuff that I don't ask about."

"Oh right, um, yes. Work stuff." He stops, scratching the middle of his head as he closes both eyes. "Right, well, he usually answers, and it's unlike him not to."

I rinse my bowl out in the sink before shutting the water off. I turn, wiping my hands on one of the dishcloths, and face Chuck. "What do you want me to do? Light a flare? Smoke signal him?"

"Aren't you worried?" he asks.

"About Erebus? No. Why should I be? He's literally older than...well, everything. Who is going to hurt him? The last person who tried to kill him is standing in this kitchen."

Chuck steps closer, his voice barely a whisper, like he doesn't want to be overheard. "But what about the people we are looking for? You know, the scary ones like you?"

I narrow my eyes at Chuck, and he gulps and backs away from me. The *people* he is talking about are not people at all. No, he is talking about the Titan Kronos and Primordial Chronos that I so happily helped escape when I first came back to Olympus. Chuck has been helping me track them. We've been going through my list of enemies and following up on any leads. Problem is that list could stretch across this world and the next. I blow a breath through my nose and tap my fingers against my hip.

"How many days has it been?"

Chuck looks at the ceiling as he counts off on his fingers. "I spoke to him the other day, and since then, I've left voicemails. I would say, maybe twelve hours."

I chew the inside of my lip for a second. "Hold that thought."

I disappear from the kitchen and reappear in my room. I grab my phone and rematerialize downstairs, right behind Chuck.

He jumps as I startle him and clutches at his chest. "I hate when you do that."

I ignore his comment and unlock my phone, going through my messages. Hmm, he isn't wrong. Erebus hasn't contacted me either, although I usually leave him on read. The last text he sent me said he would be gone an extra day and back around noon the following. I glance at the clock on the stove. Yup, late. He is never late or says things he doesn't mean, even if they are annoying things that make my stupid heart do flips. An idea crosses my mind. I lift my shirt and take a picture of my breasts before hitting send.

"Oh my God, Atë!" Chuck yells, covering his eyes.

"What?" I ask, curling my lip at him. "You've seen tits before."

Chuck mumbles something, but I barely hear him. I wait for the little dots to pop up, telling me he has seen and is just ignoring Chuck because, well, it's Chuck. I chew the inside of my thumb for what feels like an eternity, but nothing changes. *Fuck.* Inaudible chatter takes me out of my haze as I look up and see Chuck still talking.

"...I mean, if he doesn't respond, then he's probably dead. Can you guys die?"

"He's not dead," I snap. *Hopefully.* I shake my head, placing my phone on the counter. "Keep an eye on that. I need to change clothes."

"Wait on your phone. Wait, why are you changing clothes?" Chuck calls as I turn to walk out of the kitchen.

"Because if he doesn't respond, we are going to find him and kill him ourselves," I call back.

"Oh, this isn't good," I hear Chuck murmur as I reach my room.

No, Chuck, it's not.

It has been a whole day with no response from Erebus, and my stomach is in knots. He always replies. He is usually the one that religiously checks on me, not the other way around. Also, I may have sent some threatening messages after he didn't respond to my picture. At this point, I am losing my grip on my more homicidal tendencies. Take, for example, that I am currently forcing a mortal to learn to breathe underwater.

I lift her head out of the full sink in her studio apartment. I think Tracy is her name, but I don't remember.

"Tell me again the last time you talked to him?"

She coughs before squinting at me with one eye. "I told you it was a few days ago. I sent him info on another gig, and that was it."

Ugh. I toss her to the ground as she continues to cough and gasp for air. Gig. Right, because Erebus DJs. He likes music. I remember how his eyes lit up when he was telling me about the stupid rock music on our awkward yoga date. I also remember how he smiled when he told me little parts about himself or inquired more about me. And especially how he looked at me when he thought I wasn't looking, no matter where we were. And now I am so afraid that won't happen again. Tears prickle my eyes, which only pisses me off more.

"Do you think a broken arm will make you sing like a bird?" I ask as she scurries away from me.

Chuck steps in front of me, holding his hands up. "Okay, I know she's not lying. Why would she? I also know you are worried and upset, given your crazy gold eyes are now shining, but maybe we need to look at a different lead."

I rub my hands over my eyes, snapping at Chuck, "I don't have any fucking leads, Chuck! You think someone is just going to text me like, *Hey, guess what? We have Erebus.*"

"Well—"

He doesn't finish his next sentence as my phone lights up, playing a small tune. I rip it out of my pocket. Erebus's name shines, and I accept the call, screaming into the phone line.

"I swear to gods if you aren't tied up or half-dead, I will personally make sure you are!"

"Well, that's a rude way to answer the phone," a voice I don't recognize replies. "Although I don't expect much from you, Atë."

"Who is this, and why do you have Erebus's phone?" I bite the words out as Chuck looks at me, concerned.

33

"Meet me at 406 Anvalla Drive," he says before hanging up.

The address belongs to some old, abandoned warehouse. I roll my eyes so hard I think I see my brain. Typical bad guy 101, no one uses warehouses anymore. Fucking mortals. I put the car in park harder than I mean to and hop out, chuck following close behind.

"You sure you want to come inside?" I ask as we jog across the street, and I rip the chain-link fence in half.

Chuck walks through first. "Yes. What if it's a trap? We don't even know if he is in there."

I nod at Chuck. He likes to carry a gun with him for protection, and no matter what I tell him, he insists on tagging along. I think he is starting to like the adrenaline rush. I also don't tell him that I know Erebus is in there. I am elated until we get closer, and I realize something feels wrong. We've always had a weird connection. I have felt it from the beginning, even though we were not the least bit interested in exploring it. As we get closer to the old warehouse, I feel him again. Only it isn't the warm, fuzzy, tingling feeling I usually get. This one makes my head pound, signaling his distress, and worry fills me.

I step in front of Chuck, taking the lead. "Just stay behind me, and if I tell you to run, you run, okay?"

He nods, and I turn back towards the warehouse. The front door is rotten and what is left of it crumbles beneath my touch. I step over a few piles of trash as we enter. Chuck holds a small, compact flashlight over his gun as he scans the room. I don't have the heart to tell him the coast is clear. I am convinced the guy actually likes and cares about Erebus and me.

Water drips from the ceiling as we continue further inside. Pieces of metal hang in different places, but the pulsing in my head tells me Erebus is upstairs. I wave Chuck along, telling him to go check down the far hallway, and I will check the second floor. I don't want him following me. It is really hard to find a good assistant. He nods and continues deeper into the warehouse. I make sure he is out of eyesight before I disappear and reappear upstairs. I raise my foot and kick the large metal door, sending it flying into the room beyond. I could have opened it, but hey, I'm dramatic and pissed. I walk in, expecting to see Erebus tied up or something, but there is no one in here. A table is set in the center of the room with a TV in the middle. I tilt my head and walk closer. I see a note with the words *Play Me* taped to the top of a DVD player. I roll my eyes again at the terrible villain portrayal but follow the instructions.

The screen goes fuzzy for a second before an old familiar face pops up.

"Atë, it's good to see you. Although technically I can't see you, but I'm sure you get the gist. How long has it been since you, you know, ruined my business?"

35

Parker? Or is it Peter? Damn, I really am bad with mortal names. His face lights up the screen, and I remember him from my first stint back. He'd owned the art gallery I'd stolen the statue of Zeus from before I wired it up and sent it to Olympus to spy. It had come in handy, giving me enough information to know who I needed to track down to release the Titans. The last time I saw him, I had left him tied to a bed and then called the police so he wouldn't be in the way.

"You are probably surprised to see me since our last encounter. I have met some really nice friends of yours, who like you just as much as me. They were kind enough to help me kidnap your boyfriend, which by the way, *bravo!*" He pauses to clap sarcastically. "They always say you can't turn a hoe into a housewife but look at you. You two have been playing house for months now, even going on dates. Which yes, we saw that, too. We have been watching for a while. You really fucked over a lot of people. Tsk tsk. Anyway, I hate to ramble. I have other plans to get to that involve the ones you love so much. You took everything from me, Atë, and I plan to do the same. Although your boyfriend is probably going to rip you in half in about," he pauses, checking his watch, "oh, three minutes from now. I thought it was poetic. Okay, I gotta run. I hear there is a certain muse who you love like a daughter."

The screen goes black, and it takes me a second to realize the beating drum I am hearing is my heart. Fucking Peter. I should have killed him. Also, what enemies? Where is Erebus? How does he know about Clio? I run my hands through my hair and then pick up the TV, shattering it against the nearest wall. The table follows as I let out a scream of frustration. I tilt my head back, placing my hands on my hips as I let out a shaky breath. That's when I realize I am no longer alone. Shadows creep up the walls as the room fills with energy. It is Erebus, but not like he usually is. The hairs on the back of my neck stand up, signaling danger, which is not the usual response my body has to him. As I slowly turn, the already darkened space seems to be swallowed by the abyss, with no outside light or sound penetrating.

The person, if that's what you want to call him, that greets me isn't *my* Erebus. No, this is pure Primordial. He has no features except the lines and angles that tell you his appearance is male. Constellations dance where his eyes are, and a sharp-pointed spear tipped shadow bristles around him. It is pure darkness in its truest form. I have only seen him like this once before. Back when the Titans were first released, and every god fought to send them back to Tartarus.

I instinctively reach towards his face as I whisper, "What have they done to you?"

His cosmic eyes glance towards my hand and back, a look of pure disgust gracing his shadowy features. He answers my question by grabbing my wrist and throwing me through the wall.

My back hits the floor, and I groan, rolling to my side. Okay, fighting him is not the answer. Plus, I am a hundred percent sure every time we have fought, he has held back. Just ask my cracked rib. I push myself to my feet and limp toward the far door. Leaning against the wall, I catch my breath as parts of my body pop back into place. A loud thud tells me he has entered the room I just crawled out of. Closing my eyes, I dissipate and reform, putting more distance between us. Now I know something is definitely off. He has always been able to control my ability to shift. The logical part of my brain tells me he doesn't even realize it is me. I hear the building groan as if different pieces of the metal structure are being ripped and thrown. His shadows are growing restless and more destructive as they search for me. I slowly step back, keeping my eyes on the door and one arm across my abdomen.

I let out a sharp yelp as I trip over something heavy and land on my ass. Leaning up, I see Chuck lying unconscious on the dirty floor. "Oh, Chuck, he found you first." I crawl to him and place my fingers against his throat, happy to feel a tiny pulse. "Okay, at least you aren't dead, but you can't stay here, buddy," I whisper and look at the door once more, then back to Chuck. I grab him by his right arm and stand up with him, disappearing from the warehouse and back to the car. Digging in my pocket as I reform, I grab the keys and unlock the door, placing Chuck as gently as I can in the backseat. He has a gash on his head that has stopped bleeding and probably a few broken bones. None of his injuries seem life-threatening, which tells me Erebus is still in there somewhere.

Chuck groans as he tries to sit up. "Where am I?" He reaches up, wincing as he touches his forehead.

"Outside of the warehouse. Stay here, okay? I'll be back. Maybe." I turn to leave, and he grabs my arm. The look I give him makes him second guess that impulsiveness.

"Where are you going?"

I look at him like he is crazy. "I have to go back."

"No, we have to go get help or something."

I shake my head and say firmly, "I can't leave him."

"But—"

Chuck starts to say something else, but I throw a punch, knocking him unconscious. I belatedly realize that probably wasn't great for his concussion, but he was wasting my time. I need to get back before Erebus realizes I am not there.

Sighing, I close the car door and turn back to the old warehouse. I have an idea, but it is more than likely going to get me killed.

I reform back inside the warehouse, leaning against a wall as the darkened embodiment of Erebus stands in the middle. Thousands of shadows jut out of him, some searching and others tipping like daggers, waiting to impale anything that gets close to him. As soon as I solidify in the room, every part of him stops moving, and he spins to face me. One of the dagger-like shadows shoots forward. I dodge it, and it impales the wall behind me.

I stand back up and look at him. "You know I am really starting to think you don't like me anymore." Another shadow comes for me, and I disappear, reappearing across the room. "Is this about the yoga date because I thought we agreed we would try something different?"

He turns quickly, as if he is about to send several more shadow-like daggers toward me, but falters. His head tilts for a split second at my words, as if they snuck in past whatever Peter had used to make him a killing machine. And at that moment, I know my plan will work. I just need to get close enough to use it. In the next moment, his eyes glow, and I drop to the ground, rolling out of the way of the ceiling, he tried to bring down on top of me.

I stand, wiping off my jeans. "This is a new experience for us. I haven't even tried to drop a building on you, and you've attempted like twice now."

Another shadow dagger flies toward me, and I spin out of the way.

"That's how I know this isn't really you. You would never hurt me. You never have. I know you are in there somewhere. You didn't even kill Chuck, and that's saying something. I mean, he can be annoying. Villain 101, everyone is expendable."

I see the area where his eyes squint a moment before he raises his arms, and a large black wall forms behind him. I have a second to think before that wall comes rushing towards me and sends me back several feet. The wind is knocked out of me once again as I hit the first floor of the warehouse. I cough up dust as I try to catch my breath. Erebus lands heavily beside me with a loud thud. He reaches down, picking me up by the collar of my shirt. I grab onto his arms, steadying myself as my feet dangle.

"You know," I croak, "Eros goes on and on about this stupid thing that if you really care about someone, you don't leave. So, I'm not leaving. No matter how many times you try to kill me. I know you are still in there."

His face contorts for a second, his brow furrowing as he hisses in pain. I can feel it, too. Every time I say something, the hold on him weakens a little more. At that moment, I know what I have to do. It is something I hate doing, but what choice do I have? I can't live without him, and so I have to admit my feelings.

"Erebus, this isn't you, okay? They got into your head somehow and made you see things. It's me. It's Atë." I struggle a little more in his grip. "You wouldn't hurt me. You never have, okay? I need you. Just like I said that night. I meant it. I can't do this whole life thing without you."

The reaction I get is not the one I expect as he drops me straight on my ass. He stumbles back, grabbing at his head as an ungodly wail echoes off the walls. Shadows bend and twist around him as if they are in pain, too. I push myself to my feet, and the wind picks up in the warehouse. It is the howl of darkness, pure and simple, fighting itself.

I hold a single hand over my face, squinting from the force of the power struggling in the room. I try to walk towards him, having to yell even to be heard over the continued wails. "Erebus, I know you can hear me, but you have to fight this! I know you can. You are one of the strongest and most annoying people I know. You are too stubborn to let some mortal control you!"

My words seem like they are working and have some effect. I just have to keep pushing. He never gave up on me, so I will not give up on him. "You said it, Erebus. You told me you and I are more right for each other than anyone you know."

He keeps moving backward, gripping his head as his shadows and the darkness in the room seem to vibrate out of rhythm. Their shapes jagged and serrated stab at anything too close. I know I should be scared. Scared of him, scared of dying, but I am only afraid of losing him.

"Trust me, I have lived for thousands of years, Erebus, and one thing I am certain of is that you are it for me. You are all I have in this fucked up world! So, I am not leaving until you snap out of it!"

I shout the last part, and in a response, a sharp pain rips through my chest. My body lurches forward, and I look down to see one of the shadow daggers protruding from my chest. The sounds in the room die as the darkened figure that is him stands in front of me. Erebus, like always, has touched my heart, only this time literally. It feels like how I thought it would, a searing pain. I know that if he moves, he can rip me to pieces, but isn't that what love is? Isn't it trusting someone else not to destroy you? I lean closer and use the little bit of strength I have left to cradle his face in my hands. If I am going to die, I want him to know it isn't his fault.

"I want you to know," I struggle, my teeth gritting as I hold on to the piece of him so closely connected to my heart, "if I die, I will die knowing that your life was the best part of my life. And I am so, so sorry I got you involved in this. I should have left the second I got out of Tartarus b-but I couldn't," I groan as I struggle to catch my breath, "because I love you."

The hollow wail that fills the room quiets, and I am pretty sure I am dying. I don't see a better way to go, though. I have lived my life caring practically for no one, and here I might die by the one I love. Hey, like Peter said, it's poetic, isn't it? I watch the cosmic swirl that makes up Erebus's eyes slowly return to normal, and the black mass that encompasses his form retreats into him. The shadow-like weapons slowly fade, and the room lightens. As the blade leaves my body, I fall forward, coughing and gripping my chest in pain. He catches me almost instinctively, cradling me to him. Blinking a few times, he looks around the room before his gaze falls to mine.

"Atë?" he asks. "Where are we?" He pauses again, looking me over once more. "You're hurt."

He hurriedly takes off his jacket and wraps me up in it. I nod before closing my eyes, feeling my skin trying to knit itself back together. "Yeah, well, you stabbed me, so I guess in the long run, we are even."

"What!? I stabbed you? When?" he asks frantically. He picks me up, holding me against him.

I groan at the sudden movement, my arms wrapping around his neck. "It's a very long story, and one I will tell you far away from here."

Back at the house, I shower and change clothes. I talked to Eros earlier, and he said Clio was fine and that they hadn't been visited by ghosts of my past. Chuck is asleep and nestled comfortably in my bed. He has a wound on his head but nothing major. The car ride home was anything but pleasant. Every bump had my chest hurting, and I occasionally rub it even now. It is the closest I have come to death, and it made me realize a few things.

I don a satin pajama set and a long matching robe before going to find Erebus. The house itself seems eerily quiet as I make my way downstairs. The nightgoyles lift their heads when I enter and make a snort like sound, looking toward the balcony door. I turn, seeing the sliding glass door wide open and the long curtains blowing in the night air. I pad silently across the room, Erebus's back coming into view. He leans against the railing wearing a white T-shirt and dark pajama pants, a drink in his hand.

"Hey, killer." I hear him make what sounds like a mix between a groan and snort. "Too soon?"

"Not funny," he responds as he takes a sip of some dark liquor. Well, someone has been raiding the cabinets.

I shrug, leaning on the railing next to him. "I thought it was."

He turns to me, his temper apparent. "Atë, I almost killed you. Why are you making jokes?"

My eyes soften as I reach out and touch his shoulder. "Because you didn't."

He doesn't say anything as he finishes his glass and sets it down. I trail my hand from his shoulder to his arm, making him face me. He sighs when he turns, and I know he is more upset about hurting me than anything else. I open my robe, exposing the smooth skin above my breast, where a scar should be.

"See? All healed up." I smile at him, although his expression doesn't change.

He reaches forward, the tip of his fingers grazing the same spot as his brow furrows. "You should have left me."

I shake my head. "I couldn't leave you. I didn't know if I would be able to find you again or if they would come back for you." I swallow at the thought. "Speaking of which, how much do you remember?"

He drops his hand before his eyes meet mine. "I remember getting a text message from you to meet you somewhere. I remember arriving, and after that, it gets blurry. Next thing I am at the warehouse with you, and you're bleeding because of me."

Okay, well, that answers my question then. I had been wondering since we left how much he remembered. If he actually heard what I

45

had confessed. A part of me is relieved. I can continue to play up my ruse. Pretend he means nothing to me, but who am I kidding? I can lie to him, my friends, even the world, but I can't lie to myself. Not anymore.

I curl a piece of hair behind my ear as I bite my bottom lip. "That's kind of what happened, but I need to tell you something."

"You can tell me anything. You know that."

I nod before I swallow, a huge lump suddenly forming in my throat. "I have enemies. Lots of them. Some you met tonight, even though you don't remember clearly. I have made a thousand or plus mistakes in my lifetime, but the one right thing was meeting you. I know we have a complicated past, but you mean something to me, and they know it." I pause. "They tried to use that against me tonight, and I have been lying to you. I have been pushing you away because I have to. Because you are the one thing that I am afraid to lose."

My eyes water as Erebus steps forward. His big hands cup my face, and I reach up, holding them with my own.

"You are the only thing in this world. I don't want to ruin it, Erebus, and I am so afraid I will. The way I feel about you. I know we don't always get along and that this is new for you and me but after tonight..." I shake my head, trying to find the words to tell him everything I've felt and hidden. "I know I am not good at feelings. It's not me. That is way more Eros, but that's the thing. I have been friends with Eros forever, even before my fall, so I know love. I've seen it. I know love isn't selfish. It isn't cruel. I've witnessed thousands fall before his arrows in the name of it. I've witnessed immense joy and tragic ruin in the name of it. But only the truest version makes you bare your soul. Makes you fight for it. Makes you die for it. And that's what I did tonight. I couldn't leave you. I'll never leave you, even if you killed me. So, in that I know without a shadow of a doubt that I, Atë, Goddess of Ruin and traitor to Olympus, love...you."

His eyes soften as his thumb caresses my cheek. "I know. I heard you the first time."

I feel the tears rolling down my face and don't get a chance to form my next thought before his lips slam onto mine. His kiss is hot and electric, like everything I'd said was what he was dying to hear, and he knows I mean it. I wrap my arms around the back of his neck as I deepen the kiss, drinking him in. The fear I feel over losing him increases my desire tenfold. I don't know how long we stay there, wrapped in each other, before he pulls back a few inches. He brushes the hair from my face as he looks at me, his touch filled with reverence.

"Wait?" I ask, slightly confused. "You heard me the first time? In the warehouse?"

"That you love me? Yes. I just wanted to see if you would say it again or try to deny your feelings."

I playfully slap his chest. "You ass! I thought your memories were all screwed up."

"I mean yes, but I heard what you said. Every bit of it. I love you, Atë. I have for a while."

I knew how he felt. He had shown me several times by the simplest gestures. Even though I tried to ignore them and push him away, he never gave up on me, and that's why I will never give up on him. I smile a real smile for the first time in a while. I am just happy to have him back and whole again. Then another thought crosses my mind, and I tilt my head back towards the house. "You know Chuck has my room," I whisper innocently, sliding my fingers into his hair.

A mischievous glint lights his dark eyes, and a sultry smile plays over his lips. "Well, that is terribly inconvenient, isn't it?"

I nod before my laughter cuts through the cool night air as he lifts me in one easy motion. My lips meet his, letting him taste my happiness. I wrap my legs around his waist, and he takes us back into the house.

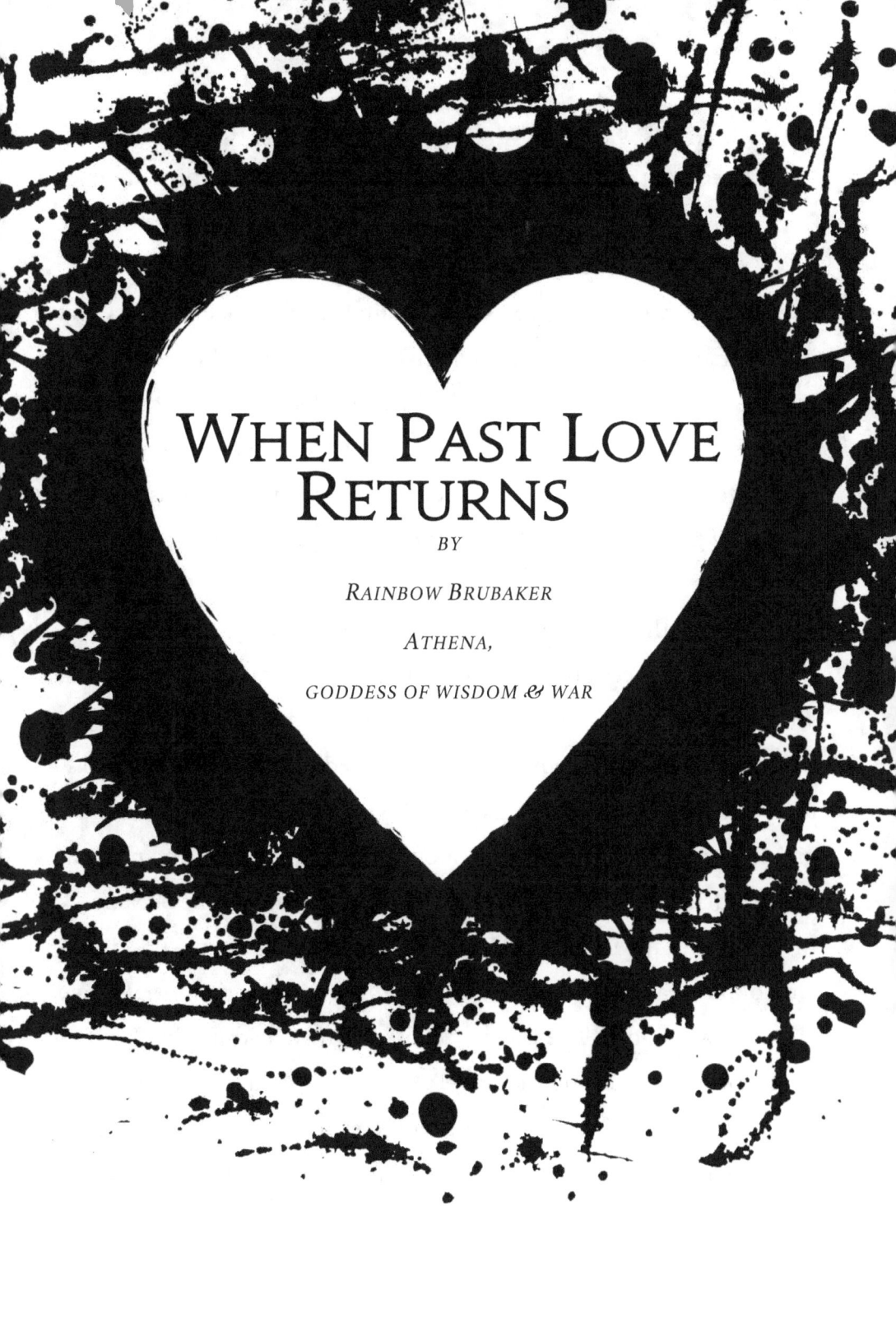

WHEN PAST LOVE RETURNS

BY

RAINBOW BRUBAKER

ATHENA,

GODDESS OF WISDOM & WAR

W e have all heard the age-old saying that if you love someone, set them free. If they don't return, then they were never yours. I never really understood what the expression meant, especially since it doesn't specify how long you should wait. Days? Weeks? Years? What if the person you loved died and then came back? Would their resurrection change how you feel? How they feel? Can love truly conquer death? I know it sounds far-fetched, but then again, you are talking to a goddess. Far-fetched seems to be the norm for us deities. We rarely give oddities a second thought and just accept it as the way things are.

One thing that is certain for both mortals and immortals alike is that second chances are rare. If you are blessed enough to have a second chance, you would be a fool not to take advantage of it.

The woman I loved eons ago has returned to me. Back then, I was too young and stupid to realize what loving her truly meant. I didn't give her the time and care that I should have. My neglect and pursuit of the glories of man left her alone and wanting more. She became involved with my uncle. You have probably heard of him—Poseidon, God of the Sea. I understand why she fell for him, many mortals have, but she was *my* love. The jealousy drove me mad. I admit that I lost my temper, and she paid the price. Out of anger and hurt, I turned her into a gorgon, vowing that no one would ever have her. The curse strengthened her and gave her powers over man. I didn't want her to fall prey to the grim fate that many mortals suffer when they become involved with the gods.

At the time, all she saw was the curse, and I understood her pain and anger. I still do.

Despite her extra defenses and abilities, she was slain. Her beautiful head was mounted on a shield, in all of its gorgon glory, and presented it to me as a gift. I cannot count the number of times I stared into her eyes, frozen wide and lifeless, wishing she could return to me. I know it's gross, but it's true. I kept her close to me in all the morbid glory of carrying someone's severed head around. I took that shield with me into battle, and it kept me safe...she kept me safe. She had died, but it was a dark reminder of the only person I had ever loved. Sure, I loved my adopted son, but that was a maternal love and not romantic. The two cannot be compared.

Regardless of the how, I have been given a second chance at love. This time I am going to do my best not to fuck it up. I did that once and have the emotional scars to prove it.

So here I am. My love has returned from the dead, resurrected as the immortal gorgon. She is the Medusa of legend, and I am so thankful that she exists. Our reunion was unexpected. We were thrown together when we were asked to work on the same case for the police department. Sometimes our unique talents were useful to the mortals in solving the worst of their crimes. She wasn't happy to see me at first, but I was overjoyed to see her. Medusa showed up at a crime scene that I was investigating, adorably flustered and full of spirit. She wanted to be angry at me but couldn't manage to stay that way. I am sure that my rushing to her and wrapping her in a tight embrace had something to do with it. Of course, my apologizing and honesty didn't hurt. I didn't care who was watching. Let them watch. I was lost in a world that was just hers and mine. All the feelings I had kept bottled up from long before she was killed came flooding out of me in a giant tsunami. I couldn't have stopped it even if I had wanted to, and I hadn't even tried.

Our first time seeing each other after so long had its challenges and awkward moments. We have spent a little time together since, but now what? Where do I go from here? I need to be with her. I crave her to the depths of my soul. I wish it were easy, but nothing worthwhile ever is.

I know that I have to take the next step, but my palms sweat, and my heart races at the mere thought of her. Part of the perks of skipping childhood and adolescence was bypassing puberty and all the mess that accompanies it. I have been a grown woman my entire life. I would never have believed that at my age, I would be going through all this now. I feel like a teenage mortal gushing over my first love...probably because she *is* my first love. I have thought, dreamed, and longed for her for so long. Now that she has returned, I feel like a fool because I have no idea what I am doing. Some goddess I am.

Releasing the breath I didn't realize I was holding, I pull my cell phone from my pocket and stare at it. Almost as if by doing so, the answers I seek will appear on the small piece of technology held within my sweaty grip. It didn't. Well, hells, I guess I need to leap and hope to fly. Tapping the speed dial for Medusa, I patiently await the sound of ringing to start. Yes, I have her on speed dial—no comments on how that makes me look.

"Hello?" Medusa's voice drifts through the receiver, sending shivers of anticipation down my spine.

"Hello?" her repeating her greeting brought me back to reality. *What am I doing? Right, I am wooing Medusa!*

"Hey, it's Athena. I wanted to know if you had a moment to talk?" I can feel the warmth spreading over my cheeks. Great! I am blushing like a fool over *hello*.

"Sure, I have a moment. What's up?" she replies. I can feel the joy in her voice. Is she as happy as I am about talking?

"Hello, Athena? Are you still there?"

"Yes, sorry." Now I know I am full-on blushing. *Zeus help me.*

"I was wondering if you had plans on Friday night?"

"No, I don't think so. Why? Do you need me to help on a case?"

She thinks I am calling for a case…just great. Choking down the frog in my throat and trying to seem even halfway intelligent, I respond, "Um…no…I…um…I wanted to know if you would go out with me…on a…you know…date?"

She giggles at me, stammering and falling over my words. Just great, Athena. Now she knows how off your game you are. If I am being an honest goddess, I would admit that she is the only one ever to do this to me.

"Yes, I would like that."

A rush of relief flows through me. She said, yes! In this moment, if my heart had the ability, it would have freed itself from my chest. Clawing its way from me and leaping through the phone to be with her. Hells, I would follow it.

"Um, Athena, are you there?"

Shit, I did it again.

"Yes, sorry. Okay, so meet at the complex at eight PM?"

"Sounds great. I'll see you then."

"Wonderful! I'll see you later." Without giving her time to reconsider, I say goodbye and hang up.

See, that wasn't so bad, was it? Gah, sometimes I really don't like myself. All I can do now is plan the perfect date and hope that she doesn't come to her senses and cancel on me. Maybe if I just turn my phone off and teleport it miles away, that won't happen. No, that won't work. Damn.

Remembering how much she loves the ocean and seafood I know what I will plan for our date. A romantic night on a private yacht, secluded on the sea. I can cook all her favorites, set the mood with candles, enough roses to choke on, and romantic music. Let the wooing begin!

The blaring sound of my alarm reminds me it is time to prepare to meet Medusa at the God Complex. Not that I need reminding or have stopped thinking about her and our date for a single second since I asked. Getting up from my desk, I stretch before teleporting home. I want to look my best. I want her to know that I want her.

After a thorough shower, I exit the large bathroom and walk across my master bedroom to where I had laid out the new clothes I'd bought for the occasion. I slip into the matching black lingerie set, complete with garters. I catch sight of myself in the mirror and realize I look like a professional call girl. The lacy material emphasizes my lean legs and toned backside. The flare of my hips tuck in at my waist, my torso bare except for the dark bra cupping the curve of ample breasts. The fabric is sheer enough to hide very little from the imagination but thick enough to conceal my nipples. I want to be dressed for the occasion to get undressed if the date goes that far. I don a royal blue dress to bring out the blue in my eyes. It clings in all the right places and is short enough to show off my thighs. I want her to see my every curve. The hem and sleeves are trimmed with black lace that matches my bra and panties. I decide not to wear any jewelry, but a pair of strappy black stilettos complete the look.

I spin before the mirror more times than I am comfortable admitting before sitting down to apply some smoky tones for eyeshadow, eyeliner, mascara, and luscious red, non-smudge lipstick. I blow out my long golden locks, and they fall in waves around my face and shoulders. I would normally wear it in a pretty up-do, but decide I want my hair free for her to tangle her hands in as we kiss. Warmth pools low in my belly, and I take a deep calming breath. *Slow down, Athena. This is a marathon, not a sprint.*

My newfound sexuality has me ready to pounce and eager to give and receive pleasure. I am aroused at the mere thought of Medusa and am instantly glad that I am not a man. Not just because I love my body, but because walking around with perpetual erections does not sound fun. At least as a woman, I can hide my arousal…for the most part, anyway. A final look in the mirror, and I teleport to the God Complex.

I arrive, and my eyes land on Medusa. She is leaning against a wall playing on her phone. If she is nervous, I can't tell. She is stunning, and I mean jaw drop to the floor stunning. Her short, sparkling green dress hangs off her beautiful shoulders and is ravishing on her. The colors grace her sun-kissed skin and accent her every delicious feature. I smile because she has worn her hair down, too. Mentally, I begin to undress her. *Damn it, Athena! Stop it! One step at a time!*

I walk as gracefully as possible and do my best to make sure that I don't fumble and trip over myself.

"I'm so glad you came," I greet her.

"Did you think I wouldn't?" The edges of her lips quirk up. Damn, she must know the effect she has on me.

"I had hoped that you would." I lean in and kiss her cheek. "Ready to go?"

"Yes, but where are we going? Somewhere in the city?" She looks around as if trying to guess what I have planned. I bring my body close to hers and wrap an arm around her waist.

"You will have to wait and see, Gorgie." This time I playfully kiss her nose before teleporting us to the yacht.

We arrive, and a small gasp escapes her lips. My arm is still wrapped around her, holding her closer than I really needed to for the teleport. The truth is, I just want to be close to her, to feel her skin against mine. For a moment, we stand in silence, taking in the clear night sky and the breathtaking display of the stars as they glimmer and glisten off the ocean. For miles, all you can see are the stars and the water.

The soft sounds of the waves lap at the boat, and a cool breeze drifts around us. Out here, on the calm sea with the moon above, is one of my favorite places. It's the main reason that I bought this yacht. So I could come out here whenever I wanted, completely unhindered. I have named it Immortal Love after my love for her.

"Do you like it?" I ask, hoping that she is happy with my choice of a date. Since this is our first one, I want it to be perfect.

"Oh, Athena, it's breathtaking," she whispers as she leans into my embrace. Standing there, holding her, I know I could spend an eternity here. Forever spent with her, and no one else would be as close to perfect as one could ever get. I don't want the moment to end. I am reluctant to break the tight embrace, but I know the food I'd prepared will get cold. I don't want to serve her anything less than magnificence tonight.

"Are you hungry?" I whisper into her ear. Sure, I could have asked normally, but I am wooing her.

"Starving."

Gently, I release her waist and take her hand in mine. I lead her into the yacht, where I have a candlelit dinner set and soft music playing. I made a special playlist for tonight with all the great singers of love songs, including Sinatra, Elvis, Flack, Houston, the Carpenters, and Savage Garden, among many others. I wanted enough to last us through the night and into the morning. I have a backup list if things get steamy, featuring Marvin Gaye, R. Kelly, and Usher. Honestly, I hope to get to play the second one, but maybe that's my libido talking.

I pull out her chair and wait for her to sit. Once I have her pushed in, I remove the silver covers to reveal our dinner. The plates are filled with buttered lobster tail, shrimp, clams, mussels, and angel hair pasta. A large salad and cheddar biscuits round out the meal. I pick up the bottle of aerated wine and pour each of us a glass. I have planned out everything to the finest detail. I have her favorite colors in the decorations and around two hundred red roses, either in vases or as petals I'd strewn around the room. Candles give the atmosphere its romantic glow. Taking my seat across from her, I contemplate playing footsie under the table.

"This looks delicious," Medusa says as she gives me one of her dazzling smiles. Maybe it's dazzling because it's her and she couldn't be anything else. To me, she is the very standard of perfection. I know, I know, I'm gushing again. I can't help it. She does that to me.

"Thank you. I hope that you like it."

Her eyes widen. "Did you cook this?"

Now it's my turn to smile.

"Yes, I cooked and prepared everything for this evening myself."

"You have changed, Athena."

"Is that good?" My face must have given away my insecurities because she extends her lovely arm across the table and takes my hand in hers.

"I think you are wonderful just the way you are."

I let out a sigh of relief.

"I think you are perfect just as you are, Gorgie."

"I am not perfect," she scoffs slightly. I reach out and lightly caress her cheek to reassure her.

"You are to me." We share a moment of silent appreciation for one another.

"Shall we eat? I am famished. It has been a crazy week," she says with a smirk. She wants to lighten the mood, and I can't be more thankful for her.

"Yes, let's."

The food is as delicious as it smells, and she seems to enjoy it. For the next hour, we eat and talk about our week, exchanging stories and jokes. Laughing as if no time has passed, and we were always this way. Something about it just feels right. Like this is how it always should have been. The rest of the world and its never-ending problems melt away, and all that is left is Medusa, me, and my boat.

Our meals finished, I excuse myself to fetch dessert. I return with two bowls, each containing a warm piece of chocolate lava cake and a scoop of vanilla ice cream topped with fudge, salted caramel, and nuts.

"I hope you like chocolate and ice cream."

"I haven't met a goddess who doesn't. This looks amazing."

"Thank you, Gorgie."

We savor the dessert and linger over our drinks, talking and laughing. I rise from my seat and hold out a hand to her.

"Dance with me?" She places her hand in mine, and I lead her out onto the deck where the music is a little louder. Pulling her close, we sway together. The melody and rhythm pulse through our bodies, vibrating from one to the other and back again. I can feel her warm breath on my neck, and it sends shivers through me. Breathing in her scent, I close my eyes, savoring her. The song ends, and another starts as we move, our legs in between each other's and breasts caressing. I keep her hand in mine and hold it as if my life would end if I let go. Not a crushing grip, but enough for her to know how much I need her. *I need her.* The realization hits me, and for once, I am not scared of needing someone else. Instead, I am happy.

She presses her forehead to mine as we continue to dance. I slowly pull back enough to study her beautiful blue-green eyes, memorizing them. I wonder if she is feeling the same devastating emotions that I am. As if reading my mind, she leans in close, and our lips meet. We kiss slowly and deeply. She opens and allows me in, and I explore her mouth, letting the passion take hold. She tastes as sweet as she smells. I could get drunk off of her and still crave more. Like a moth to a flame, I am drawn to her. I break the kiss, gently biting her lower lip before returning to our dance.

I want her to love me as I love her. Then it hits me. I am *in* love with her. I can feel the tears threaten to come to the surface as the revelation fills me with joy.

"What's wrong, Athena?" We have stopped dancing, and Medusa is looking deeply into my eyes. Concern furrows her brow, mistaking the tears filling my eyes as sadness. I want to tell her, but what if she doesn't feel the same? What if she doesn't love me in return? I want badly to have her, but I also know that she may not ever completely forgive me for all that I have done. Love makes you stupid, and tonight I am stupid.

"Gorgie…I'm in love with you."

The worry leaves her eyes, and she pulls me close again.

"I never stopped loving you," she whispers against my lips before kissing me deeply.

This time the kiss is full of passion, need flaring hot between us and pulsating through our bodies. I slide a hand up her back and into her hair. Her snakes are out and seem to be happy as they twine about my fingers. I have never seen her as a monster, and her gorgon form is beautiful to me. She is exquisite no matter which form she is in, but I do love her snakes. I love all of her. There it is again...*love*.

Our bodies press against one another, breast to breast, legs rubbing in the most intimate of places. The silk of her panties caresses my thigh as we move in a silent dance of passionate kisses. By the time we come up for air, our lips are swollen, and our bodies are left hungering for more.

I guide her to the large, overstuffed seats that line the deck of the yacht. Sitting down, I pull her into my lap, caressing her bare arms lightly. As much as I want to undress her and explore her body with my mouth, I need her to know that I want her and not just sex. Although sex would be amazing, I need her to know that I want more. I don't expect her to be monogamous. After all, we are just starting our relationship. I know she has a thing with the mortal named Luke, and it doesn't bother me in the slightest. I don't care about being exclusive as long as I get her. Mortals don't live that long anyway, and I hope to have an eternity to woo her and explore her body with my own. An eternity of passion and companionship, and she doesn't need to be just mine for that. Hells, I would even love to experience her, Luke, me, and the Captain. The thought makes me smile.

Visions of our naked bodies entangled play in my mind as I gently caress her arm, sliding my hand to the top of her thigh. I gently stroke the soft skin and savor the feel of her beneath my fingers as I inch my touch higher. Neither of us is worried about modesty, and even if we were, there isn't another soul for miles. I trail my soft lips from her shoulder, up her neck to her earlobe. I stop there to nibble before moving back down again. She cradles the back of my head and leans into my kisses.

My touch moves closer to her inner thigh, and I caress the sensitive skin. A small moan escapes her throat, letting me know that she is enjoying my attentions. Slowly I bring my hand up to cradle her breast through the fabric of her dress. She nearly purrs into the kiss as she arches into my touch. I could stay in this moment forever, touching her and listening to her sounds of pleasure. The feel and taste of her leaves me wanting more. Like a woman dying of thirst, I want to drink her in, needing her.

"I want you," I whisper into her hair and lightly bite her neck.

"Then take me," she replies before twisting on my lap to face me. Her lips crush mine as she pulls me into a passionate kiss. Her body rubs against mine as she rocks her hips against me, driving me crazy with need. Pulling her in tighter, I drink her in and satisfy the ache that we both feel.

Tonight, will be a night that we both remember as the moment our love story started again. This time I will not let anyone fuck it up. No mortal, god, or goddess. This time I will give myself to her and not hold back.

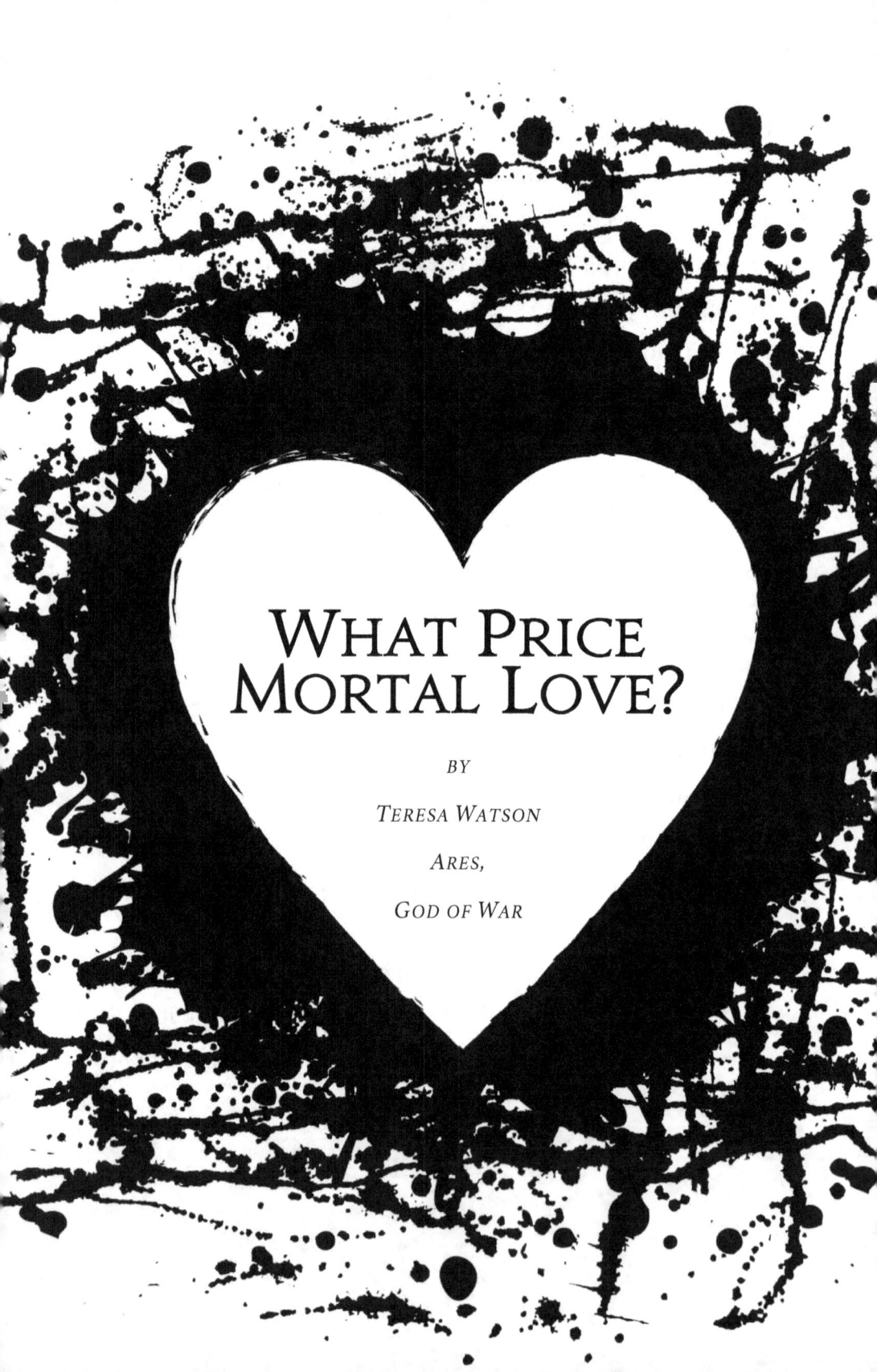

WHAT PRICE MORTAL LOVE?

BY

TERESA WATSON

ARES,

GOD OF WAR

My phone rang; it was Eleni. "We've got a problem," she said breathlessly. "Markos, the head of the Ultimate Power, the man you wanted me to keep an eye on, just got a text on his phone, freaked out, and left."

"I know," I replied. "Whatever they've got planned is starting to go down."

"We've been following him, so I have a couple of ideas about where to look for him. I'm headed over to get my partner and…"

"And what? Where are you going? Tell me, and I'll meet you there," I demanded. "We need to work as a united front right now, not separate entities."

Her voice became cold on the other end. I could hear her anger. "My partner is dead."

"What? How?"

"Hang on." I heard footsteps, something being shoved aside, and then some breathing. "She's been garroted."

"Who?"

"Cyndi," she said tersely. "Markos or one of his men must have killed her."

"Look around the area. Do you see any clues?" More scuffling noises, followed by very colorful language, which was totally understandable, given the circumstances. "Tell me what you see."

"A bloody mess," Eleni said. "There are papers everywhere, like he was looking for something. Not sure what he expected to find, or if he found it. I can't imagine there being anything here that would do him any good. I'm going to take a look at the body."

"Are you sure you want to do that?" I asked.

"If it means justice for Cyndi, then yes. Personal feelings can't interfere in an investigation. I'll deal with them later."

"And you wonder why I gave you such a plum assignment," I jokingly said.

"Screw you, Ares. The garrote is still around her neck. Somebody has been watching too many *Godfather* movies. Wait, there's something in her hand. It's a long strand of red hair."

For a moment, I thought my heart stopped, and an icy chill went up my spine. My girlfriend, Cassandra, had long red hair. "I gotta go."

"What's wrong?" Eleni said.

"I don't know. I've got a bad feeling. I hope I'm wrong."

Sometimes it was good to be a god. With a pop, I was in front of Cassie's house, and the door was partially open. I didn't have my gun with me, so brawn was going to have to deal with whatever I found inside.

Nudging the door open with my foot, I listened for noises but heard nothing. I moved quietly through the foyer and into the living room. My heart dropped into my stomach. It couldn't be…

Cassandra was on the floor with her beautiful red hair splayed out around her head. A knife protruded from the middle of her chest. She was gasping for air as I quickly knelt beside her. "Cassie," I said, gently caressing her cheek.

"A...Ares..." she gasped.

"Don't talk. I'm going to get you some help. Don't move. Lie still."

She looked at me with a mixture of sadness and pity. "I-I...l-love...y-you..." Cassie whispered.

"I love you, too. More than anything." I texted Hestia, pleading for help and sending her the address. "You're going to be fine." I took off my shirt, wrapped it around the wound without moving the knife, and applied pressure. "I've been thinking. We should go back to Paris. Go to all our favorite places again, don't you think?"

I heard a noise from behind me and looked over my shoulder at Eleni. "What can I do?" she asked. I didn't ask how she knew where to find me. As one of my most trusted priestesses, she always knew where I was, even when I desired privacy. Many times she had walked in unannounced, interrupting a private moment with a beautiful woman. But this was one time I was happy to see her.

"Wait outside for Hestia. I texted her and asked her to come."

She knelt next to Cassandra and felt for a pulse. "She's gone, Ares. There's nothing Hestia can do for her now."

I looked at this beautiful woman, who I had blithely discarded so many years ago. When I had come to my senses, she opened her heart to me, giving me another chance. She had given me so much, but getting close to me had cost her life.

They say a heart can turn cold, but it's always been something that I've scoffed at. Until now. There was a rage building inside of me, a rage that I had not felt for a long time.

Standing up, I walked out the door, Eleni right behind me. "Hey, look, there's a note on the door. Didn't you see it when you came in?"

"No, I didn't," I replied.

Let the games begin, God of War. Do you have the guts to fight, or have you truly turned into a coward, as others have said? I say coward. After all, you let a mortal get to your heart. Rather poetic that I drove my knife into her heart, isn't it? Grab your sword and your armor. Let's go to war.

Markos

I hadn't planned on taking anyone with me to face Markos. Ever since the gods had come back to Olympus, he and his group had been doing their best to sabotage everything we tried to do. I had always been a few steps behind, not quite sure if he was involved. But something told me that I needed to keep an eye on him. I had finally gotten too close, and he decided to push for a showdown by killing Cassie.

This was my fight, my revenge. But Artemis and Nike convinced me that it was better for me to have backup. I kept the number of people involved small: my son, Dinlas, Nike, Artemis, and her dragon, Sayeh.

Dinlas had tracked Markos and his men to the forest outside of town. We split up to surround them, and the battle was on. My sisters, as usual, fought like the warrior women they were. Nike sliced and diced her way through men like they were sticks of butter, and Artemis took aim with her bow and arrow, all of her shots true and on target.

Artemis dropped another body before approaching me. "Half ran off once the serious fighting started," she said. "But we still killed many of them. I'd say at least twenty to thirty." A flash of fire lit up the field to our right, followed by screams. "Sounds like Sayeh got a few more."

Nike dropped out of the sky, her wings folding behind her back. "I think the man you are looking for is over there. I spotted him near a tree, watching the fight but not participating. It's a cowardly act to let others do your fighting for you."

I looked over at the man Nike had pointed out. He strolled toward us, pulling his sword out as he walked. I pushed Artemis and Nike in Dinlas's direction. "Keep them over there with you," I called out to him.

"But Ares," Artemis started to say.

Glaring at her, I shook my head. "I will kill him myself, Arty," I said, my voice cold and distant. "This part isn't about family. It's very personal. Stay out of my way."

"I see you brought some help," Markos said when he got closer.

"And you lost a lot of your help," I replied. "You should have trained them better on how to be warriors on the field of battle."

"Yes, you know all about that, don't you, *God of War?*" he retorted.

We slowly walked in a circle. He twirled his sword in his hand. I had seen that move in hundreds of movies. Amateur. Mine was firmly grasped in my fist, blood dripping off its end. "Why? Tell me that."

"You and your kind became irrelevant thousands of years ago, and mankind was better for it," Markos said. "We have thrived. Without you lot around, we learned about fire—"

"That was given to you by Prometheus," I reminded him.

"Against the wishes of your father," he threw back at me. "At least there was one amongst you to stand up to the old blowhard."

"Technically, Prometheus is a Titan, not an Olympian. But I will give you that he did stand up to Zeus. He paid for his disobedience, however. You may have gotten along fine without us, but you've made a mess of things. We're here to help you clean it up and put you back on the right path."

"Meaning you want us to worship at your feet again," Markos scoffed. "That will never happen."

"I have never asked such a thing from any mortal."

"Who would worship you?" he laughed. "You're a bully and a coward. Your concubine is your brother's wife. And that stupid woman I killed this evening was a foolish twit who fell under your spell."

"Cassandra was her own woman who did what she wanted. I cast no spell over her. She was not afraid to stand up to me and tell me off. Now, are we going to talk all night, or are we going to fight?"

Holding out his hand, he waved his fingers at me. "Bring it, *coward.*"

We rushed forward at the same time, swords swinging. The clash of metal on metal sent sparks flying into the air. He feinted, and I followed. He brought his sword up, cutting deep into my right arm. It stung a little, but I ignored it. "What are you planning to do, slice and dice me to death?" I taunted.

"If that's what it takes," Markos said, lunging at me again.

I stepped to the side, swinging my sword in a downward motion, slicing into his leg. He gasped and grabbed it with his free hand. I swatted him on the butt with the flat side of the blade. "What's the matter, mortal? Afraid of a little blood?"

Spinning around, he came at me again, yelling like a banshee. This time, I cut his left arm. The anger on his face when he looked at me was pure evil. "I will not die today, Ares," he growled. "It will be you who is defeated this day."

"Is this the best you can do?" I said, faking a yawn. "Your men gave me a better fight than this. Makes me wonder who taught you how to fight, your mother? Perhaps it was your wet nurse. You should have suckled at her breast more."

He charged at me. I'd had enough. Bracing myself, I met his incoming swing with a parry and kicked him in the chest, knocking him to the ground. Moving quickly, I stepped on his sword hand before bending over and yanking it from his grip. I tossed it aside and placed the tip of my blade against his throat. "Why did you really kill Cassandra?"

"Because I knew it would be the one thing that would piss you off enough to fight me."

"Well, that was the only thing you've been right about." I raised my sword in the air. Looking him in the eyes, I said, "This is for her." I drove the blade into his chest, just as he had driven his knife into Cassie.

He gasped, and his body tensed up, then relaxed as I yanked the sword out. He coughed up some blood as he put his hands over the wound. Suddenly, he started laughing. "Killing me won't stop this," he said, spitting out some blood. "There are more of us. And we aren't just here. We're everywhere. You'll never see it coming, *coward*. Someone will find a way to kill you."

"You forgot the part about immortality, *mortal*."

He laughed again. "Anyone can die, even an immortal." He coughed, took one big breath, then died.

The other three joined me as I stood looking down at his body. Nike reached into her small pouch, pulled out a bandage, and wrapped it around my wounded arm. It would heal on its own in time. "Are any of you hurt?" I asked.

"Just the usual bumps and bruises," Artemis said. "Nothing that a nice, hot bath and a cup of Hestia's special tea won't cure." She shook her head. "Are you okay?"

"I'm fine. Why wouldn't I be?"

She started to say something but changed her mind. "We need to get rid of these bodies," she said. "A fire would be the best way to do it."

As we built the funeral pyre, I gave no thoughts to the families of the men we killed. Half of them had fought bravely, if for a foolish reason, and therefore deserved to be honored. But I refused to throw Markos's body on the pyre. He had killed innocents, and there was no honor in that. Even I knew that, although in the old days, I had done the same thing. Talk about the pot calling the kettle black.

By the time the flames had burned themselves out, it was dawn. Wild animals would soon be foraging for food. I left them Markos's body. Rather appropriate that an animal should be eaten by animals.

I shook Dinlas' hand. "Thank you, Son. What you did for me this night...it meant a lot."

I watched the emotions flash across his face. He was unsure of how to handle my gratitude. "You're welcome. It was an honor to fight next to you. But let's not make a habit of it. People might think we actually like each other." He walked away, whistling.

Nike gave me a hug. "I'll be there if you need to talk, Brother. You're not as tough as you'd like people to believe. I can feel your pain." She gently touched my cheek. Stepping back, she spread her wings and flew off.

"What will you do now?" Artemis asked me as we walked toward Sayeh.

"I don't know. Run my security company. I'm sure I'll have plenty to keep me busy."

"Nike is right, you know," she replied. "You're a bit vulnerable right now. You let love into your heart, pure love. Now you're feeling the loss and the pain. Let us help you deal with it. Don't do your usual macho thing and take off to deal with it yourself." She gave me a hug before climbing onto Sayeh's back. "You know how to find me. You can always spend some time here in my forest if you seek peace and quiet."

"Thank you, Arty," I replied. "I'll think about it."

"I love you, my brother."

"I love you, too, my sister."

She flew off, leaving me standing alone at the edge of the field.

"You know, I've had a wonderful time this week," Cassie said to me as we walked in the Parc des Buttes-Chaumont.

"As have I," I admitted. I pulled her close and kissed her. "I never thought I'd have such a wonderful time with anyone again after..."

"After what?" she asked me.

I shook my head. "It's not important."

Cassie chuckled. "She must have been pretty special."

"Once upon a time, I suppose she was," I conceded. "But that was a long time ago." I looked into her eyes. "This is now, and no one is more important than you at this moment."

She blushed, kissed me quickly, then took my hand in hers. We continued strolling through the park as the skies turned dark, and millions of stars began to twinkle and dance.

"Have you ever thought about getting married?" she asked out of the blue.

I stopped in my tracks. "Why would you ask me that?"

"Don't panic. I'm not about to propose to you or anything," Cassie laughed. "But is it something that you would consider in the near future?"

We started walking again. "If the right woman came along, yes, I would seriously consider it."

"It would have to be a pretty strong woman that could keep you from straying," she replied.

"That is true," I replied, "but I'm sure that you could rise to the challenge."

"Nice to know you think I'm that strong."

I pulled her close again. "Yes, I think you are," I said, gently tucking a strand of hair behind her ear. "I wouldn't mind growing old with you."

"Really?" She seemed surprised by my answer.

"Really," I said, kissing her lips.

We started walking again. "How many children would you like to have?" Cassie said. "I'd like at least one boy and one girl."

"I'm good with that, although our daughter won't date until she's thirty."

She laughed. "Oh, you're going to be one of those dads, are you?"

"Damn right, I am."

She pulled me toward a bench, and we sat down and gazed at the night sky. "I can't wait to grow old with you." She sighed, putting her head on my shoulder.

I stood in the rain, the collar of my jacket pulled up around my neck. The bench where we had sat that night was just in front of me. A small blue urn was tucked under my left arm, and a single red rose in my right hand. I had scattered parts of Cassandra's ashes in some of our favorite places and had left a rose as well. This was my last stop.

It was dark, as it was the last time we were here, but I could not see the stars this time. Just as well. This was not a time for stargazing. I scattered the remainder of her ashes around the bench before I sat down.

"This isn't how I pictured the way things would end," I said out loud. "I knew that you would die someday, but I pictured you old and grey, wrapped in my arms, with me telling you over and over how much I loved you as you slipped away. I never thought that you'd die alone at the hand of a man I didn't even know was my enemy."

It rained harder, as if Nyx were crying for Cassandra.

"You made me feel alive, Cassie. You made me feel so loved. Granted, Aphrodite is the Goddess of Love, but with you, it was different. I'm not sure I understand it. Maybe Artemis said it best—it was a pure love. If she is right, then I have no complaints. You gave me the best part of you, and you made me a better man because of it."

I looked at the red rose in my hand, gently stroking a petal. Standing up, I kissed it and placed it on the bench.

Then I turned and walked away, leaving her and my heart behind.

PHILIA
AFFECTIONATE
LOVE

A WEEK IN KORINTH

BY

NATALIE BARTLEY

AMPHITRITE,

GODDESS OF THE SEAS

Life had been a chore these last six hundred years or so. The king had abandoned my kingdom, and the wound that was left needed healing. I knew he liked to hang around the mortals, so I made my way to the surface. I wasn't planning on being away from Atlantis for long. She couldn't survive without a ruler, but this was something I needed to do. Keeping Poseidon in check was never my job, but he'd been gone too long this time, longer than any of his past *indiscretions.* It's odd, but that sort of thing never bothered me like it did some of the *wives.* Maybe that's because P and I never married? I didn't know, and I didn't care if he was fucking half of Greece. Atlantis was missing her king. And honestly, I missed my love.

My heart hadn't been in the ruling of the kingdom for the last few centuries. It felt cold, empty, and barren. Parties raged around me, but the realm knew what it was missing, and I was desperate to bring him back.

I approached the surface near Athens and my instincts guided me west to Korinth. I decided to start at the Temple of Poseidon. I found a quiet cove and grew my legs in place of my tail, remembering at the last moment to add clothing.

Walking into town, I smiled as I realized that no one recognized me. No one was harassing me for things or trying to entice more benefits and ranking out of me. I was completely anonymous. It was amazing, and I did a small dance in the street. When people began to stare, I blushed softly and wandered. This new freedom was intoxicating, and I found myself wondering why I had never done this before. I'd walked among the mortals, but generally as myself, and always with Poseidon. Today it was just me, and I was free. I didn't know what to do with myself.

I continued with my plan and arrived at Poseidon's temple. The priest didn't question me when I requested sanctuary as a priestess. I must smell like the sea because he took one look at me and nodded. I followed him to where some of the priestesses stayed and found myself among kindred women, those who loved Poseidon dearly. Oh, I could tell them stories. However, I refrained and found a place to rest. "What is your name, young one?" one of the ladies asked me. Did I look so young? I thought I had chosen the visage of a mature woman, but perhaps not.

"Efterpi," I replied softly, the name rolling off my tongue without much thought.

"It's nice to have you here. Tomorrow, you'll be out in the streets, doing good work for our Lord Poseidon, so get some rest." She didn't introduce herself, and I didn't ask. I nodded and laid down my meager surroundings vastly different from what I'd left behind in Atlantis.

The next morning, I was paired with a young girl named Korinna. She was sweet, kind, and innocent. They set us loose on the streets of Korinth, trying to pull worshippers into the temple. I found the whole thing more than a little silly.

81

Even though Korinna had been in the temple longer than I, I took her under my wing. She reminded me of my daughter, Rhodes, and I knew I needed to guide and protect her. "Korinna, when was the last time anyone felt Poseidon answer their prayers?"

She smiled up at me as we walked up to the AkroKorinth. "Back in the Persian war, in the battle of Salamis. I heard it was glorious." I stopped for a moment, remembering a storm off the coast a few decades back, but I didn't think it was him. I couldn't tell her that, though.

I nodded and continued walking. "And before that?"

"I'm not sure, Efterpi. He must have, or the priests wouldn't keep making offerings to him. Would they?"

I shook my head and shrugged. "I'm not sure, Korinna. I've been looking for a very long time. I had hoped I would find some trace of him here," I commented off-hand.

I think she heard the pain in my voice because Korinna pulled on my arm. "Come with me. There's something I want to show you." I sighed and followed the young girl as she dragged me to the temple of Aphrodite. I wondered why she was bringing me here, but then I saw them—the hetaerae. Not working in the temple, but just outside it, still within their goddess' watchful eye. It wasn't the hetaerae that caught my attention, but the men who were visiting. This was a place that Poseidon might visit. Not that he was ever short of a conquest either back home or up here.

"You wanted me to see the working women of Korinth?" I asked her.

Korinna laughed. "No, the men. Sometimes," her voice grew hushed as she pulled me into some bushes, "I come up here and watch them. There's one I've taken a liking to. But he'll never notice me. I'm just a lowly priestess."

I looked over at her. "Korinna, you are young, pretty, and smart." Not that intelligence in a woman was highly prized, but whatever. "Any of those men would be lucky to take you home. Which one do you have your eye on?" I asked, really hoping that it wasn't one of the older men.

Thankfully, she pointed at a younger man, at least one closer to her age, and I sighed with relief. "Alright." I stood up suddenly and motioned for her to stay there despite her protests.

As the man left the company of the hetaerae, I slid up beside him. "Hi there." The poor lad nearly jumped out of his skin. "I was wondering why you visited the hetaerae. You're a strapping young man, have you not thought about taking a wife? What's your name?"

He looked up at me, and I think my age or motherly maturity was showing through because even though he was nervous and confused, he still answered. "Hilarion, ma'am." He coughed and sighed. "Of course, I've thought about it, but this is Korinth, where all the women are hetaerae or old."

"And what of the priestesses? I'm sure if you petitioned one of the priests, he could help?" I commented, wondering why I was getting involved in this. Perhaps because I could do nothing to bring my love back, so I would help someone find theirs?

"Most of the priestesses are out of marrying age or so devoted to their god they would never leave." I looked at Hilarion as I sat on a bench, not far from where Korinna was hiding.

"And what if I told you, one pretty priestess, not far off from your age, was willing to leave the service of Poseidon?" I asked pointedly. I really shouldn't be helping a priestess leave the service, but this was an opportunity to see *someone* happy.

Hilarion's eyes bulged at the thought. "Are you sure? I thought I had seen all the ladies in the area. I'd very much like to meet her."

I smiled, half cocky, half pleased, and nodded. "I'll bring her by tonight, here on this bench, and you two can meet. How does that sound?"

Hilarion nodded and ran away gleefully. I hoped he would work off the tension he had built up. He wouldn't want to scare off Korinna before they'd even met. I leaned back, and Korinna came out of her hiding spot to sit beside me. "Efterpi. What just happened?"

I looked over at the young girl. "I believe I set you up on a date to meet Hilarion. Isn't that what you wanted?"

Korinna sputtered, but her smile was genuine. "I...yes...of course it is!" She hugged me tightly, and I smiled softly. "But I have nothing, no home, no family, nothing."

My heart broke for her, and I hugged her again. "I'll be your family, your *mater*." Korinna began to cry, I held her tight in my arms and stroked her hair. "Shush, child. If you cry now, you'll look horrible for Hilarion tonight." She laughed and nodded, pulling back to wipe her face. "Now go back to the temple, tell the priest, and get cleaned up. You will want to look your best, right?"

"Oh, yes! Of course!" Korinna jumped up and giggled as she ran down the hillside toward the Temple of Poseidon. I shook my head and watched her go, lost in memories of my own youthful joy.

It wasn't until a voice sounded from behind me that I reined in my thoughts. "That was a nice thing you did there." The voice was male, and I felt power behind it. I turned to face him and met a stunning pair of brown eyes. I held his gaze almost reluctantly. This feeling of desire building within me was one I was familiar with, and one I hadn't experienced in a very long time.

"It seemed the right thing to do," I replied slowly. The man sat down beside me, almost touching my knee, and I scooted away a bit. He was making me uncomfortable for all the wrong reasons.

"You're not one of the hetaerae, are you?" he asked, and I shook my head. "No, I've never seen you here before, and yet, here you are. Up at the temple of the Goddess of Love herself. Why, you could be her."

I sprang to my feet and shook my head. The man stood as well, as if expecting this reaction, and smiled. "No, I am not the Goddess Aphrodite. She is…well…she and I are well acquainted with each other, but no, I am not her. And I would thank you not to call me that again. Bad things happen to mortals when they are compared to the gods." The man laughed, and the sound of his voice rolled like the ocean. "Pos-" I caught myself and sighed. No, it couldn't be that simple. I wouldn't find him here, after one day of searching.

"What's your name?" the man asked softly, indicating for me to sit again.

I did so and sighed softly. I wasn't getting out of this conversation quickly. "Efterpi, and yours?"

"Leandros," he replied cockily. I rolled my eyes. Of course it was. "And what brings you to Korinth, Efterpi? Other than facilitating young love?"

I looked up at Leandros. He was taller than me, even sitting down. "Would you believe me if I said love? I was here to find love?" It wasn't even a lie. I was finding love, my love, that stupid god I fell for thousands of years ago on Naxos.

"I can believe that. What I can't believe is that you haven't found it yet," Leandros stated.

I looked over, my mouth open to speak, but then closed it. I couldn't precisely explain. "Yes, well, not all of us are so lucky. And what about you? Did you come to stare at the hetaerae and harass lonely women?"

Leandros looked playfully affronted. "Harass? Harass?! I'll have you know, Efterpi, that I only speak to the women who look like they need cheering up. That is generally *not* a hetaera." I stared at him. Was my pain written all over my face?

"Alright then, Leandros," I toyed his name out, and he sat up a little straighter, "tell me what you see since you've so keen an eye."

86

He leaned forward, getting close, and I felt myself blush under his gaze. "Other than your beauty, on which I have already commented, I sense a strength within you. You have the ability to do jobs that would normally fall outside your realm. I see a great ocean of love, and a deep sea of hate, or at least, the capacity for it." My eyes bulged. How could he know? Before I could respond, Leandros's finger pressed against my lips. I stopped breathing, his scent exhilarating. "I also see great passion in you and a blockage. You stopped giving into your desires a long time ago. Why?"

I looked, *really* looked at him. I could see Poseidon clear as day in him, but I knew it wasn't him. "I was left behind." The words were out of my mouth before I realized I'd said them. I clapped my hands over that idiot hole in my face and stood up, almost smacking my head off Leandros's. I looked down at him, his eyes staring into mine. "I…I can't. Bye."

I rushed back to the temple where I found Korinna arguing with the older priestess, whose name I had learned was Tanis. "What's going on here?" I demanded, authority pouring off of me.

Tanis and the priest, Alecto, stared at me, anger filling the silence before Tanis spoke, "This child wants to leave the temple. She can't leave the service."

"And why not?" I asked angrily. "I know for a fact that Poseidon doesn't require his priests to remain chaste. Why should he expect it of his priestesses?" They looked at me, clueless. "If necessary, I will take her with me, adopt her, and then she can do what she wills."

87

Alecto's mouth fell open, his gaze filled with hatred. "And who are you to take one of Poseidon's priestesses?"

I snarled, dark and angry, "One he abandoned. I sought sanctuary here, but if you are not willing to help those who need it, I *will* make sure he hears about it. If you keep Korinna here against her will, believe you me, I will make this place a living Tartarus for you all." I was getting my point across because they both shrank away from me.

Tanis recovered her wits and slapped me across the face. I didn't recoil, and I barely registered the pain. I stared her down, a storm forming in my eyes. "You don't know what you've done, Tanis. Let us leave, or I will bring this building down and explain to my husband why I did it."

That's when her mouth fell open, and that's when they all realized what was going on. Tanis attempted to speak, but Alecto placed his arm on hers and nodded to the door. "Take her and go, my lady. I hope you find what, or who, it is that you are looking for."

I simply nodded and hauled Korinna out of there. I hadn't intended to reveal anything, but here I was. "Wait, Efterpi!" Korinna called out, and I stopped. I hadn't realized we were walking so fast, but the poor girl was out of breath. I had pulled us down to the beach, not far from where I surfaced. "Are you..." With a sigh, I turned and looked at her, trying to keep my face calm, but I could feel my eyes betraying me. She dropped to her knees in reverence and babbled, "My lady."

"Oh, goodness! Please, Korinna, stand up. If I wanted attention, I would have come as myself. Please, forget it's me. I just..." I sat down and stared at the water, Korinna sitting a few feet away. I think I'd scared her. "I came looking for him, and instead, I found you." *And Leandros*, but I wasn't going there...was I? "Something pulled me here to Korinth, and I intend to find out what. I hope to help you discover where your heart belongs if you'll still let me?"

Korinna looked at me, her face blank, but I could see her mind working. "Alright, I am not afraid to admit I need some help, my lady."

My face must have radiated joy because Korinna smiled at me and nodded. "Please, Korinna, just Efterpi? I don't want the whole town knowing I'm here. I'm going to have to go back and speak with Alecto and Tanis about it. If they disagree, well, I'm sure I can reason with them." She giggled softly, and it made my heart swell. She reminded me of Rhodes when my daughter was younger. "Okay," I said as I stood, and Korinna joined me, "night is falling. Let's get you back up to the Temple of Aphrodite so you can meet your future."

I saw the blush creep across her face and smiled once more as we linked arms, making our way back to the temple. We got to the bench a little early, but Hilarion was already there, along with Leandros. I couldn't look at him, the one who reminded me so much of Poseidon, so I focused on the young couple. "Ah, good, you're here." I brought Korinna over and watched as Hilarion's face lit up. Excellent, the attraction was mutual. "Korinna, this is Hilarion. Hilarion, Korinna, recently released from the service of Poseidon."

"And entered the service of Amphitrite," Korinna interjected smugly.

I coughed and stared down at her. "Excuse me?" I begged the question.

Korinna glanced up at me, her broad smile setting me at ease. "You are her priestess, right?" I nodded slowly, wondering where she was going with this. "And she is a much better goddess to be in service to, rather than Poseidon. You won't keep me from love, will you?" I shook my head. "Perfect. I'm sure she'd have me as a priestess and still allow me to marry someday."

It was Hilarion's turn to cough. I nodded and whispered to her, "Sneaky. Alright then, why don't you two go over there and talk, get to know one another. I'll sit here and *pray*...to Amphitrite for guidance."

Hilarion held out an arm for Korinna. They walked a little way away, speaking in low tones. I sat down and sighed, Leandros resting beside me. "That surprised you. Why?"

I looked at him, my eyes tired, and my body suddenly weary. "Amphitrite isn't used to being worshipped. Even though she is Poseidon's consort and Queen of the Sea, people do not tend an altar for her. They do not leave offerings, and she has all but been forgotten. By man and by Poseidon." I looked up at Leandros, his face sad, and I shook my head again. "I'm sorry. It's not my life," *it was*, "it shouldn't be affecting me so much."

"How could it not, Efterpi? I can see you love both your goddess and Poseidon with all your heart. How could it not affect you?" He sat a little closer, and this time I didn't move away. "Why are you really in Korinth, Efterpi? It's not just to find love, is it? Is it to find *him*?"

I stared at him with tears brimming in my eyes and nodded. "I've been looking for Poseidon for years. My Lady Amphitrite picked me back up when I thought I had lost it all." It wasn't entirely a lie, and I did pick myself up. That's why I was there. I had planned to drag Poseidon home once I found him. "I think…I'm going to give up on him. I'll live here in Korinth until the end of my days. I think I could be happy with that. Watch Korinna get married and start a family, grow into old age, be alone until I die." I was sore, I hurt, I was tired, and I was angry. Mostly at myself for thinking that I mattered anymore. I'd go home, install Triton as regent until his father decided to return, and come back here.

A hand rested on my knee, and I looked at Leandros. "I'm sure if Poseidon knew how much you loved him, he would come rushing back to you. But, if it helps, you don't need to be alone. You can stay with me. You know a woman can't live by herself." I nodded, not even thinking about it. I wanted to keep this man near me for as long as I could.

91

"Thank you, Leandros. I think that would be nice. But why are you still here? I thought for sure you would have left when I stormed off earlier," I asked curiously.

He laughed then, and my heart sank. Somehow, he was channeling Poseidon, whether consciously or not. That laugh, his face, they were too similar. It would be a puzzle for another day, though. "I knew you would be back, and I knew that would not be the end of our conversations. I have a feeling you're going to keep me on my toes."

I giggled, I chuckled, I burst out laughing, and Leandros laughed with me. "Me, I'm nothing. I'm not likely to keep anyone on their toes."

The look he gave me sent a shiver down my spine. "Then off them, Efterpi." I blushed and smiled softly.

"We'll see Leandros. We'll see," I replied as I placed my hand over his. I felt a tingle at the contact and looked at him, wondering if he felt it, too. Perhaps it was being near the Temple of Aphrodite, or maybe I had a connection with him. But this, *he* was what had been pulling me towards Korinth, that much I knew.

"Efterpi!" Korinna came racing over, her long brown hair falling out of her loose braids. "Will you marry us?"

I nearly fell off the bench, but Leandros pulled me closer and whispered into my ear, "Steady." His breath gave me shivers, and I nodded.

"I..." I looked between Korinna, whose eyes shone with hope, Hilarion, who had run up as Korinna was speaking, and Leandros, who was attempting to both calm me and keep from laughing. "Why me?" I queried quietly.

"Because we're both priestesses of Amphitrite, and I think it would mean more to have you do it. You brought us together," she explained quickly.

I sighed. "Wouldn't it be more appropriate to get married by one of Hera's or Aphrodite's priests?" I countered. It wasn't that I didn't want to, but I wanted them to be sure about it.

Hilarion was the one who spoke up this time, "I agree with Korinna. You gave me hope, and you brought her to me. It could only be you."

My mouth fell open, and Leandros closed it back up. I shot a look at him. "Don't look at me. I think you got yourself in this fine mess," he said with a chuckle.

I rolled my eyes and nodded. "Fine, but not now, not tonight. I'm bone-tired from—" I almost spoke about the incident at the temple but caught myself. "It's been a long and interesting day. Why don't we speak more about it tomorrow? I need to find somewhere for Korinna and me to stay."

"Nonsense, you are staying with me, remember?" Leandros commented.

"And Korinna is more than welcome at my parent's house," Hilarion added. I sighed and nodded. It wasn't ideal to have Korinna and Hilarion under the same roof, but then I didn't know how living with Leandros would go. It was all an experiment for sure.

"Alright, why don't we take the next few days and think things over. You two get to know each other a little better." I stood and wobbled a little. Channeling even that small amount of my power was hurting. Leandros was by my side immediately and picked me up in his arms. Korinna watched us, her eyes lit with happiness. She led Hilarion away, the two of them disappearing into the evening, Leandros turned and walked in the opposite direction, and I held on. Even though his arms felt tight around me, I still worried.

"You've been through a lot, Efterpi. Let's get you home, and you can rest." I stared up at him again, wondering how much he knew. I think he could see my questioning gaze, and he smiled down at me, placing a soft kiss on my forehead. "I'll explain when we're inside, dear."

I nodded and sighed. As we made our way into the elite's district of Korinth, I began wondering who this guy was. He carried me into a beautiful home and laid me down on one of the couches. The smell of wine was everywhere, and I wondered if I had missed a symposium. "Did you have…did you skip out on a symposium?" I asked softly.

Leandros sat down near my knees and smiled down at me. "I may have. Something else had caught my eye today, and I wanted to see if she was worth it."

I blushed, hoping he meant me. "And was she? Worth it?" I countered, biting my lower lip a little.

"That remains to be seen. She's an enigma, one I intend to figure out." As he spoke, Leandros leaned down and pressed a gentle kiss to my lips. I almost evaporated then and there. Even as soft and brief as it was, I could feel passion and desire building behind it. I desperately wanted to know more. I didn't react much more than leaning into it, and Leandros smiled as he pulled away. "So far, she's worth it."

I caught my breath and focused on him, his features. Soft brown hair pulled back in braids. Dark brown eyes that pierced into my soul, as though he could see right through me. Muscular, he must be a general, or at least an officer, for you could see scars on his body. I traced a finger along the inside of his arm, watched him shiver, and smiled. "Leandros, you were going to explain why you can see through me. Why you know as much as you do."

He nodded and took a deep breath. "I know who you are, Amphitrite." I stilled and said nothing. "I was on a walk down by the beach when a woman swam up on the rocks. She was the most beautiful thing I had ever seen." I blushed furiously. "And then she changed into the form of a woman, the one I see before me now. You immediately entranced me. I knew you had to be here for a reason, so I followed you. I'm not afraid to admit it. Why *are* you here?"

I held nothing back this time, telling him everything I'd skipped over earlier. Including the fact that he reminded me of Poseidon. How I felt a connection between us. I explained all my fears of being left alone in Atlantis and my decision to return only briefly and then come back to Korinth to stay.

"You can't stay, Amphitrite. Atlantis needs you," he replied sadly.

95

I shook my head. "Atlantis needs her king, not some knock off queen." Leandros's hands were suddenly on my shoulders, and he pulled me towards him.

"You are strong, Amphitrite. You are the Queen of the Sea. Poseidon wouldn't have picked you, wouldn't have taken you as his queen if you were not." I stared at him while he continued. "I want you to stay with me, gods know I do, but I cannot be selfish here. A balance must be maintained." My mouth fell open, and Leandros's lips met mine, crashing down on me. I could feel the strain it took for him not to push it forward, and I appreciated it.

When we finally broke apart, I pressed my forehead against his and smiled. "I'm not going anywhere just yet. I still need to marry Korinna and Hilarion."

Leandros laughed and nodded. "You've decided to do it then?"

"I have, and you're right, Leandros. Atlantis needs someone. I'll go back, be the queen she needs, once the ceremony is over," I replied.

"Good." Leandros smiled, kissed my forehead, and stood up.

"Goodnight, Amphitrite."

"Goodnight, Leandros," I murmured as sleep took me.

The next few days were a flurry of planning. Korinna wanted her wedding down at the beach, and since I didn't have a temple, I agreed. It would be better for me. And it was what she wanted. I explained to her that I wouldn't be staying, but she would be in good hands. She would be busy with her new husband and life. Korinna would always be my only priestess, and I think she felt unique because of it.

The day of the ceremony arrived. Korinna, Hilarion, Leandros, and a handful of others were beside the sea. I had no idea how to marry them, but the love they showed each other and me was all the inspiration I needed. "Be good to each other." Korinna and Hilarion nodded and kissed. I smiled in both joy and sadness. "It's time, Korinna," I stated simply.

The young woman walked up to me and pulled me into a hug, and I almost started crying. "Will you come back?" she asked quietly.

"I don't know, child. I don't know that I'll be," I looked over at Leandros and sighed, "able to visit much. If I can, I will." Korinna nodded, sighed, and stepped back into Hilarion's arms. As I walked into the surf, Leandros caught my arm, spun me around, and kissed me softly. "Come with me?" I asked into the kiss.

"Are you sure?" he replied. I could already tell he was debating his answer.

I smiled at him. "I wouldn't have asked if I wasn't."

He simply nodded and walked into the surf. I waved goodbye and took Leandros's hand. Together we swam off, heading for the gateway that led to Atlantis. I watched in shock as his body changed, taking on mer form, the bright green tail catching me by surprise.

"Good, I can be myself. My queen, please, call me Rommel. I will be forever at your service."

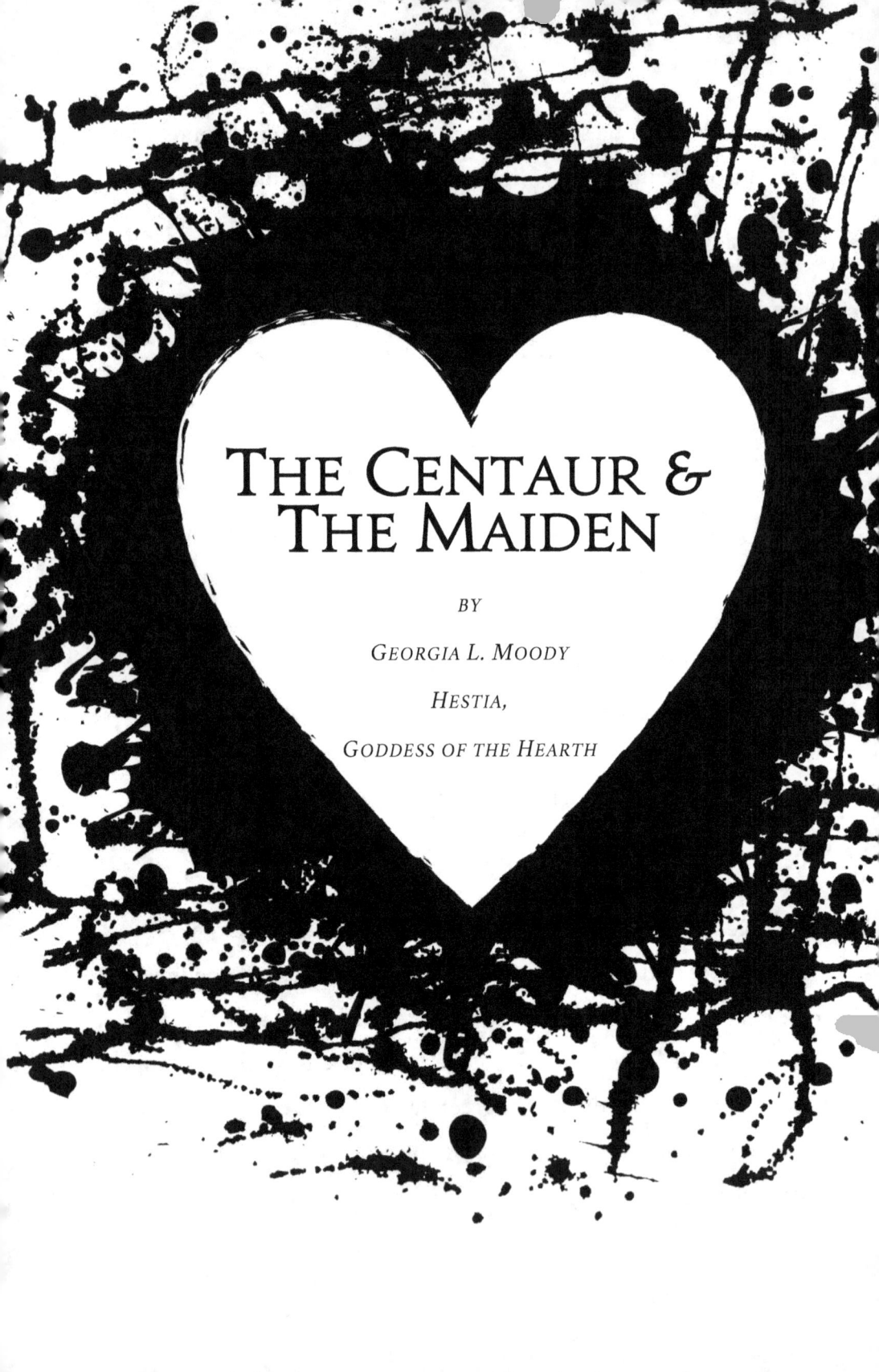

THE CENTAUR & THE MAIDEN

BY

GEORGIA L. MOODY

HESTIA,

GODDESS OF THE HEARTH

How did the most famous virgin on Olympus end up spending two millennia with a centaur? That's an excellent question.

Contrary to what historians would tell you, I was actually courted by several Olympian Gods, but I wouldn't take second place to any of them. It comes from being the eldest of the Kronos children—I kneel to no one, not even my brothers and sisters. I keep the flame of divinity, and they would be nothing without me. Considering the opinions on headstrong females in ancient Olympus, this explains why I remained unmarried. I may tend the hearth of the gods, but I'm no meek housewife. I mean, even Hera shuts up if Zeus yells enough, whereas I just roll my eyes and continue what I'm doing.

As Chiron used to say, it takes a special kind of person to put up with a goddess who has turned down three Olympian gods as suitors. Luckily for me, a centaur who had dealt with an arrogant teenage Achilles was barely fazed by a somewhat grumpy elder hearth goddess.

After Olympus fell—or so I thought—I ended up in the lush green lands populated by satyrs and strange, unearthly beautiful beings that flitted between the trees, always avoiding my gaze. To this day, I don't know how Chiron ended up there. We never discussed it.

I had been following a small stream to my favorite grove of oak trees, and there he was, sitting with all four legs folded, reading a scroll to the little satyr boys and nymph girls. It was the story of

Narcissus, if I remember correctly, or was it Adonis? One of the beautiful ones who got tangled up with the Olympians and died, anyway.

My Chiron had a beautiful speaking voice, and I stopped to listen. He looked up and smiled at me without interrupting his story. They were all spellbound, even the little nymph girl who was braiding a flower chain into his tail. He finished the story, and there was a round of enthusiastic juvenile applause before he dismissed them back to their duties of picking berries and gathering herbs.

He got to his feet as they dispersed and made his way to where I lingered at the edge of the clearing.

"Lady Hestia, you honor me with your attention. I wasn't aware that any of the Elders survived. It gladdens my heart to know that I am not alone in this exile, but that I shall have your gracious self for companionship in this strange new place. Your presence will, as always, be a comfort to those who find themselves lost and alone." He reached out and took my hand in his, and sinking into the uniquely graceful centaur bow, down on one foreleg, he kissed the back of my hand. I smiled back and blushed despite myself. I've always had a secret soft spot for sincere gallantry.

I had always seen Chiron as a fixture in the gardens of Olympus, frequently attended by a gaggle of students who were paying a greater or lesser amount of attention to the lessons he gave. I knew sometimes he retreated to a cave on the lower slopes to teach humans the mystical ways of healing with herbs. We had always been cordial to each other, but I wouldn't call us close. However, in this wild place so far from home, I was grateful for any hint of familiarity.

"What distresses you, lady?" he asked, in that soft, rich baritone that I would eventually come to characterize as his *healer* voice. This was not the first time I had heard it—despite being gods, we can and do hurt ourselves, if through unusual means—but it was the first time it had been focused on me, and I liked it.

"I'm glad to see someone from home," I replied and smiled. "I've been a bit lonely, if I'm being honest."

"This is indeed a different place, my lady. May I walk with you so that we can enjoy each other's company a while longer?"

I crossed my hands over the handle of my basket, considering. "I suppose that can be allowed," I answered, teasing. "After all, I seem to be bereft of an appropriate escort." Ancient Greek was a gloriously formal and occasionally incandescently obscene language, nearly as playful as modern English, and we both laughed.

"May I?" he asked, gesturing towards my basket. "Where are you bound today?"

"No, thank you. I think I can manage a basket on my own. I'm going to collect acorns in the oak glen where the stream curls back on itself," I answered, and he nodded. He turned with me and began to walk majestically down the mossy banks of the stream, keeping pace with me. Despite his dinner-plate-sized hooves, he stepped delicately enough that the streamside plants barely swayed at his passing. Not overly burdened with grace, I stumbled and nearly went into the icy water. I attempted to catch myself on an overhanging rock and flailed my arms to try to reset my balance.

A strong hand closed around my upper arm and stopped me just before I went headlong onto the rocks. I flailed with my free hand and found my footing, just in time to get pulled back into Chiron's arms.

"We can't be having the Lady of Flames getting damp, now can we?" he said, with a rumbling laugh that was infectious. I couldn't help but giggle. "Up you get."

"Thank you," I said, readjusting the fall of my dress and settling the basket back over my arm from where I had dropped it. His touch lingered just a moment until he was sure I was steady on my feet, and I felt my cheeks turn a bit pink. "Shall we go on?"

That was the first of many thousands of walks together through the glens, hills, forests, and hidden places of Caledonia.

The first winter caught me off guard, accustomed as I was to the Greek climate and the unchanging seasons of Olympus. The satyrs had warned me that I would need a place for when the snows came. I had been distracted, though, by what I can't remember and hadn't gotten around to building more than a slight shelter to keep the rain off. It worked well enough, but I was woefully unprepared for what Caledonia was going to throw at me.

Have you ever been to Scotland in November? The wind comes off the North Sea and cuts you right to the soul. Even I, she who keeps the fire of divinity within herself, got so cold my fingertips were turning blue as I tried to keep a little fire going in a depression lined with rocks. The wind was screaming like the Erinyes on the hunt, loud enough that I couldn't hear anything beyond my own cursing. Something sharp and spiky slammed into the side of my head. It was a pinecone, one of the millions of pinecones that were everywhere you looked and everywhere underfoot. It knocked one of my hairpins loose, and my hair began to swirl into my eyes and mouth. My veil disappeared into the forest, flapping like a gigantic red bat and taking the rest of my pins with it. I spat a lock out, cursing again when the tiny spark I had nestled down into a bed of pine needles flew away with the wind.

"My lady!"

A thin sound, almost lost in the storm. I wasn't sure I had heard it at all. I turned into the wind, allowing it to blow my hair from my face, and was greeted with a slap of stinging sleet. The sky was full of pearl-grey clouds, rounded bellies pregnant with the incipient blizzard. It wasn't more than midafternoon, but it looked like sunset.

"Lady Hestia!" Chiron cantered into the clearing, hooves cracking fallen branches like snapping bones under his feet, an oil-soaked torch held high in one hand. "You must come with me! The satyrs say there's going to be two feet of snow by morning."

"I'll b-be fine," I said, through chattering teeth. "All I n-need is a fire. Loan me your torch."

Chiron looked at my little lean-to under the spreading branches. As we watched, the wind caught the edges of the shelter and spun one of the dry boughs loose, right into our faces. We ducked in unison as it whizzed overhead. The torch lost the battle against the wind, and there in my little cove of trees, we were plunged into stormlight gloom. The look on his face as he turned to look at me said it all—I was an idiot, but he wasn't going to let me freeze to death because I was stubborn. He didn't look at me directly but rather past me into the forest.

"Will you come with me voluntarily, or do I need to carry you away like the satyrs do their nymphs?" he asked, raising his voice to be heard over the rising wind. The softness was gone from his tone as he stomped over to where I stood.

"Your argument has some merit," I said, attempting to regain what little dignity I could muster under the circumstances. "Fine, I'll go with you. Let me gather my things."

As I went to pick up my little brazier and the bag that contained most of my worldly possessions, I saw him head off into the forest and caught a glimmer of movement out of the corner of my eye. A stray sunbeam broke through the clouds, and I saw him rear up on his hind legs and reach into the boughs of a tree to retrieve my veil. The horse portion of him was a beautiful rich reddish-brown, and he positively glowed in the momentary brightness. A branch snagged in his hair, and it came loose from its bindings. It cascaded down his back to well past his waist, black as the feathers around his hooves, and it made me smile to see it. Let someone else have to deal with unmanageable hair for once. He thudded back down to all fours and returned to me, still not looking directly at me.

"Your veil," he said and waited while I pinned it back to my braids. Once I had done that, he looked back at me again, and a little bit of the grimness was gone from his expression. I hadn't realized how uncomfortable it made him, seeing me unveiled. I reached into my pack and pulled out a leather string before I slung the bag over my shoulder.

"Do you want me to tie yours back?" I asked, holding it out. "You'll have to kneel, though. I can't reach that high."

He took the string from my hand and held it for a moment, looking as though he was considering something. "No, I can manage...but thank you."

Snow was beginning to fall, and I shivered. He scooped the brazier out of my arms and walked over near a fallen log that I had been using as a table.

"Come on then. We're losing the light."

"I'm ready when you are," I said, bouncing the bag against my back and wrapping my veil more tightly around me.

"No, don't be silly. I can move much faster than you, and your shoes are practically gone. Come over here and get on." He set down the brazier, then reached up and pulled his hair back into a knot, looping the leather strip tightly around the base and securing it with a hard tug.

I was rendered speechless. No one *rode* centaurs, let alone Chiron himself. It was considered immensely rude to even joke about it. Rude to the point of bloodshed, in point of fact. Even Achilles had learned that lesson the hard way.

"Are you sure?" I hadn't moved.

"I wouldn't have offered if I didn't mean it," he replied. "Now, please." He picked up the brazier again and tucked it under his arm.

I trotted over and climbed up onto the log, then gingerly slid one leg across his back, settling my weight just behind where the horse met the man. He was broader than I thought he would be, and I felt very stable even as I wriggled a bit to get some little padding between my legs and his shoulders. His tail flicked once or twice as I found my balance, but he stood like a rock.

"Put your arms around my waist, but don't pull my hair," he said, taking a couple of steps to see how bad of a rider I was. I had always enjoyed going for a ride with Poseidon, so I managed not to disgrace myself. "Hold on tight, it's a good long way to my cave, and I don't want to break an ankle in the dark. If you fall off, just scream, and I'll come get you."

Not bloody likely, I said and wrapped my arms tightly around his torso. "Let's get going before I freeze to your back," I quipped and immediately regretted it.

He reared up just enough to make me slide backward, then took off in a blazingly fast gallop. I barely managed not to slide off onto my ass and pulled myself back up to my spot. I ended up burying my face between his shoulders and praying to whoever was listening that he would remember I was there and wouldn't scrape me off on a low-hanging branch for a laugh. If you've ever ridden a horse at a breakneck gallop down a forested slope, imagine the experience with one that is laughing at you.

We ended up at his cave down in the glen just as the snow started to get really serious about smothering the world in whiteness. I slid off his back onto legs made mostly of jelly and managed to wobble just past the entrance of the cave. He had partially smothered his fire before he left, so it took just a few moments to raise it back to a cheerful blaze. I sat as close to the flames as I could and steamed as the snow melted off my veil. I heard a splashing outside, and he came in carrying two great big buckets of water from the stream he had hurdled right before he slid to a stop. He set them down and dipped a bronze pot into one of them, filling it and setting it down near the coals to heat up.

After I felt the ground stop moving under me, I looked around a bit. There were fresh cut rushes underfoot, which smelled lovely and sweet, and a rack for his scrolls. Quills and ink sat near to what was obviously his bed. Rush-dip lights were everywhere, and even some oil lamps that I recognized from home. He, unlike I, obviously had time to pack before leaving Greece. I smiled and held my hands out over the fire.

"Thank you," I said, meaning it. "Not for attempting to shake my kidneys out my ears, but for coming to get me. It was very kind of you."

"Not at all," he said and returned the smile as he settled down by the fire. *He really does have a sweet smile*, I thought. "I'm glad for the company. The satyrs don't know what to think of me, really. Our outlooks on life are just too different."

"Tell me about it," I replied with feeling. "As if my brothers weren't enough of an object lesson on what happens when you live your life entirely focused on pleasure, the satyrs raise that to an art form. Nothing wrong with it, they are the way they are, but it's not for me."

"And what is for you, your ladyship?" he asked, looking at me. "If that's not too impertinent."

"Please, just call me Hestia. After that wild ride, if we're not on first name terms, I don't want to know what it would take. I like taking care of people, of being the source of comfort and security," I said, gesturing at the fire. "Speaking of being the way one is inclined to be. I've always been the refuge. Everyone comes to me, sooner or later. What about you, o teacher of heroes?"

He snorted. "Achilles was a demigod who got lucky. I would rather share my knowledge with healers and craftspeople. I've had to learn a great deal since I came here. The herbs are different, the auguries are different, the land is different—but I learn, and I share my knowledge with all who ask for it."

I shivered again as a gust of wind cut through the growing warmth and slid icy fingers into the damp folds of my veil. He stood, walked to one side of the cave, and brought over a basket of the hard, shiny coal that the satyrs were so fond of. He dumped about half the basket onto the wood embers and gestured for me to take his place away from the draft. A few more steps, and a screen of woven reeds cascaded from the ceiling, concealing the passageway to the cave mouth. The temperature in the cave immediately rose, and I sighed. He came back and sat behind me, giving me something to lean against while the coals caught.

I was almost asleep when he nudged me to wakefulness. "The coals are ready," he said. "You can fill your brazier now."

I jerked awake at the thought and pushed myself to my feet. He had set it down when I dismounted, and I had completely forgotten about it. Flexing my fingers, I scooped up handfuls of the burning coals, impressed at the clear light they gave off, and dumped them into the bronze basin. He had moved it close enough to the fire that it had warmed gently, so the heat wouldn't make it crack. It was wrought by one of the Titans, back in the days before time, so it wasn't likely that thermal shock would damage it, but the gesture was thoughtful in the extreme.

"Thank you," I said, sincerely grateful. "I can't believe I almost went to sleep with the fire out."

"Well, the fire is lit and will burn until daylight. Come, rest yourself. I'll keep watch."

That was the best offer I had had in decades. I dusted the ashes off my hands and walked back over to my spot, leaning up against his belly. My veil had dried while I dozed, and I wrapped up in the soft linen, leaned back against Chiron's warmth, letting myself go to sleep.

That was the first of thousands of nights we spent together. More often than not, we would stay up talking about whatever caught our fancies, only falling briefly asleep as the sky lightened before sunrise. I never went back to my little makeshift camp.

In an amazingly short time, I realized I had deep feelings for Chiron, and he for me, but we never spoke of love. When I decided to try to make a new version of my ambrosia, he helped gather the herbs, attempting to replicate what had been lost on Olympus. We both taught the children, and when the humans came along and found the satyr's glen, we taught them, too. I kept his hearth, and he kept me fed.

When the humans came for the satyrs, hundreds of years later, we stood against them. We sheltered who we could, hid even more, provided gold and silver to get others away from the rampaging mortals. From that first night in the cave together, while I slept against his belly and the storm buried the world in thigh-deep snow, we rarely spent a night away from each other. When we did, it was usually because he was called away to attend an injury or a birth. The time we spent apart after Zeus called me back to the new Olympus was the longest we had been separated. We had never spoken of marriage. He knew of my vow, and he never pushed for more. Children had never been a possibility. Even had we been so inclined, I didn't possess the shapeshifting ability of my baby brother. I had had my dalliances from time to time, usually with the satyr bucks, and Chiron encouraged me in them. He was always happy to see me relaxed and enjoying myself, far from the meddling, overbearing machinations of my family.

When Connor showed up on Olympus to tell me Chiron had passed away, it crushed me. I had secretly been relieved that Connor had passed out once he delivered the message. I had retreated into my distillation room and sobbed, raging at all the gods and circumstances that had pulled me away from him. We had had a deep and loving relationship that had lasted longer than the Roman Empire, and his loss left a gaping hole in my heart.

When I had seen him briefly at Eventide, it had gone a long, long way towards my recovery. I loved Connor, but it was a fiery love, full of passion and joy and excitement. My love for Chiron had been slow to grow, a gradual warmth rather than a bonfire. It had been more about comfort, deep contentment, a certain survivor's bond, and camaraderie. We both remembered the old days on Olympus, whereas Connor had learned about them as much from fantasy novels and dusty mythology textbooks as he had from Chiron and me. The single knowing nod and sweet smile from Chiron's shade had reassured me that I was, in fact, on the right path.

It was okay to move on. He would be happy for me, like he always was, and sooner or later, in the fullness of time, we would meet again. I'm certain of it.

THE RETURN OF JUSTICE

BY

JAYLYNN WATKINS

DIKÊ,

GODDESS OF JUSTICE

TOUK, VTOUK

VTOUK, VTOUK-VTOUK, VTOUK

Have you ever listened to a heartbeat?

Life, quite literally, has its own rhythm. Within these rhythms lie the chords of balance. Balance, as we know, is the strength on which Justice stands.

On which *I* stand.

I am Dikê, Goddess of Justice, and I've been away for far too long.

In the darkness of the universe, I existed as Virgo. The constellation outlined by the light of Spica shining down. Before that, when Justice was venerated and accepted, I walked the earth. That was when my sole purpose was to bring about the balance and justice humanity craved. When that changed, when it became apparent mortals were willing to follow inequity instead of balance, I left.

Then mortals evolved beyond the point of understanding what balance and justice truly meant. Humanity's evolution led them to believe they understood everything of this earth and all the secrets of the universe. That perceived understanding fed a desire to manipulate the scales.

Greed.

Corruption.

Savagery.

These practices ran free and rampant. The presence and energy of *Adikia* were strong and unbearable forces. My father, Zeus, was always more focused on and concerned with the gods, doing little to help me turn the tides. So…I exited the vast ocean of mortal deviance rather than succumbing or being drowned by it.

I left the world and mortals to be what they would be. I allowed them to shape their balance how they would. I escaped the pain of the constant, bubbling rage that filled me daily. Sitting in judgment was not easy, even for a goddess.

My escape led me from the gravitational pull of the earth and through the array of stars lining the skies. I went past the hue of Selene's glow and Helios's heat to the peace of Virgo. Close by, but far enough away, I watched and waited for the world to be ready for justice again. That time never came. The imbalance and injustices just continued to grow. Connected still, I saw and felt these changes. My heart ached, and with each atrocity to the natural order, the ichor boiled in my veins.

Then I heard it. The heartbeat. It was not a singular beat, but the collective one of the world.

VTOUK, VTOUK-VTOUK, VTOUK

It sounded like pain, calamity, hopelessness. It sounded like the fear of a *point-of-no-return*.

VTOUK, VTOUK-VTOUK, VTOUK

I had been waiting for the world to be ready for justice again. Instead, it had reached a point where the world *needed* justice more than ever.

VTOUK, VTOUK-VTOUK, VTOUK

So, like stardust, I rained down in glowing flurries, hoping to cover this place with my essence—the peace of justice.

Warriors had formed, wearing different gear, ready to fight in my name. Yet, it still felt as if the world was covered in an impenetrable cloak, making them resistant to the balance justice supplied.

I had been back a little over a week before it became clear my return had been orchestrated from on high. Big Daddy Zeus had issued a summons, beckoning us all home to Olympus. For me, the call sounded via the heartbeat of the world, crying out for justice. My father and his messengers were nothing if not dramatic.

I was nothing if not stubborn. So, I ignored the summons. The history between Zeus and I did not lend itself to me happily taking his orders. I chose to walk among the mortals instead. I strolled the streets of New York, trying to get my bearings in a world that looked new to me. My walk among those streets is where I met *her*.

Our meeting happened when I was already physically ill with the imbalance of the world. However, she gave me hope. Her internal beauty and aura radiated almost as bright as a collapsing star. They were only overshadowed by her bright smile, full lips, gorgeous brown eyes, and russet brown skin.

"Justice for Addison Wright! Say her name!" She was so busy yelling as people rushed past her, she didn't realize the wall of human traffic had slowly shuttled her into the middle of the street.

I watched from a corner, both concerned for her and appalled by everyone else's lack of concern. I didn't know who Addison Wright was, but the exclamation of *Justice for her!* and *Say her name!* had garnered my attention. Watching the beautiful bumbling woman lumber closer and closer to her death in the name of some version of *justice* was both fulfilling and disturbing.

Deciding my return should be less bloody than my exit, I made quick work of easing into the intersection and shuttling the woman back to the curb.

"Who the fuck—"

I arched an eyebrow and stepped back, out of swinging range. "Your savior. Thank me later," I stated, pushing my black curls behind my ear. I pointed to the intersection and the cars that were racing through where she'd just been standing. Cars, traffic, and the high-tech world where they were normalized were completely new for me. Studying history since my return had made my adjustment period swift, and I evolved as I learned. It didn't mean all I'd discovered of the progress of humanity wasn't astounding. It made it clear that evolution was destined to be their downfall. I only hoped I had returned in time to slow it down.

The beauty grunted a thanks, absently nodded her head in my direction, then walked away.

Her aura smacked me as she turned. Obviously not literally, but the blow to my energy felt damn near physical. She radiated sadness, anger, and purity meshed together within a simmering cloud of indignant rage. I wanted to step back out of her sphere, but at the same time, I longed to drink of her essence.

Whoa.

I found myself intrigued and hesitant, even as I jogged down the street after her. "Hey, excuse me."

She turned to look at me. Her face was questioning, and her lips turned down in a scowl. "Yeah, what's up? I said thanks. What more do you need?"

"Tell me about Addison."

She paused, scanning my body, stopping at my eyes and probing. She was looking for truth, so I allowed mine to shine freely. She jumped back a good five feet as my brown eyes pulsed silver.

"What the fuck?"

"Tell me about Addison. How do we bring her Justice? Why should we say her name?"

"Am I being punked? Did Ebony send you here? Is this their way of getting me to stop? I won't stop. Not until her murderer is behind bars. Not until the system is changed. Not until they are willing to say her name and admit what they did to her was wrong...horribly wrong."

She broke down then. Tears streamed down her face as she shook her head, turning to walk away from me.

I followed in silence for blocks. I slowly walked behind her as she altered between calls of *Justice for Addison* and moments of wailing into the sleeve of her sweatshirt. I needed answers, though I wasn't entirely sure what the questions were. I knew the mortal beauty intrigued me. I knew it was fascinating that she hadn't run when she saw the pulse of power in my eyes. I knew, without a doubt, she was a warrior. Just as I knew she was doing battle in the name of justice. In my name.

I had questions, and even without those answers, I knew I couldn't just walk away.

So, I followed. Eventually, she stopped at a cafe called *Feed the Blues*. "Well, Creepy, you might as well come in. Let me buy you a cup of coffee since you've followed me this far," she said, walking up to the door and holding it open for me. She waved me in slowly. "After you."

A smirk curved my lips as her energy swirled around me. Even with tear stains and black streaks of makeup lining her face, she was radiant. I nodded, walking into the small but bustling cafe. The staff all mumbled or grumbled *hello* to acknowledge our entry.

"Grab a seat. One of us will get right to you," an older lady called from behind the counter. I saw her wipe her hands on her white apron as Addison's warrior ushered us to a table in the back to the left side of the counter.

"Here's good," she said, sliding into the booth with her back to the wall of the shop, leaving her a full view of the side windows and front door.

Was she paranoid, cautious, or just smart? It was a hard judgment to make. The irony of that was not lost on me at all.

I slid into the booth across from her, leaning back against the mildly uncomfortable plastic seating. It crunched as I shifted, trying to get more comfortable. "So, will you tell me about Addison now?"

She frowned at me, and the pain searing through me felt like my heart was breaking. I'd seen her yelling, indignant, crying, and forceful. Something about that frown caught me like a punch to the gut. "Do you really want to know, or is this a sick ass game? 'Cus, I am not playing. This is real for me. I know Ebony and them want me to let this go. I know they want me just to accept the outcome and come back to the movement, but I can't. They say there are bigger fish to fry, that I should look at the whole picture. But if we let one go, if we stop shouting Addison's name, are we any better than them? Doesn't that mean we are just playing into their game?"

It was my turn to frown. I felt the creases as they trailed across my forehead. I had no idea what she was talking about, but the rawness of her pain was evident. The passion she emanated was something that couldn't be missed with a ten-foot pole. Even without using my *sight* to taste for the truth, I knew her words were brutally real and pure.

"You don't know me, but I promise you I am asking with honorable intentions. I am not here on behalf of anyone else. I am not

120

seeking you out for any ulterior motive or mission. Meeting you was happenstance. Now that I have, I would like to know more about Addison."

She nodded, just as the woman from behind the counter shuffled over to the table.

"What will you two dumplins have?"

I smiled politely. There was a piece of paper beside me on the table. It was obviously a list of the eatery's offerings, but I pushed it aside. I looked over at my companion. "What would you suggest?"

"Coffee is great. Pie is excellent. Chicken platter is amazing. You pretty much can't go wrong, honestly."

"What do you think you're having?" I asked, my lips parting slightly, my eyes focused on her lips as I waited for her answer.

She looked up and smiled, her eyes bright and clear for the first time. "Aunt Janet knows my order."

Her smile was full-bodied, soul-warming, and like a second punch to my soul as it transformed her face from beautifully tragic to radiantly beautiful. The third punch came when I looked over at the waitress. The answering smile she beamed back toward my companion was just as genuine and warm. "That, I do. Maple Chicken Tenders and black coffee, with a slice of sweet potato pie to go."

Aunt Janet turned, looking at me, her smile still beaming. "And you, dumplin? What you having?"

I frowned slightly, my lips pursing, as I glanced quickly at the paper offerings, then away. "I'll have the same."

121

Aunt Janet nodded, turned, and shuffled away.

"So, what's up with the eyes?" she asked as soon as Aunt Janet was out of earshot.

Turning my attention back to her, I offered a slight shrug before reclining as far back in the booth as I could. "What's up with Addison?"

Her head tilted slightly, as though she were trying to see me from a different vantage point. She sighed, biting at her bottom lip. I patiently watched as she began flipping sugar packets between her fingers, her eyes following the random bounces of each as it rolled over her knuckles. "I haven't really slept. Not since it happened, ya know?" She looked up, her damp brown eyes locking on mine. "I'm willing to lay good odds that I am imagining all of this. What happened to your eyes earlier, your presence period, the two of us, here and now…all of it is just a figment of my imagination. That includes the energy flowing between us, which feels like it's making my skin vibrate and pulse."

I sucked in a deep breath, my eyes locking with hers across the table. She felt it, too. Interesting.

I didn't comment. I just stared back, letting her talk as I allowed my posture to relax a little. I leaned forward, easing closer to the table, closer to her.

"Since I am imagining this, or dreaming it, or hell, mid psychotic break, I'm just going to go with it, okay? I'm just going to act as though it's real, even though I know it's not. And when I wake up, and you're gone—"

I shook my head, suddenly obsessed with convincing her I was real. I was immortal, a goddess, Justice itself. But I was real and not some trick of her mind.

She shook her head in response to my gesture and raised her hand to stop me from speaking. "When you're gone, to wherever it is you will go, just don't forget Addison or me. Wherever you are just...say our names."

I smiled, somewhat sadly, fearing the remnants of some fated prophecy were slipping between her lips. "How can I say your name if I do not know it?"

She grinned then, grabbing two more packets to twist between her fingers in her flipping game. "My name is Carla. What's yours?"

"Dikê."

Without even a moment of hesitation, she responded, "Justice. Ahh, how fitting. Nice to meet you, Dikê."

I nodded, my eyebrows arching in question. "You know Greek?"

"Yes. Fluent in classics. Once, I wanted to tour the world, see all there was to see. I wanted to learn from history's mysteries within the beauty of the present and find all the answers to balance the world."

Balance the world. The phrasing made me pause as tingles danced along my spine. The feeling was short-lived as I thought of the other word she'd used. *Classics.* Well, that was one way to make a goddess feel every stitch of her immortality.

"What happened to those plans?"

"Life. It's hard to travel the world, searching for answers when there are problems to solve and fires to put out in your own backyard. Should I leave my city burning while I go off to study monuments in another land?"

"You're human, it's all your land, but I understand the argument. Balance is about picking your part of the war, especially if you cannot see the full battleground."

"Yes, and we are at war. Addy knew that."

"Did she?"

Carla nodded solemnly, knocking down the pyramid of sugar packets she had created as a slight sigh escaped. "Yeah, she did. She wanted change. She wanted to make the playing field as even as possible so she could and turn the world on its ear. She worked full-time while taking night classes for her JD at Tech. She said she wanted to be hands-on with the information, so she traveled all the way across town for classes. I told her she could get the same degree and faster going through one of those online schools, ya know?"

I shook my head, my brow crinkling.

Carla frowned, "You're not from here, are you?"

"Yes, and no. I will tell you only the truth, so be careful what you ask if truth is not what you really seek."

"Who are you?"

"Justice."

"Not your name. Who are you? Like, really? Cop? Reporter? Investigator? Who are you?"

"Justice."

Carla sighed, leaning back against the booth. She effectively put as much distance between us as she was able. The loss caused my heart to skip a beat.

Vtouk-Vtouk

Vtouk

Vtouk-Vtouk-Vtouk

"I thought you promised me no games."

"I did. You know my name. You said my name. I am she. She, who was named Justice. The Goddess. The embodiment."

"Ooooh," she rolled her eyes, "so you're *that* justice. The goddess. Got it."

"Yes. I haven't lied to you."

"Then, do it again."

"Do what?"

"Your eyes. Change your eyes."

I shook my head. "No. I am not a game or a parlor trick. My words are my truth, accept them, or do not."

Aunt Janet returned, her hands in mitts, carrying two piping hot plates. Gingerly, she sat them each on the table before stepping aside so the young girl behind her could place two mugs of charcoal black brew on the table near the plates. The girl moved away as Aunt Janet produced utensils and napkins from her apron, carefully placing them on the table. "Y'all dumplins enjoy," she said, turning and shuffling away again.

"You're justice?" Carla threw out as soon as Aunt Janet was out of range once again.

"Yes," I answered succinctly as I took in the aroma wafting up at me from my plate. It was sweet, swirling in savory, highlighted by some sort of temptation of which I was not yet aware. I was suddenly ravenous.

Carla pulled me from my hunger as she hunched forward angrily. She slid her plate to the side before asking, "Then where the fuck were you when Addison needed you? Where the fuck have you been for the last 400-plus years while my people have been enslaved, broken down, persecuted, and tormented? Where were you -"

"Among the stars, crying tears of shame, hoping humanity could heal itself and see the error of its ways."

"Yeah, well, how did that work out for you?"

I sighed deeply, pushing my plate away as well. "Pretty horrible, given what I have seen since I returned. When I left, I never imagined the world could get worse than it already was, yet it seems to have degenerated at an incredibly rapid pace."

"Understatement of the century," she growled, glaring at me angrily. Whatever connection existed between us, it sizzled and burned. It felt like I could feel every fiery emotion she'd ever possessed. I wanted to wrap her up, keep her safe, and take away her pain. The only way to do that was to give her the justice she craved for Addison. Hopefully, that would heal the part of herself that had been damaged along with her friend.

"Carla, tell me about Addison."

She nodded, sighing deeply as she began to weave the tale. I closed my eyes, allowing my breathing to slow as I let her words guide me into a trance-like state. Each syllable and verbal hum swirled and vibrated with the colors of her aura and the basic essence of her being. I could see any lie she shared, and I would taste every truth.

"Addison was a big fan of giving second chances. She was an empath. She felt everything and loved to take care of people. She carried this world on her shoulders, and we didn't deserve her." Carla sighed before continuing, "Justin wasn't any different. She gave him way too many chances. Technically, they were never really together. So, he wasn't actually an ex, but that's how he acted—like a jealous ex. For him, it was never about loving Addy or even liking her. It was about possessing her. He was this rich, entitled, white kid who everyone treated like a god, except Addy. She never deferred to him and couldn't have cared less about his money."

Carla's voice trailed off until eventually she just stopped speaking. I opened my eyes slowly, allowing myself to readjust as the world shifted to accommodate me. She was staring out the window, turned away from me. "Love and passion are rough, ya know? They get all tangled. Addy got mixed up, and Justin wouldn't let her go."

"You loved her?" I asked, knowing the truth before I even heard the words.

127

"More than life. She was simply everything. You know that person that is *your* person. She was my friend, my confidant, my family. There was a brief period when she was my lover, and I would have sworn one day she would have been my wife." Carla paused then, looking at me with a wistful smile curving her lips. "For years, for me, Addison has been synonymous with love. One of those beings that make you feel how inadequate those four letters are when it comes to truly describing the depth of what you are feeling."

I nodded. "Yes, this modern language of yours has tried to...to...όριο...um, limit the depth of its meaning by compiling its breadth of meaning down to one tiny word. I truly do not understand it."

She shrugged. "Humanity is stupid."

I hoped she didn't want me to argue. "Please, finish."

Another deep sigh slid through her bow-shaped lips before she began again.

I weighed her words, letting them swirl around me as she told me of the whirlwind that was Addison and Justin. "Eventually, Addison became tired of the constant battling with Justin. She called it quits, even though," Carla's voice turned sharp, "Addison was adamant they had never actually been a couple. Justin couldn't handle the idea of Addison being with anyone else. One night, it all came to a head," Carla said, a fresh set of tears causing her eyes to go damp.

"What happened?"

Carla hunched her shoulders before shredding the packets of sugar in her hand and covering the table in white. "He killed her. Witnesses saw them arguing in the middle of fifth avenue. They testified to watching him punch her and throw her to the ground. The case was dismissed. The judge wouldn't allow mention of his prior harassment charges, cited lack of proof, and deemed the witnesses unreliable."

I frowned. My pulse raced as the beat of my heart throbbed against my skin. My rage was building.

Carla looked up angrily. "Three witnesses, a history of harassment, and a pattern of documented jealousy weren't enough proof. According to the bench sitter, there wasn't enough evidence to try, let alone convict him. So, a chance was never given to let a jury decide. I am sure the judge's decision had nothing to do with the fact that he and Justin's daddy are old college friends. Rich white men take care of their own, and black women like Addison, like me, are left to rot."

I knew then what needed to be done. I could feel the sorrow emanating from Carla. I had been gone from mortals so long that calibrating to their emotions again was taking its toll. It made me slower in processing some of their feelings. So much so, I'd just realized I'd been incorrect in my reading of the energy pulsing between us. I was drawn to Carla. An overwhelming need lived in my spirit to pull her close to me and keep her safe. The spark I felt and assumed was returned, I had at first interpreted to be desire.

Now I knew her desire *was* love for me, but for me in my truest and rawest form. Carla was a Justice Warrior. She was fighting for

Addison, for her friend, but also for an unadulterated truth that could only be found within the realm of the just.

She gave me hope I wasn't aware I had abandoned.

"Tell me their names."

She tilted her head a little, her eyes narrowing as she looked at me. "Who? Why?"

"I cannot speak for your courts, but I have listened to the truth in your words. I will give you the justice Addison was denied but surely deserves."

Carla frowned, lifting her mug for the first time to take a large gulp of the lukewarm brew before glancing toward Aunt Janet and back. "If I remember my classics, the mentions of you, dear Dikê, speak of your battles with Adikia. They tell of how you would, literally, rage and club injustice, dragging Adikia through the streets for all to see."

I nodded. "Yes. What I have seen of this world since my return lets me know that Adikia still roams freely and is active in the nature of man."

"Yes, because injustice cannot just be clubbed out with rage. It will feed off of that and find a new way to return."

My eyes locked with hers as I let my growing rage ignite my power within. The silver of my irises was vibrant when I didn't force the power down. Carla gasped, scooting away to curl into the corner of the booth." You really are Justice."

"I am."

"And y-you want to bring Justin and the judge t-to—"

"Justice. To heel. Justin and all his accomplices should be made to face their actions and the inequity and imbalance they put into the world. I stand for balance and equity. I shine light down on ultimate truths."

Carla nodded, leaning forward, her body inches from mine as she lay halfway across the table. "I need you to promise me you will never take their lives."

"I will not lie to you."

"Would you make me a murderer?"

My breath caught, my rage oozing away as the silver drained from my eyes, leaving only a hue of brown confusion in its wake. "I do not know what—"

"I thought this, and you were a dream. I told you this. I would have never told you if I had known who—what—you really are. If you act on that knowledge, if you harm them or take their lives, it's my fault. I don't want that on my head. I won't wear that imbalance on my soul."

"I am justice, Carla. I am judgment. I am balance. I bring equity. I force those to face the errors they have made. What would you have me do?"

"I would," she paused then, leaning even closer. I could smell strawberries shrouded in hope and peace. Just as my brow crinkled in confusion, her lips touched mine, and I was lost. The world spun around and around, but I was gone. I was once again cloaked in the brightness of Spica, hidden amongst the beauty of the stars. I'd lived millennia among the constellations, and she'd given me the universe in one kiss.

"Now I know," she whispered, pulling back and falling against her seat.

"Now, you know what?" I asked, my voice a little gruff.

"The true taste of justice."

I smiled.

"Do not taint yourself and spoil that for me. Do not make me a murderer, even if it is in my own mind."

My fingers traced the edge of the table as I tried not to focus on the lingering taste of her kiss. "Again, what would you have me do?"

"Find a new way. Teach this world, *my world*, justice without invoking your old ways. Try the method of finesse. Work within the systems to dismantle them, making them just and whole again. That's what Addison wanted. She wanted to be a lawyer so she could play the game knowing all the rules." She grinned slightly, her fingers running across her lips. "Learn the game and help those that need to be helped."

I breathed deeply, letting a sigh overcome me. I knew she was right. This world was new, and the injustices were vast and ran deep. I couldn't just go on a killing spree, as some of my other relatives would have. I needed to be smart. I needed to act differently.

Within a few moments, I had a plan. I would start a business, *Blind Equity*. I'd use it as a place to help people like Carla and Addison. Justice would be obtained, and we'd make sure we did it in the names of all the fallen. I'd make sure the world continued to rise and say their names.

"Are you sure?" I asked Carla, who now looked at me with deference and awe. "I can tell how much you wanted retribution for Addison, how much you loved her.

She nodded and smiled. "I never said I wanted retribution. I said Addison deserved justice. I love her with all of me. I just…" she paused, her words trailing off, "I want to fight beside you. I want you to lead us to something better and to balance the scales. It's what Addison would want. It's what she would demand. And in the end, Dikê, my goddess…"

"Yes?"

"In the end, Bell Hooks said it best, 'Without justice, there can be no love.'"

AGAPE

SELFLESS

LOVE

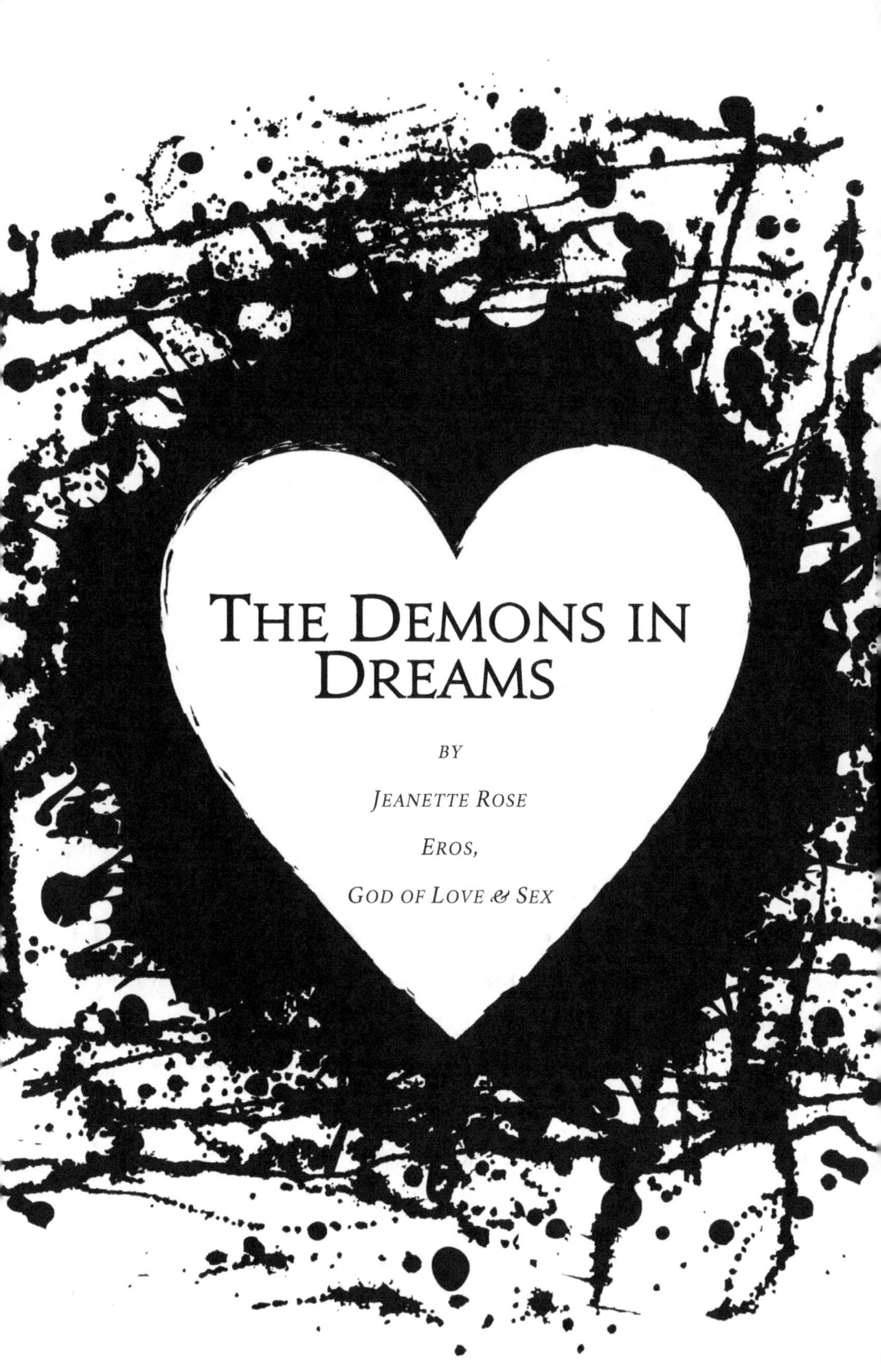

THE DEMONS IN DREAMS

BY

JEANETTE ROSE

EROS,

GOD OF LOVE & SEX

I blink heavily behind my sunglasses. My eyes feel like they have hard sandpaper over them. I haven't slept in...days? Weeks? I'm losing track. I don't *need* to sleep, at least not as much as a human. So, it's not a big deal.

The part that's making it worse is hiding it from my wife. *Clio. Psyche.* My head still reels from the idea that the wife I pined for was in front of me all along, hidden behind false memories and preconceived notions.

She didn't take my wings. She is innocent of all I once accused her of, both of us played by her controlling mother. In every life, I'd found her, loved her, and lost her. This time will be different. It has to be.

She doesn't know I'm not sleeping. And pretending to fall asleep next to her in bed every night is a challenge. Usually, I just lie awake through the night, staring at the ceiling and counting down the minutes. I focus on her every breath until she wakes, and I am sure she is safe. Keeping all of this from her is even harder when she's the most intelligent creature I've ever met, not to mention she's both the Muse of History *and* the Goddess of the Soul.

I need a distraction before I go mad. Wandering down the street, I pull out my phone, playing the security footage for the building. My twin, Dinlas, the God of Hate and Jealousy, installed the security system for the entire God Complex. I created a backdoor at the same time, but I doubt that surprises anyone. How is a trickster supposed to cause trouble if he doesn't know where to strike?

I'm not using it for that at the moment. I'm using it to watch the hallway between my floor and the elevator. I left Clio sleeping, and I'm hoping she'll remain that way until I'm done. I took her at least ten times before she begged for a reprieve. She needs the rest.

I'm a bit *greedy*. You don't get to be the God of Love and Sex without a voracious appetite. And I just got my wife back after two thousand years. So yeah. I *kind* of want to fuck her into the next millennia. Sue me.

If she's exhausted from me, then she can't leave me, right? Focus, Eros. You're trying to surprise her, remember?

Oh right.

The armed security guard at the entrance looks at me as I pull open the first store door. I nod passively at him and immediately realize I have no idea what the fuck I'm doing. My feet root to the marble floor, and I repeatedly blink behind my sunglasses.

Sensing blood in the water, a well-groomed saleswoman saunters up to me. "Sir, do you need help? Are you looking for something special?"

Slipping my sunglasses to the top of my head, I barely notice the way the mortal's breath catches at the sight of my eyes. Even without sleep, I'm still the fairest of all the gods. Mortals tend to *forget* themselves around me.

She composes herself after a moment, waiting for an answer. An answer I don't have.

Fuck. Why didn't I ask Din to come?

"Just looking," I croak.

She nods at me, moving back to the counter, and following me around the store as I look.

And look.

And look.

I don't stop looking, not in that store or the seventeen that follow it. Nothing is screaming at me. Fuck, I should have tried this after I slept. It's all blurring together. It doesn't help that I'm always checking the feed on my phone, my palms sweating, praying each time to whatever god will listen. *Please...don't let her leave me while I'm gone.*

Something catches my eye as I lower my phone.

This is it. I can feel it practically vibrate. The same strings of fate that bind Clio and I are wrapped around it. I need it.

There's a hazy exchange of money, and it's mine. I'm a little more awake now that it's in my possession. One more stop, and then I can finally do what I should have done millennia ago.

Back in the God Complex, I step into the elevator and press the button for my floor. I close my weary eyes. Even the fluorescent lights are a little too bright. My hand finds my new purchase in my pocket, and I rub it with my thumb like a talisman.

The elevator stops, and I step off, entering my apartment with a hiss of relief. I head towards the bedroom but pause at the second door. I knock, and my daughter answers immediately. I smile softly at her, staring into her extraordinary eyes, and fleetingly wish for all the things I can't have. I can never see my daughter grow up. Never see her first words, her first steps. I only get to have her new experiences. Her new world, the one we create together.

I speak with Hedone for just a few minutes before pressing a kiss to her forehead and continuing to my bedroom. Pushing open the door, I smile softly at Clio. She's still passed out, and for a moment, I just look at her.

My *Aren*, my little lamb. She must have woken up sometime during my errands because she has on one of my shirts. She wears them more than I do.

"*Aren?*" I call softly to her, and she groans before stirring. Picking her head up, she looks over her shoulder at me, locking me with those magnificent rainbow eyes of hers.

"*Lykos?* What time is it?" she whispers, looking around for a clock.

"It's almost noon," I answer, coming to her side of the bed and sitting on the edge, looking down at her.

"Noon?!"

I laugh lightly, stopping her from jumping out of bed. "You don't have anywhere to be, *Aren*. The museum is closed because of the virus, remember?"

She sighs heavily. "You're right. I forgot."

She sits up, allowing me to fluff her pillows behind her so she can lean back against them. Her nose scrunches, and she giggles nervously at me, making me wipe my hands on my jeans again.

"Are you okay, *Lykos?*"

Fuck, am I that transparent?

"Me? I'm fine. How are you?"

Rhea, preserve me! Who am I, fucking Han Solo?

She laughs lightly again. "I am doing much better now that you're here."

Reaching forward, I swipe my thumb across her lower lip in thought, murmuring, "I'm not whole without you, *Aren*. Not ever."

She reaches out, placing a hand on my cheek. I drop my hand from her face as she leans in to kiss me deeply. She pulls back to whisper against my lips, "All those years we were apart…I felt a hole in my soul. Now I know why. I am so happy to be with you again, to be whole again."

My throat is tight, and I have to clear it a couple of times to croak out, "*Aren*."

She mimics my serious voice when she responds, "*Lykos*."

I wipe my hands on my pants again. "*Aren*…Fuck, I said that already." I run my hand through my hair. "Okay, hold on." My eyes lock on hers, and I take a deep breath. "Clio. Psyche. *Princissika. Aren*. My muse. My love. My life. My soul."

She giggles again. "Yes?"

"I wanted to do this right. Once." Fumbling with the ring box in my pocket, I pull it out, dropping to one knee next to the bed. "In every life, in every form, it's always been you. You for me. Me for you. Never have I loved another, and never will I love another. I married you twice before, once as a mortal and once as a goddess.

140

Yet, neither time did I actually ask you formally to marry me. I figured the third time would be the chance to fix that." I thumb the box open, revealing the ring that took me eighteen stores to find. It has a massive oval diamond surrounded by a halo of kaleidoscope gems, forming the same rainbow that sparkles in her eyes.

"Will you marry me?"

She gasps, her hands cover her mouth, and her eyes well up with tears. It's an agonizing couple of minutes before she nods her head.

"Yes."

I feel my eyes glow with excitement, and I freeze, needing to know that I heard her correctly. "Yes? You will?"

She nods quickly once more. "Yes, I will. Eros, *Lykos*, husband. My love."

She lunges at me, throwing her arms around my neck, and I barely catch the box in time to keep it from falling. With the ring in one hand, I wrap my arms tightly around her and stand.

"Oh, the ring, I wanted to show you…"

She stands on the bed, pulling back as little as possible from me. Without words, I know she's as loathe to let go of me as I am of her. I tug the ring free and set the box aside, holding the ring out. I wait for her to slip it on.

She slips her finger through the band, tears flowing down her cheeks. "It's beautiful, *Lykos*."

There's the sound of a tiger whining at the door, and I kiss Clio hard before calling over my shoulder, "You can come in now, *Thavsma!*"

Clio smiles at me, her lips twitching, wiping tears from her face. "What did you do?"

Hedone throws the door open, and there is a blur of blonde hair as she leaps onto the bed. Din, Las, and Duck all right behind her, and when the two massive tigers and the tiny fox make their way onto the bed, I immediately protest, "Off the bed!"

All of them, including my wife and child, ignore me.

"Let me see the ring!" Hedone squeals at her mother, bouncing on the bed with her.

Clio laughs as Duck paws at her leg, begging to be picked up. She holds her hand out to Hedone.

My daughter coos, "Soooo shiny."

"Your pater picked a good one."

"He came and asked for my blessing to ask you."

Clio's gaze snaps to mine. "You did?"

I smile softly at both of them. "Of course, I couldn't propose without your daughter's blessing."

"I made him tell me about his intentions." Hedone giggles.

Clio laughs. "And what did he say?"

"I said they were distinctly ignoble, and that I intended to ravish you at least four times a day for the rest of our lives."

Clio blushes deeply. "*Lykos!*"

I only laugh because there, with my daughter and wife/fiancé, I can't think of anything that could make this better, except *maybe* the ability to sleep.

I struggle through the day, groggy and exhausted even through my joy. I know I can't just pretend to sleep next to her tonight. My body is breaking down and demanding rest, but there is no way I will risk sleeping next to Clio. So, I drag my feet to the couch and collapse face-first into it. Closing my eyes, I drift off.

It's the same dream. It always is. The dream that dogs my steps, making it unsafe to sleep in the same bed as my wife.

I don't remember waking up or even moving. I suppose sleepwalking is like that. But when I do snap to consciousness, I have trouble understanding what exactly I'm seeing. Clio's pinned beneath me, my hands locked around her throat, and I'm squeezing as she begs.

"*A-Aren?*" I whisper brokenly before throwing myself away from her. This is just more of the nightmare. This can't be real. I would never hurt, Clio. Even in sleep.

Well, that's not exactly true, is it? There's a reason you're sleeping on the couch. You can't trust yourself not to do this very thing.

I scramble away from her, my back hitting the wall of the living room. She sits up slowly, coughing and touching her throat.

This is a dream. It has to be another nightmare. Looking down at my hands, I see golden blood spilling from the scratches on my forearms. Closing my eyes, I force myself to wake up. But when I open them again, nothing's changed.

I try again.

And again.

And again.

No, no, no, this can't be real. Please, gods, don't let this be real.

"*Lykos?*" She coughs. And I wince at the sound of her voice struggling through her traumatized vocal cords.

I can't look at her. I can only stare at the slowly healing scratches she's left on my arms. She must have clawed to get free.

What did I do? No, no, this is just another nightmare. It must be a new one, the first one in two thousand years.

She crawls closer to me, and I can barely hear her voice over the roaring in my ears.

"*Lykos?* What happened?" I flinch again at the sound of her damaged throat.

Finally, looking up at her, I try to move further away, cornering myself against the entertainment center and the wall, shrinking in on myself.

"I-I hurt you?"

Say it wasn't me. Say this is a dream. Say anything else.

"You did…"

No. Please, no.

Scrambling to a stand, I demand, "What were you doing out here, *Aren?* You were in bed!"

Why didn't you sleep? Why didn't you just stay away! Then I wouldn't have hurt you.

She stands slowly, chewing her bottom lip. "I woke up, and you weren't there. Why are you sleeping out here?"

"You should have stayed in bed!"

Then none of this would have happened. She'd still be safe from me.

Her lips turn down at my shout. "Why weren't you in bed?"

Looking down at my hands, I wish I could cut them off so all traces of this would be gone. I can't even wait for the couple of hours it will take for the marks to heal.

"I hurt you…" I whisper brokenly. My eyes snap from my hands to her neck, where the red marks I left behind are forming into dark bruises.

She cuts off my view by placing her hand on her neck, her eyes shimmer with understanding, and it only makes me hate myself more.

"Not on purpose, *Lykos*," she whispers. "I'll be okay."

"Aren't…aren't you scared of me?"

Because I'm scared of me.

"Of course not," she whispers, but the way her voice cracks belies her own statement.

"I hurt you." My back hits the wall again, and I slide back down, looking at my hands. Hating that I used them to hurt the one thing I need more than air. I want them gone. I ache for any sharp instrument to remove them. To hack the appendages off, so I don't have to look at them anymore.

My ass hits the ground again, and I can barely hear Clio's question. "Why were you sleeping out here?"

"It's dangerous for me to sleep near you."

She stands up, and I tense, expecting her to leave. Moving slowly, she sits next to me, leaving a little space between us. Why isn't she running? Why isn't she telling me how much she hates me for hurting her? What if she wants to leave me? I'll be alone again. Without her, I'm nothing.

"How long has this been going on?"

"What? The nightmares?"

She shakes her head, inching closer to me again. "That you have been sleeping out here."

"I can't sleep near you." I knew this would happen. I can't control myself when I sleep, and I've dreamed the same dream for two thousand years.

"Why?" she asks, scooting closer to me. I force myself to keep from flinching away.

"I can't stop...the things in my head."

When I dream, the enemy wears your face.

She forces my legs down enough to crawl into my lap, wrapping her arms around my neck. I should stop her and push her away. But this might be the last time she allows me to touch her like this.

Burrowing my head into her neck, I breathe in her scent, taking it into me.

"What's in your head?" she whispers, her hands locked around me.

"Nightmares."

Nightmares that I always have, but I've never needed to worry about hurting someone near me. For two thousand years, I've slept alone.

She holds me even tighter. "What kind of nightmares?"

"I…" I begin, but I can't bring myself to say it.

We remain silent for a few minutes, my face buried in her neck, her hands sifting through my hair. I hurt her, yet she's the one soothing me.

"I'm so sorry."

"It's okay, *Lykos*," she whispers, kissing the side of my head.

"But I hurt you. How could I hurt you?"

You're everything to me, my entire world.

"Why don't you hate me?"

I hate me.

"What do you mean?" she asks, pulling back to look at my face.

My gaze drops from her eyes to her neck, my hands shaking as my fingertips line up with the bruises still forming.

"That wasn't you."

My body starts to shake. "I won't hurt you again, I swear it. You can trust me."

Please don't leave me. I didn't mean it, and I won't let it happen again. I need you. Gods, do I need you.

147

"I trust you, *Lykos*, but right now, I want to focus on helping you."

"You don't want to leave me?"

Fuck, did I say that out loud?

"Of course not! Why would you ever think that!"

Because I hurt you, and I hate myself for it.

My hands drop from her neck, and I wrap my arms around her. I can't let her go. Even when she slowly starts to snore, I don't release her.

Instead, I stand and carry her back to our bed. I lay beside her, watching her sleep.

The hours pass, and the bruises only become darker. They are a clear testimony to how I hurt her.

What if she wakes up and wants to leave? I dread each passing minute and savor every breath she takes. I lay and listen, entertained by the T-Rex noises that come from her diminutive frame.

The sun is rising when she wakes again. She stretches, then winces slightly. Her magnificent eyes blink open. She looks at me and whispers brokenly, "Hi."

She gives me a small smile, trying to reassure me, but it only takes my fears to an even higher level.

"Do you...do you want to leave?"

Her eyes water slightly, and she reaches out, putting her hand on my chest. I know she can feel my racing heart against her palm.

"Never."

But what if this is only the beginning?

"Are you sure?" I cover her hand on my chest. "I...I don't know how you can stand to be near me."

I can't stand to look at myself. How can you?

"I'm sure, *Lykos*," she murmurs, chewing her lip. "Tell me what happened."

No, no, no. I can't do that. Her knowing the truth of what lurks in my head will destroy her. And I don't want her to know my deepest shame.

So, I stiffen and pull away. "*Aren*, I'm...I'm handling it."

I will be better at hiding my lack of sleep. Maybe I will move to the guest room when I absolutely need to pass out.

Her brow furrows, her bow lips turning downwards. "Wait. How long has this been going on?"

"It's nothing. I know better now."

It's fine. I just won't sleep near you.

Her eyes narrow on me. "What do you mean, you know better now?"

"This happens when I sleep, I just...I just won't sleep near you."

"What?"

"*Aren*, I won't hurt you again." *I'd die first.*

"There must be some way to help you. I'm sure we can figure this out."

"It's fine. I won't sleep near you again. You can trust me."

Slowly, I sit up in bed, but Clio rises as well, grabbing my arm.

"*Lykos*, we can't just sleep separately forever. We will figure out what is causing those nightmares."

"I said I'm handling it," I murmur. "Everything's fine, *Aren*."

Stop pushing, just trust me to never sleep near you, and then I won't have to tell you what's in my head.

It will kill her to know. I can take this on and sacrifice the absolute contentment I feel when I sleep in her arms. Though the memory is vague, I remember. When she was Psyche, I never felt so *complete* as I did when I slept with her in the cocoon of my embrace.

But I can forget that if it spares her this.

She sits back from me. "Really? Because it doesn't seem like you are."

"Last night was an anomaly. It was fine before—"

Fuck, I should not have said that.

"Before what?" she says, and my shoulders tense, silently trying to retract my slip up. Except I physically can't lie. I can't say I didn't mean it, or it was a lie. *Love always speaks true.*

Swinging my legs off the bed, I stand and head towards the closet. As if, somehow, that would be the end of the conversation.

"Eros, answer me," she demands. *Eros.* She never calls me that unless she's serious. It's always *Lykos.* I have to answer her.

With my back to her, I pause at the entry of our walk-in closet, muttering, "Before tonight."

I try to escape into the closet, but I know she'll follow me. Her voice whips out as I yank on a T-shirt, ruffling my hair with my hand as I do.

"So, this has been happening for a long time, and you didn't tell me?"

"It's not a big deal." It's really not. I'm a god, and I can go days without sleep.

"It is! You haven't been sleeping at night, have you?"

Bracing myself, I turn to face her, the back of my neck heating. "Not...not every night."

Her brows get that stubborn look I typically adore. "We will figure this out—"

"It's fine. It's figured out." I just won't sleep near her, and she'll never have to know.

"It's not fine, Eros!"

Eros again. Something about the sound of my name from her lips feels wrong. I'm Eros to everyone else. Usually, I'm *that fucking dick Eros.* But to her, I'm more. Or I used to be.

"Is this because I hurt you?"

Do you not love me anymore?

"It's because you are suffering, and you don't want me to help you!"

"I'm not suffering!"

I'm not. I can go without sleep. There are far worse things. Involuntarily, my gaze drops to her neck, the marks left there by my own hands mocking me, torturing me with the knowledge that I hurt the only thing in the world I ever cared about.

"Why won't you let me help you?!"

"I don't need help!"

She flinches back at that, her eyes swirling with her own riotous emotions. I went too far. I pushed too hard. I know that, but I can't take the words back because I'm sparing her. The knowledge of what I dream about every time I sleep will destroy her.

I just...I didn't understand the cost.

Moving slowly, she looks down at the engagement ring I gave her yesterday. Is she thinking about us? About letting this go, so we can pretend like this is fine? Is she finally going to listen to me?

Then she slips the ring off her finger, closing the distance between us and pressing it into my hand.

And my world shatters.

"I didn't mean to hurt you, *Aren.* I can do better, be better, please. I won't hurt you again, I swear," I ramble, my emotions spiraling out of control. Any kind of hold on them vanished the second she took the ring off. "I'll be whatever you want. I...I won't touch you again if you're scared of me."

She chokes back what sounds like a sob, but I can barely hear her. The ringing in my ears is too loud. "It's not because of any of that, Eros."

"Are you...do you not love me anymore?" I can't take my eyes off the ring in my hand, and my vision blurs. But it's not tears. It's numbness. My body is going into survival mode, cold washing over me, "I need you. You're my soul."

I can't push it off. My knees hit the ground so hard I think I shatter them. But I don't feel it. I don't feel *anything.* Just cold. Staring out

152

blankly, I can't even seem to find who was right in front of me. My vision is a blank canvas, and I'm lost in the idea of filling it. There's a distant sensation of someone touching my face, like someone walking over my grave, but there's no one there.

I'm alone again, just like always. I'm...*cold.*

The ringing in my ears lessens enough to hear someone talking to me, but I don't recognize the voice.

"Why won't you let me help with your nightmares?"

They know about them? How? No one knows. No one can *ever* know.

"It's dark in them, too dark. They take my soul from me," I whisper, not sure if I actually say the words out loud or if they are just in my mind.

"Eros, listen to me. You and I are a team. A team works together. I love you so fucking much, and all I want to do is help you. You help me, and I help you. Okay?" They sound like they're talking through tears. What happened to them? Their words don't make any sense to me.

"The darkness took my *Aren* from me. It took her." She's gone, and I'm adrift without her.

"What did the darkness do?" the voice asks.

"It's...in my head, always there. It wants my *Aren*. It makes me see the same thing over and over. It took her from me. Will you get her back for me?"

153

"I can. What does the darkness show you?" Just the confirmation that I can get her back cuts away some of the numbness, a single drop of warmth in the ocean of ice in me.

"My soul. My wings. Every night it's the same. Round and round. I need my soul."

"What happens to your soul?" the voice asks, and I distantly sense their hands on my face, warming me even more.

"She takes them from me. Every night. She comes for me in the dark."

"I will figure this out, my heart. I promise you that." The voice is...female? And it sounds like they're talking through tears.

"She's gone. I hurt her, and she's gone."

The cold numbness is seeping away from me into the floorboards beneath me. My surroundings slowly register, but everything is a haze of shapes and partial impressions.

"She isn't gone..."

She isn't? Hope flickers, cutting away more of the coldness, and I can feel the pain in my knees. I must have hurt myself somehow.

"Where is she?"

The voice kisses me, and my vision clears even more. I'm in my closet? "Will she stay?"

Then my eyes focus, and I look around at a loss. I'm kneeling on the floor of our closet. Clio is in front of me on her knees. Tears are falling down her face, and she's patting my cheeks.

What happened? How did I get here?

"*Aren*, what happened?" I ask, trying to remember how I got on the closet floor and coming up blank.

"Um…" she whispers, wiping away tears from her face. Why is she crying?

"The last thing I remember is…" My eyes catch her hand, and her ring sparkles on her finger. "Huh."

Slowly I wince, standing up, my knees knitting back together, healing. I hold my hands out for her, helping her to her feet. "Did something happen, *Aren*? I-I don't remember."

She shakes her head, going on her tiptoes, kissing me gently. "I need some fresh air. I'll be back."

What just happened?

HIS NIGHTMARES

BY

ALICE CALLISTO

CLIO,

MUSE OF HISTORY & GODDESS

OF THE SOUL

His nightmares. At first, I had no idea what they could be, but I managed to get the information from him when he went catatonic in the closet. His *soul*, a name he often calls me, takes his wings. *I cut off his wings!* I saw this once before. When I returned home, I accidentally looked into Eros's past and saw the memory of Psyche committing the unspeakable act. At the time, I had not realized that Psyche and I were the same person.

When I was younger, my mother found out about my relationship with Eros. Mnemosyne is the Titaness of Memories and would often use me to test her abilities. She wanted to see how long my memory lapses lasted after she placed a black cloud in my mind. Maybe even worse was when she added memories that were not my own. She knew I would marry Eros, and with his strength, I would have broken the toxic connection I had with her. That together, I would finally have the power to keep her from using my mind for practice.

She erased both of our memories as punishment and trapped my essence in a dagger. My mother had no intention of releasing me, but I managed to escape. My soul entered the unborn infant of a mortal queen to be reborn. She named me Psyche, and as I grew, I caused enough ruckus with the mortals that Aphrodite ordered Eros to deal with me. Eros and I are soul mates, and in a story as old as time, we fell in love, pledging our immortal lives to each other. My mother found me on the night of our wedding and stole me from our bed.

She disguised herself as me, and in a final act of cruelty, cut off his wings.

I wrap my arms tightly around my torso. Every night he sees the same nightmare. For two thousand years. How can he stand to be near me?

I need to help him. I can't let him have these nightmares anymore. It is tearing us apart. It terrifies me that twice he was beyond my reach. I tried everything to bring him back during his episode in the closet, but nothing worked. Luckily, he snapped out of it. But what if he hadn't?

I step into the elevator, staring at all the buttons. Who could help me with this? My eyes become blurry again, and I pull out my phone. I scroll, and my finger lands on one contact. *The King of Bacon.* The name I bestowed on Erebus, the Primordial of Darkness, a long time ago. Back in ancient Greece, the two of us formed an unlikely friendship while tracking down something that belonged to him. Did I mention he attempted to outbid me in buying a piglet to eat? Anyway, since then, the two of us have kept in contact. Erebus is one of my best friends and helped me get through a few major historical events. He comforted me when the memories of my old friends were erased. He isn't as mean as he looks but don't tell him I said that.

The phone rings, and it takes a few seconds before he answers.

"What's up, chicken wing?" Erebus answers.

"I need to talk to you about something. It's serious."

He clears his throat. "Are you okay?"

Tears threaten to pour down my face. "No...not exactly. I'll meet you at your place in twenty minutes?"

"Okay, I'll head over there now."

Hanging up, I press the button to Erebus's floor. I arrive, dragging my feet to his door. I lean against the wall, slide to the ground, and bury my face into my hands. A little less than twenty minutes later, I hear the elevator ding and heavy footsteps make their way towards me. Erebus slides down the wall, sitting beside me.

"Hi, old friend," he says.

"Hi," I say, looking up at him, my lip trembling.

Erebus slides an arm around me, pulling me into a hug. "Whoa, whoa, what's happening? Talk to me, Clio."

The tears pour down my face. "I-It's Eros."

Erebus's eyes go wide as his gaze fixates on my neck, and rage vibrates off him. "Are those bruises on your neck?!"

I attempt to cover them, but he lifts my chin to the side. "It's n-nothing!"

"That is not nothing! Has Eros seen this?"

I squeeze my eyes shut. "He uh...was the one who...um..."

His jaw drops. "Excuse me?"

"He was having a nightmare, and when I tried to wake him, he s-strangled m-me," I say, chewing my bottom lip.

Erebus stands me up, opening his door. "Let's go inside."

I nod, following him into his apartment. He sits me on his couch. "Can I get you something? Tea? A blanket? How about a warm cloth?"

159

"That would be n-nice, thank you."

Erebus disappears for a few minutes before returning with the items. He applies the warm damp cloth to my forehead, placing the tea on the table.

"Th-thank you." I smile sadly at him.

"Okay," Erebus takes a deep breath, grinding his teeth. "Why would Eros strangle you? What kind of nightmare would cause him to do that?"

I let out a shaky breath, sipping the tea. "I don't know. He wasn't awake when he did this, and trust me...he feels horrible."

"I'm sure he does." He nods, taking the cloth off my head and wrapping the blanket around my shoulders. "Are you angry at him? You have every right to be, but this is so not like him. I am really concerned for the both of you, Clio."

"I'm not mad. I am worried about him. He has had the same nightmare for two thousand years and won't get help."

"Two thousand years? I'm so sorry, Clio. I had no idea," Erebus says, his brow furrowing. "What do you mean he won't get help?"

My lip trembles. "He says he is fine and that he is handling it. His solution is to not sleep in the same bed as me."

"Fuck that!" Erebus gets up, his face going red. "That is not dealing with it."

He takes his phone from his back pocket. "I'm going to give that idiot a piece of my mind. What the hell is he thinking?!"

I scramble from the couch, grabbing Erebus's arm. "Breathe."

He stops and takes a deep breath before putting his phone back into his pocket.

"I was thinking...you can talk to him about how to get rid of the nightmares," I say.

"Me?" Erebus asks, confused.

I nod. "Eros won't listen to me. Maybe he will listen to someone who has also experienced nightmares?"

Erebus shudders before looking at me. "I'll talk to him, but I can't make any promises. Everyone dreams differently. You know that, Clio."

He places a comforting hand over my shaking one. "I know. It doesn't help that the nightmare is of me h-hurting him."

"That could be a problem." Erebus raises a brow.

My eyes water. "He doesn't want to hurt me..."

"I know that, chickie," Erebus says, holding his arm out to me. "That man would go to the ends of this world and next for you. We will get down to the root of this. And if that asshat still doesn't want to listen, then I may just have to lock him up until he sees who's right."

A small smile curves my lips, and I loop my arm through his. "Have I ever told you that you are a good friend?"

"Not nearly enough." He smirks, leading us out of the flat and to the elevator. I press the button, looking up at him anxiously.

"He isn't going to be happy about this," I say as we step into the elevator, pressing the button to my floor.

Erebus chuckles. "Do I look concerned about Eros right now?"

He raises his hand to touch the bruises on my neck, but I quickly cover them with my hands.

"No, you don't."

The elevator quickly makes it up to my floor, and we both exit. Erebus lets go of my arm and kicks the door to my apartment open.

"Erebus?!" Eros shouts from inside. "You're paying for that door!"

I grab onto Erebus's arm. "Breathe."

This time he doesn't stop. He pulls away from me and storms over to my husband. "Is this funny to you?"

"You breaking my door down?" Eros looks over at me before his gaze darts away. "A little."

"No, you little shit!" Erebus shouts.

Suddenly, Erebus's shadows burst from him. My eyes widen as they create a barrier between the men and me. I know what he is about to do. He knows I will not be happy about it and will try to stop him. I watch helplessly as Erebus's hand shoots out, gripping Eros by the neck, squeezing and lifting him off the ground. Eros claws at Erebus's arm, twisting and kicking his legs as he chokes.

"Erebus!" I shout, stomping my foot. Tears sting my eyes, and I hit Erebus's shadows.

"Listen and listen closely," Erebus hisses. "You are going to get help! Don't you think for one minute that you have this under control. Look at your wife. Does that look like you have this under control?"

162

Eros looks over at me, his face flushing red before looking away. He gasps out, "I…I didn't m-mean t-to."

Erebus lets him go. "Don't you think I know that!?"

"I…I…" Eros chokes.

Erebus points at me. "This will not happen again!"

"Never," Eros says, looking over at me again. Tears are rolling down my face. I don't want to upset him any more than he already is. "I'll get help."

Erebus smacks Eros across the face, and I wince. "Get your shit together."

"Okay, I'll get help!" Eros says, rubbing his face. "No need to add insult to injury."

Erebus pushes Eros in the chest. "Go see Melinoë and fix it."

Eros coughs. "Always delighted to see you, E."

Slowly, the shadows return to Erebus, and he turns to look at me with a slight smile. I give him a disappointed look, shaking my head.

"You know, you never agree with my methods," he says with a shrug.

"Methods?!" Eros coughs, rubbing his neck.

Erebus snarls at him, "This is how I get my shit done."

Eros looks at me in disbelief as Erebus makes his way to the door. He stops a few steps from the exit, turning back to us and pointing his finger at Eros.

"Don't forget!" Erebus walks out, leaving me alone with my husband.

Eros chokes slightly and begins picking up the remnants of the splintered door. My heart sinks deeper into my chest. I didn't want to make him feel bad. I just want him to get help.

"You went to him?" Eros asks, breaking the silence.

I gulp, nodding slowly. "I did."

He looks away from me, picking up another piece of the door. "Why? I-I scared you? You don't trust me anymore. Y-y-you don't love me anymore."

I walk over to him, tears rolling down my face. "I do love you, *Lykos*. But you weren't listening to me. I didn't know what else to do."

His entire face goes red. "I-I...I just didn't want you to know."

"I know."

Eros's eyes snap up to mine. "Y-y-you do?"

I squeeze my eyes shut for a moment, realizing he doesn't remember telling me.

"In the closet, you mentioned your soul taking your wings."

"Oh." He chokes, squeezing his eyes shut. A single tear drops from his eye, and I place my hands on his cheek, wiping it away.

"Please. Let me help you."

Eros opens his crystal blue eyes, locking them with mine as another tear falls. "That's not all."

"Tell me," I whisper.

"I-I-I...give up." Another tear falls, and I wrap my arms around him, holding him tightly.

"Oh, *Lykos*."

"I didn't want t-to live in a world where you didn't love me anymore." He chokes back a sob, shaking violently in my arms. Tears roll down my face as I kiss the side of his head.

"I love you so much, Eros. We are going to fix this, okay? We are going to get rid of these nightmares and then we don't have to worry about this anymore."

Eros drops to his knees, pulling me down with him. He lands hard onto the ground, and I wince.

"I didn't want...want you to know."

"Shhh," I hush him, running my fingers through his hair.

"I just didn't...I wanted to keep you safe." He shakes his head.

"I know," I say, kissing his cheek.

He presses his head into my chest, sobs wracking his body. We stay like this most of the night, holding each other.

A knock at our makeshift door pulls me away from my inner turmoil. I hardly slept, my thoughts only on Eros. We called Melinoë early this morning, asking her to help us with the nightmares. It was the logical thing to do, but we are both anxious. I try to keep positive, even though my worries try to push through. What if this doesn't work? What if this permanently scars him? I let out a shaky breath, pulling myself in before my thoughts go wild.

I walk over to the door, opening it wide, and Melinoë stands on the other side. She looks at me, her dark eyes studying my features. Melinoë's black and blonde hair is tied back into a messy bun, her baby hairs curled. Her black cardigan almost touches the ground as she wraps it tightly around her body.

"Hi, Melinoë. Thank you so much for coming," I say, moving to the side.

"Hello, Clio," she replies, her face softening as she steps into the apartment. "How are you two feeling?"

I look behind me towards the bedroom where I left Eros to rest. I know he isn't sleeping. He is still awake, probably dwelling on what he did to me. I turn back to Melinoë, blinking back my tears.

"Could be better," I mumble.

Melinoë nods. "Where is your kitchen?"

"Follow me." I sigh and lead her to the kitchen. Melinoë pulls things from her bag, placing them on the counter. I set her up with a pot of boiling water as she explains what is going to happen. I am to enter Eros's nightmare. Well, my soul is. I need to show his sleeping state that all the images he is seeing are just a dream. I am sure my mother had something to do with this, and I need to help him break free of whatever darkness she put on his sleeping state. A curse to keep him away from me and to ruin our love. Well, Mother, this is only going to bring us closer together.

"Once the tea has finished steeping, we can begin," Melinoë says, crushing dried poppy petals and placing them into the boiling mixture.

I nod, opening my mouth to reply, only to startle when Eros interrupts me.

"*Aren*…I don't know about this," he whispers, coming up behind me. His sunken eyes and pale face wrench at my heart. I have to do this for him.

I give Eros a small smile, kissing his cheek. "It will be okay."

Melinoë walks over to us, teapot in hand. "Go ahead and take a seat."

We both nod, and I grab three teacups before we make our way to the couch. Melinoë pours the tea, and I try to hide my shaking hands from Eros.

Stay strong for him. You can do this.

"*Aren?*" Eros whispers. I turn my head to look up at him, and my heart sinks. His eyes are still grey, like a storm is brewing in them. Would they ever go back to normal?

"Yes?"

"Remember what I told you? M-my darkest…" he stutters and trails off.

"I know, Eros," I whisper, kissing his cheek softly.

Melinoë clears her throat, and we both look at her. Her cool demeanor calms my anxieties. If anything happens, she will be here. I fully trust that Melinoë has the capability to pull us out if things get bad. I am just hoping everything goes smoothly.

"You both need to be in a comfortable position. Eros, I suggest you lay down since we will be working on your nightmares," Melinoë instructs. "Please drink, Eros."

Eros nods nervously before taking a sip of tea. He coughs slightly before gulping the rest down. I smile at him reassuringly before he lays his head in my lap. I gently run my fingers through his hair as his breathing slows, indicating sleep.

"The tea's effect is quick. You will find yourself in the dream world shortly, Eros," Melinoë whispers. She waits a few seconds before looking up at me. "Now, Clio, you need to understand that there is a chance that things can go south very quickly. I may not be able to pull you from the nightmare, and you will be stuck in the Dreamworld forever. Do you still want to continue?"

I open and close my mouth a few times, my hands shaking once more. Looking down at my husband, I sigh, and a tear rolls down my cheek. He is my world, my soulmate. Eros would do anything for our daughter and me. It's time for me to do the same. Kissing his forehead, I look up at Melinoë and nod. "I need to do this. I *can* do this."

"Okay." Melinoë nods, indicating the drink.

I look down at the blue liquid before gulping it down. The taste of poppy and other flowers tingle on my tongue. There is no turning back now. I place the cup on the table before resting my head back and closing my eyes.

"I will guide your soul to his nightmare. The rest is up to you, Clio." Melinoë whispers, her voice already far away.

At first, all I see is darkness. My soul is the only thing that illuminates the black. A blue glow surrounds my entire body, making my skin translucent. I look down at my shaky hands, clench them into fists, and start walking. The scene around me changes, and I'm back in Eros's apartment. Not the one we have now, but his apartment back in Ancient Greece. The one we planned to live in together, where we dreamt of raising our future children. I let out a shaky breath as I run my hands over the wall. Even as Psyche, I knew something was wrong. Memories of my life as Clio were slowly returning to me. If my mother hadn't stolen me away the second time, I am sure I would have figured it out. But no, I was taken right after our wedding, and now, I will see what happened to him on that fateful night.

Slowly, the nightmare materializes, and I choke back a sob, covering my mouth. I see Eros, sitting on the side of his bed. His eyes wild as gold ichor drips down his back, staining the sheets.

"Princissika?" He stands. I try to yell out to him, saying I am here, but I can't find my voice. Eros collapses to his knees, and I clutch my chest. A shadow looms above him, and I focus on the figure. My heart stops when I realize who it is. It's...it's me. I knew this already, but it takes me a second to register what is happening. In the imposter's hand is Thanatos's scythe and Eros's blood drips from it. His feathers cling to the gold ichor on the blade. My stomach turns.

Din and Las appear at Eros's side. They snarl at the imposter, baring their sharp teeth.

That's my boys.

The imposter backs away from them, and Eros struggles back to his feet.

"Princissika, whatever has happened, we can face it together," he pleads, his hand reaching out towards her. Why is he forgiving her...me? The imposter cut off his wings. And yet he is willing to put this behind him? I choke back a sob once more.

"Princissika," the imposter snaps at him, dragging out the nickname. "I always hated that you called me that. You never expected that anyone could not fall in love with you? The perfect God of Love."

You bitch, I snarl in my head, trying to move towards them, but I can't. I look down at my legs and see inky darkness crawling up them, holding me in place. No. No. No. This isn't good. I look back up, watching as the imposter swipes the scythe at the tigers.

"Well, how do you feel now?" the imposter continues. "Wingless and soon to be headless, at the hands of the only woman you ever loved."

Eros falls to his knees once more, lowering his head and awaiting his death. He really did give up. My chest burns, and my eyes sting as I continue to watch.

"Gods, you're pathetic! You can't even put up a good fight, can you?" she growls, raising the scythe above her head.

Before she has time to lower it, I wrench myself free from the darkness and charge at the imposter. My body is low, and my shoulder impacts her stomach, tackling her to the ground. She topples onto her back, hitting the

170

floor hard. I land on top of her, and she glares up at me in shock. We grapple
with each other, struggling for control. With a quick twist of her body, she
flips us, pushing me onto my back. She straddles me, locking her knees
around my torso and pressing her full weight on top of me, digging the stem
of the scythe into my neck. I gasp for air and kick my legs, trying to free
myself.

"Weak," the imposter hisses. My entire body burns from the lack of
oxygen as black spots start to fill my vision. A surge of adrenaline flows
through me, and I slam my fists against her arms, loosening her grip enough
that I can yank the shaft from her. I toss the weapon aside and twist, pushing
her off me. I crawl, scrabbling to the scythe. I grab it from the ground and
leap to my feet. I pivot quickly to face the imposter, watching in horror as she
morphs into a group of three imps. They smile evilly at me.

"Fuck you," I spit, slashing the first imp, slicing its guts open. It lets out a
piercing wail as its life force is drained. Pulling the blade from it, I spin to
the next. It bares its fangs at me, and I swing the scythe, severing its head
clean off. I pivot to face the last imp, chopping straight down, cutting it into
two pieces.

Slowly the bodies of the imps melt into black goop, becoming absorbed by
the dream. I drop the weapon, my breathing ragged as I turn to look for Eros.
He is still on the ground, his head bowed and waiting for death. I collapse to
my knees, crawling to him. Tears spill down my cheeks as I look up at him.

"Lykos?" I murmur soothingly, and his eyes connect with mine. I gasp,
covering my mouth. Nothing. I see nothing in his eyes, not even a spark of

171

emotion. Not the glimmer of happiness I am so used to seeing. They are empty and dull.

"You can take my head, Princissika. It's yours," he whispers.

"Lykos, I am not going to take your head." My lip trembles, and I fix a strand of his hair before pointing at the decomposing imps. "It's over now."

Eros's eyes slowly flicker. "A-Aren?"

I give him a quick nod before wrapping my arms tightly around him. "It's me."

His arms enfold me, and he buries his face against my neck. "You...you saved me."

"Yes, Lykos. I never, ever would hurt you," I whisper.

"I-I..." he stutters, cupping my face in his hands. "I see you, my soul."

A tear rolls down his face as he presses his forehead to mine.

"I see you," he whispers.

The world around us dematerializes, and I open my eyes. We are back in our living room, and my face is damp from my tears. I look down at my lap to find Eros blinking up at me.

"Did it work?" I ask hopefully.

"Yes. It did," Melinoë says, and I hiss out a breath of relief.

"Thank you, Melinoë," Eros says groggily.

"Yes, thank you so much," I say.

"Not a problem," the Goddess of Nightmares says, getting up from her chair.

I look back down at Eros as she quietly lets herself out. "How are you feeling?"

"I...I feel strung out," he whispers, squeezing his eyes shut. "You saw it."

My chest stings at the reminder of the nightmare. "I did."

He shakes his head, tears rolling down his face. It breaks me to see him like this. I shift his head off my lap and lay beside him. He rests his cheek against my chest as I run my fingers through his hair.

"I-I wish I could take the memory from you, and I'm a fucking monster for wishing that." He chokes out on a whisper, his entire body shaking.

"You are not a monster. You have never been a monster."

"I am! Because I want you to forget!" He shakes even more. "I'm sorry, *Aren*. You must hate me."

I stay silent for a few minutes, closing my eyes. My memory has been something that has been manipulated multiple times in my life. He knows this. He knows how much it upsets me. I press my lips to his forehead.

"I will never hate you, okay?" I whisper. "I love you."

Eros looks up at me, his eyes connecting with mine. They are shining like a child's when they need reassurance. "Even now? Knowing everything? You still love me?"

"I still love you, and I always will. Even after everything." I smile at him.

His eyes continue to tear up as he leans in, kissing me hard. "I love you so fucking much."

"I love you so fucking much, too. Now, you should try to sleep." I giggle.

He laughs brokenly. "I'm scared, *Aren*."

"I know, but I am here if you need me."

Eros stands, taking my hand and leading me to our bedroom. His body is still shaking, but I know a good night's rest will help him. Eros pulls me onto the bed, covering us both.

"I need you..." he begins. "I-I need you to sing me to sleep."

I tilt my head, looking up at him. "What would you like me to sing?"

He pulls me close to his chest, resting my head on his heart. The rhythm is still a little frantic, and I close my eyes, willing him to calm.

"W-what would you sing to our daughter if she needed it?" he asks.

"Well, she does like those Disney movies..."

Eros stays silent, kissing the top of my head.

"Flowers gleam and glow..." I sing, running my fingers up and down his chest. In the movie, Rapunzel uses this song to heal Flynn. Maybe this song will help heal him. Once I finish singing, I look up at him and smile.

"Really? *Tangled?* That is your choice?" he says, smiling softly.

I scrunch my nose. "Well, I was going to sing the lullaby from *Frozen Two*."

He laughs softly, stroking my hair. "I can sing to you, *Aren*..."

"Please do," I whisper.

Eros's voice drops low as he sings, soothing my emotions. I find it hard to keep my eyes open, and I feel myself drift off into a peaceful sleep.

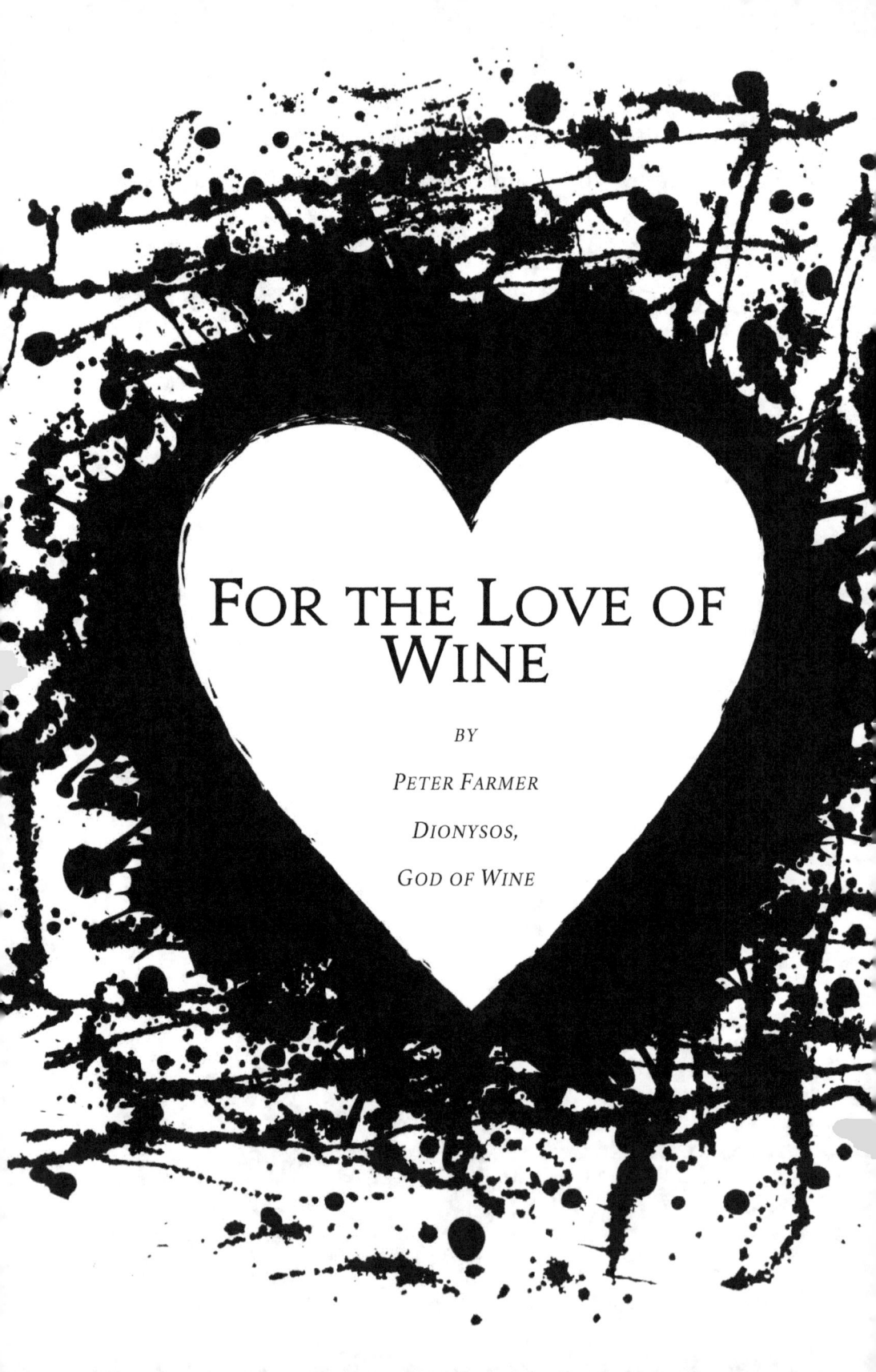

For the Love of Wine

BY

Peter Farmer

Dionysos,

God of Wine

We were on the final leg of the journey and about an hour and a half from landing in Napa County Airport, just south of the city. The convention would be held at the Napa Valley Expo on the edge of town and just east of the Napa River. Luis already secured our stay at the Poetry Inn just up the road on Silverado Trail. The location was perfect, in the heart of the local vineyards. Initially, he tried to fight me on the price, suggesting that we could just rent The Farmhouse, a smaller structure on the inn's property. At $25,000 for the month, it had ample space to accommodate the team we would need to ensure the completion of the Master Plan. Still, I told him just to book the entire complex for a month, just in case we needed the extra room. The local wine expo was the reason for flying in, but it was no longer the *main* priority.

I had poured over the three files in front of me in the last two hours. It was never easy for me to make this decision. I knew that everyone familiar with the name Dionysos would automatically think of the God of Wine and Frenzy. That had given me the image of a rebel and a party goer. Most people did not know about my kind of frenzy because there was order in the chaos, and there was reason to the rhyme. I wanted my celebrations to be the epicenter of a ripple in time that would touch people throughout their lives. Some would be affected positively, and some would be affected negatively to keep the balance. The choice was mine to make and to be sure that all affected would be rightly so.

This list of three was of local vineyards. All three were small family affairs. They all showed promise, but all three were struggling economically to make it through these times of mega-corporations and economic chaos. The big fish had always eaten the small fish, but it seemed that there were so few little fish left in the sea. I had to pick one of these vineyards and give them a helping hand. Whether as a shadow investor, a partner, or an outright buyout with recurring stakes.

I would bless one of these companies and help them grow, flourish, and prosper like grapes on the vine in my own way. I had done this countless times over millennia. Every time, with few exceptions, the family I blessed became yet another branch in the mortal family I had created. Who knew? The next vineyard I chose to bless might bring me the next Luis, when this Luis decides to step down and rest for his remaining days.

Once I finally made my decision, I moved all other papers away from me, re-reading what I had already re-read a handful of times. There was this tiny vineyard just south of Lake Hennessey that was operated by a family of five and a handful of farmhands. Grandfather, parents, and their two kids. The head of the family was still the grandfather, Antonio. He had passed the business to his daughter, Fran, and her husband, James. The vineyard was called *La Dolce Vita*, which fit because their wines were on the sweet side. He had opened his vineyard in 1960, which made him a pioneer of this area.

178

Antonio was a post World War II refugee who had run away from home instead of being part of an army for a cause he did not believe in. Eventually, he had found his way to the US and settled down in the area. He had taken a wife, and even though he was older, he started a family. He had grown up in his family vineyard in Sicily, so he had gone back to his first love. Grapes. To anyone reading this file, it was obvious that Antonio had the love.

Early on, *La Dolce Vita* had a good amount of success, and things were looking up. The success would be translated to expansion and hopefully some international recognition, but that was not what The Fates had in store. Soon after giving birth to their daughter, Antonio's wife, Milla, contracted some rare disease that kept her bed-ridden for many years before succumbing to the pain. Weighed down by grief, loss, and medical bills, all talk of expansion was put aside. It took decades of toiling before most of the debts were paid, but that meant the business struggled to keep up. Now, in his late 80s, I figured that Antonio was due.

I had Luis reach out to Fran, and they were expecting us later this evening. Traveling west meant that we were traveling with the sun and chasing daylight. It was a bit easier on the jet lag as long as you kept your strength up, but it was hard to sleep during the day. Not that I was ever a morning person. I had always felt more grounded in my energies at night because every breath was instilled with a little spark of mystery.

My biggest fear was that the voices would choose to be rowdy, and I needed to have my sanity intact for this task. I was not worried about a breakout or anything. Those were extremely rare, and there was no reason for the pot to boil over. I was most concerned about exposing the madness that I carried in the edges of my being to Antonio and his family. I doubted they would be willing to accept help from someone that giggled to himself, so I would have to remember to avoid the giggles and the self three-sixties until after their meeting.

I took what little time of peace I had left and closed my eyes, pushing the voices back with an inward hiss and a growl. There was a time when all I needed to do to silence them completely was close my eyes and concentrate for a few seconds. Not lately. Just like Antonio, I was also due, but for something else. Hopefully, the upcoming events would either satiate the impending breakout, so it stayed dormant longer, or accelerate it to the point of release. One way or the other, I sensed a change coming.

As soon as my feet touched the ground in Napa, I was overcome with a glorious feeling. I decided to head to the vineyard right away instead of stopping by the inn to rest. It was early evening when we landed, and Luis and I got into one car and headed out to while his assistants took the other and headed to check us in at the hotel. The drive was quiet as I laid back in the seat and closed my eyes. I took the short time it would take us to get there to center myself and concentrate. More times than not, that dampened the voices in my head. As entertaining as they could be, a business transaction was not the ideal setting for them to come out in full force.

When we arrived, the gates were open, and Steve was outside on the round driveway waiting for us. The house looked big but modest, with a wrap-around balcony and double doors instead of windows. It had an old-style red ceramic roof, with ivy crawling on one side of the house, which pleased me even more. This house was meant to be a little slice of the old country. It took all my strength not to do a little dance when I got out of the car. Steve welcomed us with a nice, firm handshake and led us straight to the dining room. Everyone else was already seated around the beautifully set table.

I took a short bow and waved at everyone. Luis did the same, and I made introductions. I used the name Dion for simplicity's sake. Using my full name always brought up questions, and I was not one to lie. Steve offered me one of the two seats considered to be the head of the table, directly across from Antonio. I took it with a nod, accepting the honor given me with open appreciation.

Steve sat in the empty chair to my right, and Luis took the remaining spot to my left. With that, Steve raised his glass and said, "I am sure you are tired from your long trip, and we are all honored that you chose to visit our humble home and business. I hope you don't mind that we eat and drink first. We have it as bad luck to do business on an empty stomach."

To that, I raised my glass in return and said, "Thank you for accepting us into your home. For that, and for your meal, we are honored and pleased. There is nothing better for getting to know someone than breaking bread with them." That pleased everyone, and the creases on Antonio's face deepened as he broke into a small smile.

The main course was veal osso buco. Judging by the smell of the pancetta, the fresh thyme, and the silky texture of the polenta that came with the plate, this was an authentic dish passed down within the family from generation to generation. The way the kids dove into the food hinted that it was not a meal served often. I could sense the family stealing glances toward me, and when gazes were met, they were followed by warm smiles. When I picked up one of the shanks, put my lips over the opening, and started sucking out the marrow loudly, the little ones giggled. Antonio raised his shank as if toasting me and followed suit.

I must say that I enjoyed the food, and while no one was looking, I added a few drops of water from my flask into the wine to get a better taste. The flavor was light, the scent aromatic, and the aftertaste not too sour. I could tell by the smell alone that the grapes were young and that what I was drinking was from last year's stock. Probably from the personal family barrels. The temperature was cool but not cold. Cooler than red wine was usually served, but I did not mind. It reminded me of the days when people kept their barrels in the cellar, and if I were a betting man, I would put money on this family doing just that for their private stock. I knew I did the same with mine.

After we ate, the kids cleared the table and left the dining room. After a moment of silence, I took it upon myself to start. I looked first

182

to Antonio, then Fran, and finally her husband, Steve. I held their gazes for a few seconds before moving from one to the other. Without even having to use my gift, I could sense both excitement and trepidation coming from all three. I placed my hands flat on the table and began.

"I want to thank you again for the warm company and the great meal. It is not how most business is done these days anymore, even though it ought to be. Now I will not waste any more of your time and get to the *marrow* of why I am here. I am sure my associate Luis has explained some of this, but I would like to go into it myself. After I am done, you can ask me anything you want. The one thing I need you to keep in mind is that there is no downside for you in this. All you have to say is *no thank you,* and we both shall move on with our lives."

"First, I will go over what I want to do *for* you. Many factors have brought me here, but the main one is that I no longer need money. I have forged my empire over the years through the vine. I have all I need and more from that. I do not see what I have created as a company, but as a family. Once in a while, I come across people like you, people that love vine and family, and I choose to help them. Be it with funds, knowledge, technology, marketing, or whatever sources my trusted team thinks will help best." I glanced at Luis, and with a warm smile, nodded in his direction.

"Your reciprocation to this help is strictly voluntary. You can completely reject it, and we go our separate ways. You can accept it and say thank you, and we also go our separate ways. You can also accept it, keep lines of communication open, and if and when *you* see fit, *you* can decide to join the family. Before you ask me what I have to gain from this, I will tell you that I do not need to gain anything. Family helps family. Teacher helps student. The only thing that I *do* need is an answer from you before I walk away tonight. I am willing to help you, but if you choose to reject my offer, I want to give someone else the opportunity to get the help they could use."

As I paused, I tried to keep everyone in my gaze, Steve looked at Fran, Fran looked at Antonio, and Antonio looked at me. This would make for a fine Mexican stand-off except for the fact that we were one too many, and neither of us was Mexican. Fran cleared her throat slightly and broke the silence.

"I also would like to thank you for reaching out to us and giving us this opportunity. Chances like these do not come very often. Regardless of the saying it is too good to be true, Luis and I have talked over the phone multiple times already, and we have covered all the bases of this agreement. I hope you understand the hesitation since offers like this one do not come by in the world we live in. The decision has more or less been made, but before we get to that, my father would like to say a few things."

I arched an eyebrow, or maybe I winked, I am not sure which. I nodded for her to continue. This was either really good news or really bad news. Usually, mortals do not make such weighty decisions so quickly. I was expecting a barrage of questions and the silence threw

184

me off for a minute. Getting thrown off is not a fun experience. I remember that time in the rodeo in San Jose. I tried to ride this maverick called Rambo on a dare, and he threw me clear across…

I closed my eyes for a second and tried to disguise shaking my head back on track by stretching my neck muscles. I opened my eyes and nodded again. All eyes rested upon Antonio. The old man, weighed down by the passing of time, took a breath and straightened up more than he probably had done in decades. He looked directly at me with an air of pride and strength, licked his lips, and started speaking.

"When my Francesca came to me with this news, I was adamant that we have this dinner so I could meet you. You see, I passed this place and business to her a long time ago, but I insisted on this, and to her credit," he turned to her and went silent for a second as a tear formed in his left eye, "she did not deny this old man's wishes." Biting his lip lightly in an effort to keep his composure, he turned back to me and continued.

"Considering all I know and all I have heard you say, this offer sounds like a sort of miracle. *Un dono di Dio,* as we say back home. We have other things we say back home, as well. About a generous god that walked the earth, teaching people about pleasure and the love of wine. Un Dio che ama il vino." With that, he struggled to stand and placed his hands on the table. He leaned forward as if to get a better look at me. "So, who are you really, Mr. Dion? You come to us with this *dono di Dio,* but you don't look like Bacchus. *Chi sei veramente?"*

185

I leaned back in my chair and laughed heartily at that. It was not a nervous laugh or a condescending laugh. It was loud and deep and authentic, taking everyone by surprise. Even Luis looked at me in shock and blinked. By the time I was done, I had tears in my eyes. That was a good thing. It allowed for a few tears of sadness to escape, as well. I was starting to really like Antonio, and I was saddened that at his age, he would not be around much longer. I wiped my tears away and looked at him, a faint smile playing on my lips.

"Bravo, Antonio! Sei vicino alla verità. So very close. Bacchus è la faccia opposta della stessa moneta. Two faces, same coin. Say my name and finish it."

"Bacchus in the same coin? Ma questo è impossibile. Dion, as in Dionysos?" His arms and legs wavered. He sank back down into his chair and looked at me. "So, you are really *him*? The Greek God of Wine?"

"Il Greco e l'Italiano sono una razza, una faccia. One race, one face? I am sure you have heard that before. The same story, when told by different people, changes. Add to that the passing of time, the lines in the story get even more muddled."

"What do you want from us? To worship you?"

"Per favore, Antonio. You have worshiped me almost all your life through your love of wine and vine. I am still here because of people like you. What I want is to repay the kindness. Let me bless your vines. Let me help your family. They will not have to worry about profits and bills anymore. La tua famiglia prospererà."

The old man clapped his hands once and laughed, the sound warming my heart. I already knew the answer, even though I heard it a few seconds later. "How life changes from one moment to the next! Dionysos sitting across from me at my dining room table, eating osso buco. Un dio dell 'Olimpo! Yes! Of course, yes to your blessings and your help!"

"Hold on one minute," Fran interrupted, raising a hand. "God of Wine or not, miracle or not, this being a dream or not, I want to read the paperwork before I sign anything."

"There is no paperwork, so you have nothing to sign. The company is, and always will be, yours. Stay in contact with Luis, and he and his associates will explain everything to you. The blessing of the vines will also be yours. As long as you want it to be so."

Fran's mouth moved up and down, but no words came out. It was always nice to see that sometimes mortals copied me without even realizing it. Finally, she broke into a giggle and wiped away a tear that had rolled down her cheek. I could sense her mind trying to absorb everything. Even though it would have been easy for me to help her get there, I just pushed my chair back and stood. There were no malicious thoughts in this family. No anger about abandoned gods, and no thoughts of riches rooted in greed. I knew I had made the right choice.

With a nod of her head and a smile that looked almost as wild as one of mine, Fran said in a soft tone. "You do not only bless our vines, but you also bless us. I have no words to express how happy I am for this opportunity. Yes! We accept your gift and are grateful for it!"

Without any warning and without giving them time to do anything more than stand in return, Luis and I got up and took our leave from the table. We walked out into the night air, and I told Luis to wait for me in the car as I slowly made my way deeper into the vineyard. The spacing between the vines was following a more modern method. It was further apart than in the olden days, allowing space for access to machinery. I placed a hand on the first trunk and closed my eyes, concentrating and reaching out with my senses.

How do I explain something this personal to someone that has no experience with something like this? The blessing is a way of communing on a very base level. People tend to forget common knowledge, and they need to be reminded that plants are indeed living beings. When I reach out to a plant, and of course, a vine, I communicate with it. We do not speak in words but in feelings, thoughts, and mental images. The healthier the vine, the more exhilarating the experience. The more damaged, the more draining.

Antonio's vines were very loved and cared for, and they knew it. I got flickering images of kids laughing and playing, warm hands caressing the vine and holding the grape, music, humming, and an overall sense of wonder. There were a few flickers of unrest here and there, stemming from not getting the right angle of light or being colder than they should be on those dry winter nights. Nothing that could not be easily fixed with attention directed to the right place.

Just as I reached out and took, I also reached in and gave. In my own way, I let the vines know there would be a few changes, but they would be for the better. I showed them that from then forward. They were blessed and would be loved and cared for. I would help them rise, expand, and make the best grapes possible to give their gift to the masses. I sent out all my love, care, and protection to them. The Beatles had it right when they said love is all you need.

When I walked away from the vines, I felt like I was floating. There was nothing like getting in touch with something you love dearly and that loves you back, especially when the love is on that prime, natural, and base level. I made my way to the car, and we drove away. We were not even on the main road before I heard sniffling from the driver's seat. I looked over and saw Luis trying to drive through the tears streaming from his eyes.

"It truly is a wondrous thing that you are doing for them, master. No matter how many times I have witnessed you impart your gift, it never fails to amaze me."

"Oh, shut up, you old goat, and pay attention to the road!" I snapped at Luis in my God Voice and huffed at his display. "I still need you for the next week or so. Do try to get us to our resting place without climbing up a pole." I huffed again and turned to look out the window, wiping away a solitary tear of my own.

TORTURED LOVE

BY

D.M. WHITE

PROMETHEUS,
TITAN OF FORETHOUGHT

Y ou probably don't know me.

But you should.

I am Prometheus, the God of Forethought, and I created you. Not you specifically. I wouldn't rob your parents of that miracle. I mean humankind.

This is my story. It's not a pleasant tale filled with romance and passion. If that's what you're looking for, skip these pages. They're not for you. This love story goes out to the lonely and the sad.

It all started hundreds of thousands of years ago. A time before time, when life was simple, and I was young. It was a time when the earth was new and brimming with potential, just waiting to be uncovered.

Being the mightiest and wiliest Titan, the gods entrusted me to distribute gifts to all the living creatures. It was no small task, so I asked for help from my brother, Epimetheus. Together we set to work dishing out skills and abilities: speed to a cheetah, bounce to a kangaroo, and bite to a crocodile. But Epimetheus was wasteful with his generosity, and we soon ran out of gifts to share, which left me short-handed for the second, and more significant task the gods had entrusted to me.

You see, despite all the fancy gifts we had distributed, the animals on earth all carried the same major flaw. They couldn't worship the gods. And that just wouldn't do. What is the point of being high and mighty if those you rule over don't even know you exist?

So, I was tasked with creating a creature lower than the gods but with knowledge and wisdom far beyond that of the birds, the fish, and the beasts. Undeterred by the lack of implements available to me, I took some clay from the ground at my feet, moistened it with water, and set to work fashioning it into something the gods would be proud of.

I played around and formed creatures with two heads, or four arms, or even—on one of my more adventurous attempts—seven legs. Every time I finished, I looked at my creation in dismay and squashed it back into a ball. And then I had a thought. What if I made something in the form of the gods? Yes, that might just work…

A feeling of excitement rippled through my body as I worked the cold clay between my fingers. The proportions had to be perfect. No, the head was too big. Two legs, definitely only two. Ten fingers and ten toes. That's it. Almost there…

Voila!

Once I'd finished, I stood back and marveled at my creation. I was immensely proud. It was perfect. I'm not afraid to say that I had a tear in my eye when Athena breathed life into my masterpiece. But, alas, we had no gifts to give this new life-form. There this new being stood, naked and unprotected, the most helpless beast on earth. What had I brought it into? What a pitiless existence.

When hunted, it could not fly like a bird, run like a gazelle, or climb like a monkey. When it was cold, it froze. When it was warm, it burned. And when it went into the sea, it drowned.

I could only look on, helpless, as my creation died in droves, my heart a pit of sorrow. Imagine, dear reader, having to watch your children needlessly slaughtered in front of you every day. Would you not want to do something? Would you not want to help? Of course you would. You would do everything you possibly could to stop it.

If I could just give my creation something that would help it thrive and achieve its potential, something that could protect it. I looked up and saw Helios as he drove his chariot through the sky, and suddenly I knew what that something was. Fire!

I approached Zeus, whom I considered a brother after having stood side-by-side with him during the war against the Titans. The war which put most of my family in the pit of torment and suffering they call Tartarus. The war which put Zeus on the throne. Surely, he would help. Had I not shown myself to be a loyal and devoted servant? Did he not owe me this?

But Zeus had no compassion. I had decided to call my invention humans, but he didn't care about them. We argued, and the earth shook as our voices thundered, but he would not move. He had his own plans, and humans weren't a part of them.

I couldn't leave it, though. My children needed me. I heard their cries and felt their tears every day. I had to do something. Sometimes love drives you to do the unthinkable, and there is nothing stronger or more unbreakable than the love of a parent for their child.

I bided my time and waited. Then, one night, when the gods were feasting and drunk, I snuck into Mount Olympus. Loud snores told me that Helios was asleep, having completed his daily journey through the sky. I tiptoed my way into his stables to find his four milk-white steeds feeding greedily on hay. They were Eos, Aethon, Bronte, and Astrape, and they were stunning. They had bright manes and wreaths of sweet-smelling amaranths and asphodels from the heavenly gardens hanging from their necks.

Never before had I been so close to the legendary creatures, and every sinew in my body strained to stroke their muscular backs. But I knew they would only respond to their master. Any attempt to befriend them would cause carnage, and so I kept my distance. If anyone discovered me, my plan would come to naught.

Instead, I looked for Helios's flaming carriage, which was easy to find with its piercing heat and intense glow. I borrowed—some say I stole, but they are wrong—a flame from the sun cart by hiding it in a fennel stalk. I knew that I was acting in defiance of Zeus, but I thought he would approve once he saw what humans were capable of. How could he not?

I hastened back to earth with my gift. At first, my children were afraid, but then they saw the power my gift harnessed and rejoiced. Now they could light the caves in the dark of night. They could drive fear into the animals that hunted them. They could defy the cold on winter nights. But that was only the start. Soon, they learned how to cook, forge weapons, and craft. There was no end to what they could achieve.

I stayed on earth and watched my creation grow and develop. There has never been a prouder parent. But why stop there? I had only scratched the surface. My humans had shown themselves to be creatures capable of so much more. So, I showed them the stars and told them how to use them for navigation. I explained how the seasons changed and how to plant and grow crops. I showed them how to build houses and ships and explained the mysteries that lay hidden beneath the ground. Gold, silver, iron.

With this wisdom, humans built cities and navigated the seas. They were no longer pitiful, groveling beasts, but intelligent beings, perhaps even capable of challenging the gods.

My meddling didn't go unnoticed.

From his throne on Mount Olympus, Zeus looked down and saw black smoke curling towards the sky. When he looked closer, he saw that it came from red and golden flames. Around those flames, swarms of people gathered, laughing and dancing merrily. He scratched his thick beard and wondered what strange creature had developed so swiftly under his nose. And then he realized my treachery.

His wrath was swift and severe.

Speedily, he assembled a council of the gods to determine an appropriate punishment for my blasphemy. They decided what better way to chasten me than to make a creature so beautiful and enchanting that she would first steal my heart and then cause the downfall of humankind. They created a woman as beautiful as

Aphrodite, as wise as Athena, and as cunning as Hera. They called her Pandora.

Hermes, the Messenger God, presented her to me one day. It was unusual for the gods to visit me on earth, so his sudden appearance put me on edge.

"A gift from the gods," he told me as his winged sandals touched the ground.

I stared into the violet-blue eyes of my gift. I could almost taste her innocent lips, and I felt my heart flutter. "And why would the gods present me with a gift?" I asked, turning my attention to Hermes. He had a quick and deceitful tongue, and I didn't trust him.

"Why the suspicion?" he asked. "Are we not all friends? Why would the gods not wish to share a gift with you? She is beautiful, is she not? Her name is Pandora."

I looked at Pandora again, and she smiled at me. It was an invitation, but to what I didn't know. "I cannot accept your gift," I said, although the words didn't want to come out.

"You wish me to tell the gods you reject their gift?" Hermes asked, folding his arms, his eyebrows raised. "You realize that the gods will not take this slight lightly. I am but a messenger, but I fear you have taken leave of your senses. You have spent too long down here on earth with these...creatures of yours." He scrunched his nose up as though he smelled something vile.

"I am not *rejecting* their gift," I stressed, ignoring his insult. "I just cannot accept it straight away. Not without having something to give in return. The gods have been very generous, and whilst I would like nothing better than to take the beautiful Pandora off your hands, I would forever be in their debt. That would weigh heavily on my conscience. I'm sure the gods would not want to tarnish the gift so?"

Hermes had a quick tongue, but I, too, could think on my feet. Being the God of Forethought, I knew I needed to be cautious.

"Very well," Hermes muttered, looking away and breathing in deeply. "I will return to the gods and let them know your response."

I took one last look at Pandora, who looked hurt by my rejection, and then watched as she disappeared with Hermes.

The gift was too perfect, too exquisite, to be without motive, and I knew that I had merited the anger of Zeus. What treachery did he have planned? I knew that wouldn't be the end of it, so I told Epimetheus of what had happened and warned him to be wary of the gifts of the gods, for they might also target him.

Zeus's rage at my insolence shook the mountains. Not only had I stolen—borrowed—fire, I had rejected his gift. His next move was blunt and devastating. For defying his will and giving to humans what he had denied them, Zeus ordered that I be bound with chains of adamant so strong not even a Titan could break them. I would then be tied to a barren rock on Mount Caucasus, a savage and remote land where no creature dwelt. In the summer, there was no protection against the sun, which beat down in fierce waves. In the freezing winter, pitiless rain fell constantly.

I listened to my punishment without emotion. I knew I had wronged Zeus, but I also knew I had no other option. I did it for my children, and their love for me gave me the strength to face whatever hell was coming for me.

But Zeus hadn't finished. He'd saved the worst bit for last.

He decreed that an eagle would visit me each day and feast on my liver while I lie chained to the rock. It was cold, callous, and utterly excessive, but he wanted to make a statement at my expense. Still, I didn't care. So long as my children could thrive, that knowledge would protect me from my torment.

I did not fight or argue when they came to take me. There was no point. I went willingly with my head held high, proud of my actions. Zeus would eventually see that I was right to have acted how I did. My children would show him.

It was Hephaestus who bound me. "I take no pleasure in this," he told me. "Here, chained and bolted to this rock, you shall not see your children's faces or hear their voices. You will suffer the blaze of the sun and the chill of the wind. Year after year, you will keep this lonely watch in this joyless place, without sleep and help. You will be in endless pain, tormented by an eagle every day, with no-one to hear your screams. This is the punishment for your crime."

With one final blow of his hammer, Hephaestus fixed the last chain and gave me a sympathetic smile. Then he was gone.

The next face I saw was that of the eagle sent to torment me. It swooped down onto my rock and landed a few meters away. It looked at me with its evil, black eyes and rested. It wasn't in a rush. It knew that I couldn't go anywhere, that no matter how hard I strained and pulled, the chains that bound me would hold true.

Slowly it approached. It walked around me, inspecting what was on offer, I was a surprising treat. I shouted at it, trying to scare it off, but it made no difference. It didn't even flinch. Eventually, it climbed on top of me and sunk its cold talons into my skin, kneading my muscles like it was making bread.

I screamed out, begging it to leave me alone, but it was deaf to my pleas. When it finished playing, it stared at me for a while, as though savoring the moment. Then it sunk its beak into my stomach, tearing away at my skin until it opened me up. I was completely and utterly helpless as it tucked into its meal, devouring my liver.

As the monster ate me alive, I disappeared into another world. I thought about the look of adoration my children had given me when I taught them how to cook. I thought of how they had cheered the first time I helped them sail a ship across the mighty sea. I thought of how they celebrated as a community every time a child was born. Love will always overpower hate if you let it.

When the eagle finished, it looked up at me, its face and beak dripping with my blood. Then it flew off with a promise to return the same time the next day. I didn't care. The love of my children protected me. This was for them.

And so, it continued. Every day the same. Sometimes I received a visitor. My good friend, Oceanus, once visited me in his winged chariot to console me, but he caught me at a bad time. My hatred of Zeus was seething, and he swiftly left when I started cursing the Sky God. Others with ill will towards Zeus took pity on me and brought me food and water, but they were few and far between. Most of the gods didn't want to be seen siding with me, so they kept their distance.

Then one day, Hermes fluttered down. I was in no mood for talking to anyone, especially him.

"Good day," he said, his manner upbeat. "Is it good? I suppose they're all the same for you. Or do you have good and bad days?"

"What is it you want, Hermes?" I spat through gritted teeth and gently prised an eye open.

"No small talk? You know, I get a feeling you don't like me, Prometheus. Just a hunch."

"What do you want?" I asked again.

"I'm here to deliver an invitation to you."

"An invitation?" I asked, suspicious. I wanted no part in it.

"Yes! No need to be so apprehensive. I can see why you would be in your predicament, but this is good news. You should be happy."

"Depends on what the invitation is for," I muttered and then groaned as a wave of pain pulsated through my body.

"A wedding, my poor Prometheus. It is a wedding invitation. And not just any wedding. Your brother Epimetheus is getting married."

Hermes hopped from foot to foot as he delivered the news, and I wondered what the catch was. I was happy for Epimetheus, but I felt like Hermes was holding something back.

"So, you're going to release me for the wedding?" I asked.

Hermes laughed. It was high-pitched and hysterical, his winged sandals raising him into the air as he hooted. "Of course not, dear Prometheus. Ever the optimist. No, no, but he has invited you and so I will send your apologies. It's the least I can do."

"Why are you here, then?" I shouted, surprising myself that I had the energy.

"Are you not interested in who your brother is marrying?"

I hadn't even considered who Epimetheus might be marrying, and I didn't much care, but Hermes desperately wanted to tell me. "Who then? I'm sure you're going to tell me whether or not I ask."

Hermes chuckled to himself. "Can you remember the lovely Pandora?"

My mind flashed back to the day I saw her, and I envied my brother then. "Of course, I remember her," I said flatly.

"Well, it seems your brother was not so wary of her. Bet you wish you'd just accepted the gift now," Hermes hummed. "And the gods have created a wonderful wedding present for them. One which I'm sure even you will hear about, even from this dreadful rock. Perhaps even see it…" He let the sentence hang and looked at me out of the corner of his eye, desperate to say more.

I groaned, this time not in pain, but knowing that this was somehow part two of my punishment. I took a deep breath. "What's the present?" I asked.

"I wouldn't want to ruin the surprise. Who knows who you might tell?" Hermes made a point of looking around as though waiting for someone to show up. "Anyway, we are both busy, so I won't keep you any longer. I know you have burnt skin to peel and a liver to re-grow, so I'll leave you to it."

I pulled on my chains in anger and then grimaced as they cut into me. Hermes tutted and shook his head. He gave me one last look and then flew away.

I waited anxiously, Hermes' words ringing in my head. Sure enough, a few days later, I witnessed a great explosion of light in the sky, like a sinister warped version of the northern lights. I knew that the dastardly deed had been done, but I didn't yet know the outcome.

I could only wait, the feeling of dread swelling in my stomach.

The first I knew of anything was when a family walked past my rock. They were skeletal and dressed in rags, and as they walked, they argued amongst themselves. The sight of them made me bridle. What could have happened to them? My poor children.

"You there," I shouted.

They looked at me in disgust, surprised to find anyone else on the barren rock.

"Who are you?" the man who I took to be the father asked, aghast and staring at my chains.

"I am Prometheus," I said, expecting some recognition. I got none, and that cut me deeper than the eagle's beak ever could. "What has happened to you?" I asked and realized how absurd it must look for someone tied to a rock to be asking that question.

"We were at war," spat the man. "And we lost. They killed my family, and this is all that is left of us. Now we are searching for a new home, but we are hungry and thirsty."

My brain did cartwheels. Humankind knew nothing of war, or murder, or famine. How could it be so? "Who killed your family?" I asked, unable to process what the man was saying, praying it was a cheap trick of the gods.

"A tribe from a nearby village. Their chief said my son raped his daughter, so he killed him. But he couldn't have done it because my son was hunting with me." The man was too tired to be angry or upset, and the words fell out of his mouth plainly, as though he was describing the weather. The man turned to his group and said, "We need to keep going." There was a collective groan, but they kept moving, uninterested in my plight.

Later that day, Hermes visited me again.

"Did you see it?" he beamed.

"What did you do?" I snarled.

"Nothing," he replied, struggling to keep a straight face. "We did *warn* them not to open it," he giggled.

"Open what?"

"The wedding present. Lovely wedding, by the way."

"What was the wedding present?" I mumbled, already tired from the conversation.

"Just a jar. Nothing special. Although, we might have stored a few things in the jar…"

I closed my eyes. I didn't like where the conversation was going. "Like what?" I asked after a pause.

Hermes grinned. "You know…sickness and pain, strife and war, theft and violence, grief and sorrow, and all the other evils of the world. We did warn them not to open it, though," he added again, defensively. "We can't be accountable for Pandora's curiosity!"

I had warned Epimetheus! *Beware of the gifts of the gods*, I had said. But he had always been foolhardy. My advice had fallen on deaf ears. Had it not been for Epimetheus, I would have had gifts leftover to give to humankind, and I wouldn't have had to have taken the fire. Had it not been for Epimetheus, I wouldn't have been tied to a rock suffering eternal torture. And did he ever call for my favor? Of course, he didn't. Not even my own brother dared to approach Zeus to ask for my pardon.

"Of course," Hermes considered, pacing slowly up and down, "there's no taking it back now. The damage has been done. I suppose it'll all be too much for those humans of yours to cope with. Shame, really. Just as they were developing so well, and now I suspect they will forget you or hate you for abandoning them in their time of need. I'll let you muse on that…"

This, then, was the real punishment. My scream was so loud it shook the rock. I didn't see Hermes leave, and he didn't visit me again.

Knowing what the gods had made my children endure made my plight insufferable. Every second was agony, my pain mixed with anger and grief. I called on Zeus to come down to strike a bargain. I called on any god who would listen. They all ignored me. As Hermes predicted, my children forgot about me and about what I did for them. I could feel it in my soul. Their love for me died, and with it, my resolve. I had nothing.

Eventually, the mighty Heracles, demigod and son of Zeus, released me. It comforted me to know my tormentor's son had freed me. But that is a story for another day. What was I to do now? I was unable to return to the gods, for they hated me for my past deeds. I couldn't face the humans knowing what had happened to them and how they had been made to suffer without me, knowing how they must hate me. My heart was in pieces, so I hid in the shadows, a fragment of my former self. There I stayed for years, lost and alone.

But then, one day, I discovered two humans walking. They were laughing and in love. How could it be so? With all the pain and suffering that had been unleashed on the world, how had these two people managed to find happiness? I approached them, and they told me they were heading to a city called Athens, so I joined them. There I found thousands of humans living a full and joyous existence. They had skills and abilities far beyond the level I had left them with all those years ago.

I laughed and then cried tears of joy. My creation had thrived despite the gods. Rather than destroy humankind, the evils of the world had taught them how to be stronger, more resourceful, and resilient. My name might have been forgotten, but my lessons had not. I lived on in the heart and soul of every being. Everything I had endured had been worth it!

As I watch you now, continuing to grow and adapt in a world filled with woe, I know that I would face my punishment again in a heartbeat so that you could live on in defiance.

So, dear reader, this love story—if you want to call it that—is about you. If you are ever feeling downhearted or alone and unloved in this vast world, remember that I am here. Blame the gods for your faults, not yourself, and do not be ashamed. They are what makes you…you. My love for you is pure. It will not be diluted by time or usurped by a rival emotion. It is endless and unassuming. It is without question. It is present whether you care for me or not. And I do not ask that you love me back. But I would ask one thing…

Remember me.

STORGE

FAMILIAL

LOVE

NEW MOON RISING

BY

RASHMI P. MENON

ARTEMIS,

GODDESS OF THE HUNT

Thousands of years had passed since the tragic event. Yet, the pain of loss and betrayal was fresh in my mind. I inhaled deeply, wiping beads of sweat from my forehead. The nightmares never stopped, and neither did the guilt of his death at my hands.

"So much for sleep," I murmured and swung out of bed. I walked out of my chamber to the temple's central hall. A massive brass statue of my likeness stood on the altar, surrounded by a small fountain decorated with chimes. A soft glow from the candles illuminated the room, casting a halo on the statue. The fragrance of incense hung thick in the pillared hall.

"The same nightmare?" I startled at the voice and wheeled around to see Iphigenia standing with a glass of water in her hand. Iphigenia became the head priestess of my temple the day I made her an immortal. Long before that, she was my nymph, one of the very few who knew everything about me.

"Geni, did I wake you?" I asked, taking the water.

"Not really. You know I'm a light sleeper." She shrugged, watching me take large gulps.

"I'm sorry. I couldn't sleep and thought some fresh air would be good."

"I can join you," she offered. I nodded in response. We walked out together toward the woods behind the temple. A chilly breeze loosened a few strands of hair from my braid. I tucked it behind my ear, securing it in place. Iphigenia pulled her stole closer around her slim frame. She broke the silence, "Artemis, it's been a long time. Don't you think it's time to move on?"

I glared at her. "You want me to forget and simply move on?" I took quick breaths as my anger built. "How can I forgive Apollo after what he did? And for what? To ensure I remained a Virgin Goddess?" My fingers unwittingly curled into a fist.

"I am not asking you to forget his betrayal. I am asking you to forgive yourself for Orion's death. You bear his burden, and it weighs you down," Iphigenia said, stopping to study my face in the moonlight. "You deserve happiness, my goddess."

I could not argue with her, but I had no idea how I could ever move on. I was incapable of love. I had left my heart behind with Orion on the beach that fateful day. My destiny was set for an immortal life as the Goddess of Maidens and Wildlife.

Iphigenia scrutinized me and shook her head. "Nothing I say makes a difference, does it?"

I did not blame her for trying. She didn't know that I had completely shut down my heart. So much so that I could no longer feel the *twin sense* with Apollo and no longer felt my brother's pain. "I'm sorry, Geni. I know you care about me, but I'm fine. At some point, even the nightmares shall pass," I said more to myself than her.

"It will be dawn in a few hours. I should head back to the temple and prepare for the morning rituals," Iphigenia said. I watched her retreating figure and wondered what I would've done without her. She was one of the few nymphs who remained by my side when I left

Olympus that day. Ever since, she has proven to be more of a counsel and friend than a nymph or priestess.

I walked through the verdant woodland. The virescent beauty of the coppice soothed my soul. The ground swerved into a narrow gorge and ran for around ten miles before sloping back up. The scent of wet earth and freshly sprouted grass rose from the ground. The forest was the heart of my world and a part of my soul. I laid on my back and stared at the starlit sky. My eyes traced the line of Orion's constellation before it rested on the moon. The silver beams lit brightly against the starry background as it began to descend, giving way to the golden petals stretching into the light blue hues of dawn. The sun came into view over the horizon.

My thoughts returned to the latter half of that ill-fated day. I'd begged my father, Zeus, to bring Orion back after my arrow marked the end of his life. He had looked at me with apologetic eyes. Even the King of Gods had limits. Instead, to appease me, he turned Orion into a constellation of stars spread across the sky. "You can see each other every night," he had said. I wiped a stray tear from the corner of my eye.

The woodland around me came alive, ending my solitude. It was time for me to return to my sanctuary. Iphigenia had finished her morning prayers and rituals and greeted me as I entered.

"Hermès came by, left a message for you. It's on the counter," she said from behind the altar.

"It's too early for messages from Hermès," I said, dismissing it.

"I think it's from your father," Iphigenia replied, giving me a, *you shouldn't ignore a message from the King of Gods,* look. I rolled my eyes and retrieved the message from the marble counter. My father was throwing another party in honor of his wife, Hera, Queen of Gods, and everyone *must* attend.

"There's another party in Olympus," I said, sighing deeply. "Ugh. Do I have to go?"

"I figured you wouldn't want to go because of Apollo, but I'm sure Selene will be there, too," she said, giving me a shrug and walking back to the altar.

"For sure, I'm not looking forward to meeting Apollo, but what on Olympus has Selene got to do with this?" I asked. My thoughts invariably went to the Titaness and our recent meeting. A slight heat rose in my core as I thought of her silvery steel eyes and perfect heart-shaped face.

Iphigenia stepped in front of me. "You have been avoiding Apollo forever," she said, jabbing her finger into my chest. "And don't think I didn't see the way you looked at Selene during your mother's gathering last month."

"Fine, I'll go, but only to prove that I'm not uncomfortable in either of their presence," I said. "And you're coming with me. Why should I be the only one suffering?"

Iphigenia squealed, clapping her hands like a little girl. "Oh, trust me, my goddess. I will be doing everything except suffering at that party."

"Some priestess!" I murmured under my breath, leaving the hall.

"I heard that," she called out.

"I meant for you to hear it," I retorted.

The day of the party arrived sooner than I liked. I stood studying my reflection in the mirror, wearing an elegant midnight blue gown. The sheer mesh fabric layered over the silk base had tiny silver stars embroidered from the waist to the trails. I ran my hands over the stars, and my heart ached for him. My antler diadem finished the look, perched on a chic updo of my long wavy hair. I met Iphigenia at the entrance to the temple. She wore a classic one-shouldered number in pale-gray embroidered silk that accentuated her dusky olive skin. She paired the look with diamond jewelry that reflected off her hazel eyes. She was beautiful!

"Ready for the drama?" I asked. She chuckled and nodded, and I opened a portal to Olympus from the edge of the woods. We reached the galleria within Mt. Olympus. It was a sight to behold, decorated in the evening's theme of blue and silver. We stopped to greet family and friends on our way to the large main ballroom. The ceiling stretched a few hundred feet above my head. Dozens of crystal chandeliers spiraled down, sending lovely diffused golden light over the beings below.

My father and his queen sat upon their thrones on a dais, looking regal as always. I walked towards the royal couple and wished them my best. Iphigenia greeted the king and queen before moving on to talk to the other nymphs. I strode across the ballroom, avoiding the dancing couples, and headed for the bar. A familiar voice called out my name. My fingers dug into the palm of my hands, and I turned, knowing well whom to expect.

"Artemis, how are you?" he croaked in a weak tone. Apollo stood before me, shifting uncomfortably on his feet. My eyes found his, and I noticed the shadows that had formed under them. He seemed older, somehow, as though he had aged. My brows furrowed in confusion. He reached out, extending his arms, and I stepped back, raising my hands in defense.

"Please leave me alone, Apollo," I said and turned my back, heading to the bar. I climbed onto a stool and ordered a drink. Before I could take a sip, a sharp throbbing sprouted in my heart and traveled over my body. My hands inadvertently went to my chest. Coming here was a mistake. The memories I have been trying to bury for eons gushed out, spreading their venom all over me. Seeing Apollo only made it worse. My throat constricted as the room closed in on me. Picking up my glass, I headed to the balcony. The chilly mountain air greeted me, raising goosebumps on my skin. I rested my elbows on the railing and leaned over, breathing deeply. I ignored the shuffling of feet behind me and hoped it was not Apollo. I was in no mood to talk, not now, not ever.

"It's a beautiful night," Selene said, leaning over the railing. A few strands of her platinum hair curled and fell over her cheeks, accentuating her cheekbones. The silver dress she wore sparkled, matching the twinkle in her eyes.

214

I recovered from gawking in time to respond. "Hmm. I guess."

"You're not enjoying yourself?" she asked.

"Not really. I prefer the quiet of the wild to large gatherings."

"I know! I've seen you in your woods," she said.

"You have?" I asked, my brows raised.

"You seem surprised. I saw you last week, too," she replied. Her lips curled in a smile.

"I didn't know you were watching," I said. My face felt warm as I remembered staring at the moon from the valley.

She chuckled but said nothing. We stood in silence, staring at the city lights for a few minutes. "After all that food, I could use a walk. Would you like to join me?" she asked, and I almost choked on my drink.

I wanted to get out of that party, but I wasn't sure if I should leave with her. My hands traced along the stars on my dress as the constellation in the night sky seized me. Yet, the set of sparkling eyes that stared at me in invitation tugged me in her direction. One part of me was holding on to Orion, while the other part yearned to know what it'd be like to be free of pain. Somehow, the light emanating from her calmed the tightening in my chest. Before I could overthink and complicate it, I replied with a nod. My dreary evening seemed better already. I wrote a note for Iphigenia telling her she didn't have to wait for me and bid goodbye to my father and his guests. I felt a slight pang when I saw Apollo alone, leaning against the bar nursing a drink, but quickly pushed the thought away.

We teleported to the woods and walked to the spot where I had laid staring at the sky last time. We sat at the edge of the valley, admiring the stream beneath us. "I can never get enough of this view," I said.

"It's beautiful!" Selene exclaimed, looking at me. I flushed as warmth rose in my core, quickly followed by a pang of guilt. I rested my elbows on the ground and stretched back, staring at the night sky.

"You miss him," she said, following my gaze.

I bit the inside of my cheeks at the mention of Orion. "Sometimes. It's been so long. I barely remember what it was like with him."

She placed her hand over mine and squeezed it. "I understand. Truly."

"I'm sorry about Endymion," I said, knowing she was referring to her ex-husband.

Her mouth curled into a sad smile, and she looked down. A few moments passed in silence before she raised her face. "He's in another realm, and I've made my peace with it."

"How do you do it? Make your peace, that is."

"You take one step at a time towards healing and learn to move on. Holding on to the past will only drown you in misery," Selene said with a knowing glance.

I dropped my eyes from hers and ran a hand through my hair, pulling it free from the bun. It fluttered in the breeze as I gathered it into a side braid. Selene's eyes remained on me throughout, waiting for me to talk.

"Orion was important to me, but so was Apollo. It was the betrayal that I cannot seem to forgive," I said.

Selene nodded with genuine concern in her eyes. "I understand. You lost two of the most important people at the same time. And to the action of one of them. That's not easy to forget." she said. I looked up at her with a small smile. She didn't wait for me to speak. "You may not be ready to forgive Apollo for his betrayal, but it is high time you forgive yourself, Artemis."

"Forgive myself," I scoffed.

"Yes, from the guilt of your role in Orion's death."

I stared at Selene for a while before laughing. "You sound like those mortal therapists."

Selene joined in the laughter. "Well...I am a healer."

Silvery beams of light streamed through the dark velvety sky, bouncing off the stream below. My rage and confusion had darkened my mind over the years, and I had forgotten to laugh. Looking at her for the first time in years, I felt a beacon of hope that could cast away the shadows from my heart.

We spent the night in the valley talking. The next morning Selene accompanied me to the temple, and I introduced her to Iphigenia. The two of them hit it off like they were long-lost friends. Unexpectedly, I felt a pang of jealousy and wondered about my growing feelings for Selene. She kept glancing sideways at me, and when our eyes met, there was need in them. Selene turned to face me. "Artemis, I wonder if you can tell me where I can find accommodations for the next few weeks. I have some business in town and will need a place to stay."

"You're welcome to stay here. If the temple's chambers suit your needs," I said.

"I wouldn't want to impose," Selene replied.

"You're no imposition at all. It'd be our pleasure," I said, feeling a little flutter in my stomach.

Over the next few weeks, Selene and I spent time hiking the trails of the woods, hunting in the valley, and swimming in the rivers of Olympus. We took long walks after dinner and talked about our pasts. But I never mentioned my nightmares. Some nights I found her rushing to hold me after I woke up screaming. During the day, Selene disappeared to the city for a few hours. I never asked her where she went or what business brought her here. I figured she'd tell me if I needed to know. The more time we spent, the closer we became. I wondered if she noticed my longing glances and lingering touches.

One night we were strolling through the woods and reached the waterfall across the valley. Selene giggled as the moisture-laden breeze grazed her face. "Artemis, this view... it's beautiful!" she exclaimed. Her voice softened as her gaze locked with mine, "Just like you." I flushed and looked away into the starlit sky, confused but happy. The guilt that I expected didn't make an appearance this time.

Breathing deeply, I spoke, "The day I lost Orion and Apollo. It was a stupid game. At least I thought it was a game. Apollo had challenged me to a round of archery." Selene took my hand in hers and squeezed them lightly, urging me to go on. "I trusted him, Selene. Never once did I doubt Apollo had other intentions. He pointed to a large boulder far out on the beach and dared me to hit the target in the center. And I just aimed and released the arrow. I proudly watched as it whizzed past the trees and pierced the center of the stone."

I covered my face with my hands as guilt and shame overtook my senses. Selene draped an arm over my shoulder. "It was when I heard the soul-piercing scream that I realized I had hit a living being. My victim cried out again, and I knew…I recognized the voice. I wished it wasn't him. I heard Apollo begging me not to look, but I ignored him and ran. I will never forget the gut-wrenching cry and the look on Orion's face as the life drained out of him…by…by my hands," I cried.

My body rocked as I sobbed in Selene's arms, shedding tears I had held back for centuries. She didn't try to stop me. She simply held me and let me get it all out. "I demanded Apollo explain himself, but he just stood there looking guilty in his betrayal. He said he was sorry and that he had to do it to protect me. From what? He had no answer. Just a deadpan look in his eyes." I continued sobbing, tears gushing down my cheeks. "And just like that, I lost my partner and my brother." I wiped my tears and turned to face Selene. "It's Orion's scream and Apollo's eyes that wake me every night," I said, feeling naked and exposed as I bared my soul to her.

Selene understood how difficult it was for me to open up. She draped her arms around me, pulling me into a tight hug. "I understand your pain, Huntress. I think you're very brave for talking about it." She rubbed my back as I rested my head on her shoulder. We sat in silence, holding each other, the moon bright and full in the night sky.

I stared at Selene. "It's a full moon tonight," I whispered.

Selene shook her head and took my face in her hands. I slowly turned, meeting her gaze. "It's hunter's moon tonight," she said, her voice husky. The shine of desire in her eyes reflected in mine, electrifying the air around us. A coy smile played on Selene's lips, and she shifted closer to me, resting a hand at my waist. She tucked a stray strand of hair behind my ear and leaned in to kiss me lightly on the nose. Goosebumps raised on my skin as a shiver ran through my body. Instinctively, I reached for her. My hands settled on her hips, pulling her in closer, surprising us both. She smiled and pressed into me, brushing her lips against mine, teasing me with a small nip at my lower lip. The slight sting had me locking my mouth over hers in a fiery, demanding passion that yearned for more than a kiss. Selene's eyes twinkled as she looked at me with a longing that matched mine.

I exhaled with a soft growl as desire blazed through my soul, a passion I had kept bottled for centuries. We explored all night long, working in excruciating slow designs to learn each other's bodies, pleasures, and needs. Sometime late into the night, I fell into a satisfied, comfortable sleep in her arms. For the first time in eons, I slept through the night.

We returned to the temple in the morning, holding hands. Iphigenia eyed us with raised eyebrows, a huge grin, and a nod of approval.

"I'm going to shower and change," Selene said, planting a kiss on my cheek.

"Maybe I should move your stuff to Artemis's chamber?" Iphigenia called out.

"Geni!" I scowled.

"That's a good idea," Selene retorted as she walked across the hall toward her chamber, leaving my mouth hanging open.

Iphigenia laughed, seeing the expression on my face. "Hermès left a few messages for you and Selene." She pointed to the counter where he usually left them.

I picked up the cards Hermès left and sorted mine from Selene's when one addressed to her caught my attention. I recognized the hand, and against my better judgment, I turned it over to read the sender's name.

From, Apollo

My heart thumped against my chest as I considered possibilities for a message from Apollo to Selene. I wanted to believe it was nothing, but my mind conjured the worst possible scenarios. My breath came out in short, heavy gusts as I tried to bite down the rising fury.

"Any messages for me?" Selene's voice came from behind me. I turned, holding the note from Apollo, and extended it to her without saying a word. Her brows creased, perplexed by my coldness. She took the envelope, and her face drained of color as she saw the name on the card. Her head flipped in my direction, but I was already walking away from her.

"Artemis!" she called, but I wasn't listening. "Artemis, please, I can explain," she ran behind me, taking my hand.

I pulled free from her grasp, seething, the fury visible in the red rim of my eyes. "Was any of it real? Or were you simply working for him?" I spat.

Selene gasped at the venom in my words. "How could you even ask me that?" she asked, her voice breaking. I shook my head and turned to leave. "Yea, of course, you leave. That's what you do best, isn't it? Run away?" she said as I retreated from her.

I stopped, her words cutting deep. Maybe I was afraid of being hurt again. Maybe I thought she'd betray me like Apollo and running away was the better option. I didn't know when I had started taking the easy way out but disappearing seemed a lot safer than standing there listening to her. Perhaps it was time for me to face my fears. I turned back to her and crossed my arms over my chest. "I'm listening," I said.

Selene took a deep breath. She was struggling to form the right words. "Artemis, it's true I approached you for Apollo," she started, and I turned my face away to hide the pain. "But everything else between us is real," she pleaded. When I said nothing, she continued. "I'm working with Apollo as his healer."

My attention snapped back to her, our gazes locking. "Why does Apollo need a healer? He has healing abilities himself," I demanded.

"He believed that you'd forgive him someday, but when you closed yourself to him and the twin sense, he shut down his heart. The *twin sense* started working against him. You are the second half, but weren't there to control it, and he started aging. When he couldn't control the deterioration, he came to me for help. He wanted to stay alive until he had a chance to explain everything to you," she said, looking at me with sad eyes.

"How…how bad is it?" I asked. I almost didn't want to know the answer.

"It's not good," she replied. "But I am hopeful we can bring him back with your help." Selene moved closer to me and took my hand in hers. I flinched at the touch, but I let her hold me. "I approached you for your help with Apollo, but I wasn't expecting to fall for you. Yet I did, and that part is true. I did fall for you, Artemis, and it's as real as night and day," she said, looking into my eyes. Her expression imploring, searching for something from me in return.

"I don't want him to suffer," I whispered, tears running down my cheeks. I didn't address the part of the conversation that she insisted was real. I wasn't ready for that. Not yet, at least.

"I know you don't. I know you still love him," Selene said. If she noticed I hadn't responded about our relationship status, she didn't show any reaction to it. She simply answered my question and let me decide.

223

I took a few deep breaths. "What do you need from me to help Apollo?" I asked.

"I will need you to use your *twin sense* with him," she said. "He's still at his place in Olympus. If you're ready, we can leave now."

I pulled my hands free from Selene and took a few steps back. I wanted to help Apollo. His image from when I saw him at the Olympus party came into my mind. He did look frail, and it had shocked me, yet I hadn't dwelled on it. Now, standing here, getting ready to face him, I felt the intensity of his anguish. I turned to Selene and nodded.

We teleported to Apollo's mansion in Olympus. The once bright and shiny house of the God of Sun now had an eerie, deserted appearance. Nature embraced it from all sides, the unkempt gardens overgrown with creepers and weeds. Grime and dirt covered the glass windows. I looked at Selene, my eyes wide, surprised by the state of his residence. Apollo was nothing if not swank and fashionable in his luxuries. It was part of his charm. He knew how to impress without looking like he was even trying. This was not him.

Selene sighed and walked through the main door into the foyer. It had been a while since I was here. We reached the master bedroom, and Selene knocked on the mighty oak door.

"Come in," Apollo answered. His voice was croaky with fatigue. Selene pushed the handle and walked in. I stayed behind, gathering my nerves before following her into the bedroom. Apollo stood by an open window. The drapes billowed as the cool breeze swayed into the room. He had lost more weight since I saw him at the party. He looked older and weak.

Selene cleared her throat. "I got your message," she said.

"Thank you for coming so soon, Selene. I want to ask another favor of you. You're already doing a lot for me, but I request you to do this one last thing," he said without turning to look at her. "I want you to let Arty...uh...Artemis know that I never stopped loving her. Tell her she'll always be my twin and my best friend."

"Why don't you tell her yourself?" Selene asked while I silently watched Apollo.

He took a few deep breaths to steady himself. I felt the familiar tug of my heartstrings, the ones that connected me to him—our *twin sense*. Apollo must've felt it, too. He whirled around and stared at me with his mouth open.

"Arty..." he croaked, stumbling a few steps forward. I rushed to hold him and wrapped my arms around his shoulder, steadying him. He stroked my cheek with his thumb as if to ensure this wasn't a dream. "You're really here."

"Yes," I answered weakly. At that moment, all I cared about was his healing. Selene helped me lay him on the massive bed in the center of the room. The nightstand had various bottles of ambrosia, left untouched.

"Why haven't you taken the ambrosia, Polo?" I asked, addressing him by the name only I used.

He flipped his head to me, eyes wide, with a ghost of a smile. He hadn't heard me address him as Polo since that day at the beach. "I couldn't find the will to carry on without you, Arty. I tried for all these years, but when you shut the twin sense off, I couldn't take any more."

I took a bottle of ambrosia and urged him to drink from it. The immortal drink would help restore his energy while Selene worked on him. "Well, I'm here now. I can't lose you again, Polo," I pleaded with him. He opened his mouth to take the drink from me. He looked at Selene and nodded as she sat by him on the opposite side of the bed.

Selene took his hand in hers. She tipped her head once in my direction, asking to use the *twin sense*. Looking at Apollo, I opened to him completely. An invisible thread of connection formed between us, and I was hit by the full blast of his pain while my energy flowed into him. I shuddered, rocking back and forth to steady myself. I looked at Selene and gasped. She was glowing. Silvery beams of light poured from her body. The energy found its way into Apollo, reflecting off me, and I could feel him getting stronger. The brighter Selene shone, the stronger he got. A few minutes passed, and Apollo fell into a deep healing sleep. Selene's light dimmed, and I saw the fatigue in her. I ran to her side and wrapped her in my arms when she slumped from the exercise.

"Don't worry. I get a little tired whenever I use my powers on an immortal. With their strength and the conflicting powers, it requires a lot of energy. I'll be fine in a few hours," she said, smiling at me.

"I don't want anything happening to you," I said, stroking her face. Our eyes met, and my heart thumped, beating against my chest.

"He'll be awake in an hour or so," she said, getting off the bed intending to leave. I reached out to stop her. I didn't want her to leave, not without finishing our conversation. Yet, I couldn't leave Apollo. Selene must've seen my anguish. "We can talk after. I'll wait outside," she said, giving me a quick hug before walking out of the room.

It was almost evening when Apollo woke. He took my hand in his and sat up, looking stronger despite the shade under his eyes. "Arty, I want to apologize about that day," he started, and I flinched. My heart ached with grief and guilt.

I looked up at his face and saw genuine concern in his eyes. He took a long breath and got up from the bed, leaning against the poster, his head bowed. "I did it to protect you, to save you."

"From what?" I asked, confused.

"From Mother Gaia," he answered without looking up.

"Mother Gaia? She'd never hurt me!" I said, defiantly.

"No, she didn't want to hurt you in particular. But Orion. He'd been boasting about being the greatest hunter of all times, and with you by his side, he'd hunt down any creature, including Gaia herself," he said, pausing to watch me.

I looked at him, my eyes wide, unable to comprehend what I had just heard. "Orion challenged Mother Gaia?" I asked. Saying it out loud made it even worse. There was not one immortal alive today, including my father, the King of Gods, who'd challenge Gaia. And Orion, a mortal hunter, had done that? My pulse ran faster as Apollo's words registered.

Apollo noticed my surprise. "He never told you any of this?" he asked, and I shook my head.

I tried to process the new information. I had no idea this had happened. "How did you find out about this?" I asked. "And it still doesn't explain why you made me shoot Orion."

Apollo shifted his weight from one foot to the other. "Dad heard about Gaia's plans. He went to her, asking to spare your life. He couldn't lose you," he answered.

"Dad knew? All this time, he knew, and he never said anything to me?" I asked, getting off the bed and pacing the room in frustration.

"He couldn't say anything. It was part of the deal. Dad promised Gaia he'd have you take out Orion, thereby eliminating him and sparing your life with the smaller punishment. Gaia wouldn't have it any other way. Dad knew you'd never agree, so he told me. He said there was no other way to save you from Gaia's wrath. And all I could think about at that moment was to save your life," Apollo said. He drew in a sharp breath and looked at me with pleading eyes.

I walked back to the bed and sat on the edge. I knew there was no escape from Gaia's wrath. I understood his need to save me. Perhaps, if the roles were reserved, I would've done the same for him. Yet, here I was, trying to come to terms with Orion's loss and Apollo's betrayal, even if said betrayal was to save me. Apollo knelt beside me and stroked the back of my hand with his. "Forgive me, Arty. I never wanted to hurt you. I'm sorry. Truly," he said.

I stroked his hair and closed my eyes. Tears ran down my cheeks, and he wiped it gently with his thumb. I nodded slowly. "I forgive you, Polo." He pulled me into a tight embrace. It wouldn't be easy to let go of the pain I had held onto for centuries. But despite everything, I still loved Apollo. We promised to work on our relationship over time before I left.

I found Selene pacing in the lobby. I had to set things right by her. If it weren't for her, I would've never realized how much I was punishing myself by trying to punish Apollo.

"Now that your twin sense is working, I think it's time for me to leave," she said before I could say anything.

"So, you just leave, and that's the end of it?" I asked, walking up to her. I took her hand in mine and tipped her chin to meet her eyes. "You said it was real. What we had."

"Everything between us is real, Artemis. I have feelings for you. But I wasn't sure if you'd want me after all this," Selene said, her eyes downcast.

"You have given me the best gift by bringing Apollo back into my life. I agree your methods were unconventional, but your intentions were honorable and that I can respect," I said. Her eyes glistened with unshed tears, and I saw the selflessness behind it. I had lost out on love once, but I was determined not to lose it again. This time, I was going to do whatever it took. "Can we start over?" I asked.

Selene smiled, wiping a tear from the corner of her eye as she fell into my arms. "I'd like that."

LOVE & LOSS: A MOTHER'S GRIEF

BY

ASHLYN GREY

DEMETER,

GODDESS OF THE HARVEST

Smoke filled Demeter's nostrils as she stared blankly at the burning apple tree. She swayed slightly, greasy strands of her auburn hair glued to her face. The flames consumed the tree and spread rapidly to the dried grass around it. The wood began popping and cracking, pieces of ash hitting her face. While most people would have run, Demeter stood emotionless and gazed at the fire. After several minutes, she picked up her sickle whilst balancing the lit torch in her other hand.

Yes, she had started the fire, and she didn't care. She was the Goddess of Harvest and Grain. She was the one that gave fertility to the earth. And today, she felt nothing. A few moments earlier, she'd had the fleeting thought that if she started another fire, it would make her feel something…anything. It didn't.

"This is bullshit," Demeter muttered as she turned and walked away into the darkness. "Time to make more noise."

It had been eight days since her daughter went missing. Demeter wasn't sure if she was dead or alive. She knew nothing. No one knew anything. One moment her beautiful daughter was picking flowers in their favorite meadow, and in the next, she was gone. The only clues Demeter could find were a few wilted daisies strewn on the grass.

How could no one *know what happened to her?* Demeter clenched her jaw, thinking over the recent events.

Demeter's love for Persephone was more than unconditional. Her daughter was more than her heart and soul. She was her life force. Everywhere she went, she brought fair-haired Persephone with her.

The child was the light and warmth of her life. Demeter had shown her how to tend to the land. And oh, how the earth loved Persephone! Flowers sprung up in her wake, and woodland creatures followed her. Once, a herd of deer brought a bouquet of daffodils to her feet. Persephone was so flattered and delighted that thousands of pink flowers bloomed in the meadow. Pink was her favorite color.

I should have known then that she was gaining too much attention, Demeter thought. *What type of mother am I for not realizing?*

Demeter felt an immense amount of guilt, and tears welled in her eyes. She stopped walking and slumped forward in defeat. Demeter dropped her hands to her sides, closed her eyes, and wept.

I wish I could be released from this pain, she thought as her temples pounded.

As if Zeus heard her wish, she felt a warmth to her right. In a rash moment of excitement, Demeter thought it was the warmth of her daughter. But when she flicked her eyes open, the sight of flames greeted her instead. She had started another fire.

"Persephone!" Demeter screamed her daughter's name, every syllable coated in her grief. She gripped the torch and turned, blowing the flames in a wide circle to encompass her.

Maybe this is how it should be.

Demeter stood encircled by the fire with her head raised high. Smoke filled her nostrils, and through the flames, she could see a faint color of pink rising above the horizon.

Is this a sign? Could she be alive?

Demeter panicked as the blaze grew closer. She cursed her rashness.

*I can't give up. I **will** find her. I **have** to. Otherwise, no one will.*

"I will find you, Daughter!" Demeter cried out to the sky and walked through the blazing flames. She batted out the cinders that had formed on her cloak. With her free hand, she shielded her eyes from the sun as it peered over the horizon. And as if in penance for failing her daughter, Demeter knew she had to continue walking.

Today marks day nine.

She wasn't sure where she was anymore, but she needed to continue looking for Persephone, so she marched forward. She searched frantically, as she had for days, and kept her ears perked for any sign from her daughter. She gripped the torch and tipped it slightly to her right, setting another bone-dry field ablaze.

How much longer can I keep this up?

She peered around her. Everything was dry. No creatures were stirring, not even a single chirp from a cricket. She could feel the crunch underneath her boots of dead plants as she made her pathway alone. Her tongue stuck to the top of her mouth, and she realized the extreme drought of her surroundings.

I am parched. I need water.

Her grip tightened on the torch, and Demeter felt the splinters pierce her hand, blood trickling into her sleeve. The goddess plunged the torch into the soil as more hot tears bathed her face, and she began to feel light-headed. Demeter's pale cheekbones were sunken in, and her lush auburn hair was now completely gray. She suddenly grabbed her chest, struck with such a sharp pain that she fell to her knees.

How can I be concerned about water when my daughter has been missing for nine days? I failed her as her mother and as her only protector. Oh, such heartache.

Stricken with guilt, she cursed again. Her muscles tightened and cramped as she glared at the sun. Her heart ached, her feet hurt, and now her hand was bleeding.

How much longer can I keep this up?

She pushed the hair from her face, leaving streaks of blood over her cheeks, and forced herself back to her feet. She wavered but stayed upright, clenching her jaw until her teeth ached and continued on her lonely trek. It was almost mid-day when she saw a small town through the mix of her tears and sweat.

Demeter reached the village and immediately went in search of something to drink. She found a pail of water outside the inn and glanced into its depths before taking a sip. She saw the reflection of a weathered, haggard woman looking back at her. She raised a hand to touch a lock of her silver hair as her green eyes turned a dark brown and welled with tears. In her grief, she had lost herself.

"Where is she?" Demeter cried out in anguish and covered her eyes. The goddess fell hard upon her knees again, wincing in pain.

"Ms. Demeter," a soft voice whispered behind her.

She sat back on her heels and dropped her hands to her lap. She tilted her head towards the voice. Demeter's eyes were glazed over, willing to accept whatever the fates tipped toward her. "Yes?" she softly answered back.

"I have been watching you for days," the voice said, as a radiant light stung her eyes. "I have seen your torment. And I have been a coward with keeping knowledge you should have."

Demeter wiped away the seemingly endless tears to gaze upon the brightness of Helios, the Titan God of Sun. Her brow furrowed.

"I must confess. I saw what happened when your daughter was taken." Helios sighed heavily.

As if a ton of bricks finally fell off her chest, Demeter held her breath in anticipation.

"For many years, I have watched and observed your daughter grow into a beautiful young lady. She has gained attention from many admirers," he let out a long sigh before continuing, "even myself. I was drawn to her youthful spirit. So, for my love of the earth, I will confess, Ms. Demeter. I will tell you who it was that abducted her if you stop torching the land."

He is trying to stop me? *Does he not understand the anguish and torment tearing me apart?*

Demeter stumbled to her feet and reached for her torch. "Why, after all of this time, would you confess to me now?" Her eyes turned a dark hazel.

"You have changed, Goddess of Harvest. Don't you see what you have become?"

She pulled the torch closer to her face. "I don't care. Tell me. Now!" she commanded him.

Helios gasped, taken aback by not only her demeanor but the weathered physical appearance of the goddess. "Please, I mean you no harm. It was....it was Hades...I saw the ground open and saw..." he said, his voice trailing off. Demeter stood silently, staring with such hatred and pain. At that moment, she knew what she needed to do. Helios heard a faint *pop* as the goddess vanished.

Demeter teleported back to the meadow where her daughter went missing. She took in a few breaths as she gazed upon the wilted flowers that were the only signs that leant truth to Helios's story.

I will save you, my daughter. No matter the cost.

Demeter screamed out in agony as she drew her Sickle of Harvest from her side and swung it hard into the wilted flowers.

"Not my daughter, you bitch!"

She straightened her posture and watched as her sickle glowed. It consumed the rest of the flowers' life essence. She clenched her jaw and stood witness as the meadow's grass slowly turned to dust. The tall stalks of grain toppled over, and within minutes, the field turned to ash around her.

"Give me back my daughter!" She picked up her sickle as another section of the field turned gray in front of her. The perverse turn of the cycle Demeter had sworn to uphold filled the hole where the love for her daughter had been with hatred and bitterness.

Even knowing where her daughter was, she had no way of getting down there. Demeter was angry, and the world could starve as far as she was concerned. And thus, her stages of grief had finally moved on to wrath, but the all-encompassing loss remained.

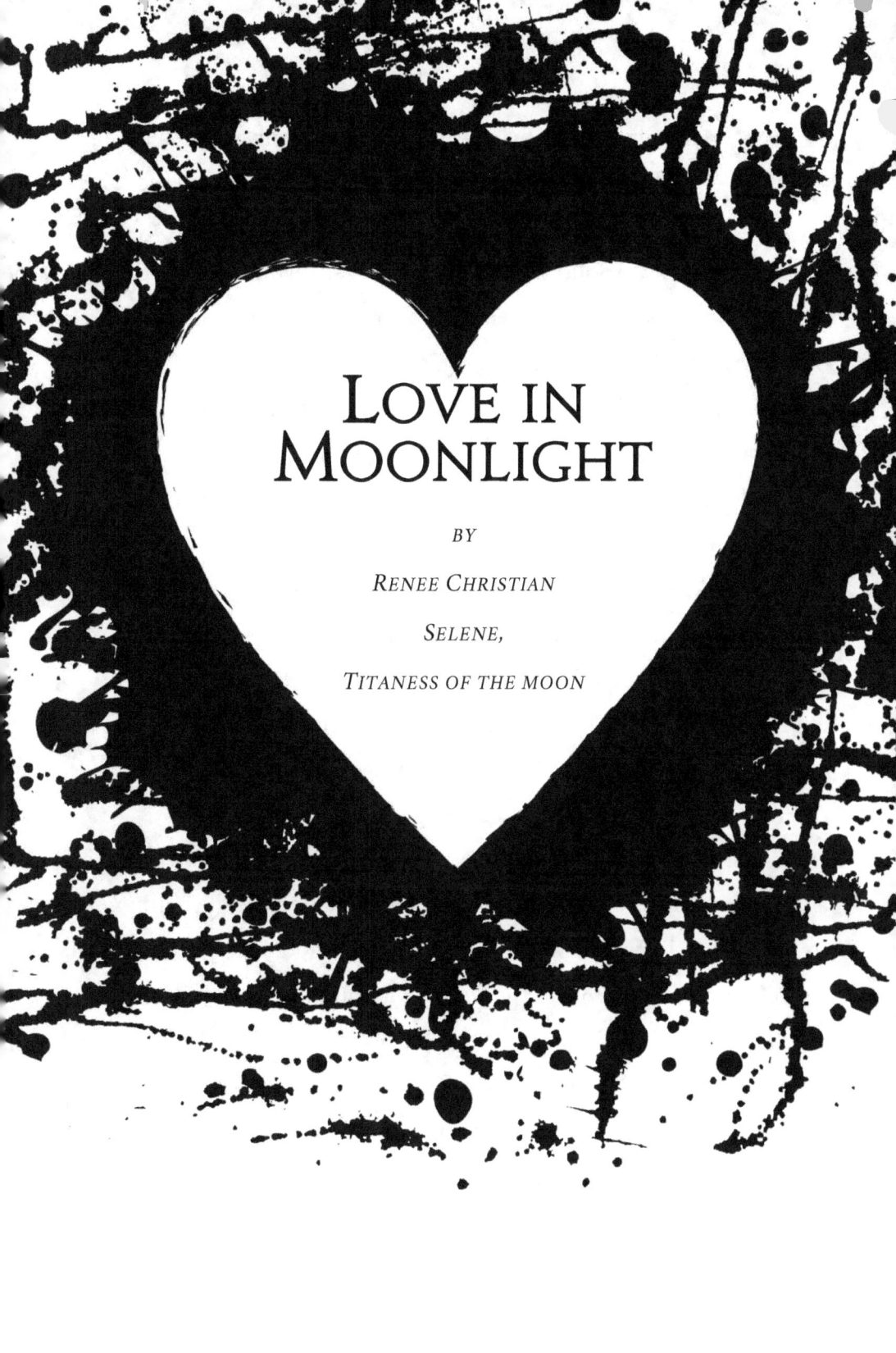

LOVE IN MOONLIGHT

BY

RENEE CHRISTIAN

SELENE,

TITANESS OF THE MOON

The mighty dragon soared through the air, wings beating as she caught the wind currents with practiced ease. The trees blurred beneath us as we raced to the clearing where the finish line lay. Apollo was waiting there, cheering us on as the referee. My steeds were wet with sweat, and the moonlight reflected off their sheen. Panting and huffing, they raced against Sayeh, Artemis's dragon. Snapping the reins, I called out to them encouragingly, "Almost there, boys! We can do this!"

Sayeh slid to a halt at our destination, stopping short to avoid crashing into the tree line. The suddenness of it threw Artemis from Sayeh's back, and she rolled across the ground, landing in a crumpled heap on the forest floor. My steeds, smaller and more nimble, maneuvered between the trees, coming to an easier, more experienced landing. I jumped from the still moving chariot and rushed to Artemis's side. "Arty! Arty! Are you okay!?"

Her body was shaking as she sat up, her back towards me. "Artemis! Oh, my gods, that looked like a bad fall." My heart thumped against my chest as I ran toward her. She turned to me, dirt clinging to her sweat-slicked skin, creating rivulets of mud. Her eyes twinkled, reflecting the moon within them. She was laughing, not crying, laughing!

"I...beat...you," she panted between breaths. "Sayeh kicked your ass." Her laughter grew louder as she rolled over and collapsed on her back. Golden ichor ran down her leg, where the ground had scraped her. "We beat your Titan ass." She chuckled, still gasping for breath.

I exhaled a sigh of relief and kicked her thigh teasingly, the impact playful and gentle. "You scared me, Arty! What the hell!?"

Apollo, instinctively knowing his twin was okay, tended my horses and brought them back into the clearing. He jogged over to us with a huge smile on his face. "That's my sis! You beat her fair and square!" He roared in laughter at his sister's victory. Clasping arms with Artemis, he helped her to her feet. Pulling her into a hug, he lifted her off the ground and spun around. I shook my head, watching their joy.

Apollo set her down, and Artemis limped slightly towards Sayeh to check on her. "You did it, girl! You beat Sel and her steeds." She stroked the beast's neck, hugging her tight.

I wandered back to my horses with a smile. "What a race, boys. You did so well! I couldn't be prouder." I patted their sweaty necks as they panted and frothed. They shook their heads in pleasure, enjoying the thrill of the race. One stomped a foot at me, and Artemis chuckled.

She walked to my steed and patted his nose, whispering something into his ear, before turning to face me. "He's not happy we won but enjoyed the race all the same." Artemis was telepathically communicating with the animals, and I appreciated her interpretation of their thoughts and emotions. I appreciated many things about Artemis, and perhaps that was one of the reasons our relationship was so special. Many assumed since she was a *replacement* goddess in the pantheon, I would have ill thoughts towards her, but they were wrong. Very wrong. Now, I would admit, when she and Apollo began

241

taking the praise and admiration of my believers, it had stung a bit. I felt replaced and useless, perhaps even jealous. It felt like a younger, prettier version of me was on the scene. But as she grew and matured, so did her character. I realized how amazing she was when we started spending more time together. It was then that my feelings towards her shifted. I have Apollo. to thank for being the catalyst that brought her into my sphere. If he had not approached me for my help in healing his broken heart, I might never have had a chance to work with her. While my relationship with Artemis quickly grew from friendship to love, Helios and Apollo were not so lucky. They still saw each other as rivals, and as such, never really got along. Men are such petty beasts.

Artemis adjusted the reins, loosening them from my chariot, and helped me unbridle the horses so they could breathe easier. I glanced over at her with a smile so radiant I glowed. Her wild spirit was completely enamoring. I realized, maybe not for the first time, just how important she had become to me. I shook the thoughts out of my head and went back to unhitching the steeds from my chariot so they could wander, cool down, and find some water.

Helios joined us, and a friendly, or not so friendly, wrestling match began between him and Apollo. Realizing this was escalating, Artemis and I tried to break them up. "Helios! Stop this. We all had fun. There is no sense in this. Now back off!"

He glowered at Apollo over my shoulder, ignoring me altogether. I grabbed his attention telepathically and bore into him. *"Sol! Stop it! I* *do not understand why you cannot grow the fuck up! He is not replacing you, just a younger and less experienced version. He is still a reflection of you and needs you to do his job. Can you not see that? We **are** the sun and moon. They are the god and goddess **of** the sun and moon. We are not the same. Now stop this!"*

Helios looked at me, the marigold aura in his eyes receding as he breathed heavily, calming down from the fight. Artemis and Apollo seemed to be having a similar conversation behind us. Sayeh nuzzled against Apollo, shifting his attention to her. "You're right, Sayeh. It was foolish of me." He turned to her, stroking her side. Let's go get you some water, too." He bounded away, and Sayeh followed him.

Artemis returned to my side and placed a gentle hand on my shoulder. "Boys. Damn, when will they grow up?" Her hand felt soft yet strong on my bare flesh, making butterflies rise in my stomach. She'd had that effect on me from the first time she touched me. Before I could respond, Endymion's image filled my mind. I pinched the bridge of my nose, surprised by the suddenness of it. It had been a while since I had visited him, and a pang of guilt settled over my heart, suppressing the earlier flutters of joy. Artemis's brow creased, and she eyed me. "Everything okay?" she asked, her voice laced with concern.

I pushed my thoughts away and turned to face her. "Today was supposed to be fun, not another fighting match."

She smiled and cupped my face pulling me closer. "They'll learn to be friends. I'm sure of it," she said, winking at me. Smiling warmly, I held her hand and squeezed it gently. We spent the next few hours enjoying the day and each other's company, but the image of Endy lingered at the edges of my mind.

On my way home, I decided to visit Endymion. The cave where he lay was hidden from the mortals, marked as an official archaeology dig site. Zeus had infused the entrances with an enchantment when he'd gifted Endymion eternal sleep. Beside my love, I had stored my drachma, mementos from the past, and secrets kept.

I illuminated the room as I entered, running my fingers along bits of clothing and the golden laurel wreaths my girls wore when they were young. Memories of them running and playing in the fields flickered through my mind, and a grin curved my lips. I strolled deeper into the cave to where Endymion lay. Sitting on the edge of his bed, I ran my hand gently along his ever-youthful face and leaned in to kiss him gently on the forehead.

"Oh, my sweet Endymion, my love. I will always love you. I know I haven't visited often in the past few years. Please do not think that I have been ignoring you. Artemis and I," I paused, trying to find the right words. "You know we have been lovers for a while now. She is so amazing, and I love how she makes me feel. It reminds me of our time together." I caressed the back of his hand with mine, remembering the old days and the first time I saw Endymion.

I was passing across Greece one night, looked down, and saw the most delicious looking mortal tending sheep in an Olympian field. I landed my chariot and sauntered over, introducing myself like I was the answer to all his prayers.

He took my hand as we walked along the shore, and I stopped and turned to face him, saying, "I want this to last forever."

He replied, "Me too, Luna, but I will age and die."

My resulting deal with Zeus turned our dream into a nightmare. He granted Endymion eternal youth and life, but the price was that he would sleep, never to wake.

Sitting beside his lifeless form, I said, "After you, I never thought it possible for me to fall in love again. But, Endy, my sweet love, I think I am in love with her, so much so that I wish to call her my wife." The words left my mouth before I could even think about it. I stopped, hearing what I had just said. I brushed his perfect face with the back of my hand and sighed. "I haven't felt this way about anyone since you. For centuries, I came to see you every night without fail. I raised our girls alone. I love you. I do...but I so desire *life*, and Artemis...she is everything I need."

Images of Artemis flashed through my thoughts. Her smile warmed me, and her touch was divine. I longed to undo her braid and run my fingers through her hair. Glancing back at Endymion, I realized I had to tell Artemis how I felt about her. I knew her as the wild, untamable woman, and perhaps it was this knowledge that had so far stopped me from taking our relationship to the next level. A nervous flutter raced through me. I wondered about her reaction, wondering how I would react if she did not feel as strongly for me as I did for her. "What do I do, Endy?" I asked, leaning over to kiss him softly. I stayed by his side for a few hours before returning to Olympus.

I found her where I normally did—in the forests of Olympus. She came running from her temple as I landed my chariot in the field. "Selene. I wasn't expecting to see you so soon. Is everything okay?" Concern was evident in her voice at my untimely visit.

I smiled reassuringly. "Everything is fine. I just wanted to see you again." Climbing down, I greeted her with a small embrace.

"And Endymion? Did you see him?" Her gaze searched my face for answers to my visit.

"He is the same." My smile dropped a little. "But I came to ask you something. May we talk a bit?"

"Of course, Sel. What's up? You're worrying me." She took my arm and walked me back to the entrance, sitting on the steps.

I took a seat next to her, settling close and turning to face her. My heart pounded in my ears, and I inhaled a steadying breath, the scent of the forest easing my nerves. A breeze danced through the temple, whipping a dark tendril of her hair into her face. She tried to contain those silky strands with her braid, but just like her, they were wild and untamable. I drank her in with my gaze and tucked that errant lock behind her ear. My palm caressed the soft curve of her cheek as I lingered, admiring the silky texture of her skin. I held my breath, loathe to break this moment, my body warming as our gazes locked. I could see the answering heat in her eyes and the electricity licking at my fingertips where they touched her skin.

I bit my lower lip, part of me not wanting to ask the question, afraid of her answer. If I were wrong, it would hurt. It would hurt so much, but I had to know. "Arty, gods, I hope this is not a mistake, but…" I paused, trying to calm my nerves. I watched her as her shoulders stiffened, and she bounced her knee up and down. Her eyes darted from my face to her feet several times. Doubt filled my mind at what I was about to do. I would have to think this over more. I did not want to rush her. A being as wild and free as Artemis would hate to be bound by love, and I was the last person who would want to impede her freedoms. I didn't know how to say what was in my heart without making it feel like I was trying to tie her to me. She took my hand in hers and squeezed it gently, urging me to go on. I inhaled sharply. "You make me so happy with your smile, your laugh, your...your touch. I love being around you. I...I love you, Arty," I said, instead.

I watched, transfixed, as her luscious lips curled up into a smile. Artemis leaned into the caress, inhaling deeply. Her shoulders relaxed as she gazed back at me, a fire alight in her eyes. "Sel, my dear, you make me happy, and you know I love you, too." The heat from her touch filled me to my very soul and the fluttering in my core intensified. I closed the distance between us, the scent of pine and fur radiating from her as my lips brushed hers. The weight of the next few moments set like a stone on my chest as I waited for her to shift away. Instead, she deepened the kiss, pulling me closer. Her tongue teased against my lips, and I opened, savoring the exotic, wild spice of her.

My head spun, and I reluctantly broke the kiss, tugging gently at her lower lip with my teeth before releasing it. I rested my forehead against hers, searching her eyes for any hint of regret as I tried to catch my breath. I found only fiery passion and a hunger that called to my own. I trailed my fingers along her jaw and down the graceful arch of her neck, pausing over her throbbing pulse. I pushed the disappointment I was feeling for lying by omission deep into the recess of my heart.

Artemis wrapped her arms around me, her kiss-swollen lips teasing against mine as she whispered, "Let's go inside." My breath quickened, and I slid my hand over her soft chestnut hair, aching to feel the silky length slide between my fingers. She released me and took my hand. In one graceful motion, she stood, pulling me to my feet. I loved the way she moved. Her every movement was a seductive invitation as she turned toward her temple. I accepted and followed her willingly, eagerly, into the depths of the cave.

When we emerged, night was falling, and I had to ride.

Our visits to each other became daily, and we spent more and more time together. Helios often caught me watching her with a longing in my eyes that he did not seem to understand. One dawn, as I returned from my nightly ride, he caught me by surprise. "Luna, you know I can feel you. Tell me what's bothering you?" Helios asked. His voice was soft, not accusatory. "You love her, do you not?"

I nodded, glowing slightly. "I do, Sol. I have not felt this way in a very long time." Crossing my arms, I rubbed my biceps, afraid of his reaction.

Placing his hands over mine, he held me at arm's length, gazing into my eyes and soul. "I know, Luna, I know. And you should know how I feel about it." His pride, love, and worry poured into me through our bond.

"Oh, Sol, she lights up my world. She is like the sun on a rainy day." The warmth she brought me spilled over and reflected in my aura, filling the both of us with peace and calm.

"Then why is it that you're afraid to ask her to be your wife?" he asked.

"She is brilliant, strong, an amazing spirit and wildness that is such a contrast to my cool and calm soul. I am older and at a stage where I am ready to commit, but she is young, wild, and untamed. I do not want her to feel bound to me by her love. I want her to feel what I feel for her," I explained. Helios nodded, but his brows remained furrowed.

"Why do you worry for me, Sol? I am sure someday she will realize my commitment and return my feelings."

"No, Luna, it is not that. I worry about what her family will say or do. Hell, you have children with her father! Has that not crossed your love-sick mind?" The worry pulsed from him in waves. "She is Zeus's *child,* for god's sake!"

"I know that, Sol. Artemis and I have talked about that a lot since we started dating, and she feels her father will not interfere. He would want her to be happy, especially after the Orion episode. And Zeus knows me. Hopefully, he knows that I am trustworthy. Fuck, Eros can test me if so inclined. I *love* her! With every fiber of my being."

Helios shook his head, sighed, and hugged me tightly before placing a kiss on my forehead. "I just worry about you, Sel. I don't want to see you hurt. Please be careful." He released me and, with one last smile, returned to his duties.

I met up with Artemis the next day, and we took a walk in the outlying forest of Olympus. "Sol asked me about us yesterday. He thinks we are too much into each other."

"Oh? Apollo has been pressing me about what was different. Says he's felt a change." Crimson peppered her face as we talked, strolling hand in hand.

Suddenly, she stopped in her tracks, pulling at my hand. Knowing her senses were on high alert, I froze and looked around for the threat. We crouched, scanning our surroundings. Instinctively, we spun on the balls of our feet, lining up back-to-back. Then something happened I never expected. I *heard* her, like I hear Helios. She was speaking to me telepathically.

I leaned my head back against hers. *"Did you just...?"* She nodded once and repeated her statement.

"Pay attention this time. Something is off. The animals are restless and manic in behavior. We aren't alone."

"Where?" I continued scanning the forest, struggling to focus as this new depth of intimacy threw me off my game.

"Give me a second and hush. I'm concentrating." The reproach stung, but she was right. I waited with bated breath, returning my focus to the treeline. *"There, found it. A hundred meters or so east and heading towards us."*

Goosebumps sheeted my flesh as I felt him. An heir of Lycaon stalked us. The utter gall of him to approach me here, in my own home, was unnerving. *"He's here for me, Akti. This is not your fight."*

"Like hell, it isn't. Your fight is my fight, Seli. You can't get rid of me that easily." Her tone was steady, and I knew she would not leave me. A sense of pride overtook me. I was not alone. *"He still isn't aware we know he is here. Let him think we are oblivious. Stand, let's return to verbal conversation but keep the thoughts between us."*

Artemis and I stood and continued along the path. The strain was apparent in our voices, even as we attempted to act normal. "So, where would you like to go today?"

"Anywhere you lead me, Arty." We did not look at each other as we continued to feel out the lycanthrope's location.

As he drew closer, the bloodlust in him blazed through his scent. The primal snarls emanating from his throat became more and more unhinged as my powers warped his wolfen mind. His body morphed, unable to resist my pull, the pull of the moon. His muscles expanded, and bones lengthened. The transformation complete, he leapt at us, clearing the gap in one bound. The earth quaked a little as he landed. I brought my arms up, ready to defend myself.

A base survival instinct flooded my Titan body with adrenaline, and I grabbed a fistful of his pelt, throwing him into a nearby tree. Shaking it off, he stood and paced around us. *You subdue him, and I'll get my arrow ready,"* Artemis relayed to me.

Artemis touched her silver quiver necklace, and it materialized into her silver bow, the quiver filled with her signature arrows. She pulled curare from her hip pouch and dipped the arrowhead in it. I nodded and sank into a fighting stance, holding his attention. I lunged at him, and he snarled, taking a step back before leaping at me again. I grabbed him by his maw to prevent him from sinking his teeth into my flesh and kicked him back, sending him careening into the underbrush. Artemis spun, taking the opening, and fired. True to form, her shot met her target, sinking into the thigh of the lycanthrope. Aided by his racing heart, the toxin spread through his system quickly. He collapsed to the ground, paralyzed. We joined him in the trees and watched him struggle to breathe. Artemis removed the arrow, wiping the blood and toxin off the tip before replacing it in her quiver. "Why did he attack you? I thought lycanthrope worshipped the moon?" she asked.

I sighed deeply. "Normally, yes. But I had a personal clash with this one's clan a few years ago. My daughter Dreyla fell in love with Lycaon's second son, Acontes. Lycaon found out and was livid that his heir was even acknowledging one of our kind. The fact that she was my daughter just made it exponentially worse. Lycaon, along with half a dozen of his sons, found and cornered them not too far from here. Acontes was trying to protect Dreyla, but my presence changed him. He lost control and turned on Drey. Knowing they outnumbered us, I called my mother, as well as yours, and a few other Titans for help."

"Oh, Sel, what happened?"

"We fought, Lycaon lost, and Acontes died saving your mother. This clan has been after me for vengeance ever since. I am surprised Leto has not told you of this. She probably did not want you to worry over her." Adrenaline still coursed through us as we gazed into each other's eyes. My heart raced, pounding in my ears as I cupped her face gently. "Thank you for today, and I am so sorry I put you in danger, Arty. You would not have had to face this if it were not for me. I would never be able to forgive myself if something were to happen to you," I said, my eyes downcast.

"Sel, my dear, when will you understand that your problems are mine? When I said I love you, I made a commitment to you, and that means I am yours until you wish me away," Artemis said, speaking softly and raising my chin to face her.

My eyes twinkled with a hint of tears hearing her words. This meant she was ready to commit. Heck, she said she was already committed to me. This meant I could finally ask her to be mine without fear or doubts. I smiled warmly, wiping the tears with the back of my hand, and nodded.

"What do we do about him?" I said, glancing over at the lycanthrope.

"No, take him to the west. Romania, perhaps," she suggested, and I agreed.

Heaving the immobilized creature over my shoulder, I carried him to my chariot and flew to Romania. I landed deep in the forest and gently unloaded the lycanthrope. I made sure he was still breathing before returning to Olympus and Artemis. I did make one stop along the way.

She ran to greet me. "Well, that'll be a story to tell our brothers." Kissing me on the cheek, she wrapped her arms around me with a smile that lit up her face.

Stepping back from her embrace, I held her gaze. "What a rush! I can't believe you were involved in my mess."

"Your mess? I told you your mess is my mess. We're in this together, are we not?" she asked, her eyes imploring. Artemis laced her fingers with mine and began walking us back to her temple as I narrated the details of my trip.

Inside the temple, I tugged her to a stop. She turned to face me, brows furrowed. "I made another stop on my way back," I said, fishing my hands into my pocket and pulling out the ring from its velvet box. "Arty, I...I know you're a nomad, the wild one, not grounded as I am. But I also feel like I understand the depth of our feelings for one another. And I thought...it might...you might…" Gods, I was rambling now.

Artemis leaned in and hushed me with a kiss. The warmth and softness of her lips set my soul on fire, and I pushed into her. A small moan escaped her as she pulled away. Gazing into my eyes, she said, "Sel! Yes!" She offered me her hand, and I gently slid the ring onto her finger. She admired it lovingly. "It's beautiful." Tilting her head towards the cave, she beckoned me to join her. I slid my arm around her, and we eagerly made our way inside.

It was some time later that we emerged from the temple hand in hand. A glow I had not had in centuries emanated from me. Artemis looked radiant herself, but that could have been the way I saw her...in a new light, if you will. "We'll have to tell our brothers." She sighed.

"Our brothers? I am thinking of the look on your father's face, my Akti."

She blanched. "Oh, shit! I hadn't even thought of that." The color returned as well as the twinkle in her eye. "Your Akti?" She smirked. "I'm your moon?"

I cupped her face and kissed her softly. "*My* Akti Selínis. My moonbeam."

MANIA

OBSESSIVE

LOVE

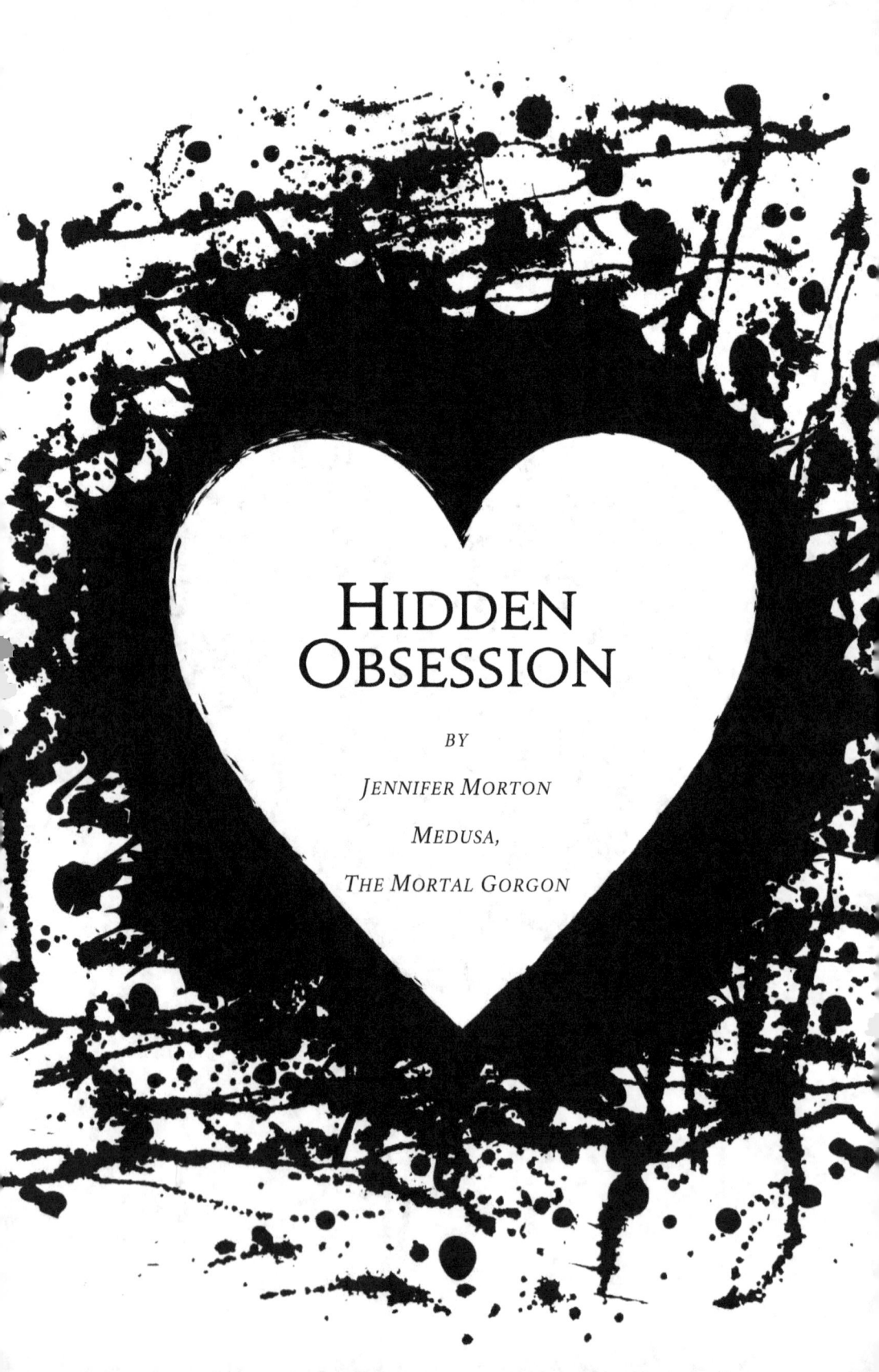

HIDDEN OBSESSION

BY

JENNIFER MORTON

MEDUSA,

THE MORTAL GORGON

It had been a long day, and I wanted nothing more than to crawl into bed. When the elevator opened, I noticed a brightly wrapped package sitting outside my door. Smiling, I gently picked it up, holding it on my hip. I got my key out of my purse and put it in the doorknob, only to find it unlocked. Damn, I must have forgotten to lock it again. I really needed to work on that. I went straight to the kitchen and placed the box on the table, looking for a tag or shipping label. It was wrapped in flowery paper, and there wasn't anything on it but a bow.

It must have been hand-delivered. I wondered if it was Athena or Luke. It still amazed me to have Athena back in my life. I never in my wildest dreams would have thought we'd find our way back to each other.

It could have been from Luke. Saying he was my best friend didn't even begin to describe what he was to me. Surprising me with a gift was something he would do and actually had done on many occasions. Quickly ripping off the paper, I pulled the top from the box to reveal about two dozen roses that had been cut from the stems. I leaned in to inhale the fragrant blooms and felt a wave of dizziness wash over me, but it passed as quickly as it came.

I reached in and pulled out a handful of the beautiful flowers and watched as the loose petals and buds slipped between my fingers. It was definitely different, but it was still a very thoughtful gesture. Moving to the cabinet over the counter, I pulled out a large crystal bowl and tipped the box of flowers into it, leaving it as a centerpiece on the kitchen table. I flopped down on the couch, wondering which of the two incredible people in my life had sent me the gift.

A glance around the room left me feeling like something was out of place, but I couldn't quite put my finger on it. It was unsettling, but I quickly brushed it off. The happiness from receiving such an unexpected gift filled me with peace, and I wanted to savor it.

The setting sun streaming through the window cast a warm glow over my living room, and I smiled as I picked up my phone to call Luke.

He answered after the second ring. "Hey, I was just thinking about you."

"Why didn't you stick around?" I asked, expecting him to knock on my door any second.

"What do you mean? I'm just locking up my office now. I was planning on stopping by, though." Confusion laced his words.

"You didn't leave a present at my door?"

"No, I didn't. Did it have a tag?" he asked, sounding concerned.

"If it had a tag, I wouldn't be asking if you left it." I laughed.

"Don't open it. I'll be right there," he ordered.

"I already opened it. It was just flowers, so there's no need to freak out." Shaking my head, I frowned at his commanding tone. He could be a little overprotective at times, but as unnecessary as it was, it came from a place of love.

Softening his voice, he assured me, "Hey, I worry. Besides, I'm in private security. You know I can't help it."

"I'll see you when you get here." I ended the call and dialed Athena, but it went straight to her voicemail. I disconnected without leaving a message. Luke's unease left me doubting the gift was from her. My mind drifted to my unlocked door, and I briefly wondered if there were cause for concern. I have been known to forget to lock up, but this was a secure building, and it was just flowers.

I put my phone down and laid my head back. Exhaustion made my limbs heavy as I reached for the blanket I always kept folded on the arm of the couch. It wasn't there. I looked around the room, trying to remember having moved it. Not wanting to get up to look, I laid back, considering the last few weeks. This wasn't the first time I'd had the feeling that my things had been moved. At first, I had brushed it off as absentmindedness. I was working almost nonstop, splitting my time between my two businesses. But now, as an uncomfortable feeling washed over me, I wondered if someone could have been inside my home? I just couldn't wrap my mind around the possibility.

I relaxed and let my eyes fall shut. It would only be for a moment, just a quick rest.

A steady pounding had me struggling to open my eyes. I obviously hadn't been getting enough sleep. I hated feeling so tired. I pushed my way to my feet and made my way to the front door, pulling it open. Taking in Luke's broad shoulders and the black T-shirt stretched over his biceps, I felt my breath catch at the sight of him. "Wow, impatient much?" I asked, still feeling a little groggy. I never liked being woken up, even from a nap.

"I've been knocking for a few minutes, and I was getting worried." He stepped inside, then pushed the door shut, slipping his arms around my waist. As he pulled me close, he brushed his nose lightly against mine.

I took a long moment to admire the ridiculously long lashes that framed his baby blue eyes. The contrast between his midnight black hair and those pale eyes never failed to take my breath away. Then, laying my head on his chest, I replied, "I'm sorry, I didn't mean to fall asleep."

He pulled back enough to search my face and asked, "Are you okay? That's not like you."

"I've been busy touring job sites. We've got more contracts than we probably should, and I've been doing the inspections."

He nodded as he released me and looked around. "Where's the box of flowers?"

"Luke, it's just flowers. Not everything is a security issue." I laughed. "If they weren't from you, they must be from Athena."

At the mention of the Goddess of War, Luke tilted his head. "Did you ask her?"

I sighed. He wasn't going to let this go. "I called, but she didn't answer. It's fine. Even if it wasn't her, it was just flowers. Everything doesn't have to be a threat."

"I know you don't notice the way people look at you, but men, women, they are all drawn to you. There are a lot of sick people out there, and I'm afraid of one of those people fixating on you." He reached out and tucked a strand of hair behind my ear. "I think that's part of the reason you keep your snakes out whenever you're in public. I don't know what you went through before, and you never have to tell me if you don't want to, but I think you use your snakes as a shield. You know your beauty has the potential to cause problems." He paused and rubbed his hands up and down my arms as he continued. "It isn't right, but we both know that the potential is there. Your snakes act as a barrier between you and the world."

I blushed at his words. "They never kept you away," I said simply, moving into the living room and flopping down on the couch. I did not want to continue that conversation.

Luke followed me and took the chair to my right, leaning back and putting his feet up on the coffee table. "I like to think it was the beauty of your soul that attracted me." He gave me a cheesy wink and crooked smile, his dimple on full display.

I laughed. "That was schmaltzy." He had the uncanny ability to make me feel good, no matter what was going on around us. I would never let him go.

"I know, and I also know you loved it," Luke replied, laughing with me.

"I still think you're paranoid. It's flowers. Someone was just doing something nice. That happens, too, doesn't it?" I was very tired of having this same talk. He knew I could take care of myself, but he had still appointed himself as my protector.

"It does." Luke bobbed his head. "There are also a lot of horrible people in this world. You've seen it."

"Yeah, I've seen more than my share." I sighed. "I still think you're overreacting." Wanting to distract him, I grabbed his hand before he could respond and pulled him towards the bedroom. Luke was my best friend, but we were close in a way that went far beyond friendship. He was accepting of me in a way I had never experienced before. My first life hadn't been easy, and it had ended horribly. My second life was just beginning, and I wasn't ready to tie myself down. At least not yet. I was incredibly lucky to have two amazing people so accepting of me.

I had been holding onto my human form, but I let my snakes slip free for a moment. They hissed in happiness, then disappeared back into my hair. As we stepped into my bedroom, Luke pulled his hand away, grabbed me around my waist, and tossed me onto the bed. I landed with a bounce and squealed as he landed next to me.

He propped himself up on his elbow and tucked his arm around my ribs, sliding me closer. Placing featherlight kisses over my lips, he murmured, "I'll never be able to get enough of you. You look exhausted, though. You need sleep."

I snuggled into him, ignoring his question and asking one of my own. "Have I told you lately how much I appreciate you?"

"You have." I could hear the smile in his voice, even if I couldn't see it.

"I think it's time you took a normal vacation. No shipwrecks, no work, and definitely no zombies."

I groaned, thinking over the last year. It had been one thing after another.

"I know what you're thinking, and you can stop. Don't go there. Just relax and get some sleep."

I tried to argue, but I was having trouble keeping my eyes open. I tucked myself against him and fell fast asleep.

I woke up alone the next morning but felt refreshed. A glance at the clock told me I had overslept, but since I was the boss, I didn't really care. I rushed through my morning routine, anxious to get to work. I couldn't leave without having my morning coffee, so I stopped in the kitchen on my way out and brewed a cup. After filling it with the appropriate amount of caramel syrup and whipped cream, I was ready to go.

I opened the door and kicked a package as I stepped out. I thought briefly of Luke's warning about accepting unknown boxes, but then curiosity won out. Setting down my cup, I knelt to pick up the gift, smiling with anticipation. Leaving the door open, I brought it inside to unwrap. It was much bigger than the last one, and I couldn't wait to see what was inside. I loved surprises.

I pulled off the wrapping paper and lifted the lid. A little puff of mist escaped. I had just enough time to think that I should have listened to Luke before I slumped to the floor unconscious.

I woke up with my head pounding and my snakes hissing angrily. I looked around an unfamiliar bedroom. I groaned, knowing that I'd never hear the end of dosing myself and getting kidnapped from Luke or Athena. Maybe no one had noticed I was gone yet. I tried to teleport to Luke's house, but my mind was still too foggy to focus enough energy on the task. I tried to swing my legs off the side of the bed and found a chain tied to my left ankle. I pulled on it, thinking I could get it off, but it was bolted to the cement floor. Great. I sat back and crossed my arms to wait for my captor to make himself known.

I didn't have long to wait. The heavy wooden door opened with a screech. The man was tall and thin, his curly hair cut short and slicked back. And I knew him.

"It was very accommodating of you to leave your door open for me. I knew you wanted me as much as I want you." He stepped inside and shut the door behind himself as he did.

"Jessie? What are you talking about? What the hell is going on?" I asked in shock.

"Oh, don't pretend. You know that you have been watching me as much as I have been watching you," Jessie said with a smile.

"Watching you...what? I haven't been watching you." I was thoroughly confused. Jessie had followed me like a puppy on my weekly inspections. He never said a word to me, though. Captain Crazypants was a foreman at the Happy Trails building, so he knew exactly who I was and what I was capable of. He had been overly clingy, but I never noticed he was a sandwich short of a picnic.

"You can stop playing hard to get. No one is around to stop you here." He sat on the chair next to the bed and pulled the cap off of a syringe. "This is just to keep you from leaving before I'm ready. You have to realize you love me first," he said in what I'm sure he thought was a soothing conversational tone.

He sounded insane, but even I knew that you never told the crazy person they were bat shit nuts. Instead, I said reasonably, "You know I have to check on the progress at the job sites. That's it. You've always been very nice, and I appreciate that. You can let me go. You don't have to use that." I motioned to the syringe he was holding.

For a moment, I thought he was going to put it down, but he was much quicker than I expected. Before I had a chance to fight back, the needle was in my leg. "Why are you doing this?" I slurred. Any human drug would work its way quickly through my system, but in the meantime, I was feeling very loopy.

"I've given you every chance, but you've been playing hard to get, and I'm tired of waiting. I'm ready for us to be together." He crossed to a dresser on the other side of the room and set down the empty syringe. "Don't try to fight it. I know what you immortals can do. This should keep you awake, but not strong enough to teleport."

When my snakes hissed, I realized I was in my Gorgon form. Even when my fuzzy mind couldn't form the thought, my body knew what to do. Shaking my head, trying to focus, I dragged my gaze to his face, expecting him to turn instantly to stone. Instead, I found his eyes shielded by mirrored sunglasses. Of course. That would have been too easy. Looking him over, I wondered how I could have possibly missed the crazy hidden behind those lenses.

"I didn't have the right dosage the first time. I've only used my special medicine on humans, so I had to guess for you. Immortals take much more," he said, interrupting the tenuous hold I had on my thoughts. My head spun when he jumped up and left the room, returning with a tray filled with different foods. He set it on a small table, picked up a chocolate-covered strawberry, and tried to feed it to me. "I thought these would be nice for our first date."

I moved my head away from his outstretched hand and scooted as far back as the chain allowed. "This isn't a date, you sick nutbag!" Crap, did I say that out loud?

Anger flashed over his face, and he threw the strawberry. It hit the wall with a splat, and I watched in fascination as it slid down, leaving a trail of chocolate. "You shouldn't talk to your soulmate like that," he sneered. Then, like a switch was flipped, he smiled. "Wine! We just need some wine. That's what people do on dates, right?" He rushed from the room, once again returning quickly, carrying a bottle and two glasses.

I sighed, and my snakes hissed wildly. I shushed them quickly and let my head fall back. Whatever poison he had dosed me with was rapidly leaving my system, and I would not give him the chance to inject me again. I was not going to lie here and pretend we were on a date either.

Crazypants turned his back on me while he poured the wine. I tried once more to teleport and was unsuccessful. A low growling noise escaped my lips. The effects of the poison were lessening, but not entirely gone.

"Here. I'm told this is an outstanding year." He sat with his back straight and his legs crossed, holding out a glass of wine with an expectant look on his face.

I kept my hands limp at my sides and let my eyes drift closed, hoping he would think I passed out. It was hard to lie quiet and still. I had to bite down on my tongue to keep the insults from escaping, having a more challenging time staying quiet than with staying still. Pissing him off would not be in my best interests just yet.

"This just won't do. This won't do at all," Jessie murmured to himself.

I heard him set the wine glasses down and wondered what he was doing. With every passing minute, anger rose like a tide until it consumed me. Hoping Jessie had his back turned and holding onto the rage. I focused all my energy on teleporting just enough to escape the chain, circling my ankle. I popped out and back within the space of a heartbeat. Not wanting him to know I was free just yet, I put my legs over the now empty manacle.

"Oh, you're awake. We can continue." He smiled pleasantly, like this was the most normal thing in the world.

"Is this something you've done before?" I asked, careful to keep my eyes on his hands. I would not allow him to inject me again. He caught me by surprise once. It would not happen again.

Tilting his head, he looked at me in confusion. "What do you mean?"

Spreading my hands out, I said, "This. Have you taken others against their will?"

"I have done no such thing." He looked offended at the very thought. "They wanted to be with me as much as you did."

"That is what I thought."

He smiled, clearly mistaking my meaning.

I looked him over. He was sitting casually wearing dark jeans and a deep green button-up shirt. He was utterly unremarkable in every way. I wondered what happened to his other dates when he was through with them. I debated trying to find out, but ultimately discarded the thought.

Throwing my legs over the side of the bed, I took satisfaction in the look of shock that crossed his face. Swinging my fist as hard as I could, I hit him in the face, sending his glasses flying.

He staggered back, and I advanced on him, snakes hissing loudly around my head. I carefully avoided his eyes. I wanted him to feel some of the fear I'm sure he'd given to the other women he'd taken. I did not doubt that there were several others.

He backed into the door and blindly fumbled at the doorknob in his haste to escape me. I let him go. He'd never be able to outrun me.

He was no match for me now that my body had flushed the drug from my system. I smiled as I teleported, knowing where he was headed.

Jessie's eyes went wide, and his face paled when he saw me leaning on the front door. "Why are you doing this?" he shrieked.

"Doing what? Freeing myself?" I asked, fighting to remain calm and watching his feet.

"Our date wasn't over yet," he whined.

His petulant tone grated. "How is knocking me out and taking me against my will a date?" I asked. "How is chaining someone up to keep them from leaving a date?"

"You just needed time to get to know me. The contract was almost over. You wouldn't have to do weekly inspections any longer. I knew you just needed a little more time to get to know me. Then you would have realized we were meant for each other. You're my soulmate."

"Really, now? And how many soulmates have you had?" I asked, keeping my voice gentle and taking a slow step towards him.

His mouth opened and closed like a fish out of water.

No longer able to contain my rage, I stalked up to him and slammed my hands against his chest, meeting his eyes. I felt him turn to stone beneath my palms and released him. Stepping back, I tried to get my breathing under control.

I stood staring at him for a few minutes, deciding what to do. I knew now that I had the power to bring him back, and as long as I didn't wait until after the sunrise, he would return with his soul. I shivered at the thought of what he would be if I waited until after sunrise. He would come back without a soul, and as sick and twisted as his mind was already, I didn't want to think about that depravity.

I glanced at the clock on the wall above the fireplace and took a good look around. I didn't know where we were, but it was clear that we were in a cabin. I tapped my lip as I considered my options. I had a few hours, so I decided to explore. I walked from room to room but didn't find anything of interest until I wandered into the kitchen. There was a door with a shiny new padlock on it.

I placed my index finger on the lock and sent a thin tendril of power into it, turning it to stone. I smiled in satisfaction, then tapped the stone lock, sending another bit of energy into it. It crumbled into dust, and I slowly opened the door, peering into the darkness. I was pretty sure of what I'd find at the bottom of the stairs, but I had to look.

I took the steps slowly, a sick feeling building in my stomach. Feeling around on the wall at the bottom of the stairs, I found a switch and flicked it on. The room lit up, revealing a dirt floor with several places of disturbed ground. I gasped and covered my mouth with my hands. Along the wall were several small, neat piles containing personal items.

I slowly moved from pile to pile, bowing my head in silent prayer for each life lost, until I came to a stop at the last one. There sat the blanket I had been looking for and the necklace Luke had surprised me with a few months ago. I knelt, lifting the quilt, and froze when one of my nightgowns and several pairs of underwear slipped out from between the folds. The blanket fell from my fingers, and I stood feeling sick. How many times had he been in my home, going through my things? Had he been there while I was sleeping? I shuddered at the thought.

I left the room in a rush, carefully avoiding the disturbed ground, and stormed up the stairs. I came to a stop in front of the statue. I debated my options for a moment before deciding to bring him back to face justice at the hands of the mortals.

Even though touching the stone repulsed me, I forced my hand out and rested my fingertips on his arm. I focused my energy on his head and closed my eyes. Before completing the transformation, I stepped back and stared at the unseeing eyes for several long moments, changing my mind.

"You stalked me and all of those other women. That is not love. That is an obsession. No one should have to live in fear, constantly looking over their shoulder, terrified of every shadow, jumping at every noise." I pushed the statue over with one last disgusted look, taking great satisfaction as it broke into several pieces. It was better than he deserved, but I couldn't bear the thought of him taking one more breath after the lives he'd taken.

I found a phone in the kitchen and called in an anonymous tip that would have the authorities storming the small cabin. I didn't want to be a part of it, though, so I teleported home after gathering my things.

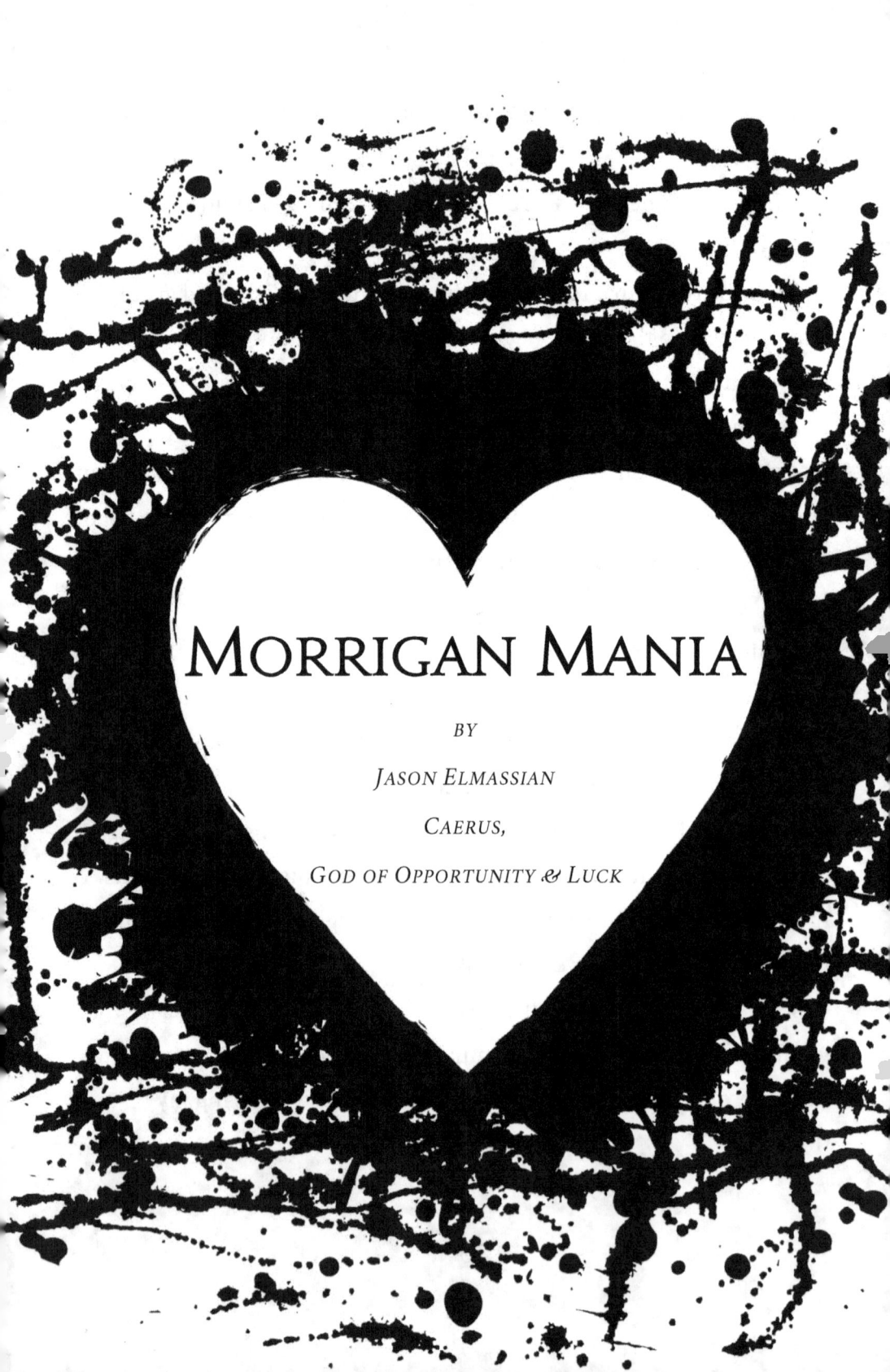

Morrigan Mania

BY

JASON ELMASSIAN

CAERUS,

GOD OF OPPORTUNITY & LUCK

I stand at the window overlooking Athens, remembering what had brought me back here, what had caused me to leave in the first place, and the heartbreak that came in between. As the God of Luck, I have a long history of eerily bad luck and a name that is largely unheard of. Caerus. As the rain pounds against the window, I think back to that fateful day. It was roughly two thousand years ago when Zeus had finally become fed up with me.

"Caerus, you are too old to be unknown like this. It is irresponsible, lazy, and embarrassing for a full-blown god to have a single, pathetic statue and no temples. Even more so, you are the son of Zeus. I will not allow you to remain on Olympus if your only ambition is to get boozed up among the mortals and make absurd bets while using your gift of luck to cheat. If a god gets a reputation for being a cheat, it sullies the deals that all of us make with mortals. Deals we rely on to remind them of our influence, among other things." Zeus's intense stare, matched by the light crackling in the air around him, did not deter me from my usual arrogance.

"I do not require your approval, Father. I do not desire great monuments and temples and thousands of worshippers begging for me to appear and *take them* as you are so fond of doing." I vulgarly humped the air, and Zeus struck me across the face. A fine gold mist sprayed the air as the ichor exploded from the new wound on my cheek. I picked myself up off the ground and spat in his face. "I'm done with you, old man. I hope you crumble into nothing and your statutes erode by the flow of time. I pray your name to be forgotten and lost to the ages. When I am the only one left who remembers who you once were, the world will once more be free from your tyranny, and a grateful people shall breathe a sigh of relief."

Zeus wound up to strike me again as I dropped my toga and bolted away. Being faster than anything on earth while naked had its advantages. I ran blindly. Buildings and people streaked past me in a blur as I pushed myself further than ever before. I hit the water and pressed onwards, my feet slamming harder into the surf with each step. I raced across the Mediterranean while saltwater splashed my face. Each footfall pounded the lifetime of bad memories further into my brain. I suddenly hit solid ground again and crashed. I skidded across the dirt, the sand and rocks pummeling my face in bitter defeat. I decided to lie there for a while and wallow in self-pity.

When I finally came to, a soldier stood above me. "Hey, you. You're finally awake. Get up. The General wants to see you." He pointed a spear at me and tossed a loincloth at my face. "Move it before I change my mind."

It would be easy to tilt his favor and knock him off his feet, but Zeus's words reverberated in the back of my mind. I meekly rose and put the clothes on, following the gruff, tanned man as he walked towards a nearby settlement. As we approached, I could see smoke rising from multiple sources. I began counting and multiplying in my head. There were at least thirty thousand troops.

Do I hear—

My thought was cut off by the roar of elephants trumpeting as they were saddled up. *Where the hell did I run to?*

I was marched at spearpoint to a large tent flanked by a picture of a triangular man worshiping a great eye above him. *Ah, Carthage. So, by General, he means the legendary Hannibal.*

"General! The man our scouts spotted is here!" The escorting soldier shoved me to my knees. I twisted my hand and tipped his scales of fortune into severe imbalance. "Better go check on your wife," I said with venom in my voice.

He looked back at me with deep concern. "What do you…how did you?" He released my shoulder and sprinted off, toppling a weapons cache as he fled.

"That is quite a trick. You will have to teach me that some time." A dark, bearded man stood before me, adorned with golden armor and a lion pommeled sword. A leopard's pelt draped his shoulders, and the symbol of an elephant was emblazoned on his chest piece. "Come, let us speak in private." He held the tent flap open and waited for me to enter. I got to my feet, bowed politely, and stepped inside.

The large tent was decorated with countless feather pillows, and the scent of sweet frankincense hung in the air. A large platter of bread and fruit sat upon a table in the center of the room. "Please, sit." Hannibal gestured to a pile of soft red pillows, and I eagerly collapsed

277

onto them. "So, tell me your name. Where do you come from, and why do several of my most trusted men swear up and down that they saw you running across the water faster than a man chased by demons?" He poured a goblet of wine and handed it to me before pouring one for himself.

"Straight to the point, I see. No fanfare or skirting around the real issues. In that case, I shall not lie. I am Caerus, God of Luck, Fortune, and Fate, Son of Zeus, Lord of the Lucky, and Master of Mischief." I bowed slightly while maintaining eye contact.

Hannibal stared intently at me for a few moments before bursting out in laughter.

"Perhaps you need a demonstration to prove how serious this is." I began to twist my hand and tilt his scales, but Hannibal stopped me.

"No need for that. You are hardly the first god I have come across. I have met your half-brother. Ares bestowed great wisdom upon me." He walked to the table and popped a grape in his mouth. "He told me, *Victory is but a small island, surrounded by an ocean of blood.*"

I laughed. "That sounds like dear Ares. No doubt he had a spear in hand and was covered in blood himself." *My sweet family, spreading tons of hope among the mortals.* "Well, I have no pearls of wisdom to bestow on you, so if you don't mind, I will be on my way."

"Oh, on the contrary, young Caerus. It is I who has the wisdom to bestow upon you." He popped another grape in his mouth and grinned as he swallowed it. While your brother has a bleak outlook, I prefer to look on the brighter side of things. So, let me share my take on Ares' saying, *Life is merely a small island of hope, surrounded by an ocean of hardship. You look like someone in the middle of the ocean. Start looking for land."* He stood up and walked to the entrance to the tent. "Now, please leave before you do what gods do best."

I sat there, stunned at what was happening. "You're not going to ask for my favor? No wishes? No pleading to bring back loved ones or turn the tide of war in your favor? What trickery are you up to?"

No mortal that I have ever come across has turned me away while asking for nothing.

His smile faded. "I take it you are largely inexperienced with humans of a wiser disposition than those that exist solely in taverns and brothels. Some of us desire more than what the world has to offer. Wise men plant trees they will never know the shade of. I intend to leave the world a better place than the one I came into, and divine favor often makes things worse for all parties involved. Ask yourself this, how many stories about your father or uncles end up happy?"

I furrowed my brow for a moment and thought. Not one single story involving Zeus, Poseidon, or Hades had what anyone would call a *happy ending.* As I walked out of the tent, rethinking everything I thought I knew, I stopped and stared intensely at Hannibal. Behind his olive skin and dark beard, I could see years of anguish and depression. This was a man who had seen real suffering and wished only to end it. I twisted my hand subtly and tilted his luck into extreme good fortune. If anyone deserved it, it was him.

279

He escorted me out of the encampment, and as I prepared to leave, I faced him once more. "What would a god find as far as *hope* goes?"

"Love. If you gods are capable of it. Love in whatever form you can muster." He turned and walked back to his tent, leaving me utterly lost and confused.

I spent the next thousand years sailing with pirates, dining with sultans, smoking opium with great thinkers, and sleeping with countless women. No matter what I tried, I still could not call any of it love. I chased adventure and company to every corner of the globe, and each time I was shattered when it was over. I chased down tales of Djinn—*shockingly real, absurdly useless.* The Fountain of Youth—*fake.* Atlantis—*vastly overrated from what Poseidon told me.* And El Dorado—*lovely people, weird beliefs.*

By 1200 AD, I had given up hope of ever finding happiness. After the disappointment of finding out that Taliesin Ben Beirdd was simply a sing-songy mortal and not a wise ancient as I was led to believe, I wandered around the Gaelic countryside. I was tilting the favor of farmers and mystics just to pass the time.

"Seems like you're in a rut. How unlucky for you," a few voices said in unison from behind me.

"Piss off. I'm in no mood." I turned to find the source of the voices but saw only an empty field and a single raven perched on top of a nearby wall.

Must have been the wind.

"We are much more than wind or imagination, young Caerus. We are seekers of power. Knowers of prophecy. Masters of magic. We are the Morrigan." A dark-haired figure with raven feather shoulder pads and blood-stained rags wrapped around her chest appeared in front of me. She held an obsidian spear in one hand, and the other was covered with tattoos and strange rings. "Come with us, and we shall give your life meaning." She stretched out her hand, and I cautiously took it. The electricity between us was immediate. I could feel a warmth in her fingertips that I had never before experienced.

She walked straight toward the woods, her touch gently leading me along with her. As we passed the tree line, I felt the world melt away. It was just her and me in the world, and everything else was inconsequential. I finally understood the mortals' hunger for things like drugs and companionship. Every fiber of my body was on fire with desire. I wanted to stay in her presence for all time, do anything to make her happy, kill anyone who stood in her way. We came to a clearing with a single monolith standing at its center, chains dangling from its top. A small retinue of purple hooded figures formed a semicircle around it, with matching swords and raven broaches.

"These are our Phantoms. They help me carry out our will and *execute* our vision." She grinned wickedly and brushed the hair out of my face. "We want you to help us lead them. They could use a bit of luck in some tight situations."

I nodded. My head was high above the clouds, and my thoughts were spinning. "Why don't I just give you all the luck? With your powers, you could do untold wonders with even a smidge of it."

Her smile softened. "If only it were that easy, our little clover. Your gift does not work on yourself, and we are similarly cursed by heretics of our own pantheon. We require lackeys and friends to do our bidding for us. Else, we would not need to entice these ne'er-do-wells with gifts." She waved her hand at the dozen or so Phantoms in the clearing. "But, with you here, we shall rule this world side by side and make all who've wronged us pay for their sins." She spat against the grey stone, and I watched it slowly trickle down to its base.

"Anything for you, my queen."

The wicked grin returned to her face. "Excellent. Come now, there is much work to be done."

Where my past was marked by chasing good times and coming up empty, the centuries following my introduction to the Morrigan were drenched in blood and the screams of people who were sacrificed at the monolith. Kings were made to kneel in the entrails of their loved ones while begging for mercy. Even minor gods were sacrificed to keep my love happy. No one was safe from her wrath. She would send a raven to whisper in my ear, and I would tilt the favor of whichever Phantoms she'd assigned to the job. As the years went on, it seemed to me that she was on the warpath rather than trying to rule. It bothered me, but I felt like it was worth it to keep her happy. She did know the fate of the entire world, after all. I truly would have done anything she asked.

One day I walked to the clearing to find all the Phantoms assembled, but Morrigan was missing. I knitted my brow and stared them down. "Where is she? Where is Morrigan? Where is my very heart?"

"That is what we are here to find out, our little clover." She appeared behind me and slipped the manacles on my wrists. The chains on the monolith drew tight, and I was brought to its base.

"Is this a joke? Do you mean to have me beg for my life before you release me?"

"The begging, yes. The releasing, no. It always had to end this way, Caerus. You see, we lied when we first met. You can tilt our fate, but in doing so, you would cause our death. When we were bound to this form, the great maker cursed us with knowledge of our own destiny. You were to be our downfall at the end of the world. Every person you have slain, every demigod whose blood you have helped spill, has created a weapon capable of shattering fate. We will no longer be its slave, and we have you to thank." She drew a golden sword and a bowl of blood. She began chanting as the blood swirled.

283

"Please, please don't do this." I strained against the shackles. "We can find a way to do this together. We can be our own weavers of fate." She ignored my pleas and continued the spell. "Morrigan! My love!" Tears streamed down my face as she took the blood and poured it over the sword.

"We never loved you, Caerus. We used you to end your life." She raised the sword over her head and plunged it into my chest. A great force exploded from the point of impact, knocking Morrigan back and killing every Phantom in sight. She rose to her feet and looked at my body, slumped against the grey stone. "Unlucky 'til the end." She spat on my corpse and transformed back into a dark raven, flying toward the horizon.

A roll of thunder shakes me from my memories, and I rub the stab wound over my heart. I still have no idea why I didn't die that day, but I don't intend on giving her a second chance. She knows I'm alive, and she knows where I am.

"It's time for some fucking revenge."

LUDUS

PLAYFUL

LOVE

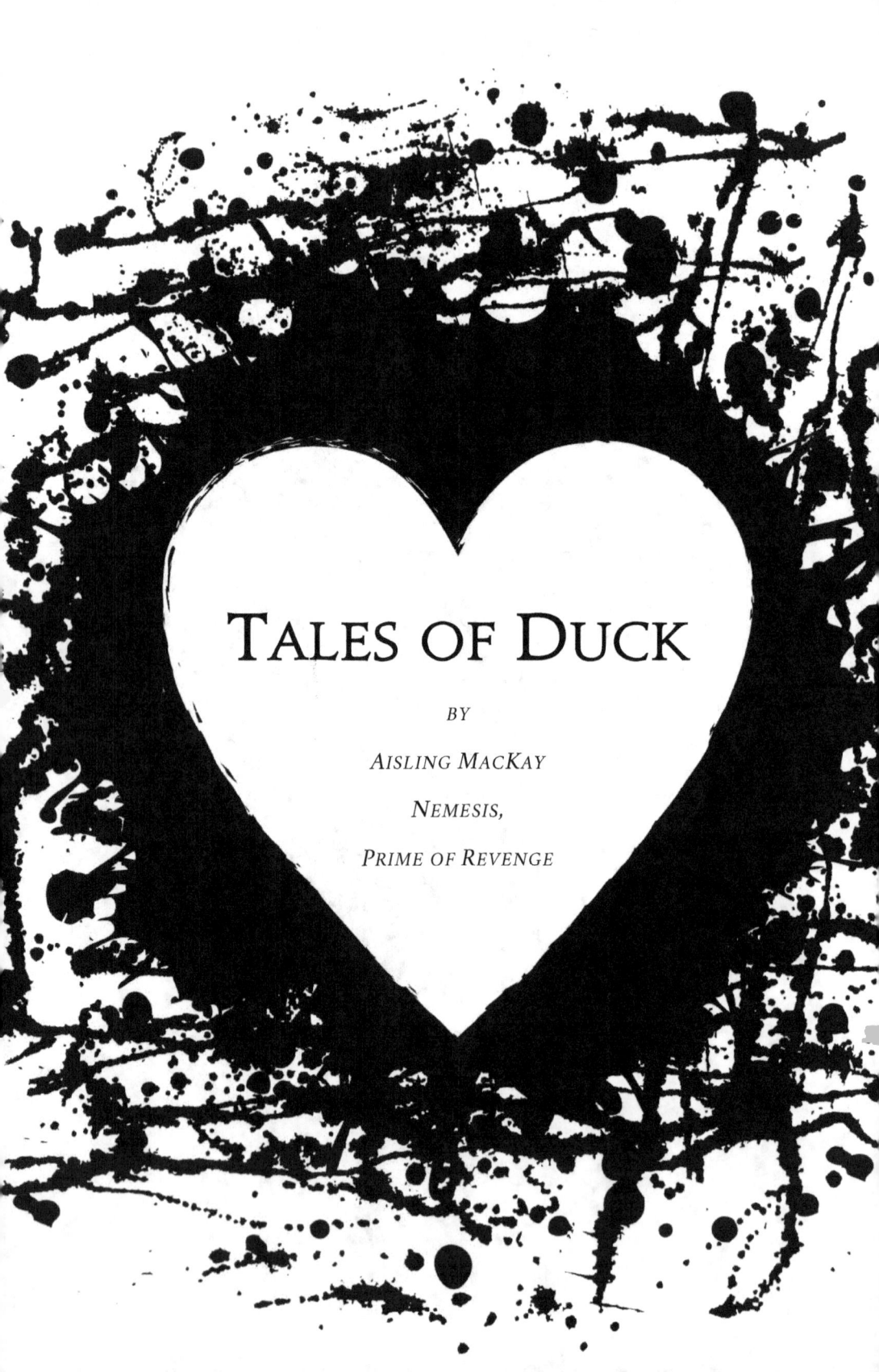

Tales of Duck

BY

Aisling MacKay

Nemesis,

Prime of Revenge

It had been a very complicated few weeks. I was not quite sure what to do with myself, and that feeling was wholly unfamiliar. Everywhere I looked, there were memories of what had happened in San Francisco. Even spending time with my brother, Thanatos, whom I loved, was painful right now. I had nearly killed him, and the memory haunted me. Hypnos, Than's twin, had managed to invade my mind and control my actions. Hypnos did not have the power or strength to take me down. Yet somehow, he had altered me enough that I acted against my very nature. It should have been impossible, and it had utterly shaken my worldview. Worse, it had shaken my faith in myself and called into doubt all that I was.

I watched Ky'Elli as she climbed to the top of the table, spread her iridescent black wings wide, and jumped, practicing her gliding. Except for the wings, she resembled a baby panther, still rounded and delicate but with the promise of great strength. I was bonded to this unique and magnificent creature in a turn of events that even I didn't fully understand. She had searched me out from another realm, and now we were linked. She was my own baby monster.

Thanatos, along with Ky'Elli, had managed to defeat Hypnos and save me in San Francisco. They brought me back to the God Complex, where things continued to devolve for me. I had recovered from that altered state, and my memory had returned. Now I was struggling and trying to process all that had happened. I needed some time away from everything.

Deciding to return home to the Underworld, I packed a small bag and readied my flat in the God Complex for my absence. I could manage some time away. It had been millennia since I had taken a break from the mortal world.

Ky'Elli and I stopped by the lounge on our way out, looking for Thanatos. I needed to let him know we would be away for a bit. If we were to disappear, he would worry.

Eros and Clio were in the break room, Duck at Clio's side. Such an odd name for a fox, but Clio had insisted that was what we should call her small pet. The little fox's ears perked, and he jumped to his feet as Ky'Elli and I entered. He bounded onto one of the chairs and bounced off, flying through the air to pounce on Ky'Elli. Her eyes went wide, and she let out a small shriek that rattled the windows just before Duck slammed into her. The two of them tumbled across the floor in a bundle of feathers and fur.

"Tartarus's flaming balls! I should have eaten him the moment I saw him!" Ky'Elli snarled in my mind.

I arched an eyebrow at her cursing, my lips twitching as Duck yipped and nuzzled at her. Trying to right herself without hurting him, she batted and snapped at him as he licked her face.

Clio laughed and called Duck to her. He released Ky'Elli and zoomed away, circling the room, seemingly unable to contain his foxy delight. Ky'Elli barely had time to right herself, her fur wet and sticking up in wayward spikes. Her feathers were rumpled, and her eyes narrow slits. She hissed at him as he headed back toward her and let out a short, high-pitched cry. He spun to a stop, shook his head, and pawed at his ears. She shot him a haughty look and gave a small, satisfied sniff as he went to his belly, his tail flicking from side to side. Ky'Elli glared up at me, then sat down to try to right her fur and feathers.

"I am covered in fox drool! It is very gross! Almost as gross as frogs!"

Duck snuck closer, crawling along with his belly on the floor, his eyes bright and intent on Ky'Elli.

As I watched the two of them, my lips curved in a genuine grin, the first in many days.

"Hello, Nemesis. It is so good to see you. How are you feeling?" Clio asked, her brightness apparent to every sense I had and her concern evident in the gentleness of her tone.

"Hey, Nem," Eros called with a jaunty salute and his usual smirk.

"Hello," I said, nodding at Eros. "I am well, Clio. Thank you for asking. I was looking for Thanatos. Have you seen him?" I knew she meant well, but I was not in a space to be comforted or to deal with her care.

"I haven't, but if I do, I will let him know you are looking for him," she said with a gentle smile. "Are you going somewhere?" she asked, looking at the bag.

Duck slid a few inches closer to Ky'Elli, going still and lying his chin on his paws. His eyes were wide and innocent when she stopped her grooming to glare at him.

I did not respond to her question, just gave a short nod. "Thank you, Clio. I wish you both well. Come on, Ky'Elli."

I saw Clio's face fall, and fresh concern filled her eyes as she glanced at Eros. I adjusted the strap on my bag and turned to the door, eager to escape the flood of emotions.

"Oh, Nem! I was just telling Eros about Duck and how he faced down a minotaur! He is such a wonderful protector. I can't thank you enough for bringing him into my life," Clio said.

That caught my attention, and I tipped my head. "A minotaur? Did some queen mate with a bull again? Great Chaos, you would think they would learn!"

"No, no," she said, "nothing like that. It was a cursed mask that turned an assistant at the museum into a minotaur. They still have not caught her. She transformed right in my office at the museum. Duck was very fierce and brave. He bit the minotaur and helped protect everyone! He is truly something special."

We all looked down at the fox who had snuck a few feet closer as we had been speaking. He was now flicking his tongue out, trying to lick the feathers at the tip of Ky'Elli's tail.

"He is…uh…very…special," Eros said, his eyes glinting with humor. Clio playfully smacked his chest.

"He is definitely worthy of a goddess. Remind me to tell you Duck's origin tale sometime," I said with a slight smile, turning toward the door.

"Nem!" Clio called again.

I looked back over my shoulder. "Yes?"

"I baked some cookies. Won't you have some with us? I would really love to hear the story."

I sighed and pushed the dark fall of my hair back from my face. "I do need to be on my way, Clio. Maybe another time." Ky'Elli and I headed for the door, only to find Duck in blocking our way. His liquid eyes were huge as he looked up at me, his black-tipped ears drooping, and his body radiating sadness.

Ky'Elli looked at him, then at me, and with resignation in her voice, said, *"Maybe just a few more minutes? I like cookies, and so do you."*

Eros patted the espresso machine. "I will make you a flat white if you stay and spill the story! Come on, Nemo. It won't take long, and it has been a while since we have had the chance to talk."

My lips quirked at the nickname he had insisted upon using for me since the gods returned. "Okay. Cookies, a flat white, and the story. But then we have to be on our way."

I dropped my bag just inside the door as Clio smiled brightly and brought the cookies to the table. Eros followed shortly with the coffee for me and tea for Clio. Ky'Elli settled close to me on the sofa. Duck settled near Clio at the other end, but his gaze tracked Ky'Elli's every movement.

I took a cookie for myself and one for Ky'Elli as Eros settled onto the arm of the couch. "So, tell us, Nemo, of the amazing tale of Duck."

I took a sip of the flat white and began.

I had taken to bringing Ky'Elli to the woods. Not only was she young and, like all young, had the energy of a thousand suns, but I could feel her unrest at being surrounded by walls. She thrived in the open air and drank in the magic of Olympus forest.

Ky'Elli would prowl her way along paths, hunting, pouncing, and rolling in the grass. She climbed the trees, sharp claws digging deep into hard bark. She perched high above the ground, her unearthly eyes surveying the surrounding land. Spreading her wings wide and flapping hard, she looked like a baby bird at the edge of its nest, strengthening the muscles of her chest and back. Her talons cut deep, holding her tight to the branch. She would release her grip and half glide, half fall to the ground. Her instincts at work, pushing her to hone inherent skills.

I wandered through the forest, keeping a light watch on her through our bond. She was very fierce and had her own unique defenses, but she was still young and small. My mind sifted through thoughts. I let them come and then let them go, a sort of moving meditation.

Ky'Elli's excitement alerted me to a change. There was a small yip of alarm and then a rustle. I figured she had found and killed her prey. Ky'Elli emerged silently onto the path, and my eyes widened.

*Her trilling voice filled my mind, **"Look what I found! It is different! I hunted it. I am going to eat it!"***

I do not know why she had not killed the small creature outright. Typically, she was fast and efficient in her kills. The big dark eyes of the tiny beast looked at me in panic and terror, its body twisting, the back of its head trapped in Ky'Elli's mouth. It yipped in desperation, unable to free itself.

*"**Ky'Elli! No! Drop that!**" She froze and looked at me in surprise. I felt her reluctance to release her prey. "**Ky'Elli, drop it now! That is not your food.**"*

She slowly lowered the small animal to the ground and released its head from her mouth, but not before placing a paw onto its tail to hold it in place. The little fox looked up at me, its large, black-tipped ears flicking back and forth and its tiny feet scrambling at the forest floor. Its auburn fur was matted and soaked with saliva. Its small sides heaved as it panted in panic. Ky'Elli looked at the kit and then back at me, her expression and mood one of disgusted annoyance.

*"**I dislike the word no. It is not a fun word.**"*

*"**I know, mikros, but this is not for eating today.**"*

*"**It is not a human. This looks nothing like a human. You only said no humans.**" Ky'Elli's mental tone was filled with displeasure.*

*"**I know, Elli, but this is not something I want you to eat. It is young, and we have to be careful about eating young animals. If we eat the young, then they cannot grow and have new young.**"*

Ky'Elli looked at me, skeptical and still somewhat disgusted with my views. I walked toward her, and she let out a small hiss as I approached, not wanting me to take her prey. I tapped her lightly on the nose.

293

"I know you are angry with me, mikros. But you may not eat this creature."

I bent and gathered up the small shaking body, wrapping the drool-soaked kit in my scarf. I stepped into the brush, hoping to find a den or a sign of where the little one belonged.

"Ky'Elli, where did you find him?" She reluctantly showed me, but there was no sign of any other fox nearby.

"He is alone. He would not survive on his own. Does that mean I can eat him?"

"No, Elli. No eating him." I tucked the fox into my pocket and then bent to pick up my outraged baby monster. *"Come on, you. Let's go home. I will make you some bacon instead."*

Ky'Elli grumbled and grumped as I teleported us all back to the God Complex. Inside, I set Ky'Elli down, and she stalked imperiously towards the kitchen, her entire demeanor one of annoyance. I sighed and followed her in, settling the baby fox into a deep box on the counter before preparing the bacon. Ky'Elli faced away from me but kept a very close eye on the box. I could hear the calculation in her mind.

"Ky'Elli," I admonished.

She bared her fangs at me over her shoulder and went back to her watchful sulking. While the bacon cooked, I cleaned up the baby fox. I gave him a quick bath, drying and brushing him until he resembled a very fluffy Pomeranian. His big eyes were dark and liquid as he surveyed me and his environment. I did not know what I was going to do with this little guy, but he was unbelievably adorable.

Ky'Elli's mood improved some after a pound of bacon and a few black

peppermints. As I gathered up the box and took it into the bedroom so I could

shower, she was still grumbling in my head. Her irritation was a dark cloud

as she skulked behind me.

I kept the kit close over the next few days and watched Ky'Elli closely. It

was not an easy task. Every time the little fox's feet hit the ground, he went

in search of her. He would shadow her every step, climb on her if she was

lying down, nip at her feathers, and pounce on her tail. Each time he came

after her, she would turn and give me a look of such annoyed outrage I could

*almost hear the implied, **You should have let me eat him.***

He simply worshipped her and did all he could to imitate her at every

turn. If she was hunting, he hunted. More often than not, scaring away her

prey. If she climbed a tree, he did his best to follow, usually making it much

higher than I would have thought possible. One night, he found the box of

holiday decorations and tightly bound both himself and her up in the

Christmas lights, or the 'evil thorn vines' as Ky'Elli called them. More than

once, she grabbed him by the scruff of the neck and tossed him

unceremoniously at my feet.

The two of them locked together in our home was a bit much to handle.

They reminded me of Thanatos and Hypnos when they were young. Either

up to mischief together or constantly fighting. I took them out to the forest

whenever possible, hoping the fresh air and exercise would tire them both

out. Ky'Elli still begrudged the little fox his every breath but had ceased

trying to eat him. She had settled into a resigned acceptance with bouts of

annoyance and anger.

One of those excursions found us wandering the paths of the deep forest. The weak winter sun barely penetrated the canopy. Ky'Elli climbed a tree, the kit jumping and scrambling at the bark, trying to get to her. She was studiously pretending that he did not exist. He finally admitted defeat, taking up a sentinel position on a large rock. He looked up at her then copied her body posture, his head held high as he looked out over the forest floor.

I settled on my own fallen log nearby, letting the two of them enjoy the chill gray day. I glanced up as Ky'Elli left her perch, half tumbling to the ground but managing to slow her descent with widespread wings. She landed hard but kept her feet under her, settling her wings against her back with an air of pride.

She disappeared into the foliage, and I went back to my book. The frisson of awareness hit me just before the low baby growl-hiss of the fox whispered in the air. I snapped to my feet and went quiet, my power slipping from me to investigate. I saw a dark shape slam into the brush. Ky'Elli's frightened and startled shriek broke the peace of the forest. I cringed as the sound hit me on both the mental and physical planes.

I was moving before I registered what the danger was. The kit had disappeared from the rock, and I spared a moment to hope he was safe. I broke through the branches to see Ky'Elli backed against the trunk of a large tree, her wings held tightly to her back, and her thin sickle teeth on display. Her eyes glowed a hot blue, but dark liquid dripped from a wound on her side, matting her fur. The promise of what she would one day become was clear. But right then she was young, she was vulnerable, and she was injured.

The creature that faced her was massive, one of the largest boars I had ever seen. It was covered with bristles with a large hump at its shoulders. A thick line of black fur over the dark gray trailed its spine in a spiky mane. Its neck was wide, the snout short. Its gaping mouth, framed by two massive tusks, revealed teeth made for gripping and crushing. Tiny red eyes seemed to glow as they focused hungrily on Ky'Elli.

I reached out and manifested my sword, the shadowy shape of it deceptive in the gray light. I lined it with my power and looked this creature over for a weakness. It swung its massive head from side to side and let out a low bellow. Ky'Elli responded with her own cry of war, the sound soul-shattering. I briefly wondered if, at some point, that shriek would have the power to kill.

The beast charged, and I could feel the vibration of his weight against the ground. I ran, my wings exploding from my back. Ky'Elli nearly glowed with light as the boar pounded closer. I leapt into the air just as a bright orange blur spun from beneath the bushes, positioning himself between the boar and Ky'Elli. The tiny fox jumped and scampered up the side of the shaggy beast. He sunk sharp needle-like teeth into the tender snout, and little claws raked at the burning eyes. The boar shook its head, howling in pain and anger. My breath caught again. The kit was so very small, but he hissed, growled, and fought like a little demon.

I landed heavily on the back of the beast, my sword a blur of black as it arced downward. With the first cut, the creature faltered, my power sucking at the life force. Smoke engulfed the boar, and my feet landed on the ground as both the kit and I fell through shadow. The fox spun, snarling, spitting, and yipping, looking for his foe. Every hair on his body stood on end, his bushy little tail straight and poofed out, his eyes crazy with battle rage.

He came to a stop in front of Ky'Elli, crouched low in a defensive posture, scanning his surroundings. Ky'Elli and I stared at him in shock. He was barely bigger than a gerbil, and yet he had the heart of a lion! I bit my lower lip to keep from laughing, not wanting to hurt his feelings. Ky'Elli sighed big and nudged at him with her nose. The little fox spun to look at her, then stepped closer. He licked at her side then nuzzled in close against her, looking for comfort and reassurance.

*Ky'Elli sighed again and looked up at me. "**You really should have let me eat him.**"*

*I chuckled softly. "**I know, mikros. I know.**" I gathered both of them up and ported us home.*

Two weeks later, I overheard a conversation in the break room at Olympus Administration. Clio, the muse of history, had just returned to the pantheon and was looking for a pet. She was gentle and highly intelligent. Her power shone with a brightness of spirit and emanated an intense protective energy. She was often lost in her thoughts but was always very aware of those around her. And she was one of those rare beings that was just kind.

She needed a protector and a companion. The kit may have been small, but he was fierce, and my instincts told me that Clio belonged to him.

I brought the kit to the lounge later that day and left him with a note. He was happily pouncing and bouncing when I left. He almost seemed aware of what was to come, as if this had been his plan all along.

I finished the flat white and the story at about the same time, looking down to find Ky'Elli and Duck curled against each other, sleeping peacefully.

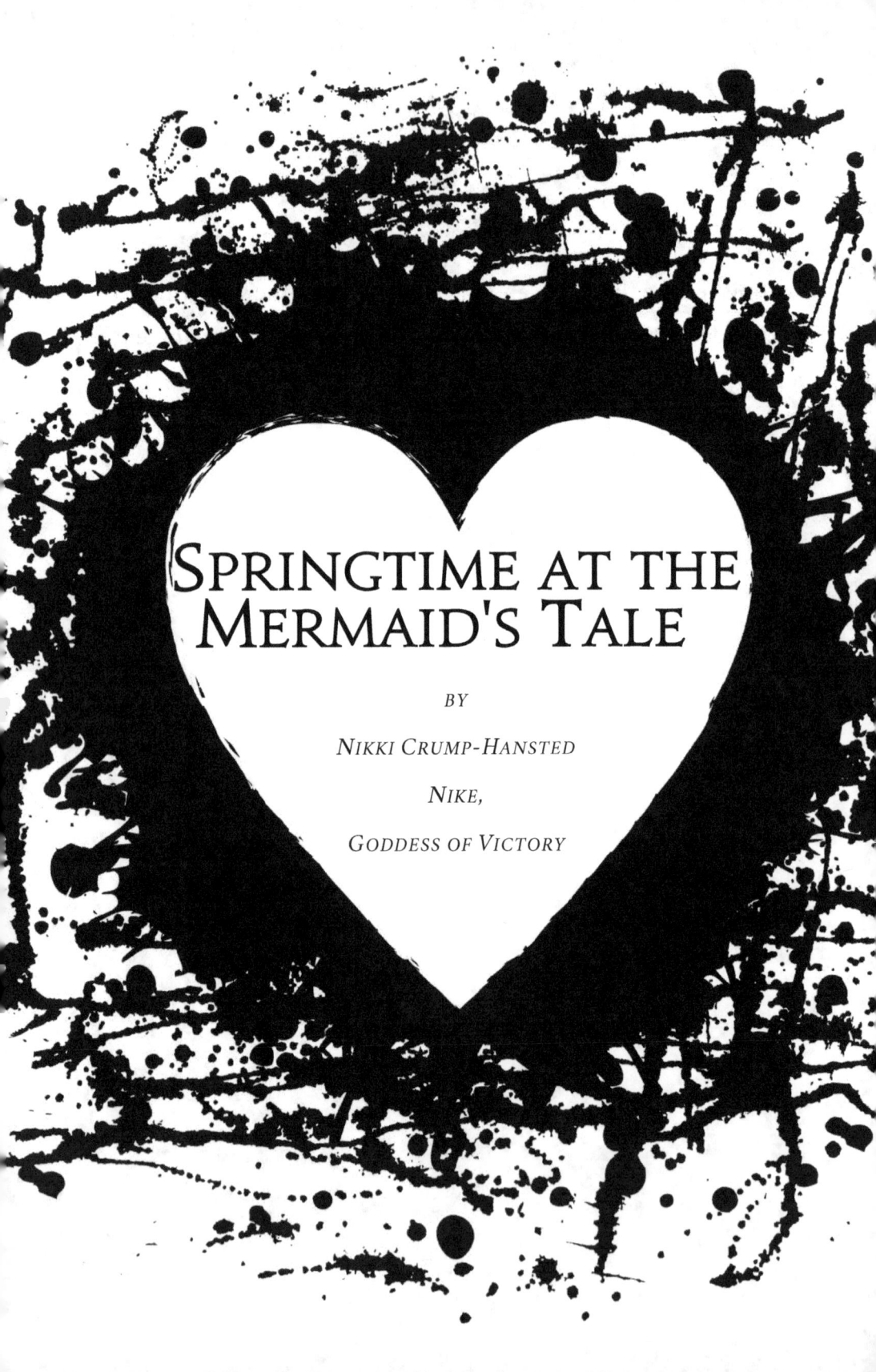

SPRINGTIME AT THE MERMAID'S TALE

BY

NIKKI CRUMP-HANSTED

NIKE,

GODDESS OF VICTORY

Springtime at the Mermaid's Tale Bar and Grill was a busy time of year, with all the conventions and the beginning of festival season. The restaurant was full from lunch service to well past supper on the weekends. The weather was beautiful, so we opened patio dining with its gorgeous views overlooking the ocean. Word of the aquarium dining in the lower level of the restaurant had traveled fast. Many guests were delighted by all the different creatures and animals that they could see. The biggest attraction was the merfolk that came to the swim-up window to be served Atlantean whiskeys and wines. The mortals were amazed at how the ocean water was held back as the merfolk enjoyed a drink at the bar.

My siblings, Kratos, Bia, Zelus, and I had been running our Uncle Poseidon's bar for a few weeks now. We had all settled into our roles and were enjoying the break from our normal duties for Olympus. Kratos looked the part of the manager with his strong jawline and deep-set eyes. Just the look of him commanded respect. Using her telepathy, Bia had figured out a way to hone in on any magic users entering the bar. Zelus used his charm and quick wit to handle the guest as he led the service team. And then there was me, Nike, Goddess of Victory. I managed the inventory of the two bars. I enjoyed watching everyone move throughout the restaurant as if we had worked together for years.

Things were running smoothly, but there was another reason Poseidon asked me to be here at the Mermaid's Tale. Foaling season for his hippocampus was underway, and as a grandchild of Oceanus and Tethys, I had a connection to the creatures of the oceans and waterways. In the time that the Greek Gods were absent from the mortal world, many of the sea creatures diminished in numbers, especially the magical ones. You could say they were on the endangered species list, and my uncle's herd had been depleting. If ever there was a creature that needed a victory, it would be these hippocampi.

Poseidon kept a whole stable of the majestic animals of the deep. They had always drawn me, and I swam with them for years in my youth. My favorite had always been the hippocampus. Poseidon kept the intelligent beasts as both mounts and protectors. These creatures fascinated me, and I devoted years to learning and interacting with them. Their heads were that of majestic horses, flowing to strong thick equine necks. Their legs flared into wing-like fins, and the strong, long back transitioned into the powerful tail of a dolphin. Colorful scales, the patterns unique to each creature, glistened in even the darkness of the depths.

Foaling season had been going well, and I snuck away every chance I got to play with the newly hatched foals. They were adorable with their soft muzzles and bright eyes. Their playful natures and excitement when they saw me always warmed my heart.

I escaped the kitchen, shaking my head and giggling as Brian, the chef, continued ranting and raving at the new line cook. I swear that man knew how to cuss in ten languages. I bit into the apple I had swiped from the counter and headed to check inventory for the bar when a high-pitched wail sang out.

My siblings and I all whipped toward the distress call. Waving my sister and brothers off, I rushed down to the swim-thru window. The urgent sound was meant only for immortal ears. All the mortals heard was a distant whistle. A group of merfolk gathered against the aquarium wall, and all of them tried to speak at once. Their voices were deafening, and their words impossible to decipher. I motioned them to be still and took off my jacket before walking to the magically contained water wall. I looked back and could see my brothers watching me. I nodded that I was fine, then turned and dove into the sea.

Once within the water, I could clearly hear the moans of the hippocampus. The merfolk explained as we quickly swam to the cave beneath the bar. One of my uncle's prized mares was about to foal, and there were complications. She was struggling to lay, the eggs trapped within. It could mean the death of both the mother and the foals.

They had set up a nesting area composed of sea kelp, sea moss, and baskets of krill to feed the foals. The handlers watched me as I swam closer. Nahiam, the male, was hovering protectively, the size and bulk of him intimidating. He was much larger than his mate, his fins and mane barbed like those of a lionfish, and thick spikes protected the length of his tail. Freah, the mare, was much more finely formed, seeming almost delicate compared to the bull. Her lines were graceful, her fins flowing like those of a betta fish, her mane a smooth raised ridge down her neck and along her tail.

I swam in a circle then lowered my head, presenting myself in a floating bow. I remained as still as possible, allowing the water to bring my scent to the mare. The bull circled, posturing and bumping against me. I waited for him to be done and for the female to signal that she would allow me close. The mare nodded to Nahiam, and he gave me one last solid bump before moving away.

Freah writhed as another contraction hit, her pained cry driving me forward. She was beautiful, with shimmering scales of purple and ocean green. Her fins and mane of gleaming iridescent gold were breathtaking. I approached her slowly, reaching out to place my hand on her sac, which was bursting. I slid my hands over Freah's belly, trying to feel the eggs within. I found one and traced its shape before moving on to examine the second. As I pressed down, I discovered the third. There wasn't supposed to be a third! In most cases, the mares only laid two. I knew what I had to do, but it would be dangerous.

I swam back to where the worried merfolk waited, and the handlers moved closer to hear.

"It looks like something is blocking the birthing vent. I will need to assist her."

Their voices rose as they all tried responding at once.

"No, you mustn't, Lady Nike!"

"She might die, and this is one of your uncle's prized mares!"

"Can you help her? She is in great pain."

"I will try. I need to get supplies from the office," I said confidently, trying to calm the handlers so the beasts wouldn't sense their distress. "Keep her comfortable and see if she will eat something. I will return."

I swam back to the bar as fast as I could, diving through the water wall and into dry air. My hair and clothes dripped, leaving a watery trail, and my shoes made wet sucking noises as I wove through the busy restaurant. I hurried to Poseidon's office and searched his desk, finally finding the small chest of Atlantean herbs. I opened the lid, and the aroma of salty spices filled the air. I sorted through the sealed vials, finally finding the one I'd been looking for. I lifted the glass, examining the glowing seeds within. Harvested from a rare flower, they would help calm and relax the mare, allowing me to do what needed to be done to help her. I carefully tipped two of the seeds into my hand, and as I replaced the box, I spotted one of Hephaestus's daggers. I picked it up, praying that I wouldn't need to use it. I skipped back down the stairs, Kratos stopping me as I ran by.

"Nike, is everything alright?"

"I hope so," I said breathlessly.

"What do you need that for?" he said, eyeing the dagger.

"The mare is holding her eggs."

"What? Nike, that's dangerous."

305

"I will try these first," I said, showing him the seeds in my other hand, "and hopefully, I won't need the knife."

"Who's going with you?" he asked, his brow furrowed and his hands on his hips.

"I can do this," I said, securing the sheathed dagger to my belt. I looked back at my overprotective brother. "Remember the hybrids of the Pegasus? I managed those just fine."

"Yes, you did, but this is underwater."

"I'm fine." I felt my eyes change again, their silvery glow mimicking the water's reflection. Kratos nodded and patted my shoulder.

"Go on." Kratos pushed me into the sea, and I dove deep to the caves. I could clearly hear Freah's moans.

I asked the handlers to keep Nahiam back, and I cautiously approached Freah. Able to sense her fear and pain, I whispered soothingly, "Easy, girl, easy."

The seeds clutched in my fist glowed brightly the moment they met the sea, and I could feel them heating against my palm. I slid my hands along the mare's neck, and with the help of the handler, managed to get the seeds into her mouth, encouraging her to swallow. Her eyes shone, and her body relaxed, her breathing evening out as the herbs took effect.

The handler looked at me with wide eyes. "Lady Nike, what did you give her? Will it harm the foals?"

I shook my head and shifted back towards the birthing vent. "No, they will be fine. The hippocampi in Atlantis often eat these seeds when laboring."

I took a deep breath of water, exhaled, and very gently slipped my hand into the birthing vent. My fingers grazed the smooth egg, and I understood why they wouldn't come. The first egg had turned and gotten stuck, blocking the others. No wonder Freah had been in such distress.

I could hear Nahiam trumpeting and calling to Freah as the handlers struggled to hold him at bay. He was a good father, and it was his duty to not only protect her and the babies, but he needed to rest with the eggs for them to hatch. The males excreted a gel inside the thin egg sack that gave the foals their pigments and coated them in his scent, protecting them in the sea from predators. Without this, the foals would not survive.

I gently pushed at the slippery orb and was able to get my fingers around it, guiding it free. I cradled the egg tenderly in my hands, and that is when Nahiam broke free. Seeing his mate so quiet and still with me holding *his* foal was too much for the bull. He charged straight for me, his massive body coiled with protective rage, his eyes glowing, all of his spikes flared, and his teeth bared. Nahiam was stopped short, curling in on himself in the water. Kratos gripped his tail and flung the bull back toward the cave entrance, calling out, "Nike, hurry! I'll keep him away, but you need to make it quick!"

307

I was surprised to see Kratos but didn't have time to question it. The bull charged again as I gently laid the egg in the nest and returned to Freah, trusting that my brother would keep us safe. Now that the first one was out, things were progressing naturally, and the second foal arrived moments later. I laid it alongside its sibling and turned back just in time to catch the third. The handler placed glowing sea kelp from Atlantis over the eggs to keep them warm.

As Freah struggled upright and moved to the nest, the handlers and I scurried out of the way. Seeing that we were a safe distance away, Kratos moved out of Nahaim's path as he charged again. Seeing the path clear to his mate and eggs, Nahaim trumpeted his victory. He sped to Freah's side and settled himself into the nest.

Within five minutes, the first egg cracked, and soon all three foals were greeting their parents. Triplets were a rare occurrence among the hippocampi, so this was a very special occasion.

"This is a blessed day!" Japho, one of the handlers, shouted.

"Lady Nike, you have brought a great victory to Lord Poseidon's herd. He will be very proud of you."

"They did all the work. I just helped," I said, beaming with joy.

"You are truly the Goddess of Victory," Kratos said proudly.

We watched as the new foals greeted their parents, and the handlers offered up the krill for them to eat. There was a loud trumpeting behind us. Mien yen, Thanuk, and their two foals arrived to greet the new foals. The two females were sisters, and they shared in each other's joyous occasions.

Mien yen's foals bayed and playfully knocked heads with their cousins. They saw me and nudged the newborns from their nest. Rushing to me, they bumped their heads to mine, showing me love. They swam around me, forming a circle. And one by one, they would charge at me. I, of course, ducked and dodged them. Each squealed with *laughter* as only a Hippocampus foal could. It was their favorite game.

This birthing brought my uncle's herd up by a baker's dozen, thirteen new hippocampus foals. I knew my uncle would be pleased.

Nahiam and Freah looked on as their foals swam around me. Their expressions of sheer happiness were familiar. They rubbed their heads together, hers below his as they rested on the nest. I had seen this look on Lord Zeus's and Lady Hera's faces many millennia ago as they watched us young gods playing in the gardens below them. Same look of pride, contentment, but most of all, love.

PRAGMA

ENDURING

LOVE

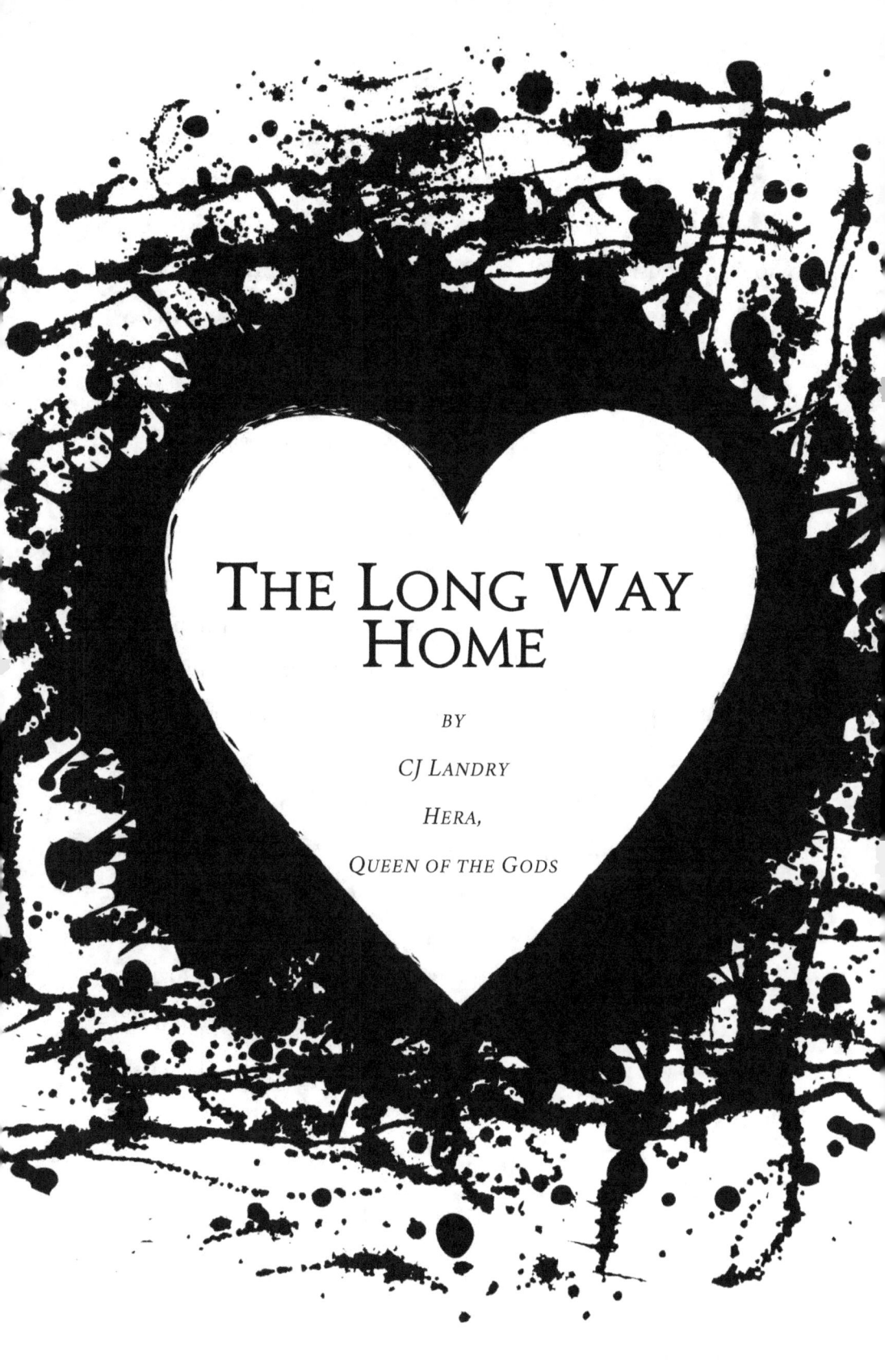

THE LONG WAY HOME

BY

CJ LANDRY

HERA,

QUEEN OF THE GODS

If you've gotten to this point in the book, I can only assume that you are here for the epic love story that is Hera and Zeus. So, let me not disappoint. To begin, I will tell you something obvious. My husband used to fuck everything that moved. Now let me tell you something that you may not already know, but that will become obvious. I take after my father.

Almost every story about every god has a good bit of exaggeration in it. Sadly, my stories do not exaggerate my levels of jealousy. I did not start out that way, though. You would think being locked in my father's pocket dimension for so many years would cause us to go crazy…even if just a little. I can't speak to my siblings' experience, but while mine was dark and lonely, it was easy to compartmentalize it as just a bad dream once I was out and in the sunlight. My husband was the biggest reason for that. He always shined so bright as to chase away my shadows, at least, until he became the cause of the shadows.

I will share some memories with you so you can follow our love story from the beginning. I ask not for your sympathy or your righteousness or even your disdain. Our story is our story, and the road we took is the reason we've stayed together so long. There is nothing about our history that I would change. Not even the bad parts.

What is it the mortals say? Buckle up because it's going to be a bumpy ride.

I was younger...not the teen I had been, but still young. I hadn't been free of my father's dimension for long, and I was still getting used to no longer being surrounded by my darkness. I sat in my room, staring out the window, watching the gods as they went about their lives. How much they took for granted. My throat tightened as I wondered what my life would have been had I not been captive all of my years.

Even now that I was free, I barely spoke to anyone. I had not used my voice much for conversation after I stopped visiting my siblings in their realms. I yearned to know how to be at ease around the other gods. I felt my chest constrict with loneliness and was about to turn away from the window lest someone see my tears when I heard my name.

"Hera!"

I looked out into the yard and saw my brothers talking. Hades was so serious, but you could still feel his capacity for love. Poseidon was loud and laughing. I don't think he would be uncomfortable anywhere. My eyes were drawn to the other god sitting with them. Zeus. The brother we didn't know. The youngest. Our savior. He saw me looking and smiled so big I could see his blue eyes sparkle even from this far away.

"My fair lady, Hera. Won't you join us today? Your face would surely brighten the darkest of days, and my heart yearns for your smile." He winked and bowed low.

I snorted. "I have no doubt that your…heart does not lack for willing smiles. You do not need mine."

"Come now, Hera. Surely you wouldn't want me to waste away to a wisp of nothing." He stood and placed his palm over his heart. "You are my life, and I cannot live without you!" He put the back of his other hand against his forehead in false sorrow. "Your smile is sustenance for my soul."

He was so ridiculously dramatic. I couldn't stop the short laugh that rushed past my lips. "If my smile is all your soul requires, I know many goddesses who would be disappointed. Take your frivolousness away. I'm saving my smiles for a god who only needs to see my face and doesn't look for it in others."

His hands clutched at his chest, and he gasped. "You wound me, my lady. Your face is all my eyes look for."

"And yet you look for it everywhere else but where it is. Go away, Zeus. I have better things to do with my time than listen to your romantic drivel."

As I was closing my shutters, I heard him laugh and say, "I will marry you one day!"

I shook my head and waited until my shutters were completely closed before I allowed myself the smile he begged for, and I so wanted to give. I knew what he was about, but my heart didn't care.

Thankfully, I ruled my heart better than he ruled his godhood. But sometimes...my heart hoped.

I was walking in our gardens picking flowers and plotting my next conversation with Zeus. I didn't want to seem desperate because a lady doesn't behave that way, even if that's how she feels. She must always appear and act as if she is just out of reach. It was difficult for me, though. Even as I was behaving like a lady and hoping to get his attention, he kept getting sidetracked with women who threw themselves at him. I wasn't too worried. I knew that the women he was with were just flings and nothing serious.

I continued my stroll through the fragrant blooms, my steps faltering when I heard hushed voices coming from a clearing just ahead of me. I was going to ignore them because it sounded like two lovers who were meeting in secret, but then I recognized their voices.

My heart dropped, and I felt the blood rushing in my ears, drowning out all sound. I wanted to freeze in place. I did not want my feet to carry me further. I did not want my eyes to see her betrayal. But I had no say in the matter. I moved forward and quietly pushed the brush aside in time to see Zeus in a passionate embrace with my sister Demeter. My world crumbled. I felt betrayed. I felt embarrassed. There was really no reason for any of these emotions because I'd never told her how I felt. I thought, as my sister, she would know. She should have been able to see the devastation on my face. My breath caught in my throat, and they pulled away from their kiss and looked in my direction. Mortified, I ran, and I kept running every time I saw Demeter.

She had no clue how I felt, and as her sister, she wanted to talk to me about her feelings for Zeus and their upcoming wedding. I couldn't bring myself to tell her how I died a little inside each time I saw them together. I also couldn't bring myself to not be there for her. She was my sister, and she deserved to be happy. I was sitting at my vanity, attempting to get ready for the day, when Demeter burst into my room.

"Sister! Oh, I'm so glad you're in here!" Demeter smiled brightly as I turned to face her.

"What can I do for you today?" I watched as she fell onto my bed with a dramatic sigh.

"I'm in love! Can you believe it? Me? In love?" She looked at the ceiling, but not before I saw the excitement in her eyes. She giggled and held her breath. "He loves me back! He asked me to marry him. Can you imagine?" She bit her lip and turned to face me again, waiting for something that I couldn't give.

After a long moment, she sat up and faced me. "Aren't you going to ask me who?"

I looked down at my dress and brushed imaginary dirt from it. I didn't need to ask. I knew who it was, and it broke my heart. I felt my chin tremble, tears threatening to fall. I was afraid to open my mouth. If I did, I wouldn't be able to stop the tears, and my sister didn't deserve them. So, I cleared my throat and tilted my head back to look at her.

"Who?"

She giggled and then sighed happily, flopping back onto the bed. "Zeus! You will be in the wedding, of course. You have to be. Nothing would make me happier!"

She went on about her plans for the wedding and what her new life would be like. She talked about the husband Zeus would be. She went on and on, and the only thing I could think of was that yet another woman would be in his bed, and I hadn't even felt the warmth of his arms.

It was painful watching their relationship. Even more so when Persephone was born. Zeus was no saint, though I suspect he tried to treat Demeter as best as he could. I wondered if Demeter realized how much like our mother she was and how much that was a factor in why he married her.

I watched them, though. A silent penance for coveting something I couldn't have. It all changed when Persephone was taken. Demeter became something…different. Not that I could blame her. I'm not sure I would have behaved any differently. But the side effect of Persephone's kidnapping was Demeter turning away from Zeus. I could see his frustration every time he tried to engage her and was ignored. Eventually, their marriage was over, and though I wanted my sister to be happy, I couldn't help but feel relieved that she was no longer with him.

You would think he would notice me after Demeter. After all, we are sisters. We spent a lot of time together. He would have laid eyes on me multiple times. So many times, in fact, that he would have to notice how I felt. You would be wrong. Years later, after Zeus and I had been together for a while, I asked him what he saw in Demeter that made him choose her over me. Do you know what he said?

"Demeter reminded me of our mother. Of all the relationships I have had over the years, the one I had with Mother was the strongest. She loved me unconditionally, regardless of what I did. There was never any judgment in her eyes or censure in her heart. She saw all of who I was and loved me despite it. I thought I would have the same relationship with Demeter."

After Zeus and Demeter split, I set about trying to get his attention. I had to make him see that I would be the best wife for him and that he needed me. I made sure I would *accidentally* run into him several times throughout the day. I dressed in such a way as to look alluring, but not easy. Everyone knows it is the chase that entices men. I saw hundreds of women throw themselves at him, and it worked. He slept with them, and if they were lucky, they got him for a handful of days, but he never stayed. There was no point. He had already gotten everything they had to give, and they had nothing more than their bodies to offer. I saw this, and I planned.

I watched Zeus as much as possible, so I could learn what was important to him. When I figured that out, I hosted dinners for my siblings. During these dinners, I sat Zeus near enough to me so we could talk about things important to him, like politics and the state of Olympus. I could tell he enjoyed our interactions. I saw the excitement in his eyes. I had hoped to keep his attention like this, but he always drew others in, especially our brothers. Though I started the conversation, I was never a part of it once the men began talking.

I attempted to get him alone by asking him to walk with me in the garden. But he would always turn me down by saying that was a woman's idea of fun, and the only time he wanted to spend in the garden was when he was getting naked. I thought he was mocking me, but eventually, I realized he didn't *see* me. I did a wonderful job of getting the conversation going for the men. So good, in fact, that Zeus didn't want to leave. It frustrated me more and more each time. I was practically throwing myself at him, and all he could think about was hanging out with our brothers.

When Mnemosyne caught his attention, I realized what I had done. I had positioned myself in his life as another brother, and he completely ignored the fact that I was a woman. Sadly, Zeus could only see women as physical beings. A place to go to rest his head and find comfort in their arms. Even though I didn't want to be seen as an object, I had done myself a disservice by ignoring my feminine attributes. Mnemosyne had no trouble using her body to get his attention, but she was smart. She lured him in by teasing him physically and then hooking him emotionally, reminiscing with him on the way things used to be. She caught him with two of his weaknesses, the female form and shared history.

I couldn't compete with that. So, I watched their courtship from afar and felt my heart break a little more every day, until I had nothing left to give. My love turned to bitterness, anger, and jealousy. These were emotions I had never had cause to feel before, and as such, I had no clue how to deal with them.

Mnemosyne and Zeus's marriage didn't last long, but they quickly had nine children. Zeus loved the act but gave no thoughts to the consequences of his carnal passions, and he couldn't even keep track of the kids he'd already fathered. Everyone knew that Mnemosyne tried to keep him around by locking him in with the babies. I saw him leave her a little more with each child, and by the time the ninth one came, he had already forgotten her name.

I was so emotionally wrecked by this time that there was really nothing for me to do but watch him jump from one bed to another. I'm sure you've heard the stories and know that he wasn't only fond of women. He sought anyone with a pretty face. Who was I to compete with that? I was so deeply in love with him and so completely broken by that love. I felt nothing but echoes of pain every time I saw him with someone new. I had no smiles for anyone and had forgotten the sound of my own laughter. I had become numb to everything. My sisters noticed but didn't know how to handle it. As I said, we had all been in our own personal hell growing up, and I had stopped visiting my siblings fairly early on. They did not understand what was going on with me, so they had no clue how to help me. I didn't confide in anyone. I couldn't remember the last time I walked past a mirror and saw a smile on my face. How would that even feel?

Oh, don't get me wrong. I wasn't innocent. I had my own dalliances before my husband. The stories always get that wrong. But my heart was never completely theirs, and it was selfish of me to demand they gave all of themselves when I belonged to him. So eventually, I stopped. I no longer went out of my way to run into Zeus. In fact, I did the opposite. I started doing my best to *not* run into him. I tried so very hard to get over him, but it seemed the Fates had other ideas.

The gods were having a party, something that wasn't a surprise. After all, what else is there to do? I had stopped going to them a long time ago, but I went to this one for some reason.

I don't remember what I wore or what I ate or who I spoke to or if I spoke to anyone at all. I remember standing off to the side of the room, lost in my thoughts and staring out into the night through a large window.

I felt someone stop beside me, and after a few minutes, he said, "It's beautiful, isn't it?"

"It's complicated." I took a deep breath and inhaled his scent, letting it fill my lungs without hesitation.

"Anything worth having is."

"It's a lie, though, and I cannot abide lies."

"How can the night be a lie?" He chuckled, and I could hear equal parts of dismissiveness and intrigue.

"What do you see when you look at it?" I rested one of my hands against my neck and tilted my head, only vaguely wanting to hear his answer.

"I think the better question would be, what do *you* see when you look at it? What is it about the night that distresses you so?"

I wasn't going to answer. I was going to ignore him as he had me all those years. I was going to leave him aching for the sound of my voice, the way I ached. My heart betrayed me, though, and I sighed. "It is simple enough to look at, I suppose. Watching Nyx and Erebus painting themselves across the sky. It's easy to not see past the first layer. But even the night has shadows, and I know what evil can hide in shadows."

"Evil?" He laughed lightheartedly. "Surely there can be no evil in something so beautiful as the night? It gives us the confidence to expose ourselves to others without having to see judgment in their eyes. It grants us a piece of safety if you will."

"Safety? Judgment? What is it you know about these two things?" I dug my nails into my palms to keep from spinning around to face him. My temper had gotten stronger, and the hold I had on it had become tenuous. "You go from bed to bed, barely learning your lovers' names, laughing at the hurt you cause. Do you see the pain that follows in your wake? No. Because by the time your lover has realized you are gone, you're with someone else. Of course, you don't see the lie in the darkness. You burn so brightly that the shadows run and hide until you're gone. Go away, Zeus. I have no more use for you."

I felt a small tear fall from my eye as I realized the truth to my final words. I had nothing left to give. No love to feel. No happiness to share. I was an empty husk, and he was too late. He was quiet for so long I thought he'd left until I heard a whisper behind me.

"I'm sorry."

I felt him hesitate, and I felt my stupid heart beat at his words. "Should the scorpion be sorry for his stinger? Should the fire be sorry for its burns? They can no more help what they are than you can. A lesson I wish I had learned sooner." I turned to him and saw a hesitation in his eyes when he looked at me. He almost made me believe he actually saw me. I knew better, though.

"It is late, and I must get some rest. Excuse me." I curtsied briefly and made my way around him and out of the party.

Some time passed after that night, and Zeus started showing up whenever I was around. He flirted with me. He tried to make me laugh like it was his new mission in life. I had seen this dance before when he met someone new that he wanted to bed. I was too jaded, though, and wasn't falling for it. It took him months before he wore me down, and I agreed to spend time with him. I should have known better.

Things were going too well. He was too solicitous, too available to me, too...well, just *too* everything. But even a victim will love her abuser given enough time. Not that I was ever a victim, but things could have gone differently. We were together several months before I finally allowed myself to relax. I had been watching his every move, waiting for him to screw up. He knew it, too, and I was sure he would behave. Or so I thought.

Up to that point, I had done everything I could to control our relationship. To make sure I didn't get hurt by his lies. He had been on his best behavior, and I couldn't find fault in anything he had done. It was as if he were a completely different god. He had *finally* sown his wild oats and was ready to settle down. He had chosen *me*. Out of everyone he could have had, he chose **me**. That was what finally wore down my defenses. On the day I realized this, I felt a crack in my heart heal. On that day, I was feeling especially giving and decided to visit him without sending word ahead. I had no reason to believe that would be a problem. As I approached his door, I heard voices inside.

"I don't care about anyone else, Zeus. Everyone knows your proclivities. But surely you realize you can't leave me now. I'm pregnant."

"Shhh. I said nothing about leaving you, but you know she won't be happy about this. She might make things difficult."

"Difficult? Everyone knows she's loved you from the beginning. Just like everyone knows you've ignored her. Of course, she's going to make this difficult! Just tell her you don't love her, and we can get on with our lives."

It got quiet. So quiet, I heard the blood pounding in my ears. The pounding got louder and louder until I could hear nothing else. My vision literally went red, and I blasted the door open to find Zeus half-naked and wrapped around a half-naked Leto. I was beyond anger now. I was beyond any emotion except for rage born from the injustice of loving a man who couldn't love me back. I. Was. Livid. My eyes latched onto Leto.

"You think I'm going to be difficult? You have no idea how weak of a word choice that was. You stole my love from me, and for that, I will steal yours from you. You will *never* give birth as long as you are on land…"

I won't bore you with the story. The old scribes captured it almost exactly. What I will tell you, though, is that I was done with Zeus ignoring me. He was going to marry me whether he liked it or not. Oddly enough, it didn't take much convincing. Much later in our marriage, he would tell me how much he loved seeing me full of power and in charge like that. If only I'd have known that from the beginning.

Let's fast forward a bit. The brothers were about to divvy up the world. Poseidon ruled the sea, Hades ruled the Underworld, and Zeus ruled the skies and the gods. There was no way I was going to let someone else rule by his side. Not after all of that pain and heartache he put me through. No. I deserved to be the Queen of the Gods, and nothing was going to stand in my way.

As the myths told, he wasn't faithful. Don't think I was unaware. A queen does what is best for her kingdom, and as long as I let him dip his godhood where he wanted, I got to rule. The only time we had issues was when he fathered *another* child. It was the only thing I asked...no, begged of him, and he couldn't even give me that.

Eventually, as all things must, he grew up, settled down, and realized he couldn't live without me. It took him way too long as far as I was concerned, but I am forever grateful to the Fates that he did. Our love has lasted through countless years of heartache and pain, and eventually, we got it right.

THE BEST THING THAT NEVER HAPPENED TO ME

BY

DAN DOLAN

ERIS,

GOD/GODDESS OF

DISCORD

Ever feel lonely?

Well, I've got good news for you. There's a secret that parents don't tell you. *Every* child is a twin.

Simply because every single time a child is born, the ideal child their parents dream they *could* be, is pushed out right alongside them.

Being the *daughter,* assigned female at birth, of the King and Queen of the Gods? Oh, my. My parents had *great* things planned for me.

I never quite lived up to those great things.

Now, it wasn't all bad. When I was young, things seemed *okay.* I mean, children don't question the nature of their reality, so to me, living in a shimmering palace floating among the clouds was not unusual. What everyone *did* agree was unusual was me. I didn't fit with the idealized picture they had painted for themselves and for who their children were supposed to be.

No one seemed to *get me,* as the modern generation of disenfranchised would say.

My parents *tried.* Well, my mother did, at least. She claimed to love me. Ultimately, it seemed like the, *I have to love you because you're my kid,* kind of love more than anything else. Dad always blew a little more hot and cold, and by *blew,* I quite literally mean actual storm clouds.

Then there were my siblings. Don't get frostbite from the warm cheer as I say that.

I'll limit my assessment to the purebloods I was raised with, the legitimate *marital* children. You know, the ones my mom didn't go full natural disaster on for simply existing. If I waxed poetic about the half-siblings, we'd be here all century.

They were, in alphabetical order: Angelos, Goddess of Purity (I know you've never heard of her but she was no angel, *believe* me!), Ares, God of War (egomaniac), Arge, a less famous Goddess of the Hunt (major Artemis envy), Enyo, Goddess of Bloodshed (she is the Diet Pepsi to my Coke Zero), Eileithyia, Goddess of Childbirth (major mommy issues), Eleutheria, Goddess of Liberty (can't get off her soapbox), Hebe, Goddess of Youth (acts like the baby), and finally Hephaestus, God of the Forge (the actual baby).

I had varying levels of disinterest to outright irritation with all of them. It was this strange paradox of being constantly surrounded and yet being totally alone. To be fair, we did occasionally try to get along, but it always ended in some *terrible* scene.

Mother would always tease us when we misbehaved. Obviously, I got it the most. "Oh, your brother Ugeus was the same way before your father destroyed him. Be careful," she'd say, "you don't want to end up like your sister, Gramia." If you're saying to yourself, *I've never even heard of Gramia.* That's the point.

She'd always say that these were our siblings that Dad hadn't just tossed out. He'd erased all memory of them. It kind of makes getting grounded seem not that bad, right?

You see, the worst thing to a god is being forgotten. Death is not something we are hardwired to fear like mortals. In some form or another, we'll always go on, but being forgotten?

That's our death.

And for the longest time, I didn't think it was that big of a deal. I mean, people forgot about me every day. Or I should say, they *tried* to.

Eileithyia would sometimes let me play with her many, many baby dolls, but she'd get mad when their heads would inevitably pop off. Angelos was too busy having nervous breakdowns. Arge would let me hunt with her occasionally but didn't like it when I rooted for the animals. Eleutheria loved my flair for drama. Apparently, I just wasn't dramatic about the *right* things. Hephaestus was a glorified fetus, and Hebe was too busy trying to steal focus from Hephaestus.

That left the two I should have had the most in common with.

It could have been any number of times. Ares and Enyo were playing war again. You would think I'd be joining in, but I *didn't do it right*, according to them. Ares on one side and Enyo on the other, their toy soldiers set up in between like the most complicated game of chess ever mounted. It was so meticulous and *ordered* that I could barely be blamed when I found myself messing it up.

"Eris!" Ares would inevitably wail. "You've ruined it!" With a stamp of his foot punctuating every syllable. Enyo was much less verbal in her reproach, the poor girl nearly foaming at the mouth.

"It's war, kiddos!" I would laugh, in part to try to get them to laugh, too. Trying to recoup this now seemingly failed attempt at sibling bonding. "You were taking all the fun out of it!"

"You're the only one spoiling a good time here, Eris," Ares seethed, which foreshadowed *years* of seething for him, let me tell you.

Enyo would snarl, and I would be forced to show her once more why Ares tolerated her and not me. I was something he couldn't control, and as he helped her up, I would walk away. It *always* ended with me having to walk away. They never had to leave, no matter who started it. Only me. I was out the door far more often than I was ever coming back through it.

One of those many times, it ended with me on a desolate cliff right at the edge of Mount Olympus. My only company was one of my blackbirds. Even back then, they flocked to me. My little omens following me, assuring me I could count on the comfort of life always being so dire.

My favorite at that time was a little roughhousing crow I called Proktókefáli, which roughly translated to Butthead. She ruffled her feathers at me indignantly as I relayed the story.

"They think that's fun? All those marching orders and plans..." I rolled my eyes. "It's so structured, and there are too many rules, and it's all just so...*boring!*"

The moment the word left my mouth, the cliff seemed to darken even as I faced nothing but the bright blue sky. The shadows twisted together, forming the shape of a female figure before falling back to reveal a woman with long pitch-black hair and piercing eyes.

"That does sound boring. So," her voice was silky as *hell*, "what would you want to do instead?"

And as far as I can remember, that's the first time someone asked me what I wanted.

"Who are you?"

"That's right. We haven't quite met. I'm Atë, Goddess of Mischief and Ruin. I'm your sister." That wasn't hard to believe, given our family tree. I'd believe any god if they claimed to be related to me. The part that was hard to believe was that she was talking to me, of her own free will.

For a moment, we were just locked in eye contact before she gestured for me to talk.

"And you are…?" She smiled, prodding me.

"I'm Eris."

Something about the name seemed to register with her, and her smile faltered before returning even wider.

"It's destiny." She laughed.

"What do you want?" I asked, my patience waning, my eyes narrowing.

"I think that's what I just asked you." She giggled again.

"Why?"

"Why?" she repeated, bewildered.

"Yeah, why are you here talking to me? Asking about…me? Why?"

"Because you're not boring." She winked at me with a smile. "So, I ask again, what do *you* want to do?"

I paused to think.

"I want to mess something up."

"We can arrange that." She smiled and took my hand.

Atë took me to a great open field filled with creatures that seemed a pale imitation of my father, brothers, and uncles. Similar in form but not in power, they didn't shine or intimidate like gods would. Instead, they were little more than bronze-colored brutes, grunting and thrashing about in an engorged show of martial strength.

"This is something Dad refers to as *humanity*," she said, disgust dripping from her voice. "Believe it or not, this is the third attempt. Gramps started the first out of gold, but they didn't last. Then Dad tried with silver, and they turned out to be spoiled little brats and got wasted. Now we have these lunkheads."

I looked out at the sea of bronze-skinned brutes with mixed emotions dancing through my mind. These *humans* were a terrible concoction of negative impulses and the most twisted of thoughts that boiled to the surface with not even the flimsiest of filters to stop them.

I found them quite delightful.

"What is their purpose?"

"Hell if I know," Atë sighed, "Dad's trying to prove he can get something right that Gramps failed gloriously at? That's the thing, Eris. Everyone is just trying to prove they are the greatest." She shrugged. Even as she said it, it occurred to me just how true that was.

We walked down toward them, and a thrill of anticipation went through me.

"There are no females?" I asked suddenly, having noticed as we walked through their ramshackle huts that all of those creatures were, at least biologically, men at first glance.

"Dad says they don't deserve them, but between you and me, I think it's the exact opposite."

"What do you mean?"

"You'll see." She said no more.

We mingled through their ranks, and soon enough, any progress they had been making was wiped out by their own hands. A whisper there, a push here, and soon they were revealed to be no more than animals. Any pretense of civilization was washed clean away.

As they thrashed and tore each other to smithereens, a warm feeling spread within me, a fullness. Something about this fed something in me that had been hungry for a *long* time. Every time I was ignored, abandoned, told to go away, and every piece of nourishment or affirmation I was denied. It felt like I was getting that *right now*.

Another illusion fell away for me. I now knew that I was to Atë as these creatures were to the gods. Watching her work was to understand what it is truly like to be the *greatest* rather than just *try* to be. She was that *twin* I was talking about. The idealized, perfect version of what I *should've* been. Everything I would never be, and yet she seemed to like me anyway.

That was enough for me.

As the years went by, Atë and I caused havoc and destruction with reckless abandon. A lot of it was done with Mom and Dad's implicit approval, much to the other gods' chagrin. However, Atë was much more in *high demand*, often going off on secret missions for Dad and avoiding Mom's wrath for being *illegitimate*.

When I was with Atë, I was something close to wonderful. I even built up something of a reputation for myself, one that Enyo once more tried to copy for herself. I became feared and worshipped, but none of it mattered because Atë had already given me the thing I had always wanted. Someone who wanted me around.

This kind of chaotic merriment went on as what these human beings would call *time* passed. Most often, I stood in awe at her strength and sheer perfection. But every once in a while, I would see a crack on her surface, and in one moment, true vulnerability.

It was then I received yet another first from her. She was truly the first person to open up to me.

"Where've you been?" she asked that fine day with a wry smile.

"The Garden of the Hesperides," I said smugly.

"Why?" She laughed.

"Well, Mom just surprised Ares and Enyo with gifts, and all I got was some nice fresh air as she walked past me. So, I decided to give myself something from her instead." I pulled out a fresh golden apple.

"Nice."

"Sometimes, I think she likes you more than she likes me, which is the opposite of how she usually interacts with her kids vs. Dad's many *other* kids. No offense."

"None taken." She smirked.

"I'm gonna plant this and make my own apples...my way..."

"Your mother can be harsh, but," a somewhat somber look crossed her face, "she loves her kids. You know that."

"She doesn't even use my name, you know," I practically whispered, my prideful voice slipping as my eyes averted.

"Oh?"

"Yeah, it's always d*ear* or even sometimes *you*." I sighed.

"You know why?" she asked, and something about the *way* she did so made me think that she already knew.

"Why?" I raised my eyes to meet hers once more.

"Eris was...my mom's name too." It was her turn for hushed tones.

"Do you think that's why he named me that?" She didn't answer, but a shared moment passed between us. "Am I like her?" I pressed on.

"How would I know?" She tried to say this flippantly but wasn't quite successful, the last syllable was almost a sob. "I barely knew her. She dropped me off on Olympus and went home with my millions of siblings that I also barely know."

For some reason, the image of her coming to me on the mountainside sprung forth in my mind.

"We could call each other nicknames...if it makes...if you want?" I smiled, trying to will the mood to lighten.

She laughed.

"Okay." She nodded, "For you, what about Malum or Mal? It means both *bad* and *apple*." She smiled and gestured to the gilded fruit in my palms.

"You'll be Kallis," I said, the word almost inaudible but I refused to break eye contact.

"That means—" she started.

"I know," I said.

And we said no more, just enjoying our moment. Together. For when we were together? I was the Kallis too... I was the greatest.

When I was alone? I tended to fall back on bad decision making.

As I said, I enjoyed people who enjoyed me. One such person—okay, *person* was a bit of a broad term in this case—was the monstrous Typhon. A volcanic force of nature, quite literally. It would turn out as he was born of Gaea and Hell itself. The Earth Mother was as angry as she usually was back then and wanted a being so powerful, he could destroy all the many gods that had failed her. She copulated with Tartarus, the living embodiment of our version of what you would call Hell, and out came Typhon.

He was actually a lot of fun.

You know what they say when you're having fun? Well, it all happened so darn fast, me and him were getting along pretty well. It was just nice to have more than one friend for a change. I even introduced him to a nice girl. Echidna was a great gal. She could unhinge her jaw and everything.

Well, before I knew it, Typhon and Dad were going at it, the world was falling apart at the seams, and everyone was upset that I didn't find that upsetting.

To me, it seemed like good family fun, at least at first. Then Typhon got Dad on the ropes, or should I say by the *sinews*. Suddenly everyone's screaming and taking off on an Egyptian vacation.

I don't know what they were all upset about, and what was with the animal head disguises? That was weird, even for us. I swear I thought we were all having a good time. Yes, he may have tried to destroy creation and specifically wipe Pops off the map, but he had a great sense of humor. And for Pete's sake, Dad was up and at 'em just a decade or two later. Well, with the help of Nike, that goodie-two-shoes he and Mom took in a while back. It all seemed like it was gonna be a blast, but by the time the dust cleared, Typhon was gone, and I was the only one smiling.

I thought for sure that was it. That was when I was gonna get obliterated, and all memory of me would be erased, just like Mom had warned me over and over again.

But then she appeared again, as she always did when I needed her most. Atë, returning from some grand mission she had been on, asked to speak with Dad alone. I didn't know what they said, but when Dad returned, he was alone and still very unhappy. He raised his hands and then darkness.

To start with, being stuck in an urn with a bunch of other dark and nasty gods wasn't as sexy as it sounds. We were all packed in like veal, and I kept getting the feeling that slaughter day was fast approaching.

I began to know what a caged tiger must feel. I'm no good like this. I need to be loose and out there! This place...this place was heavy and shadowed, like a summer night during one of Daddy's storms. No, more like a storm in a bottle. Too small and too tight. I couldn't breathe!

It was driving me mad. A car trip I would become quite familiar with as my life went along.

"You okay?" a soft, sincere voice asked. I turned to see Elpis, Goddess of Hope. She was a literal light in the darkness, and a soft glow emanated from her as she smiled brightly at me.

"How can you be grinning?" I asked as I scratched at my temples.

"I'm serving a purpose. *We* are serving a purpose." She somehow smiled even brighter, and for a moment, I could clearly see myself dismembering her. I guess she did represent hope after all.

"Eris!" someone called my name.

I turned from hope herself to see ruination, and I smiled. Frankly, I was actually a little surprised she even recognized me. I was so sure this would be the thing that made Dad wipe me out of the history books.

340

"Atë!!!" I rushed to embrace her. "How did they manage to get you?! The Kallis! The greatest of all time?!?"

"Long story, don't ask Dad about it when we get out of here. *Trust me.*" She laughed, but there was something in her eyes that told me she meant it.

"So, what's going on out there?! I've forgotten what it was like outside of this place," I said overdramatically, shaking her lightly for humorous effect.

"Dad's trying out humanity again."

"Again?!"

"I know, right? Prometheus kind of was the one to mess it up this time for a change of pace. But guess what? He's finally giving them ladies..." She smirked.

"Oh, really?"

"Yes. As a *punishment.*"

"Figures." I laughed.

"He's given them a trial run." She, too, was stifling a laugh. "He gave them one to start with. Her name's Pandora, and this urn we're in is a gift for her."

"Great... we've been reduced to a gift with purchase." I flopped down as she gave in to the laughter.

"Trust me. I think you'll like where this is going." She smiled knowingly.

I did. The stupid woman popped the lid open, and all of us inside had a blast. We popped out of that thing like we were going to a rave.

Terror and torment all around us, and this new batch of humans were losing their tiny minds. And there was Dad, laughing his head off. Maybe we weren't so different after all.

Things seemed good for a while after that. Atë and I were back in the king's good graces, and hell, even the humans managed to bounce back. I guess Dad had finally found the right recipe to get that concept off the ground.

However, one day Atë asked to meet with me in secret. If I didn't know any better, I'd have even said she seemed *spooked*. But she was the Kallis, the greatest. Nothing scared her, right?

"Listen, Dad's having another kid," she said, her tone deathly serious.

"So, what else is new?" I scoffed.

"No, this one is different! He's got a lot of plans for him," she snapped, causing me to whip my head up to lock eyes with her.

"What's wrong?"

"Nothing." She meant *something*. "It's just...your mom has asked me for a favor, and who knows, maybe this'll be my way to get on her good side?" She laughed without any mirth to it. "I just...I have a feeling, and I wanted to say, you are enough, Eris. You don't need me. You are the greatest, even without me."

"What? No. You are my Kallis...without you I—"

"You don't *need* me, Eris," she snapped. "You'll be fine on your own...if anything happens." Something about the way she said it, it was as if she knew.

"What are you even talking about?" I laughed, actually trying to disperse the tension for *once*.

She scoffed.

"Forget about it," Atë said with a smile. "Let's go kick up some ruckus."

It was just a short while later that I found myself doing my own dirty work for my mother. She'd set me on some women who had elevated other goddesses above her as patron to their sex. As someone who solely considered myself a woman back then, language hadn't evolved quite enough yet to fully express how I felt about my gender. I had mixed feelings about it, to say the least.

Nonetheless, it was some form of affection or at least *attention* from Mother, and that was a starting point.

All it took was a little *push*.

Their peace, love, and sisterhood went right out the window. Some of my family would be surprised to know what kind of violence women were capable of. A whisper here, a nudge there, and the fine ladies were taking chunks out of each other with their bare hands.

"You know they meant no harm." This voice was familiar. I turned to see Elpis, Goddess of Hope, once more glowing in my general direction. Her hand laid gently on the corpse of one of the women.

"Their intentions were not my concern." I shrugged. "Shouldn't you still be in the urn?"

"I am." She smiled calmly with a nod.

"Uh-huh." I narrowed my eyes at her, her serenity making me all the angrier.

She looked at me with an expression I could hardly describe, but I later came to realize it was pity.

I was about to rip her a new one, but a tremendous boom shook me from my rhythm. The sound was deafening. I looked to the mount behind us, and there, near the very same spot where I'd met Atë for the first time, a gigantic dark cloud loomed. Lightning sparked from its ebony billows even as the thunder roared around us.

"What in Tartarus...?"

I was mildly curious but also a little excited at the prospect of drama being kicked up. My eyes widened as the storm took on truly epic proportions. The sounds of it were unlike any storm I'd heard, more like a battle.

"Hopeless times ahead," Elpis whispered behind me. "I hope when they come, you find someone more compassionate to you than you were to these women," she said without malice, but I still wanted to bite back.

"I have someone." But even as the words left my lips, I stopped short. "I mean, I think I had a friend once...she was the greatest. Her name was..." I felt a single tear fall down my cheek as I realized...

I couldn't remember her name.

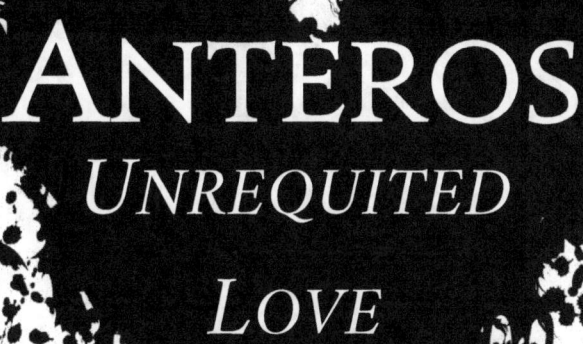

ANTEROS

UNREQUITED

LOVE

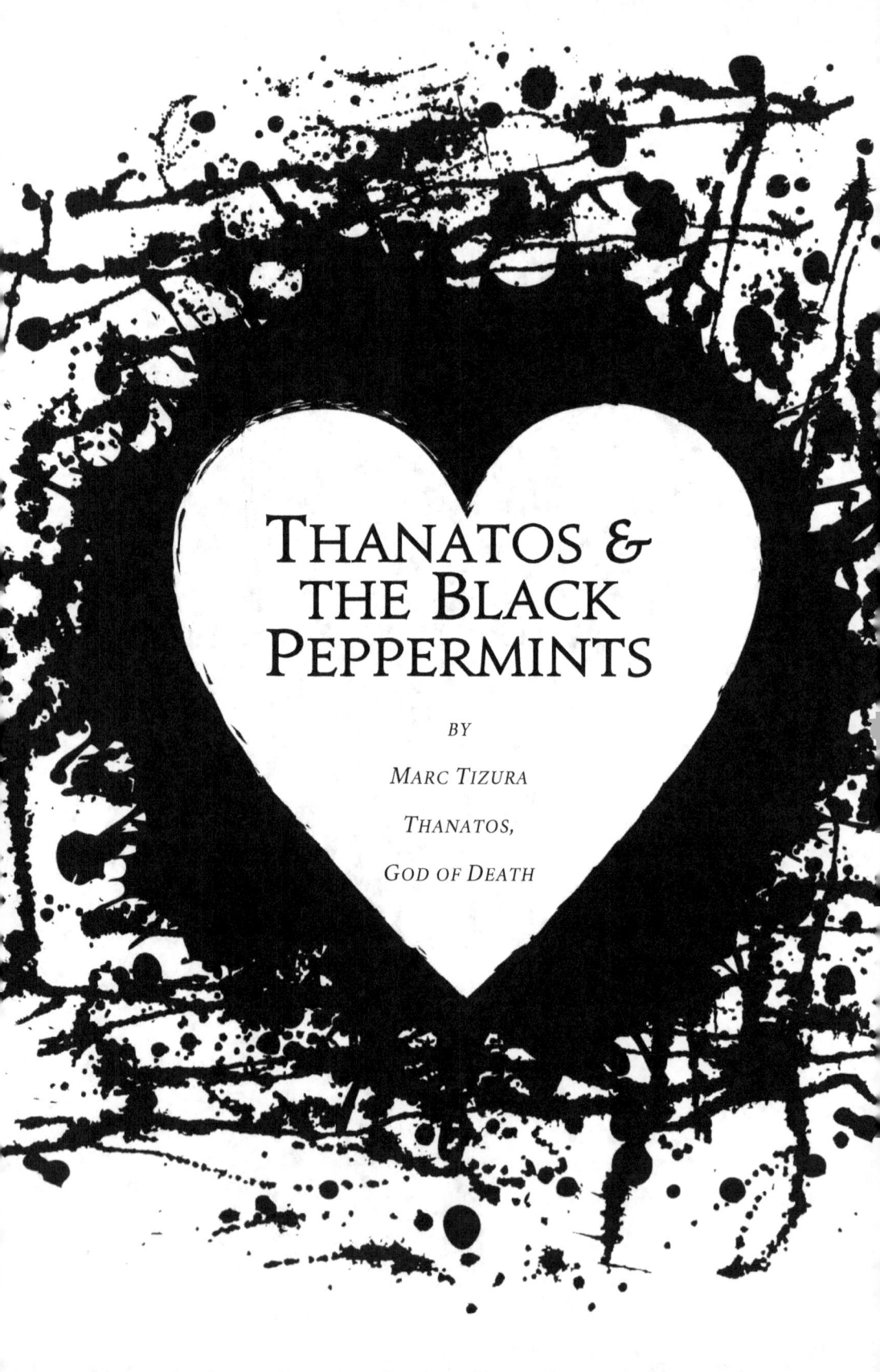

THANATOS & THE BLACK PEPPERMINTS

BY

MARC TIZURA

THANATOS,

GOD OF DEATH

Well, it's nearly Valentine's Day again, and I find myself walking across the factory floor, followed closely by my assistant, Nick. At this time of the year, my candy company releases very special edition candies—heart-shaped, black peppermints. My mind often wanders back to the moment I first tasted them, those dark and creamy-smooth, minty sweets. Black peppermints would become my favorite candy and a signature confection for my company, Mr. T's Sweet and Sundae Shoppe.

All production on the floor stops as we arrive. Ever since we opened for business, back in nineteen-eighty, I have sampled the first little black heart off the line. I always strive to recreate the original that was gifted to me so long ago. Of course, I do *love* peppermint and have since changed the recipe to increase the intensity of the peppermint flavor. As I said before, these are special to me.

Nick and I reach the end of the conveyor belt where the candies await us, and everyone on the factory floor stands around waiting for me to sample one. It is a tradition. I pick one up and run my fingers over its smooth texture. I draw it to my nose, inhaling the faint scent of mint. Just think, we used to pick mint leaves and chew them; how uncivilized, how barbaric. I hold the piece up to the light, examining it for any flaws or imperfections. It is a perfect piece, and I place it on my tongue, allowing the sweet, yet minty, confit to carry me back to...to...where was I?

Oh, yes. Paris. I was in Paris. I had rented a small room off the Seine River, back in the days of horse-drawn carriages and oil lamps. Back then, I was Monsieur Thanton, living as a simple baker's apprentice and, of course, carrying out my godly duties. It had been a long day at the bakery, and I had learned much. I came back to my small room, carrying a basket of groceries from the market. Upon entering, my nose was assaulted by aftershave cologne. Cheap cologne at that, and underlying it was the scent of musk, sweat, and body odor. I didn't turn to see who it was as I closed the door. I knew who it was from the nauseating aroma.

"Good evening, my lord!" Hermes said in an overly chipper tone.

"Is it a good evening, messenger?" I asked.

"Always! To see you, oh, great one! Oh, Lord of Death! Oh..." Hermes began.

I spun on my heel, allowing my shadow to grow large above and around me, allowing my cold aura to permeate the room. To my pleasure, his jovial, mocking face dropped as his eyes widened. He went down on both knees as I advanced to loom over him. Falling over on his butt, he scooted backward until he hit the wall. The look of fear in his wide eyes, instead of his usual glint of mischief, was satisfying to see.

"Enough of you hamming it up. If you were an actor, messenger, you would chew the scenery off the stage, I am sure. Now say what you intended and be gone with you," I said, lording over him.

Hermes cleared his throat and licked his lips before he spoke. "I have a message from your older sister, Atropos. I bring your list of collections for the evening."

He held out a sealed envelope that I snatched from his hand. I turned and stepped away, drawing in my shadow and aura at the same time. He rose slowly to his feet, using the wall as support. I tore open the letter and took my pipe from the inside of my suit coat, placing the stem in my mouth. Hermes stood there smiling, with his hand extended and open, waiting to get paid, reminding me of Charon in the Underworld. I dropped two drachmas into his outstretched hand.

His smile widened as he placed the gold coins into a pouch on his belt and flew out the open window. He hovered there and bowed to me from the waist, bidding me farewell. "Have a pleasant evening, my lord. And do remember the city of Paris is for lovers, handholding, and kissing. All things you will never know!"

Hermes broke into a fit of laughter as I glared at him from my window. He flew off, still chuckling. I thought about flying after him, but I let that go for the time being. I sat at the table, lighting the lamp and my pipe. I read over the death list, trying to determine how many clones to make from my feather and which ones I would see to personally. Somewhere in the distance, Notre Dame's bells rang out the evening vespers. My eyes fell upon three names: *George, Martha, and baby Jacques. Off the banks of the Seine, storm surge, wave, drowned at 7:15 PM.*

I pulled out my pocket watch to see it was a little more than an hour from now. Overhead, thunder rumbled, and fat raindrops smacked into my windowsill, a sound like knocking on someone's coffin. I sat back in my chair, puffing my pipe and looking at my scythe where it leaned in the corner.

"George, Martha, and baby Jacques," I said aloud to the empty room as the storm intensified.

As it happened, the wave took the pram with baby Jacques and Martha into the water. George stood on the riverwalk, crying out for help. To my pleasant surprise, people actually rushed to his aid. Martha bobbed up and down in the water, attempting to keep the baby above the waves. Despite the group trying to stop him, George declared that he could not live without them. He loved them, and he dove into the water to save them. They drowned together as the storm ceased.

I called their souls to me, and they rose from the watery depths to stand before me. His arms were wrapped around her as she cradled the baby. They smiled, staring lovingly into each other's eyes before sharing a kiss. They came with me to the Underworld without an argument, just happy to be with one another. Nothing else mattered. Not how it happened or where they went after, just as long as they were together. I was astonished as much as I was envious of such affection.

I walked back to my room beneath the full moon, thinking of my love for Artemis. She didn't know it yet, and it would be a century or two before I told her. I felt at peace, basking in the moonlight of my secret love. My heart and I felt light as a feather, a feather floating on a gentle breeze. The broad smile on my face as I strolled was well known to the city of Paris. It is the smile of every young fool in love.

I returned to my room, and once again, Hermes' scent assaulted my nose. I groaned as I turned to face him, but the room was empty. On the table, in a shaft of moonlight, was a box wrapped in brown paper. A red ribbon with a tag tied it off, with a bow on top. I walked over with that foolish lover-smile plastered to my face and ran my fingers over the present. The package bore the faint scent of perfume that I could just pick up over Hermes' musk. I pulled the tag off and read it. *Made with love.*

Still smiling, I placed the tag in the breast pocket of my suit coat. Later, I would have it framed. To this day, it sits on my desk in my office at Mr. T's. To this day, it still makes me smile.

Did Artemis send me a gift? I hoped so, but I would be too shy, too nervous ever to ask such a question from my goddess. I delicately unwrapped the package and opened the box. The scent of peppermint wafted out.

"Oh, I love peppermint. Someone knew that!?" I started laughing. Someone actually paid attention to the fact I was always chewing mint leaves.

Inside the box were black, heart-shaped candies. Black peppermints. I took one of the smooth mints out and placed it in my mouth. It was Elysium! I was in Elysium! I never knew such sweets

351

could exist. My heart soared, and from that day forward, I always had black peppermints with me. Every time I taste one, I feel like I did then.

It truly is Elysium. A simple gift that always brings back that sweet memory. The gift of knowing that I was important to someone, and that I mattered. And my heart soars all over again.

I sit at my desk now, my reminiscing coming to an end. I had approved the mints, and the production line on the floor was humming along. Holding the framed tag in my hands, I continue to read it, as I have read it time and time again.

I slip another black peppermint into my mouth, then read the words aloud, "Made with love."

But whose love? Made by whom? It is an enduring mystery in my life.

BLACK HEARTS

BY

MOXIE MALONE

MOXIE,

GODDESS OF METAMORPHOSIS

Valentine's. It's that time of year again when mortals celebrate love with grandiose gestures and small tokens of affection. Those heart-shaped boxes of chocolate and little minty message hearts remind me of a time long, long ago, when I learned to fashion uniquely shaped confections by hand.

You're probably wondering what the Goddess of Metamorphosis is doing making candy. After all, food and cooking are the domains of Demeter, Persephone, and Hestia. Lacking a material body of my own, I find the quickest and easiest way to help mortals is to share theirs. Sure, walking around in human form has some disadvantages, like not being able to walk through walls. The upside is, I get to experience what you do and learn a few handy tricks along the way.

You may be surprised to know that I've picked up many skills when borrowing human bodies. I can milk a goat, weave a tapestry, drive a chariot, throw an ax with deadly accuracy, pick a lock, twirl a fire baton, change a tire, sail a yacht and even fix a broken faucet. Pro tip: Turn the water off before changing the hoses. I learned that one the hard way.

At the time I learned how to make beautiful candies, I had taken up residence in a sweet mortal. She was caring for her sickly mother and three very young siblings. Her mother, a prostitute by trade, was ravaged with disease and unable to work. She could barely care for herself, let alone the rag-a-muffins that ran wild in their one-room hovel. The father, or fathers, were unknown. But the eldest daughter, Aurelia, was industrious, crafty, and had a natural gift for cooking and baking. Her specialty was sweetmeats, or candies as they have come to be known.

She would stay up late into the night, making sweets that she'd sell from her hand baskets at the marketplace. Between the baked goods sales and the coins she deftly lifted from the pockets of those who ventured too close, she could feed her family, pay for the rent on their tiny shack, and buy the ingredients for the next day's bakery items. It was a hand to mouth existence that I intended to change.

The plan was simple. I would help her envision and create spectacular confections that would gain her notoriety. Then, I'd use my skills to influence those with the means to patronize her. Eventually, I'd set her up in a proper shop where she could earn a decent income to care for her family.

One evening, we were making specialty candies fit for a queen—a goddess queen. Hera, my own mother, to be specific. I'd planned to make little peacock shaped dainties to send as a gift the next time Hermes came bearing news from Olympus.

Sadly, the test batch looked more like deformed, angry, blue and green ducks. As you mortals say, *Nailed it!* Those would simply never do for Mamá. You don't send ugly gifts to the Queen of the Gods, no matter how tasty they may be. Not being wasteful of the hard-earned ingredients, I reformed my ugly ducklings into a ball to try again. As I worked the doughy mixture, the colors blended, and the candy turned to a shimmery, albeit dreary, pale black.

Black like my heart...

My mind wandered back to a failed attempt to attract a god who had unknowingly captured my now-wrecked heart so many years ago. Lost in my thoughts, I reworked the dough. I remembered how, as a young goddess, I'd pine for his attention, hanging on to his every word, few though they were. I warmed, remembering those little endearments and mannerisms that charmed me so. His rare but gentle smile and how it lit up my day. His shy, quiet demeanor. Even his peculiar habit of chewing on mint leaves endeared him to me.

I stood at the rustic wooden table, remaking the sweets. I rolled and sliced and pressed, one after another, until the candle burned low and I was working by moonlight. When I finally snapped out of my reverie, I was surprised to see that I'd formed hundreds of little ebony hearts.

I cradled one in my palm, stroking a finger over the shimmery surface, holding it like he still held mine. For him. They were for him.

What had begun as a young goddess's crush still lingered. No. It was more than that. The emotion had softened and yet seemed fuller. It was no longer filled with the jagged edges of infatuation. It had grown and matured into a love that had woven itself deep into my being. Now, I saw that it was simply a part of me. He was a part of me.

He had been a part of my past and was still a part of my present. I wondered if he would ever be a part of my future. Had time changed him, too? That's when I struck upon an idea. I knew what to do with the hearts. I placed a single drop of peppermint oil onto each one.

I then set about making fresh batches of bonbons for Mamá. I made some for my foster-sister, Nike, too, forgoing any elaborate designs until we—Aurelia and I—were more skilled. When done, I carefully wrapped the boxes of candy with plain brown paper, securing them with a lovely red ribbon that Aurelia had lifted from a notions vendor in the marketplace. As a finishing touch, I fashioned little gift tags that I attached to the ribbon.

To Mamá - **Fit for a Queen**

To Nike - **Little Treats for Little One**

And the third tag read - **Made with Love**

Using the last of the brown paper, I wrote a note to each. To Mamá, I wrote about the mundane existence of mortals in the city where I was living and promised to come home soon. To Nike, I offered words of encouragement and invited her to visit, though I knew she wouldn't leave the Mount. To *him,* I confessed my love and asked that he write me back if he found that he had a soft spot in his heart for me, too. I then rolled each note and tucked it beneath the crisscrossed ribbons on each package.

The very next day, Hermes arrived bearing notes from both Mamá and Nike, as I expected. We had been exchanging monthly messages for many years by then.

Hermes spied the packages and asked, "Are these to be sent back to Olympus?"

I nodded. "Two of them. The third one may be a bit out of your way."

He read the names of the recipients, arched a brow, then pouted. "No one ever sends me gifts. Me! The messenger," he huffed petulantly.

He had a point. Hermes always carried gifts and messages to others, but who sent anything to him? Indulgently, I wandered over to the table to gather a dozen candies for him. Wrapping them in a small parcel of soft cloth, I secured it with the last remnant of the red ribbon and presented the token to him. "For you, Hermes. I hope you like them. I...well, the mortal and I made them."

He smiled faintly and nodded. "Still an afterthought, but I thank you for that, at least," he said as he opened the cloth to retrieve a sweet, dropping one on the floor. It broke in two.

He chewed noisily. "Mmm. You did well. Will there be more the next time?" He asked and kicked the broken candy to the side.

I eyed the broken sweet and frowned. "Not if you are going to be so careless."

He broke my heart...

He shrugged indifferently, picked up the third package, then stared at it for a long time. Scowling, he mumbled an off-handed remark, "Sweets for a swine."

His vitriol towards such a gentle soul stunned me. "Pardon me? What did you say?" I asked. Surely, I had misheard him.

He merely shook his head, then abruptly scooped up the three packages and left, crushing the fallen confection beneath his heel.

He crushed my heart...

That moment, the lightness of cheerful anticipation turned to a weighty foreboding. The messenger had unwittingly brought an omen, and I spent the next month vacillating between hope and dread.

To make a long story short, I did hear back from Mamá and Nike, who were both thrilled with the treats. But there was no word from *him*. Nor was there word the next month or the month after that.

Finally, I knew that I had to accept that no answer was still an answer. Once again, I had opened myself up to the possibility of love. Once again, pain replaced hope. That was when I finally let go of my silly romantic notions, and when I stopped chasing that dream.

Well, this story certainly took a dark turn, didn't it? Allow me to rectify that. After all, this isn't a tale about my unrequited love. It's about Aurelia and how I learned to make pretty confections.

The good news is, we sold the rest of the black peppermint hearts in the market for a nice price, and demand grew for Aurelia's candies. We finally perfected the peacock shaped candies and created another that looked like the golden wings of Victory herself.

Before long, word spread that Aurelia's sweets were favored by the Goddesses Hera and Nike. Soon wealthy and poor alike clambered for her beautifully sculpted, delicious confections, and she was able to open a small store. And while her family never lived in the lap of luxury, they did have a comfortable, happy life.

After her mother passed, she moved her brothers and sisters into a larger home with many rooms. Aurelia eventually married and had lovely children of her own who carried on the tradition of candy making. She found both success and love.

And that was good enough to warm the edges of my own black heart.

CYRANO DE EROS

BY

KELSEY ANNE LOVELADY

ADRESTIA,

GODDESS OF REVOLT

I had worn a ten-foot-long mini-trench into the ground beneath me. I'd been pacing a league outside of camp for fifteen minutes. I wanted to get there early to ensure that I wasn't late. It was the first time I ever regretted being so early to an event or appointment. It was also my first time experiencing that brand of anxiety. I'd never been so nervous in my life.

I was my father's daughter, and nervousness had no place in war. You had to be confident. You had to have conviction. If you doubted or hesitated, you were dead. If you worried, your worries had to manifest as fight. To freeze, fly, or fawn was to sign your death certificate.

I kept fidgeting with the piece of parchment in my hand. I flicked it over my fingers, passing it between my palms. Unfolding it only to refold it and unfold it again to read the words I'd already read about a hundred times in the last twenty-four hours.

When Discordia tossed the apple of gold and initiated the fray between The Love, The Queen, and The Wise, they acted in great error by not including you. They should have handed the golden apple to you directly, for there is no competition that can even stand a chance against your beauty, your wisdom, and your regality.

Oft have I watched you in the fit of battle and nearly lost my head to an enemy while losing my heart to you. You are the reason I have fought to survive every battle and every war. The idea of never seeing you again is too cruel to allow anyone to take me from the Underworld.

Make no mistake. I would gladly lay down my life for you with a single, unquestioned order. Yet until that order comes from your lips, my only desire is to live to see you every sunrise. Perhaps it is futile to hope that one day, you may turn your gaze to me, and it will be one of devoted desire rather than of cold focus and cunning leadership.

Nothing in this world or the next can tempt me away from you. Not even your father, the Master of War and our General, can frighten me, unworthy as he may believe I am for you. The only good opinion that I wish to create, maintain, and fear losing, is yours.

If mutual feelings on your part are even a remote possibility, please meet me outside of camp, one league to the south. I hope against hope that I will see you there tonight. If I do not, know that this will be my last night on Earth and that I will go to war tomorrow with every intention of dying with you still on my mind, heart, and lips.

Your humble soldier,

Captain Felix Decian

Felix. A captain in Father's army. One of the many captains I watched over. I never would've pegged him to be so flowery and poetic. He was always such a stoic soldier. Reliable. Sturdy. When you gave him an order or a task, he would do it with indistractable focus. That was one of the things that drew me to him.

Yes, it was true. I, Adrestia, Goddess of the Revolt and Daughter of Ares, was attracted to a mortal in my father's army, which I commanded. Of course, no one knew this. No one but Eros, and if I'd had my way, he wouldn't know either. Unfortunately, my older brother was terribly perceptive when it came to matters of the heart. Almost as perceptive as he was to matters of the genitals. It took only one visit to the battlefield for Eros to figure out my secret.

I denied his accusations when he first brought them to my feet. Stubbornness ran in the family, as we both proved. I kept refuting his claims, and he refused to back down. It was a very long night of back and forth, fighting, teasing, and yelling. The only way that conversation, *any* conversation with Eros, came to an end was by one of us wearing the other down to the point of exhaustion. I hated to admit it to myself, and I would never tell anyone else, but my brother was too good at getting what he wanted and often won fights like this. I gave in and claimed my feelings, knowing that the little shit wouldn't let me sleep peacefully until I did.

"You have to tell him how you feel," Eros said. "You're going to war. He could die any day now. Do you really want Thanatos to take him away and miss your opportunity to tell him the truth of how you feel?"

I may have been too exhausted to deny my feelings, but I had to answer to something greater than emotions when it came to confessing my love. I was still the Daughter of Ares and the captain of his army. I was Felix's commander, and he was my subordinate. It's not that I was embarrassed. At least, not embarrassed by the idea of being smitten by someone of a lower rank. But to tell someone beneath me I was interested in them in a more intimate way was controversial, at best. At any point, I could be accused of playing favorites or risking the lives of the others for this man. If this got back to Dad, who knows how he would react? I didn't have faith that it would be a positive reaction. He would either be upset with me and demote me, if not remove me from my command completely, or he could take it out on Felix. Out of the army or out of this world. Both options were viable.

Yes, I was my father's daughter. Yes, I was the voice of the revolt. Yes, I was trusted to be his captain. But I had to work twice as hard just to get that much. Phobos and Deimos had it much easier. They simply had to exist to become Dad's favorites. Okay, maybe it wasn't that simple in actuality, but it felt that way sometimes. If they did anything wrong, anything to make themselves, Dad, or the army look weak, they might get a lecture that would go in one ear and out the other. I, on the other hand, was watched with much more scrutiny. One wrong step, and what little respect and progress I had made would come crashing down around me. And fraternizing with one of the soldiers under my command would definitely be a wrong move. There was too much at stake to risk on a *maybe*.

Then one day, the *maybe* became *definitely*. I returned to my tent late after a long day of traveling and training. This poetic confession was resting on my pillow, waiting for me. I had to read it over about three times before I could believe that the letter was real. I had to read it another dozen times after that to make sure I didn't misunderstand or misread anything. And it took at least one more read-through before I actually believed what I was being told.

Once the belief had fully set in, I decided to listen to Eros for once in my life. I was going to tell Felix I felt the same way.

It wasn't as easy as it sounded, though. I couldn't just run up to him and leap into his arms in broad daylight, confessing everything as loudly as possible as the mortals' myths would've wanted me to. They were always so overly dramatic. I needed to think this through and plan as we had a battle ahead of us. Even if Felix's feelings reflected mine, we still had to worry about Dad, Deimos, and Phobos. It wasn't difficult to imagine how all three would react if they found out about us. Phobos and Deimos could either just be jerks about it, and tease the both of us, or they could go into full *protective-older-brothers* mode. It was fine if they wanted to protect me, so long as they didn't take it too far. Threatening to destroy Felix if he hurt me was one thing. Actually, outright killing him because he had the audacity to pursue a goddess was another thing altogether.

And Dad was still the wild card. The best I could honestly hope for was indifference. My father was the God of War. He had a reputation and his own ego. He could try to help Phobos and Deimos kill Felix. He could take it a step further by locking me away somewhere where no man, mortal or immortal, would ever find me. Or he could be angry with me. Being disowned and tossed aside was not outside the realm of possibility. It's not like my parents had never done that before. Mom certainly had for a far smaller offense.

So, we needed to be careful. I needed to come up with a way to meet with Felix in secret under cover of darkness, far away from camp. And I needed it to look normal. I'd ultimately settled on telling my men that Ares had ordered me to take one of them and scout ahead. When I asked for volunteers, no one raised their hands. This was good, as it added to the ruse. If Felix had just leapt to help me, it would've looked weird, and people would've become suspicious. So, I chose him at random as *punishment* for the lack of volunteers.

The groundwork had been set. Now, all I could do was wait and hope.

The parchment was already starting to come apart at the folds from how many times I had opened it, read it, and closed it again. The humidity and sweat from my palms had turned the stiff parchment flimsy as I kept passing it between my hands. Why was I so nervous? It wasn't as though I was waiting to go to my death. Hell, I would've preferred going to my death over waiting for this surprisingly sensitive soldier who had caught my eye.

I faced death almost every day of my life. I had seen some horrible things that would unnerve any other soldier, even the most hardened ones. I had seen men walk away from the battlefield with only a fraction of their original limbs as they returned to a world that was not made for them and would ostracize them for the rest of their lives. I had seen others die, not from instant, peaceful, merciful deaths. They endured disgusting, painful, agonizing diseases that forced them to go through hell and back again too many times before Thanatos finally took them. I had seen men so distraught by what they had experienced that they preferred to become residents of the Underworld than live another day.

All of this had been my burden to help humanity reach its greatest potential. And none of it scared me as much as this uncertain, uncharted territory that I was facing.

"Lady Adrestia." The velvet, baritone voice made me jump as it interrupted my anxious, distracted pacing. Fuck. Get it together, Adrestia. He's a man, not a gorgon.

"Felix," I breathed, my voice lacking the distinct authority I usually had with my soldiers. I couldn't help it. He was just so... How could I describe it? How could I describe him?

He glowed in the night, despite the fact that the moon wasn't shining. The standard-issue armor of Ares' army fit him well, as though it was specifically designed with him in mind. His skin was rough from combat and weather exposure, but it didn't look like it would feel unpleasant beneath my fingers. It was rough in that way that could arouse every nerve connected to my sense of touch in the most satisfying yet teasing ways. I imagined the joy of learning the difference between our war-torn textures.

"Are you unwell, Lady Adrestia?" Dammit. Thinking about how his skin must feel made my mind wander when I needed my wits about me. Get it together. Yes, you're in love, but you're still a captain. You're *his* captain. Compose yourself.

"Yes, Mardas. I'm fine." He was so caring and concerned. I didn't know how to handle it. People didn't ask if I was okay. They never had to because I was always fine, even when I wasn't. No one ever saw anything from me that wasn't stoic leadership or harsh anger if someone was foolish enough to get me to that point. So how could I tell him I was nervous?

"Then shall we?" Felix approached me with long strides. His brown eyes were fixed upon me like the hungry lion that almost took out Uncle Hercules. I didn't know how to feel about that focus. It was something I had never seen before, not in the eyes of anyone. No one had ever looked at me that way. The looks I got were ones of fear, respect, and sometimes angry spite. Was there the occasional fool who would show how much he underestimated me with those amused grins? Of course, but I always made sure to wipe those smirks off the soldiers' faces permanently. They never returned. So, what was I supposed to do? Part of me was so scared that I wanted to run, and that *never* happened. I was never scared. Period. And if I ever was, flight was not my natural or nurtured response.

The only reason I was scared was because this was an unknown. My lack of experience in this subject made this moment all the more frightening.

The other part of my reaction wasn't helping matters at all. The part of me that wasn't scared was experiencing something so unfamiliar to me. I thought it was a good feeling. At least, it didn't immediately make me feel anything negative. It was similar to the fear, but it was a different kind of fear...a good fear? Was there such a thing? My heart was racing, and I felt this tension in my lower abdomen. The anticipation was both excruciating and exciting. What was he going to do?

Walk right past me, apparently. Felix wasn't focusing his intense gaze on me. He was fixing it on the dark horizon behind me. What's he playing at? Does he not think that we're far enough away? I turned my gaze back towards our camp. It seemed closer than I initially thought it was. I suppose we're still kind of close. But why couldn't he just say that? He was so candid in his letter, so why be cryptic? What's the point?

Maybe he was nervous, too. He was like me, cold and stoic. This had to be new for him, as well. If I was scared, he must be terrified. I never thought I could unnerve a man in any way that wasn't connected to the battlefield. It was strange to think that I, of all the goddesses, had such a power. Mom? Sure. Me? Who would've thought? Well, Eros would be proud, at least.

I rushed to catch up to Felix, walking next to him so that our shoulders just barely brushed. That light touch of our flesh felt like a hot branding iron in the cold breeze of the night. I had to clench my whole body to keep from jumping every time we connected.

After a minute of walking, I could feel Felix slowly turn his gaze to me. I pursed my lips together and tried to keep my eyes focused on the dark horizon. After a few seconds, he was still staring at me, and I couldn't take it anymore. I turned to him and asked, "What?"

"Nothing," he lied for a moment, looking away. "But should you not be walking a little ahead? You are the captain, after all." He was right. I always walked ahead of my squad or anyone I outranked. It was a way to maintain my power and reinforce that I was still their captain. Any man who tried to step out in front of me got clotheslined to the ground, and I would make sure the force behind my arm would get increasingly stronger for the repeat offenders until they got it into their heads.

What could I say that was honest but still didn't leave me too vulnerable? What would make sense to say that wasn't overt or out of character for me? My damn pride required that I did this while still behaving in my natural state. I really needed to think my response through, so I left Felix hanging in silence for a while.

"Lady Adrestia?" he prompted.

"I trust you, Felix," I admitted. "I wouldn't have chosen you if I didn't." I had never wanted to let my guard and walls down for any one person so badly in my life. Well, Eros, I suppose, but he was family. I had no choice but to let him in, whether I wanted to or not. This was the closest I could get to the level of vulnerability that I desired.

Felix fell silent for a long moment, taking in my words. *Oh, gods. Was it that stupid to say? What is he thinking right now? It can't be good.* "I see," he stated simply, turning his gaze back to the horizon. "I'm honored."

How could two simple words that I had heard and said before so many times make my cheeks so damn hot? I turned my gaze to the ground, afraid that Felix would see the glow in my cheeks through the darkness. *No one, mortal or immortal, should have this kind of power over anyone. It's too much.*

We walked a bit further in tense silence until Felix asked, "How far are we scouting ahead? And is there anything in particular we're looking for?"

I furrowed my brows at the ground. *He's awfully dedicated to this charade. We're far enough that no one would see us. Why is he keeping it up?*

Maybe I didn't communicate well enough. Maybe he thinks that the formality of my order this morning meant that I was rejecting him and keeping things strict between us. Oh, gods! How could I mess this up so badly? Eros always made this look so easy.

What could I do or say to reassure Felix that his feelings were requited?

Only one thing came to mind, and the very thought of it terrified me.

But what else could I do?

I remembered what Eros said to me before I left for this rendezvous, *"Don't be afraid to take the lead. He may be too nervous and in awe of you to do it himself, so you may have to throw caution to the wind and initiate everything."*

Throw caution to the wind. That's what I had to do.

"Lady Adrestia?" As Felix turned towards me seeking an answer, I grabbed him by the open shoulder of his breast-plate armor. My other hand grabbed the front of the armor piece, violently yanking him into my arms.

Apparently, I was a little too violent with the yank. I pulled Felix so hard that neither of us could stop him before he slammed into me, knocking us both to the ground. The weight of him falling onto me didn't hurt, but it caught me by surprise and kept me from immediately registering the situation in the dark. All I could see was the stars in the night sky and the dark landscape around us. I didn't know which way was up, and until Felix pushed himself onto all fours, I didn't realize how compromising of a position we were in.

Instinct told me to push him off of me and act cold for the rest of the night to make up for the embarrassment I was feeling. My pride and ego were yelling at me, *Get up, you idiot! We told you this was a bad idea! No push him off, tell him he just failed a test, give him some kind of punishment, and get out of here!*

It took all my strength to ignore the fear that beat at me. I almost fell into complete and total meditation to quiet them so that the other voice in my head could speak and be heard. *Don't be afraid. You don't have to be tough or perfect. All you have to do is be honest with him and yourself. Everything is going to be alright.*

"Lady Adrestia! Are you alright?!" There was genuine concern in Felix's voice as his eyes pierced through the darkness to look down at me. He wasn't trying to get up and off of me but instead stayed on his hands and knees, hovering over me. I couldn't help but wonder if he was fighting the voices in his head, too. Was it as easy as he made it look?

I didn't immediately answer Felix's question regarding my well-being. Instead, I let silence fall between us while I tried to compose myself. *Calm down. Take it slow.* When I felt I was ready, I took a deep breath and reached both of my hands up, cupping the sides of Felix's face. My palms felt on fire as the prickly beard rubbed against them. From beneath the beard, I could feel the warmth of his skin and the hard structure of his jawline. If I were more confident and less nervous, I would've just taken my time to really feel and caress his visage. But I didn't have the time to spare. At least, I didn't feel like I did. I needed to get this first, hardest part done and done fast.

With another deep breath, I slowly pulled Felix's face to mine. "Lady Adres—" I cut Felix off, lifting my head from the ground, meeting him halfway. I pressed my closed lips to his open ones, screwing my eyes shut in dreaded excitement and shy anticipation.

We stayed like this for a long moment, neither of us daring to move. We were both equally tense. My tension was from my fear and excitement with this new experience. I couldn't say where Felix's unease came from, but he didn't pull away from me. That was good, right? That had to be good. It meant that he didn't absolutely hate it. Or maybe he was too scared of the repercussions that would come from rejecting me. *No. Stop thinking like that. He wrote you the letter. He told you how he felt. He's not rejecting you. He **won't** reject you. This is safe.*

So why didn't it feel safe?

The nervous tensions within both of us made it impossible for me to register what the kiss actually felt like. I didn't realize it until I finally pulled away from Felix, but absolutely nothing of that first kiss had been committed to memory. *Why does everyone worry and fuss over the first kiss? It's not that big of a deal.*

Or is it? Is it actually a very big deal, and I just did something wrong? Did I already screw this up? How could I ruin something so simple and easy?

I couldn't stop all of these intrusive thoughts from bombarding my head. I looked up at Felix, searching for anything that would allow me to relax and put my mind at ease. There was surprise in his eyes. I couldn't tell if it was a pleasant surprise, disgusted surprise, or any other kind of surprise, for that matter. He didn't try to stand up and get off of me. That meant he wasn't completely disgusted by my actions. Right? *Ugh! Say something! Say anything!* Even I was unsure who my mind's frustration was aimed at, Felix, myself, or both of us.

"Your letter," I finally croaked out. After clearing my throat, I repeated and completed, "Your letter was beautiful, Felix." I didn't know what else to say. All I could think was that he needed as much reassurance as I did at that moment.

"Um," Felix hesitated, pushing himself upright onto his knees. "My letter?"

I furrowed my brows, hearing the distinct questioning in his voice. I pushed myself up onto my elbows. "Yes. Your letter. The one you left in my tent."

"Lady Adrestia, I..." Felix paused his sentence as his facial expressions went on a journey. He thought better of saying whatever he was going to say. Instead, he came up with a lie that made him smile. "I'm glad you liked it," he said as he started to lower himself back down to me.

I slammed my open palm against his chest, stopping him from coming any closer to me. "You have no idea what letter I'm talking about, do you?"

"Of course I do," he lied again after hesitating. "That letter has my heart written all over it." These poetic words were stilted and unnatural coming from his lips, further confirming my suspicions.

"Really? Then you should be able to recite it word for word from heart." I didn't need to put him through this test for my own certainty. I just needed to let him know how easy it was to catch him out in a lie. "So, go ahead. Word for word. If I've memorized it by now, you must certainly know it like the back of your hand."

The silence that fell told me everything I needed to know. Felix's heart had stopped at my demand, not knowing how to cover up for his lie. "Uh," he said shakily. "You're...beauty is like none I've ever seen—Oof!" I didn't let Felix finish his half-assed, over-saturated lie. I just shot my knee up between his legs and pushed him away, so he didn't fall on top of me.

I jumped to my feet and stared down at the pathetic excuse of a man that I was stupid enough to fall for. As he writhed around with his manhood bruised, I ordered, "Latrine duty for the rest of the week, Decian. Assuming you live past tomorrow, that is." I didn't wait for him to acknowledge my orders before I stomped away, leaving him to moan in the dark.

I was grateful for the distance that we had put between ourselves and camp. I had the entire journey to allow my tears to fall. No one would see or hear me. And when I finally reached camp, I was going to kill the person who did write that stupid letter. I didn't care if he was my brother. This time, he had gone too far. I would never forgive him for this humiliation.

CAN'T GET ENOUGH OF THE GODS?
THEIR STORIES CONTINUE AT:

IN THE PANTHEON

WATCH FOR MORE ANTHOLOGIES
COMING FROM REWRITTEN
REALMS IN THE COMING MONTHS!

www.ingramcontent.com/pod-product-compliance
Lightning Source LLC
Chambersburg PA
CBHW061306170626
46817CB00001B/79